Praise for

"A stylish, atmospher... .... angelic affairs quickly reveals itself to be so much more: *The Taken* proves that Pettersson is not afraid to explore the darkest corners of the human heart—and that her gift for redemption is unsurpassed."
—Sophie Littlefield

"Exceptional. Mystery, crime-scene drama, and more than enough romance to keep the heart pumping blend seamlessly into an enthralling read that kept me glued to the pages. I can't wait for the sequel."
—Kim Harrison

"A delectably dark paranormal thriller. I've always been a fan of Pettersson's work, but she knocks it out of the park with this one."
—Kelley Armstrong

"Pettersson hits every note in the familiar duet of a 'reticent, complicated, darkly sexy man' and a luscious, plucky 'girl reporter.' . . . The resulting irresistibly good yarn proves that there's still plenty of room for brilliant innovation in urban fantasy."
—*Publishers Weekly* (starred review)

"A sure bet for urban-fantasy readers of all types, but especially fans of Carrie Vaughn, Jim Butcher, and P. N. Elrod."
—*Booklist*

"Pettersson's amazing new series is off to a rocking start with this compelling read."
—RT Book Reviews (top pick)

"Intriguing mix of paranormal, romance, and mystery with just enough suspense!"
—*Suspense* magazine

THE LOST

BOOKS BY VICKI PETTERSSON

CELESTIAL BLUES SERIES

The Taken

THE SIGN OF THE ZODIAC SERIES

The Scent of Shadows

The Taste of Night

The Touch of Twilight

City of Souls

Cheat the Grave

The Neon Graveyard

THE
LOST

CELESTIAL BLUES

Book Two

VICKI PETTERSSON

HARPER Voyager
An Imprint of HarperCollinsPublishers

THE LOST. Copyright © 2013 by Vicki Pettersson. All rights reserved. Printed in the United States of America. No part of this book may be used or reproduced in any manner whatsoever without written permission except in the case of brief quotations embodied in critical articles and reviews. For information address HarperCollins Publishers, 10 East 53rd Street, New York, NY 10022.

HarperCollins books may be purchased for educational, business, or sales promotional use. For information please write: Special Markets Department, HarperCollins Publishers, 10 East 53rd Street, New York, NY 10022.

FIRST EDITION

Library of Congress Cataloging-in-Publication Data has been applied for.

ISBN 978-0-06-206465-3

13 14 15 16 17 OV/RRD 10 9 8 7 6 5 4 3 2 1

To Larry Lee, who changed so many lives for the better.

The Tribe sorely misses you.

ACKNOWLEDGMENTS

To James, first and always. My heartfelt gratitude goes to the wonderful team at Harper Voyager, especially Liate Stehlik, Pam Jaffee, Shawn Nicholls, and Will Hinton, who've now ferried eight of my books to readers. Kaitlyn Kennedy is a dream publicist and should be carbon copied. Diana Gill's inestimable dedication, enthusiasm, and (frightening) intelligence provide a mental beacon when I'm staring down a deadline. I greatly appreciate Peter McGuigan for the new beginning, right in the middle of it all. And a final thanks to my readers, for fueling my endeavors with both light conversation and deep silence . . . and for your full and proper names so that I might kill you off in prose. Don't hate me because I live to break and mend your hearts. You know it's a two-way street.

CHAPTER ONE

I t wasn't a dream, of that he was sure. First, the only thing
Griffin Shaw dreamed of was the night he'd died, fifty
years earlier. Second, the only person he dreamed of was the
woman who'd died with him, and whom he'd been searching
for ever since.

Third, and perhaps most important, Grif damned well
didn't dream of hairy, oversize angels with heads that shone
like eight-balls, and chips on their shoulders as wide as their
wings.

No, this was *vision*, Grif thought, as he slipped his suspenders up over his shoulders, and padded barefoot through the
dark ranch house. This was the same source material of Moses
and the Apostles, and it was also the message he'd been warned
was coming. His job now was to search out the herald.

Dropping into the sunken living room, he gave a gentle

probe with his celestial eyesight, searching for a floating shimmer of silvery plasma or some other sign of angelic presence, but no one, no *thing*, waited for him there. All he saw were Kit's possessions, plentiful but not hoarded, and despite the circumstances, it made him smile. Katherine Craig—modern-day girl reporter, rockabilly chick, and the sole woman on earth, or the Everlast, able to convince Griffin Shaw that life was still worth living—only gathered items around her that had personal meaning, exceptional value, and spoke of an era long gone.

His era.

Grif couldn't much see the point in preserving what was never perfect to begin with, but there was no telling Kit that. She might be a twenty-first-century woman through and through, but she lived a rockabilly lifestyle, which meant she was retro to the core.

Spotting no sign of Pure presence in her shockingly pink kitchen, Grif headed back through the dark living room, and into the short, squat foyer. He could enter and exit any earthly property without restriction—even outside of prophetic vision—so ignoring the blinking alarm, he simply opened the door, stepped through . . . and was promptly struck in the head by a newspaper.

A youthful cackle sounded in the street. "Little piker," Grif muttered, bending to reach for the unlikely missile.

Paperboys don't deliver in the middle of the night.

He froze at the thought, and then his gaze landed on the headline. Suddenly he was running in the street.

"Hey!" Grif called after the teen. "Hey!"

Vision or not, the boy clearly hadn't thought Grif would follow. Surprise had the kid glancing back, then overcorrecting when his bag swung from his shoulder. Another loud cry

sounded in the street, this one less amused, as he then catapulted across the handlebars and performed a perfect header
into the corner stop sign.

Sighing, Grif tucked the paper under his arm.

The tightly clipped grass was crisp and soft beneath Grif's
bare feet—the sensory acuity was another sign that this was
a vision and not a dream—but summer's shadow reached up
from the base of the blades, its fingers still warm. It was early
June, and though some nights still went cool, the long grasses
and potted plants were beginning to yellow beneath the desert
sun's unforgiving gaze. Evergreens—the matured pines and
fountaining grasses studding the yard's perimeter—would
pretend not to care, but unlike mortals, Grif could hear the
cries of the nonindigenous plants. To a being both angelic
and human, it sounded like the weak final gasps of someone
expiring from dehydration. Some life-forms, he decided, were
not meant for the desert.

Just as some weren't meant for the Surface.

"What's the big idea?" Grif asked, without preamble, holding the paper out in front of the unconscious teen.

The kid's eyelids flipped open, but nothing human swirled
in the wide gaze of black granite. The voice rumbled like far-
off thunder. "What? It's a great headline. And it's what got you
bounced back to this mudflat, isn't it?"

Grif grunted. Of course it would be Frank. Short for Saint
Francis, of the Cherubim tribe, he was the Pure in charge of all
the Centurions—the angels who'd once been human. Frank
appeared to each Centurion in the Everlast via the form they
most associated with authority. For Grif, that was a sergeant in
a detectives' bullpen, a guise meant to put him at ease, though
he wasn't comforted. Grif was crummy with authority.

He flipped the paper over again, and the question that greeted him every morning, and was the last to leave him at night, blared from the top of the page: WHO KILLED GRIFFIN SHAW?

But that was all he understood. The text below that was a mixture of Sanskrit and Seraphian—angel-ese—which, despite his Centurion status, he didn't read. Glancing at his sarge, who still stared up at him through the teen's sidelong smirk, Grif resisted the urge to give him a little kick. It wasn't the kid's fault that the answer to this question wasn't on these pages. It wasn't even Sarge's fault. He didn't provide answers, only guidance.

"Little late for visiting hours," Grif finally said, offering him a hand.

Sarge accepted the help, and when they locked grips, the teen's skin was grave-cold. Summer or not, the kid would be frosted over when his displaced consciousness returned to his flesh. Grif would have felt bad about that, except that angelic possession generally left the host body with a little something extra, too—something that would benefit that individual for the rest of their mortal life. The kid's throwing arm, for instance, might suddenly turn him into the next Mickey Mantle. Or new parts of the brain, previously inaccessible, might light up like mental landing strips in his mind, making him the next Einstein. But none of that was Grif's concern.

"What's wrong, Shaw?" Sarge said, sensing his impatience. "I told you I'd be coming. Or am I disturbing something back in that warm, wide bed?"

Grif drew back, eyes narrowing. "That bed, and what goes on in it, is none of your business."

A look that was too knowing for the young face overtook

the teen's features. "It's no wonder you got no incentive to leave this mudflat."

"That's not why I'm here and you know it," Grif said, jaw clenching.

Yet the knowing look remained, and silence stretched between them. "Got a smoke?"

Grif scoffed. "I can't be seen giving the paperboy a cigar."

"That's why I came to you in a *vision*," Sarge said, and the marble eyes swirled faster. "Besides, I know you have one. I can smell it on you."

Grif did. He'd gone through the motions of putting one in his pocket as he dressed. That was the trick with visions. If you went along with them, believed and acted as though they were real, they'd reveal their secrets. If you fought them, they'd turn on you like a cornered rattler.

So Grif pulled it from his pocket, watched the swirling eyes widen, and even lit the stick for Frank. The first hit of nicotine took, and bliss gradually replaced judgment. Even angels had their vices. Then Grif asked, "What's with the paperboy guise?"

"It's not a guise. I'm actually in possession of your paperboy."

Grif was surprised. The kid looked healthy, at least in the vision. Usually only the very old, very young, or mentally incapacitated were susceptible to Pure possession.

"He's a sleepwalker," Frank supplied, closing his eyes as he inhaled again. "And I needed him to make a delivery."

Grif glanced down at the paper in his hands, and knew the real one would be waiting on the doorstep when he truly awoke. "So what do you want?"

"Same thing God wants, Shaw," Frank answered, and it was

true. As powerful as the Pure were, they had no will outside that of God's. "I want you to come Home."

Grif just jerked his head. "We agreed I get to stay until I find out who killed me."

"It's been four months," Sarge said, eyes still closed.

"Yes, and I've been working on it nonstop."

The marble gaze found his again through the smoke.

Grif raised his chin. "Fifty years is a long time. Leads dry up. The case is cold."

"So what makes you think it can ever be solved?"

Why did he think he could solve the mystery of who'd killed him fifty years earlier? Because he wasn't leaving this mudflat again until he did, that's why.

"I got an appointment with a woman. Today," he told Sarge. "I think she'll be able to help me."

Sarge tucked one arm beneath the other, propping it up, another gesture that was too old for the young body's knobby limbs. "And then what?"

"Then I follow the answers until they lead me to the killer." Or killers . . . because in the brief flashes of memory that Sarge and Company hadn't been able to wipe out, he'd seen that the man who'd attacked him that fateful night hadn't been working alone. There'd been two of them, and they'd taken his life.

They'd murdered his wife.

"I mean what happens after that?" Sarge pressed, absently scratching the boy's bony rib cage. "After you solve your life's, and afterlife's, greatest mystery?"

Grif couldn't even begin to guess. He hadn't been granted wings and the status of angelic helper because he was special. Being a Centurion had been pressed upon him because he was *broken,* unable to forget his mortal years, move past the pain of being murdered, and release the guilt of having allowed his dear Evie to be killed while standing right next to him. Assisting other newly murdered souls into the Everlast was only meant to help him move on.

But so far Grif hadn't moved forward . . . he'd moved back, the first man ever to do so. The first, he knew, to be both angelic and human.

"You should just return now," Sarge said, likely reading his mind.

"Working on it," Grif muttered, tapping out a smoke of his own.

"So maybe that'll help," Sarge said, jerking his head at Grif's paper. Then his expression turned sly. "Open it."

Holding his stick between his lips, Grif unfolded the paper again. This time he ignored the headline blaring the news of his death, as well as the black-and-white photo of him and Evie splayed beneath it, and opened it to the middle. "That's not the sports page."

Instead, it was a dossier on an individual named Jeap Yang, born only nineteen years earlier and due to die five hours from now. Yet it didn't say how. Lowering the paperwork, Grif slipped the cigarette from his lips. "Is it a Take or a case?"

Because there was a difference. If it was a Take, Grif arrived just after the mortal soul passed from the physical body— same as he had in his role as a Centurion. However, a *case* required the escorting angel to arrive just before corporeal death. This was no problem for the Pure. They had never lived, and didn't even possess souls. They couldn't begin to understand the agony of having life ripped from you.

But attending death was torture to Grif . . . and it was meant to be. He'd overstepped his duties as a Centurion—saved a woman from being murdered instead of simply watching her die—and that was really why he was here now.

He didn't regret it, though. It was why Kit—his girl, his *new* love—was still here, too.

"Why?" Sarge asked now. "Got room in your bed for another case?"

Grif gave Sarge a black look, then snuffed his cigarette butt on the corner lot's wet grass. "There a map in here?"

"Why don't you bring along your little tour guide?" Sarge said, dripping sarcasm, spitting stardust.

"I can't bring Kit on a Take and you know it." While his sense of direction on the mudflat was improving, and he'd memorized most of Las Vegas's major crossroads and intersections, he still hadn't recovered his internal sense of direction. Kit usually guided him when they were out together.

"But she's so *accepting* of you, Shaw—your job, your wings, your angelic nature. She loves you just the way you are, right? So why shouldn't she see you doing what you do best?"

"She did." Grif smiled. "Back in that warm, wide bed."

Sarge gave him a deadpan stare. "Map's in the paper. The *real* paper. And . . ."

It wasn't like Sarge to hesitate. "And?"

"This one is Lost."

Grif's breath caught in his chest, but he managed a short nod. He'd known this duty was coming.

"He might be less skittish with someone who used to be human," Sarge explained, then paused. "We can't afford to lose this one, Shaw."

"This one?"

"There were two before him. We . . . don't know where they went."

Grif blinked. The Host of angels created by and for God to do His will and protect His children . . . didn't know? Sensing it best not to voice that thought, deciding Frank already knew it anyway, Grif cleared his throat. "So how does he die?"

"Show up at sunrise and you'll see," Sarge said.

Because the lesson in Jeap's death wouldn't just be for the kid. Grif still had healing to do, too. Sighing, he turned to leave.

"You know," Sarge said, raising his voice so the treble in the teen's throat cracked. "It's not that you have a bad sense of direction, Shaw. True, you're out of your place and time, and you'll never be able to properly orient yourself on this mudflat again . . ."

Grif turned around slowly, and waited while Frank tapped ash onto the curb.

"But lots of folks are like that," he said, moving to the bike and picking it back up, gaze fastened on Grif, the dust of asteroids in his eyes. "Most people are simply inattentive. They don't see the blessings in their lives until it's too late. So you might find you have more in common with Jeap Yang than you think."

Grif clenched his jaw so tight his teeth ached. "You calling me Lost?"

"I'm saying some guys spend their entire lives searching for a place to settle."

"I'll settle when I find out who killed me."

"Will you?" Sarge blew out the last of his smoke with a hard breath, then he flicked the cigar into the street. "Because I may not know what it is to be human, but I do know one thing. A person isn't defined by their death. They're defined by their life."

Grif wanted to pretend he didn't know what that meant, but they both knew better. "We done here?"

"Just one more thing." Sarge hopped back onto the bike, and with roiling eyes no human possessed, he shot Grif a final look over his shoulder. "Try not to fuck this one up."

And though he turned away, and pumped his feet, he didn't just leave Grif staring as one of God's most powerful creations rode away on a Schwinn. As befitting a vision, he took off with a roar, ripping through the sound barrier, spewing stardust, and leaving the detritus of dead galaxies trailing behind him.

CHAPTER TWO

He always woke from his dreams soundlessly but violently.

Because of this, Kit researched sleep patterns online and made sure to be at Grif's side when he entered REM, when the nightmares were most common. If he went to bed before her, which was rare, she'd read or work at the sitting area in a low-lit corner of her bedroom. If he came to bed after her . . . well, that wasn't a problem. Over the past four months Kit had become a very light sleeper.

So when Grif jolted into a sitting position next to her, Kit and he almost rose as one. Her arms were immediately about his shoulders, gripping his tensed biceps as she rose to her knees, even before his body managed to unclench for his first gasping breath. She looked over at the clock. Three on the dot, same as the last two nights . . . and the dreams were getting worse.

Pressing her body against his back, Kit ignored the two strange knobs between his shoulder blades, ones no other mortal she knew possessed. He called them his "celestial deformation" but she didn't care about that. Her regret was that *she* didn't have wings to wrap around him so she could shield him from the memories that stalked him in sleep.

"It's okay, honey. It was just a dream. You're here with me. You're safe."

She wasn't quite sure that last part was true, but that wasn't what he took issue with. "It wasn't a dream," he said, swinging his legs over the side of the bed like he was going to rise. Yet he paused to cradle his head in his palms, and Kit continued to stroke his back, then smoothed away the errant lock of ginger hair plastered to his forehead before kneading the muscles in his neck. Gradually, he relaxed, and she slid her hands over his sweat-dampened chest, down to his waist, and fell still.

"Anything this time?" Grif asked. His voice was rough, as if shadows lay in his throat.

Kit settled back on her haunches. She didn't want to say, but his sharp glance at the ensuing silence meant he already knew. "You said her name."

His shoulders slumped. "I'm sorry."

Kit leaned forward and kissed the back of his neck, and then, because she couldn't help it—because there were other ways to help—nipped at it lightly. He shuddered, pleasantly this time, and she did it again, pleased that she could do it at all. It was a reminder that she was the one who gave him comfort in *this* life. It was a gift that he loved her well and accepted her love in return. His late wife's passing might still haunt him in ways Kit would never understand, but it was also a miracle that Grif was with *her* now, and that was enough.

Right?

"It's okay." Kit pushed the question away and shifted so she could see his face. His eyes were underscored with bruises and his brow furrowed with an emotion she couldn't pinpoint. Worry, guilt, regret . . . all of the above? Grif had a tendency to take every damned thing on himself. Angel complex, she thought, then gave him a closed-mouthed smile. "I understand."

And, objectively, she did. In the raw light of day—the time that she got to live and breathe and walk around at twenty-nine, an age Evelyn Shaw had never lived to see—she told herself that a new love couldn't be expected to replace an old one. That wasn't what new love was for. A relationship, she told anyone and everyone who would listen, had to exist for and of itself.

Besides, Kit knew it wasn't possible to forget a love deeply felt, even if the person was long gone. Most remembered that sort of passion for the whole of their lives, but Grif had carried his love for Evelyn Shaw beyond life . . . and, in a way, that was a miracle, too.

"Want to talk about it?" she prodded.

"No."

"Okay," she said, planting a soft kiss on his side. The light dusting of hair there tickled her lips, and she inhaled deeply and kissed him again. "Then just start from the beginning."

He pushed some hair into her face. "You never listen."

"Yes, I do." She blew the hair away and looked up at him. "That's what makes me such a good listener."

"Should I wait for you to get out your pen and paper? Take some notes. Turn my visions into a feature story." The errant lock of hair had slipped over his forehead again, making him

appear younger than thirty-three, the age at which he'd originally died.

"Don't be silly. I report for the *Las Vegas Tribune,* not the
National Enquirer. Mine might be a city known for its excesses,
but we're quite practical when it comes to our spiritual beliefs."

"You mean you're all heathens."

"I prefer the word 'cynics.'"

"I prefer the word 'go to sleep.'"

"That's three words . . . all of which I heard," she said, as he
rose. "Where are you going?"

"Stay here," said her grumpy angel.

So, of course, Kit followed.

Grif had to know she would. These days, they anticipated
most of each other's actions. They no longer questioned which
side of the bed they would sleep on. They'd stopped checking
on each other during the night as their days as a couple began
piling up, no longer afraid the other wouldn't be there, or awed
that they were. Their passion was now set to a low burn, yet it
could still ignite with one sidelong smoky look.

It was those burning moments that Kit loved most. She
could see Grif—both his angelic and human sides—when they
were joined in flesh. His wings flashed and flared, which had
startled her at first, but it was also amazing and awesome and
somehow holy. Besides, Kit was as grateful for his Centurion
state as his mortal one. After all, it was the only reason she was
alive and breathing in the first place.

And that, Kit thought, was the strangest, most wonderful
beginning to a love story ever.

Perplexed, she watched from the living room as Grif deac-
tivated the house alarm, opened the front door, and retrieved
something from atop the doormat.

"Is that yesterday's edition?" she asked, stepping forward. This day's hadn't even gone to press yet, and Kit would know. Her family owned the struggling paper.

"Special printing," Grif mumbled, and she tilted her head as he passed, then followed him to the kitchen. He stopped in front of her automatic coffee machine. "Coffee?"

"Decaf," she said, nudging him aside, and elbowing him again when he almost growled. "It's three in the morning. I want you to be able to sleep."

He grumbled again, but couldn't do anything about it. No matter how many times she showed him, he couldn't manage to work the "newfangled" device, but she didn't mind measuring the water, popping in the pods. Fifty years had brought a lot of change to the Surface—some welcome, some not—but he'd claimed the coffee was both recognizable and improved. He took a seat at her vintage café table and sipped it black when she handed it to him, letting its warmth and bitterness chase away the dregs of the dream.

"Well?" Kit finally said, dropping down across the table from him while she waited for her own single cup to brew. She glanced at the folded paper in his hands.

Grif just blinked.

She gave him a deadpan stare. "Don't make me interrogate you, Griffin Shaw. You know I'll win."

"I've got a new assignment," he said, clearly hoping she'd leave it at that.

"A Take?" she asked.

He inclined his head, and though she knew it was his duty— that the newly dead needed Centurions to assist them into the afterlife—she had to fight back a shudder. Someone would soon die horribly. Someone who was alive right now. "When?"

"Dawn."

"Man? Woman?"

"Man."

Her lips thinned in an alarming way, but her voice remained steady. "How?"

Grif's gaze automatically slid to the paper, but he just shrugged.

And that infuriated her.

"Don't you care?" Her voice, no longer steady, held accusation and disbelief. Because one thing about Kit, she always cared.

Grif leaned back, like that could keep the situation from escalating. "Look, when you've logged as many hours as I have ferrying souls into the Everlast, you get immune to the cause of death. My job is to help this guy cross into the Everlast, once deceased. That's all."

"But he's not deceased yet."

"Kit."

Kit shoved back from the kitchen table and crossed to the coffee machine. She slammed the mug unnecessarily hard upon the Formica, then sloshed coffee over the rim as she lifted it.

Grif waited.

Cleaning the counter gave her an excuse to rattle around some more, but when she'd finished stirring in sugar, she turned and leaned against the counter, glaring.

"Done?" Grif asked.

Kit bared her teeth, then sipped.

He sighed. "I know what you're thinking, but I can't stop it."

"So don't even ask, right?" She tilted her head. "Don't even try to save another person's life? I don't know if you noticed, Shaw, but it's my nature to at least try."

Grif shoved his own chair back, and took his mug to the sink. She edged over slightly and when he'd set the mug down— none too gently, either—he turned to her for a long stare-off. Shoving his hands into his pockets, he said, "I need you to trust that I know what I'm doing. This is the job, and yeah, it rubs that some kid's head got so jammed up that he's not going to know what he's lost until it's too late. But that's the human condition, and this death is preordained. Don't fight me on this."

Kit's shoulders slumped, but she placed her coffee on the counter and squared on him, too. "I don't want to fight at all, Grif. But this man is in pain *right now,* and we're just sitting here talking . . . drinking, like—like it has nothing to do with us."

"It doesn't."

"It *does,*" she implored, leaning forward, forcing his gaze. "It did the minute we learned about it. If you know someone is in pain and you don't try to help, then you're culpable. You're complicit!"

"No." He must have realized how cold it sounded, because he shook his head. "Look, you gotta think of it like the Pures do. Sarge always says, 'Death isn't a barrier to be knocked down. It's just a threshold everyone needs to cross.'"

"Tell that to the guy whose throat is about to get slit."

"I will," he said. "Right after it happens." And because that also must have come out harsher than intended, he added, "And it's not a murder this time. It's a drug overdose."

"So it's preventable!" Kit said.

"You ever try saving a man from himself? It'd be easier to force a river to flow in the opposite direction." Striding back to the table, Grif jammed a finger at the paper. "I wouldn't be carrying around this file if it were preventable."

"I was once in a file," she pointed out.

But Grif shook his head. "I'm just doing my job. And I can't screw this one up."

Kit set her jaw. Beyond him, she saw her reflection in the sliding glass door; her pin curls had gone loose, flowing over her shoulders like black ribbons. The silk kimono she used for a robe flared as she strode back to the table, matching the color rising in her cheeks. Setting down her mug, she glanced at the photo on the front page, and though it made her heart bump to see Grif's image splayed there along with another woman's, *Evelyn Shaw's,* what Kit was looking for was inside.

She opened to the center pages, and felt horror roll across her face like a shallow wave. Jeap Yang. Only nineteen. His stats were all there, including the place, date, and time of his death. Whirling, she held the paper up. "He's just a kid!"

Grif paced back to the sink.

"That is someone's child! Someone loved him enough to birth him and raise him and release him into the world!"

Grif shifted. "Yeah, and he threw all that good work into the world's Dumpster, then shoved *that* into a needle in his veins."

"I agree that it's a bad choice! But so is just letting him die!" And before she knew she'd moved, Kit's mug shattered against the sink's backsplash, sending coffee splattering. Grif just looked down at his previously white undershirt and sighed.

"I need to wash up," he said, and headed toward the living room.

"Make sure you straighten that halo," Kit snapped back, throwing the paper back on the table, then immediately held up her hand when he turned to stare. "I'm sorry." She sighed. "I am. You don't deserve that."

Grif hesitated a moment, then returned to her side. "Let me ask you something. What happened to your left knee?"

Frowning, she wrapped her vintage kimono more tightly across her chest.

"Your left knee," he said again, then reached down and uncovered the skin in question. She tried, futilely, to slap his hand away. "There's a mark to the left of the kneecap that's smoother and shinier than the rest of the skin."

"I fell when I was six," she said, finally edging away from him. "My dad was teaching me to ride my bike, but I hit a pothole and had to get twelve stitches."

"And why's it raised like that?"

"Because it's a *scar*, Grif," she said, impatience brimming in her voice.

"Because that's what happens when you injure your body," he countered. "Want to know what happens when you scar your soul? You can't feel anything outside your own pain, not for what it really is. The internal anguish is so great that it cripples you. And *that* scar tissue dulls your senses to the point where you find yourself wondering if you'll ever be able to feel anything again."

For the briefest of moments, Kit wondered if he was talking about himself. Then he picked up Jeap Yang's photo, and this time he showed it to her. "This man—"

"Boy," she corrected.

"*Soul*," Grif retorted sharply. "This Jeap Yang is already that injured. Something big and crippling scarred him in his past and each breath he takes adds new injury to the old. By now, he likely feels nothing at all, and that's no way to live."

Kit studied the photo for a long moment, but finally shook her head. "I lived. You saved me."

"You were different. You were slated to die because I put you in harm's way, not because you were scarred."

And because that was true, because their meeting had been accidental and not predestined, Kit finally looked away.

"I don't know why things like this happen," Grif finally said softly. "I wish it was different, but you can't make decisions for other people. They have to choose good things for themselves."

"You have scar tissue, too, you know." She wasn't angry anymore, just making an observation as she looked back up at him. He couldn't argue. He wouldn't be on the Surface if he didn't.

"Maybe I need it to do this job."

Kit nodded. Then she tilted her head. "So will it hurt?"

"I don't know. I've never died of a drug overdose." When she winced, he quickly added, "But my guess is that his greatest pain is already behind him."

"I suppose that's true."

"I can promise you this much, though," Grif said, and waited until her gaze arrowed up. "Once his soul has been freed from that tired, drug-addled body, he's going to be fine. I'll take care of him."

She studied him for a long time, and gradually the fight slipped from her shoulders. "Just . . . hold on."

Edging past him, she disappeared into the living room, returning seconds later with a hatbox in her hands. It was vintage, of course, which meant it was from his lifetime, though she'd had it artfully restored with black silk and a matching ribbed bow.

Their fingers touched as she handed over the box. "I was going to wait to give this to you for your birthday, but—"

"How do you know when my birthday is?"

"I read it in your obituary," she said. Maybe she should've found that more disturbing than she did, but she shrugged. "Open it."

But he only stared. "I can't remember the last time anyone gave me a gift," he said at last, then busied himself—and hid his pleasure, Kit thought, smiling—by pulling loose the onyx ribbon and lifting the lid. Parting the layers of crackling tissue paper, he stared again.

"It's a hat," Kit finally said.

Grif looked up. "I have a hat."

Not only that, no matter where he was in relation to that hat, come four-ten every morning, the exact time of his death, the thing would reappear atop his head. It was true for everything he'd died in—the loose-fitting suit, the crooked skinny tie. A watch. A loaded gun in his ankle strap, along with four bullets he'd never gotten a chance to use.

The photo of Evie tucked deep inside his wallet.

It was disconcerting, to say the least, to wake next to a fully dressed man after bedding down with a naked one for the night. All that was missing was his wedding ring and driver's license . . . and he swore on his second life that he'd had both on him when he died.

"I know, but this one's special." She touched a button along the brim's edge and a red light appeared, accompanied by a high-pitched chirp. "They normally fashion them in baseball caps and cowboy hats, but I had this one custom-ordered in a stingy brim. You like?"

Grif frowned. "Why is it beeping?"

Now a full smile bloomed. "Because it has a built-in compass. You program your desired coordinates, and the closer you get, the louder and more quickly it beeps."

Grif stared at her. "You want me to wear a hat that beeps?"

Kit folded her arms. "Is this a guy thing? Like asking for directions when you're driving?"

"It's a hat. That. Beeps."

Sighing, Kit reached out and took the fedora from his hands, then plunked it atop his head. "Just wear it. It'll give you peace of mind."

"That I'll find my way easily to my Takes?"

"No." Her hand lowered to caress the stubble of his cheek, and she tilted her head up. "That you'll find your way back to me when you're done."

And Grif slipped his arms around her, kissed her forehead, and inhaled deeply as he buried his face in her hair. That's how she knew their argument was over. "I love your passion, Kitty-Cat. I love how you can feel so much for a total stranger. It makes you a good reporter and a damned fine woman. And it makes me better at what I do, too."

She looked up at him.

Grif shrugged self-consciously. "It does. It helps me remember what it was to be alive *and* dying. Do this job long enough and you can get numb to the emotion of both. But you don't allow me to do that. Not anymore anyway."

"I love your passion, too," she said, lifting to her toes.

"It revolves around you," he said, returning her kiss. When it began to deepen, he pulled away and rolled his eyes upward. "So. Is this thing waterproof?"

Kit frowned, surprised. "I don't think so. Why?"

He lifted her hand, their fingers intertwining. "I still gotta find my way to that shower."

A smile began to creep across Kit's face. "I think I can help with that."

"Can ya?" Grif asked and, drawing close, whispered, "Beep."

"Beep, beep," Kit replied, and—fully smiling now—led the way back into the bedroom.

CHAPTER THREE

K it let it go. Or pretended to. She'd seen in the kitchen that Grif's mind was made up, and there was no point in trying to convince him to stop Jeap Yang's death. Not once he'd worked himself up to this level of stubbornness.

So instead, she joined him for a long shower—a surefire way to relax him—a return trip to her beautiful vintage bed—ditto—and a restful nap allowing him to gear up for the day's early start. Grif needed respite from the demands of his celestial superiors.

And Kit needed him unconscious while she made her getaway.

Back in the kitchen, Kit keyed Jeap Yang's address into the maps app on her phone, then took a moment to study the black-and-white candid staring up at her from the folds of the paper. Grif was right, of course. Jeap had set himself down this path the first time he shot up, and whatever reasons he had, as painful and excusable as they might be, it had been his choice.

But just leaving him to die was wrong, Kit thought, rubbing at her chest, just over her heart, which felt swollen and ached. If he were her son or brother or loved one, Kit would want someone to help him, and she was the only one with this information.

And, like Jeap, she had a choice.

She left the paper with Jeap's information where it was, because Grif would need it upon waking, and exited through the front door, since the alarm was already silenced. Outside, her thoughts sounded loud and dangerous in her mind, a stark contrast to the predawn stillness of the house. Intuition told her this wasn't the best idea she'd ever had, and she also knew she'd be in for it when Grif woke to find her gone.

He has wings, Kit thought defiantly, starting her car and slipping from the driveway as quietly as she could. He was using them to flit around looking for his old, dead wife, and his old, probably dead killers. So he could just use them to reach Jeap at his appointed time of death, too.

However, Kit was determined to get there well before that.

Traffic was steady as she raced toward North Las Vegas, adjacent to Las Vegas proper, but far from the lights strung like jewels along the neck of its more famous cousin. She had to cross the main drag to get there, but it was almost five A.M., the night close to fading, and even the world's most sleepless city was taking a small breather before the morning joggers and buffet crowd brought it crawling back to life. Still, neon and LED lights burned the sky, giving it false heat and an irregular throbbing pulse.

Kit had never been to Jeap Yang's neighborhood before but found it easily, using her navigation app. Yet she frowned as she wheeled her classic Duetto into a subdivision pitted with dying lawns. Yellowing newspapers littered the crumbling driveways, and bright orange stickers lay like pockmarks on empty windows and locked doors. The overt urban decay suddenly made her mission feel all the more futile.

Boomtown turned doomtown, Kit thought, sighing. It'd happened all over the valley in recent years. In the beginning, there'd been degrees of separation between the people she knew and those who'd lost their homes. Yet, before long, Kit's newspaper had been forced to rotate the phrases "financial crisis," "housing bust," and "bailouts and recession."

The hopeful FOR SALE signs never made it into neighborhoods like these. Here, people just left their homes to the banks and the squatters . . . which was probably how Jeap Yang had ended up here. She pulled in front of a house that was unstitched at the seams, though it couldn't have been more than a half-dozen years old. Silencing the car, Kit stared up at the second level and shivered. She'd been in a similar position four months earlier, staring up at a room where her best friend had just been killed, and where she'd first seen Grif.

This was different, Kit thought, forcing herself from the car before she had a chance to overthink it. This time she was here to save someone from death. This time she knew about the Everlast and Centurions. And although Jeap's predestined death was traumatic, he wasn't the victim of a homicide, so surely Kit was in no danger by simply trying to help him.

All she needed to do was knock on the door before Jeap's final, fatal hit—or so she thought. Her scant knowledge of drugs came from television dramas and the cold facts of black-

and-white newsprint. She didn't know the difference between blow, hash, heroin, or whipit. Sure, she had vices. Smoking was one of them. Her stubborn appearance at a foreclosed and abandoned home in the predawn hours against the wishes of her angelic boyfriend was probably another.

As she climbed the stairs leading to a truncated porch, Kit's fingers trailed the pebbled wall while she searched for life within the darkened window. She was surprised to find the window curtained, and was wondering if she should just try the door, when a voice boomed behind her.

"Yo, princess."

Whirling, she found the drive empty and silent, but she finally spotted a man with a dark-eyed squint leaning against a lamppost across the street. He was barefoot and shirtless, and the door to the house behind him was wide-open.

"You got business up there?" he called, jerking his head at the top floor. She wanted to tell him to hush, she didn't want to alert Jeap or any of the other neighbors, but the man kept talking. "Cuz you look like a nice girl and I can tell you. Ain't nothing nice waiting for you on the other side of that door."

Kit let out a slow sigh, and stepped to the edge of the porch. "I'm here to save a man," she replied, sotto voce.

"Man want to be saved?" the guy called, still too loud.

Kit frowned. What did that have to do with anything? "Doesn't everyone?"

He continued to stare up at her and, seeing she was serious, began to laugh. When Kit didn't move, he bent over and laughed harder. Then he turned back to his home, which stood out because its lawn was still green, the structure still well-tended, and he disappeared inside. Sighing, Kit put the laughing man out of her mind and turned as well.

What was the etiquette, she wondered, when knocking on the door of someone fated to die?

Since she was likely the first person to ever wonder that, she went with her gut and gave the door a timid tap. Nothing happened, so she knocked more loudly, then, when the home remained silent, wished for Grif's celestial ability to unlock doors with the wave of a hand. Edging to the window, she tried peering inside instead. As threadbare as the curtains were, they still obscured what they were meant to. No light or movement could be seen within.

Drawing away, she bit her lip, then smiled to herself.

"You're being stupid, Kitty-Cat," she said, using Grif's pet name for her to both chide and comfort herself, though she knew he certainly wouldn't use it on her now. But, according to him, she was already disobeying celestial law, so what was earthly law compared to that? And what did that matter when weighed against a man's life? If the wrong way of doing something was the *only* way, then was it really wrong?

The man from across the street popped his head back out of his home as she walked back down the stairs and reached her car's trunk. "I forgot something," she told him before he could speak, and hoisted a Maglite over her shoulder for her best Rosie the Riveter pose before heading back upstairs.

"Day-um, girl," the man called after her, though he didn't follow. Everyone, she thought smugly, respected Rosie.

Squared with the door once again, she gave knocking one final try. When there was still no answer, she shrugged, dropped her bag, then held her arms straight out from her body and whacked at the window's edge.

It wasn't as straightforward as it looked in the movies.

The blow made a striking *thwack,* vibrating up her arms, but did little else. A chuckle from behind turned into an insincere cough as she shot a glare over her shoulder at her amused audience of one. Early birds, she thought, turning back around. So annoying.

Pivoting, she used her wrists, elbows, and shoulders in tandem to whip the flashlight forward. This time a crack instantly splintered up the pane. Encouraged, Kit channeled her frustration, fear, and the swivel of her not-inconsiderable hips into the head of the flashlight.

Glass shattered gloriously, a tinkling destruction that made Kit wince and give thanks at the same time. Avoiding the jagged glass, Kit used the flashlight to push the dingy curtain aside, and peered into the still, soundless room. Smoke residue lingered in the air, a metallic reek like nothing Kit had ever scented before. Musty sweat hung heavy, too, and Kit spotted a lumpy mattress dropped mid-floor.

Wrinkling her nose, Kit searched for movement. "Hello?"

Her voice disappeared into the room, as if sucked into a black hole.

"See anything worth saving, sweetheart?" the man called from behind.

Kit didn't answer, but took comfort in his presence. It reassured her that there was life outside of this stale cavern.

The window was too far from the door to unlock it from outside, and too high to risk climbing through without serious injury from the glass. So, lifting the Maglite again, she began hammering at the lock. If Grif's report said that Jeap was in this home, then he was there.

Surprisingly, the knob gave way more easily than the glass, and she was pushing the door open a moment later. The toxic smoke and stranger's sweat enveloped her in an unwanted embrace, but otherwise, the stillness of the room made Kit think of Halloween and haunted mansions and rooms meant to startle. That was pretend, though, frightful experiences manufactured to emphasize the fact that you were alive. Whatever awaited her on the other side of this threshold, she knew instinctively, held true horror.

Picking up her purse, she stepped inside anyway.

The man outside stopped laughing.

Kit shuddered as the silence enveloped her, but continued edging into the home. If air could blister, this air would be rife with boils. Yet, the front room itself was less frightening than surprising. It looked much like her dad's old tool shed. Kit eyed the cans of paint thinner in the corner with confusion, gaze canvassing the household cleaners—none of which appeared to have ever been used on this room—and paused when she spotted the lighter fluid. Had Jeap and his friends been building something in here? Repainting the walls? Revarnishing furniture?

But no, the only furniture she spotted was an entertainment unit, chipped and wobbly, the top two drawers missing so that darkness loomed inside like eyeless sockets. The walls were yellowed and pocked even in the pale, intruding light, as if the harsh, acidic scent had burrowed into and peeled away the plaster. Kit covered her nose, her every sense curling inward, but continued forward.

Cigarette butts and errant syringes lay littered among potato-chip bags and fast-food containers. Dirty Tupperware was stacked against the walls, and shattered glass winked darkly along the baseboards. Kit's gaze finally fell on something familiar and innocuous: a black backpack slouched against the mattress. She reached for it, thinking it might hold some form of identification, and that's when she saw the foot.

Kit's gasp pulled in a lungful of the putrid air, and she immediately began to cough. The foot didn't move. Backing toward the dresser, she again held the Maglite like a weapon, but this time she aimed the beam and switched it on. The powerful light flooded the room, giving stark definition to the foot, and the subsequent body sprawled on the floor.

It was definitely Jeap Yang, Kit thought, swallowing hard and advancing slowly, though he remained unmoving. His face was slack and oddly gray, the features the same as those in the photo, though the shock of black hair had been recently, and badly, shorn. His clothing was nondescript—a stained white T-shirt and torn black jeans—though he could have been wearing neon and Kit wouldn't have noticed.

His body was in ruins.

Bruises littered his flesh, like someone had beaten it from the inside out. His right arm, splayed wide on the grimy carpet, boasted blackened veins beneath graying flesh. His wrist looked worse, scaly and green like he was some sort of reptile. Beside him lay a syringe clogged up with a sticky, yellowed gunk.

"J— Jeap?"

Her voice was low and sunken, the blistered air burning it from her lips. She licked them and tried again. "Jeap? Are you . . . ?"

Okay? Stupid question.

Still alive? A thoughtless one, if he was . . . and she was growing less sure of that by the second.

This is too big for me, Kit decided, pulling out her phone to call 9-1-1. Yet panic and nerves made her fumble it, and it cracked against a glass jar before landing next to Jeap's arm. Surprisingly, this sound registered with Jeap, and he startled, twitched once, and moaned.

The scaly flesh on his splayed wrist fell away to reveal infected muscle, and bone glistening with pus.

The severance must have been as painful as it looked, because Jeap's eyes shot wide. His throat moved, expelling a heartbreaking and tattered cry that rolled from him like a foghorn disappearing into an endless night. He lifted his left hand as if to cover his own mouth, but his voice cracked, and he grimaced painfully. Kit gasped, too, because that forearm was already stripped of flesh from elbow to wrist, the bone almost shiny amid the black, necrotic ruins.

"God." Kit lunged for her phone, careful not to touch Jeap's body as he began to shake. She punched at the numbers almost blindly, cursing when she misdialed. Jeap continued convulsing, body spasming like it was in nuclear meltdown. *He looks at war with himself,* she thought, staring as the tremors in his body alternated between sharp twitches and wild jerks. She'd have pulled a blanket around him, except there was no blanket, and she didn't dare touch him anyway. His whole body was an open wound.

No way had he done this to himself, she decided, and dialed again as his agonized cries roiled around her. Someone must have taken a knife to him, then left him to bleed out in this sad little room. And the drugs were clearly for the pain. Kit would damned well take drugs if her flesh was hanging from her bone in strips.

Then her phone went dead.

"Shit," she hissed. She shouldn't have unplugged it earlier in the night. It was useless now. She'd have to leave Jeap alone again just to call for help. Ignoring the smells from his seeping body, she moved to his side and bent. She wanted to reassure him first, let him know that he wasn't alone, and that she'd return. Yet she paused before touching his shoulder, not so sure the bruised gray skin wouldn't fall away as well. Instead she lay a hand on his oily, matted hair. Jeap immediately arched his back, his eyes, so wild the whites showed, rolling her way.

He looked at her, then through her, then slumped.

"I'm going to help you," she told him, but he didn't move at all. "Jeap?"

Stillness sank into the room, blanketing even the noises of the street outside. The laughing man, she realized, was gone.

Wiping her greasy palm on her capris, Kit kept her eyes on the shallow movement of Jeap's chest, as if that could somehow keep him alive. She was just about to rise, when his eyes shifted, first one and then the other. She had a fleeting thought—the muscles in those, too, must have come untethered—but then his eyebrows drew low, and the irises shrank to pinpricks, resembling nothing so much as black, four-pointed stars.

"Jeap? C— can you see me?"

"Yes," he answered, in a whisper that crawled up her arms like a spider. "It's so peculiar. You're so . . . bright. A right *deva,* you are."

Kit shivered. "Diva?" she said, and the word caused his lids to flare in surprise, the strange starry gaze pinned on her face. Yet he immediately squinted, cringing from her, and Kit held up a hand. "Hey, I'm not going to hurt you. I'm here to help."

One star-specked eye carefully edged her way again, independent of the other. It must be some sort of side effect from the drug, she thought, before he managed to croak, "You can see me? And hear me?"

Kit leaned closer to reassure him. "Of course."

"Then maybe you are a *deva*."

She shook her head, not following him at all. "I'm going to—"

"*D-E-V-A*," he spelled, cutting her off, a cracking sound accompanying every letter, like vocal cords snapping. "*Deva* means 'God,' but is also close to the word 'devil,' and both have the same root as 'divinity.' I'm very into roots."

"Roots?"

"You know, vines, trees, forests . . . roots." Jeap's head rolled away, but jerked back suddenly, like it was being held in place. Fixed, Kit thought, on her. The second eyeball followed a moment later. Bile swirled in Kit's belly.

"I wonder," Jeap said in that snapping tone, "if I can see and hear you . . . can I touch you, too?"

They both froze at the thought, and Kit—in a voice that was also unlike her own—said, "You're not Jeap Yang, are you?"

The mouth twitched, a serpent's smile, and Kit pushed back just as Jeap's body catapulted toward hers. A pained cry escaped the throat, but it was immediately smothered by a howl that was wind-washed and somehow Arctic-cold. Dead leaves fluttered through the walls of the house, and dried boughs cracked against the windows, though there was not one damned tree or leaf or branch in the room.

But there *was* a rotting arm reaching for her, and Kit threw her phone at Jeap's body as she backpedaled.

Yet she'd forgotten about the glass jars. She tripped, ankle rolling in her wedges, and the image of stray needles lacing the floor flashed through her mind. "No—"

She braced herself for the fall, and for the decaying body already collapsing atop hers.

Strong hands caught her at the waist, spinning her around. She cried out, but it was drowned out by another that squalled like a winter wind. The loosening of a thousand simultaneously unsheathed blades ripped the air behind her, and a thunderous crack sounded, like an old oak snapping at its base. Jeap's body had hit the barrier of knives as Grif flexed his shoulder blades, and his protective wingspan thrust Jeap—and whatever was in him—away. Kit had found her balance by then, but Grif—her man, her *angel*—continued to hold her tight.

Kit couldn't see his wings with her mortal vision, but his arms alone were comforting. Kit scented bar soap, powder detergent, and strong and healthy flesh. The slight whiff of licorice that always tinged his breath rolled over her as he soothed her with a quick murmur, and she tilted her head up, catching the coconut of his pomade as well. The scents, the warm and steady hands—the flaring, martial wings—centered her.

"What are you?" she heard, the question wind-whipped from behind the shielding wings. "Because you're not Pure."

Bristling, Grif's feathers clinked like knives. Kit still couldn't see them, but she could hear them as he half-turned. "Depends on who you ask."

"Are you Fallen?" The wind and chaos in the voice had died down to a cool whisper, but boughs still crackled in the question.

"More like busted," Grif answered.

Kit stared up at Grif, confused. Was he actually engaging with this . . . that . . . thing?

The splintered voice lifted. "Let me see her. I need that light again. It's been so long . . ."

Grif's arms tightened around Kit's shoulders with a clanking of metal, fine slim blades marshaling anew. "Get behind me, you piece of celestial waste. You won't touch her *or* me, because I am also one of God's own."

"Pure *and* God's child?" Icy derision funneled Kit's body in a mini-tornado. She shuddered in Grif's arms. "Not possible."

And the rush of wind rose again. Grif shifted, slivering the air with wings that'd gone blade-sharp, and Kit heard a sound like roots grinding beneath a relentless saw. Then there was an elongating cry, one stunted with the fluttering of pebbles and dead leaves, like debris roiling in a twister. The sound whipped around her, fed into the walls, and then, inexplicably, retreated out the front door.

Kit's ragged breathing was suddenly the loudest thing in the room. Grif's grip softened on her shoulders, but remained there to steady her. Eyes squeezed shut, Kit didn't move at first, but then she risked a glance over his left—wingless—shoulder, and found Jeap exactly where he'd been lying when she'd entered the room.

"Wh-what was . . . ?" But there were no words for what she'd just seen. Irises like opaque stars in eyes that moved independently of each other. Breath like a storm. A voice alive with the sounds of a forest.

"That," Grif said, jaw tight, "was an opportunist."

"It touched me, Grif. Just for a second, but . . ." She looked at him. "It felt like death itself."

She searched his face for reassurance, yet all he did was nod.

"Is he gone?" she asked, panicking all over again.

"Yes," Grif said, voice strange. "It's gone."

Kit noted the word choice, and shuddered. "It butchered him, Grif," she told him as steadily as she could. "Jeap lifted his arm and I saw bone. I saw—"

Grif cut her off with the shake of his head. "No. Jeap did this to himself."

"No way!" Pulling away, she pointed at the motionless teen. "Look at him! He can't even sit up. He's lying in his own feces!"

"Because he didn't do it today."

Kit shook her head. Though simple enough, the words didn't compute.

Something in her expression made Grif soften. "I told you it couldn't be stopped."

"You mean Jeap has been like this, by himself, for more than a day?" She shook her head, like that could make it not true.

"More than many days from the look, and smell, of things."

Horrified, she met Grif's gaze. "Jesus. Someone just left him here?"

"Likely someone as strung out as he was, yes. And that's what I need you to do now, too."

She nodded. "We'll call an ambulance. They can help—"

"Can they?" Voice raised, and angry now, Grif cut her off. "Look at him, Kit. The flesh is falling from his body. Gangrene. Can't you smell the rot?"

Kit's chest tightened, and bile soured in her throat. It was the very thought she'd been trying to keep at bay. "I thought it was that thing—"

"That *thing* was an angel, Kit."

"No way." Jerking away, she stepped back. "That was nothing like—"

"Nothing like me, no. But it was horrifying and awesome and destructive. There are angels out there who are all of those things."

Kit glanced down at her shaking hands. She needed a cigarette to get her nerves back under control. "I don't understand."

Grif clutched her shoulders again, but this time he gave her a little shake. "And I don't have time to help you. Take my phone, Kit. Go make your call, but I need to help him before, or in case, that angel comes back, and I can't do that unless you leave."

"Leave him to die?" Her voice cracked on the last word, and the shock she'd been fighting off finally found its way into her limbs. She began to shake.

"He's afraid, Kit. But he's also holding on because you're here." Grif closed his eyes, and his nostrils widened as he filled his lungs with the filth and poison in the room, along with something else Kit knew she'd never be able to smell. "He's ashamed. He wants to let go, and knows there's nothing left for him here, not even his own body, but he's not going to listen or come with me as long as you're in the room."

"How do you know that?" Kit whispered, slowly shaking her head.

Opening his eyes, Grif met her gaze. "Because I know death."

Kit stared at Grif like she'd never seen him before, but finally turned to slowly pick her way across the destroyed room. She'd return the flashlight to her trunk, get that cigarette, and call for help that would arrive too late. Meanwhile, Grif would execute his fated, unstoppable job.

Yet she paused at the threshold to the home, one hand clutching the open doorway as she glanced back over her shoulder. Grif looked the same as always in his loose-fitting suit, the fedora shading his eyes, still wingless to her human gaze. But the hard worry on his face was unfamiliar and made worse because he was looking at her and not back at Jeap.

"That angel . . . is it really gone?" Kit asked.

Grif inclined his head, but looked no less worried, and Kit knew why. She'd talked to, and interacted with, a creature not of this world. Worse, it'd talked back.

"It was dangerous," she said, speaking from her gut. She might not know the ways of the Everlast, but she'd learned long ago to trust her gut. "Not just to Jeap, but to me."

"Don't worry," Grif said, eyes narrowing. "I'm dangerous when it comes to you, too."

CHAPTER FOUR

With sweaty palms and a racing heart—and wings still unfolded and pricked to the smallest shift of the air current in the room—Grif watched Kit exit the dingy, deserted home. Every nerve in his body screamed at him to follow, and he allowed himself a shudder at the memory of the way that angel—that *thing,* as she called it—had been staring at her when Grif arrived.

It had looked ravenous. It lunged for Kit like it was about to dine.

Yet that otherworldly presence was gone, and Grif needed to forget the interaction for now. At least he knew what was happening to the missing Lost souls, and he'd report back to Frank once he hit the Everlast, but first he needed to secure this one. He'd given Jeap Yang's unwelcome visitor a good jolt, but that didn't mean it wouldn't return.

Squinting through the room's corralled chemical haze, Grif stared at Yang's abused remains. Sarge had stated that this kid and Grif had something in common, but gazing at the drug-addled body, Grif was damned if he could see what.

Yeah, they'd both been born on this great big mudflat, if decades apart. They'd both once been healthy strapping young men with promising futures, each of which had been altered by choice and fate and damning mistakes. Grif saw that much. They'd also each died in ways horrific enough to sentence them to a post-life stint in incubation, or what Grif liked to refer to as the Tube. In you went, broken and weary and weighed down with your past, and out you came, polished up enough to pass through the Pearly Gates. At least that's how it worked for most.

It hadn't for Grif, which was why he'd gotten stuck working the Centurion beat, and if Jeap were broken enough—ashamed of his life's actions, haunted by guilt, or hanging on for a chance to make it all right—then he'd end up doing the same, helping other injured souls into Paradise until he, too, healed enough to move on.

But the similarities stopped there. Newly shorn from his body, Jeap's soul was the spiritual equivalent of a newborn . . . and in this case one that was a strung-out, drug-addled, abandoned shell of a human with no hopes of locating on his own which way was up. In turn, Grif was like protective services for the soul. One that'd come through the same system, graduated without honors, and was now charged with ferrying this Lost scrap of life into the Everlast.

He had fifty years' worth of experience in dealing with the dead, plus instinct honed as a mortal P.I. before that. Right now that experience and instinct had him standing stock-still in the filth-strewn room before he pulled out his Luckies and lit a stick. It was a stalling tactic . . . and a calming one. It showed he wasn't here to judge. It also helped shield his strong sense of smell from the room's toxic chemical haze. He'd be lucky if the lining in his nostrils survived it.

Blowing out a defensive stream of smoky tar, he said to the empty room, "You can come out now. No one here but us dead people."

Jeap's shallow breathing immediately ceased, his chest falling still in mid-inhalation, as if he'd been waiting for permission to die. Nothing happened after that, though. A regular Take would rise immediately, his or her ethereal form emerging directly from the earthly remains, but maybe the Lost were different. He'd have to ask Sarge.

In any case, the kid had to know death was coming, and he'd probably overthought the experience. On top of the attempted soul-rape, Jeap was likely so scared by everything he didn't know that he'd rather hold on to the fetid remains of a decaying body than let it go for . . . well, only God knew what.

Maybe that's why Grif had been sent to Take the kid. He knew enough of both heaven's clockwork and earth's timeline to merge the two into one seamless thread. "If you're worried about the girl, don't be. She's calling for help, though she'll be back soon, and if you want to get out of here before all those people see you like this, now's your chance."

Not the most sensitive speech he'd ever given, but not the least, either. Still, nothing happened.

Frowning, Grif bent over the body, using Pure eyesight to see past flesh and bone, searching for life beneath the earthly remains. Nothing. So he took another drag from his stick, bent closer, and exhaled hard. An ethereal mingling of temporal

smoke and supernatural license washed over the corpse, causing the thin eyelids to flip open like shades. Grif stared. The
starry, otherworldly gaze was also gone.

Straightening, Grif looked around. It took a moment, one
in which he had to remember both to look and *not* look, but
then he caught the shimmery thread of plasma slithering into
a beat-up entertainment unit, the only real furniture in the
room. Tucking his stick between his lips, he crossed the room
in two strides, bent, and yanked the bottom doors open with
both hands. There, inside, were the coiled-up spiritual remains
of Jeap's newly shorn soul.

"No need to worry now, son," Grif said. "It's all over."

The soul was shivering, even though the spiritual world was
absent of heat or cold. Jeap might feel better if Grif could get
him to look in the mirror. His ethereal remains resembled the
boy he should have been, before the drugs took him hostage.
Sure, he'd be forever confined to the dingy clothes he'd died
in, and he'd made a gross error in judgment by recently cutting
his own hair with what must have been a kitchen knife, but his
skin was unblemished beneath the sad mop, his eyes clear, and
his mind was likely sharper than it'd been in years.

When Jeap realized Grif wasn't going to grab, berate, or
otherwise abuse him, he gave a jerky nod. "You made him go
away."

Nodding, Grif offered a hand, and after a moment Jeap accepted it. He straightened with a groan and wiped off the back
of his jeans. "Thank you. He was tugging at me, and it felt like
his fingers were splintering beneath my skin, but it felt like
splinters of ice, and then . . ."

"Yes?" Grif said, because Jeap had frozen, as if the memory
of those icy fingers had riveted him to the floor.

"Then it saw her. That girl you were talking to." Jeap looked at Grif, eyes going wide. He began to shake again and put a hand to his stomach like he was going to be sick. "I felt what it felt, and it wanted to snuff that light in her from existence, to infect her with illness and disease and hatred and horror . . . oh my God."

"Stop," Grif commanded, and had to will himself not to shake the kid, or slap him, anything so he'd shut the hell up about Kit. "Stop thinking about it. It's gone."

Happy to oblige, Jeap nodded sharply, but looked around the room to make sure for himself. That's when he caught sight of his corpse and winced. "Did I do all that to myself?"

"What's the last thing you remember?" Grif asked, because he didn't remember his death, either. That was the Everlast's way of protecting the dead. It kept them from reliving those final, horrifying moments over and over again, so that they could more easily move on.

Not exactly foolproof, though, was it? Grif thought, taking one final, steadying drag before flicking aside his smoke. He couldn't remember who'd killed him, yet he couldn't forget it, either.

Jeap shook his head. "I remember entering this room. It didn't look like this, though."

"What day was that?"

"Friday."

Today was Tuesday. "Which Friday?"

Jeap shrugged. "I don't know exactly, but my girl always gets paid the first of the month. So . . . last Friday, I guess."

The kid was off by a week, but Grif just nodded. No wonder he was dead. He'd been pumping this filth into his veins for almost twelve straight days. But Jeap was thinking of something else. "Come to think of it, now that I can actually think, I mean . . . I guess she wasn't really my girl. I mean, how can you really love someone if you help them do this?"

"She buy you the drugs?"

Jeap ran a hand over his head, jerked it away in surprise, then moved across the room to study his reflection in the window. Groaning, he tried to smooth out his hair, but it fell back into the matted mess from the time of his death. "Man, she introduced me to it," he finally replied, turning back to Grif. "Said I'd get the ride of my life. Guess she meant the last ride."

"Would she get high with you?"

"Yes." Then he thought about it. "No. Wait."

Grif waited as the kid's brow furrowed.

"I don't know." He stared at Grif. "Why can't I remember?"

"Because your death was violent," Grif said simply. "Even if it was self-inflicted."

"Violent. Yeah." The kid rubbed his hands up and down his arms, and shuddered. "I burned and felt dirty inside even as I was doing it. But I couldn't help it. I just couldn't stop . . ."

Grif saw where this was headed, and placed a steadying hand on Jeap's shoulder. The last thing he needed was for the kid to panic and run off-track. "The Everlast keeps you from recalling a violent death so you don't have to relive it. You're not meant to take it with you."

Jeap laughed humorlessly. "Man, I've been living this death every day for the past two years."

"Hey," Grif said sharply, causing the kid to jump. Grif softened his tone. "Guilt is an empty emotion. There's no place for it in the Everlast."

Jeap licked his lips. "You . . . sure that's where I'm going?"

"That's where I went." And Grif had enough guilt for the two of them.

"You're an angel," Jeap pointed out then. Shifting his gaze, Grif caught sight of his wings in the window across from him. Only the dead could see them. Tar-black and sharp as blades, they crested high over his shoulders, flashing ebony muscles when he flexed. They were magnificent.

"Not always," he said, returning his gaze to Jeap's. "I was murdered in 1960. So I know what you're going through."

Jeap narrowed his eyes. "That must be why you look different."

"Than what?" Grif said.

"Than me."

Glancing at the corpse, Grif huffed. He hoped so. "That's because I'm both angelic and human."

He explained to Jeap in a quick rap how he'd been forced to cram his soul back into flesh four months earlier. The dual natures had hurt at first. His blood had eventually warmed, and his coagulated veins had warmed, but he'd suffered throbbing headaches for weeks after, migraines like earthquakes. Breathing was as torturous as if he were a lunger. Memory was a plague.

But then a Pure angel transferred some of her celestial strength into him in hopes that her amplified angelic senses would drive him mad, and he'd flee back to the Everlast. The plan backfired. Earth, the mudflat, had instead become bearable again. His senses were additionally magnified, almost as strong as they'd ever been in the Everlast. He'd since gotten used to the twin feathers she'd tucked deep behind each shoulder blade, and almost never felt them.

"I'm both ageless and clothed in mortal flesh," he concluded, as Jeap listened, rapt. "I have free will, like all humans, but am still bound to the Everlast. In short, Purity lives in me, even though it shouldn't."

"So how did *you* die?" Jeap asked.

Hands tucked in his pockets, Grif shrugged. "I was stabbed in the gut. A doc probably coulda patched me back up, but one never got the chance."

"You weren't found in time?"

"I was dry-gulched right after I was stuck."

"You were what?"

"Whacked over the head with a ceramic vase."

Jeap winced, then looked back at his remains. "So what will happen to me?"

"You'll go through a process called incubation. It's . . . healing. It'll rehabilitate you so that you forget most of your earthly years. Then you can move on to Paradise."

Jeap looked over at his body and shuddered. He still had the wide-eyed aspect of the Lost, but at least he didn't look like he was going to run. "Think I'll get to come back, too?"

Grif winced before he could help it. He wouldn't wish a return to the Surface on anyone. Except himself, of course. "Aren't you tired, son?" he asked quietly.

"Exhausted," Jeap admitted, swallowing hard before he met Grif's gaze. "But I have regrets."

"'Course you do." Grif shrugged. "That's how you know you were alive."

"I did things I shouldn't have," Jeap added.

"That's how you know you were human."

Jeap thought about it. "If the afterlife—"

"Everlast," Grif corrected.

Jeap lifted his chin. "—is so great, then why are you here?"

Grif sighed, wishing the kid wasn't quite so alert now. "I'm looking for the guy who killed me," Grif finally said, then mentally corrected himself. *Guys.*

Jeap slumped. "I guess I don't have to do that."

Nope, and again, Grif wondered what Sarge thought he had in common with this gowed-up kid over half a century his junior. Jeap must have wondered the same thing, as he stared at Grif's wings, then back at his mortal remains. "And that other thing? The one that was pulling on me?"

"Once Pure." Grif shrugged. "Now Pure evil. But don't worry. It can't ascend."

"It called me lost, but I don't feel lost. In fact, I actually feel . . . good." Jeap tilted his head, and took a moment to think about that. "For the first time since I can remember, I *don't* feel like hiding."

"Good. Then you should get through incubation just fine."

"She should hide, though."

"What?"

"That girl. She needs to run, something. That . . . *thing*. It's going to circle back for her."

From far away, it seemed to Grif that he heard screaming in the night. He managed to control his voice as he spoke. "How do you know that?"

"It was in me, right?"

Grif gave a jerky nod.

Jeap tried for a nonchalant shrug, but it morphed into a shudder. "So I was in it, too."

Grif's mortal blood took up the scream, zinging through his veins, forced by his frantic heart. God, he thought. Not Kit. Not again.

"Let's go," Grif managed, needing to get this duty over with so he could get back to Kit.

But Jeap gave his earthly remains a final sad, lingering look.

"What?" Grif asked impatiently.

"I don't know. Now that I think about it, maybe under the weight of flesh and blood and, you know, free will, maybe we're all just a little bit lost."

Grif froze, staring at the kid. "C'mon," he finally said, hoping Jeap hadn't noted his hesitation. "You're beginning the Fade."

And he led Jeap toward the adjacent bathroom, where he shut the door. Jeap stopped him with a hand on his arm before he could open it again.

"You sure they'll take me? I'm . . ." Jeap looked back at his destroyed body. "Unclean."

Grif held out his hand, and because the kid needed it—because they both did—gave him a little smile. "The place would be empty if they only accepted the pure. Now come on."

And he reopened the door so they could step directly into the Everlast. Jeap gasped, sucking in stardust and solar wind, and as horns heralded his arrival, Grif led him into the Universe's welcoming arms.

Kit was neither ashamed nor surprised that she had a little breakdown before calling the cops. What the hell was she supposed to do after stumbling upon a man who was both rotting and alive, not to mention possessed by some sort of malevolent spirit? Of course it'd freaked her out. She was a reporter, not a crime scene technician. Not a clairvoyant.

Certainly not a *D-E-V-A*.

Shuddering at the memory of leaves whipping along interior walls, Kit gave in to tears that scalded her cheeks in the dawning light. Duty eventually got the best of her, and so her hiccupping sobs were gradually replaced by deep, cleansing breaths. Still, she didn't dial 9-1-1 like a normal civilian. Instead she invoked one of the perks that came with *her* job, and called Detective Dennis Carlisle.

"I like you, Craig," he said, voice dusted over with sleep. "But I'm hanging up."

"Don't you dare, Dennis. I need you," she said quickly, tucking the phone between chin and shoulder so she could shakily light a cigarette. Her hands were almost steady. "You *specifically* at a crime scene."

"Call O'Connell," he said, and Kit heard bedcovers rustling as he rolled over. "You can trust him to do the job."

Kit was as trusting of the law as anyone who reported events on both sides of it, but that wasn't the point. "I need someone who is going to care as deeply as I do."

Even over the phone, he saw right through her. "You mean who will listen to your opinion and feed you information in return."

"No reason we can't turn this investigation into a two-way street," she said lightly, and inhaled.

"Investigation?" Now he was awake. The covers rustled again as he shifted in bed, and Kit briefly found herself wondering if anyone was lying next to him. "What makes you think—"

"You'll want to bring the CIS unit, too," she said, cutting him off.

"Dammit." A pause, and the silence made her wince. "Are *you* okay?"

She warmed at the question, the way it was asked, and answered affirmative before giving him the address. Dennis hung up without a good-bye, but Kit smiled anyway. He'd moved to town a handful of years ago from Southern Cal, another locale with a strong rockabilly contingent, and as theirs was a small subculture, they'd met within weeks. They bonded over a common love of beach bands and car parks. Dennis was a cop, but more than that, he was a true friend. He'd come.

"I don't think I've ever seen you looking so slapdash" were his first words to her, and she pushed herself from the side of her Duetto as he stepped from his unmarked car.

Glancing down, Kit made a face. Her shoes and bag were all right—hard to screw that up when all you had in your closet was vintage perfection—but the capris and sweater set were boring at best, and she was barefaced, hair untidily pinned. "I was in a hurry."

Dennis frowned. Everyone in the scene knew how fastidious Kit was about her appearance. "Tell me," he said, as he made to sit next to her.

Kit jerked her head at the foreclosed home's open door. "See for yourself."

After that he was too busy to talk at all.

As hoped, Dennis gave instructions to the beat cops that he'd be doing the interviewing, so they left Kit alone while they secured the crime scene and started the door-to-doors. Kit propped herself on the hood of her car to observe the comings and goings, and to eavesdrop on the officers' conversation while she waited. She wasn't given this leeway because of him, or because she was a witness, or because she was a reporter.

Kit's father had been a cop, killed in the line of duty. The circumstances surrounding Martin Craig's death were every cop's unspoken fear: an anonymous call, a botched robbery,

a masked thief who simply didn't like men in blue. It also remained unsolved.

"What the hell was that?"

Kit jumped as Grif materialized behind her in that way he
had, as if dropped like a star from the heavens themselves. He
could reappear on the Surface any time he chose after returning from a Take—whether it was one second after he'd left, an
hour, or a week—as long as it was in the future. He'd clearly
chosen this point in time because the cops would be too busy
to question his appearance . . . and wouldn't even know he'd
been here earlier.

Kit took in his clenched jaw, stony gaze, and hard frown,
and pushed to her feet. "I've been waiting to ask you the same
thing."

He came around the car to stand with her, toe to toe, which
wasn't as romantic as it sounded. "You snuck out while I was
sleeping."

"I knew you wouldn't sleep for long. And I left you Jeap's
address."

"You left me to find my own way," he corrected.

"I left you a hat with a built-in compass."

He narrowed his eyes beneath his old fedora, and, swallowing hard, Kit took up the offense. She crossed her arms. "You
didn't tell me there were angels masquerading as monsters."

He opened his mouth like he had something more to say
about that, but then shook his head and changed the subject.
"Don't you realize what you could have done?"

"Nothing, apparently." Sighing, she stared east where the
sun had begun its stretch into the sky, its yellow yawn wide
behind the lavender-draped mountain range. Nothing she did
ever seemed to matter against fate's heavy fist.

Grif stepped forward, into Kit's personal space . . . and not in a good way. "You got yourself gummed up in something you shouldn't have, Kit. Your name's going to be attached to a death you never should have touched. Again."

Kit understood his worry. She'd been targeted for death the last time she'd had an inadvertent run-in with fate, but hey—they'd come through that okay in the end. Besides, done was done, and Kit knew she'd try to save Jeap again, given the chance. It wasn't the human element she was worried about anyway.

"That thing had black stars for eyes, Grif. It had a voice that sounded like a hurricane. It could *see* me."

And as soon as she said it, Kit could see that was why he'd been worried. His jaw clenched as he jerked his head. "It shouldn't have been able to. You're alive. You're Chosen—"

"And angels can't harm the Chosen," she said quickly, though it was really a question. "Those are the rules, right?"

"I don't know if you've noticed, but the fallen ones have a history of breaking rules."

Kit froze. She'd have reached for another cigarette if she could have moved. "But they're weaker than you guys, right? Like, neutered and scared with their tails tucked between their legs?"

"The fallen angels *hate* God and everyone on His Christmas list. They especially hate humans."

Kit held up a hand. "I appreciate the theology lesson, but right now all I want to know is why. Could. It. See. Me?"

"Better question: why could *you* see it?" Grif shook his head, but still tried to answer. "I think it's because you know so much. Too much."

The EMTs emerged just then, carefully rolling Jeap's body

from the abandoned home. Watching them go, Kit was glad Grif had Taken the boy. Jeap Yang had suffered enough.

"Dennis has no idea what that drug is," she said, lighting another cigarette. The sight of the body grounded her back in this world, but her nerves spiked all over again. "He's seen heroin, roofies, X, meth, GHB, and one or more of them combined into a lethal cocktail, but he's never seen a drug made with paint thinner and lighter fluid."

Grif glanced back at the house, and Kit watched the memory of thickly clogged needles flash in his dark gaze. The recollection of the cleaners and solvents in the corner made Kit wince, too. "He shot industrial cleaner into his body?"

"Among other things." Blowing out a skein of smoke, she pulled out her Moleskine. "Dennis did a check on the kid. He'd been going to a trade school for culinary arts. Jeap wanted to be a chef at one time, can you believe that?"

"Well he cooked up a hell of a recipe here," Grif said.

"Someone else gave it to him, though," she said, flipping the notebook shut. "And I'm going to find out who."

Tapping out his own smoke, Grif eyed her as he tucked the pack in his pocket. "Kit—"

"Don't even try—"

Grif grabbed her by the arm, cigarette forgotten. "You read a private file. You weren't even supposed to be here."

She stomped her foot. "You weren't going to do anything!"

"I was going to do my job!" Clenching his fist, he busted his cigarette, which was how she knew he wanted to grab her again.

"It's not a job," she said anyway. "Jeap is a person!"

"Not anymore." Grif held up a hand, sighing immediately, taking the sting out of her shock. He knew how it sounded.

"Just so you know, he was fine when I left him in the Everlast. Happier than he's been in over two years."

Kit goggled, but not for the reason Grif would expect. "He'd been living like that, with that fate, for two whole years?" She rubbed her free hand over her face. "And you still don't think I should have intervened?"

"Interfered," Grif corrected. "Living that way was Jeap's choice. He said as much himself."

Kit's jaw clenched reflexively. "What else did he say?"

"He said his girl introduced him to it. Recently."

Kit brightened at that. "Good, then we find out who he's been seeing recently and we have our first lead."

Grif shook his head. "We don't have a lead, because this isn't an investigation."

"Actually it is." The voice came from behind Grif, and even Kit hadn't seen Dennis's arrival. She'd been too focused on Grif's stubborn face. Grif turned, and suddenly both men were silhouetted against the rising sun, just like the mountains at their back, both formidable and unmovable as they squared off against each other.

"We're extremely interested in finding out who's dealing this drug," Dennis said. "For obvious reasons."

Kit wondered how much he'd heard of their conversation, but his face remained professionally blank.

"Obvious to some of us," Kit replied hotly, ignoring Grif's glare.

Dennis ignored it, too. He and Grif liked each other well enough, but neither of them would let that get in the way of their respective jobs.

"That's fine," Dennis said, turning to Kit. "Because you're the one I need."

"Me?" Kit said, surprised.

"Her?" Grif said, wary.

Dennis looked at Kit and cocked his brow. "You scratch my back, I'll scratch yours."

"Done," Kit said immediately.

"Kit—" Grif tried to edge between them.

Kit stepped to the side, bringing Dennis into view again. "What do you need?"

"Like crimes," said Dennis.

"It wasn't a crime," Grif tried again. "It was a—"

"It was awful," Dennis said sharply, his glare just as honed. He turned back to Kit as Grif clenched his jaw. "Worst I've ever seen. So I'm willing to trade. But I need names, dates, anything you can get from reporting sources."

"You mean anything that might not have made it into print in the past," Kit said thoughtfully, biting her lip.

"You got stuff like that?" he asked.

Kit thought of her aunt's personal files at the paper and smiled. "And in return?"

"Interviews with Jeap's immediate relatives, if he has any. Barring that, friends."

"Doesn't seem like he had any real friends," Kit commented.

"Associates, then."

"You want this in print?" she asked, as he ran a hand over his head.

"Anything you gotta do to shine a light on what happened in there. I want to find out who's dealing this shit." For a moment, his face crumpled. "His flesh was falling from his bones."

"I want in with the coroner," she said, while his defenses were still down.

Up they went again. "Kit . . ."

"Dennis," she said, her voice carrying the same warning. But she was distinctly aware that he was holding all the cards here. Just as she was aware that Grif had yet to speak. That was just as worrisome.

Dennis finally sighed. "I should be able to swing it. But I'm calling in a big marker."

"I'll do the same," she said, thinking of her aunt's files again. "Then we'll hit the major wires together and hit them hard."

"Deal," he said, and they high-fived to seal it.

"Damn," Grif said under his breath.

"Stay by the phone." Dennis threw a look behind his shoulder as an officer called him over, then began backing away. "I'll call you as soon as I get a lead."

Then he was gone, and she was left with Grif's heavy silence spoiling the morning air. It was only marginally better than the stench inside the house, Kit thought, and set her jaw before looking at him.

"You know," she told Grif, leaning against her car as he glared at her. "You could help me. Dust off your detective's hat."

"I don't have a detective's hat," he snapped. "I have a hat that beeps."

But Kit's mind was made up, so she just ignored his anger and his glare, and glanced back at the abandoned home. "How the hell did that thing get inside Jeap?"

As annoyed as he was with her, Grif joined her against the car, and eventually slipped his arm around her waist. "The Pures can possess the bodies of those who are . . . closer to God's mysteries than the rest of us. Usually very old or young."

"Sometimes a sleepwalker?" she asked, recalling what he'd told her of his vision.

He nodded. "And sometimes those weakened by drugs. I guess the fallen angels can do the same."

"I drink alcohol," Kit pointed out, then looked at the cigarette burning low in her hand. "And I smoke."

"Not to the point that you black out. Or allow the flesh to fall from your living body."

She gave him a tight smile, but flicked the cigarette away anyway.

"Hey." Grif shifted to cup Kit's face in his palms and locked his gaze on her own. "You're more alive than any person I know. And I swear on my life, I won't let that thing near you again."

It was exactly what she needed to hear. Blowing out a long breath, she leaned forward and he pressed a kiss to her forehead. For the first time since she woke in the middle of the night, she settled and smiled.

"Come on," she said, opening the driver's door. "We can't do anything for Jeap until Dennis gets back to us with sources. Let's roll."

Grif just crossed his arms.

"We have an appointment this morning, remember?"

She held out for the length of his blank stare, then smiled when he finally jolted, and edged around the nose of the car. "That's right. Mary Margaret."

They'd finally tracked down Mary Margaret DiMartino, a woman Grif believed could provide information that would help him unearth who exactly had murdered him and Evie in 1960. Unfortunately, the past fifty years hadn't been easy on Mary Margaret, which was why she'd been so hard to locate.

Still, Kit refrained from pointing out that he didn't seem to mind her investigative bent when it came to his old mystery. Mostly because it *was* the greatest mystery of both of his lives.

But also because Kit, too, had a vested interest in knowing *who killed Griffin Shaw.*

The pad was raided."

"What?" She allows the word to curl softly at the end, like the steam rising from her cup, the first of the day. And like the steam, there's no mistaking the heat from its source.

Tomas answers quickly, working to deflect her anger before it's even risen. "A girl came by early this morning. She called the cops."

The woman curses in her native tongue, not caring that Tomas—American all the way back to his pasty, backwoods, pig-fucking grandfather—can't understand. How, after she's worked for a year getting everything in place, could something go wrong *now*?

"Why didn't you stop her?" she asks, switching back to English.

"She looked like . . . somebody."

"Somebody we know?"

There is a soft rustle on the other line, and she realizes Tomas is shaking his head as if she can see him. Idiot. Though she does have an ability to see things no one else can. She is blessed this way. It's why she is who she is.

"No," Tomas finally says. "Someone who would be missed."

"Who is she?"

"I've never seen her before. She's . . . different. Healthy. Has some money, too."

Hearing another telling rustle, she can picture, with her talented mind, Tomas peering out the window of the small tract home, darting a quick glance at the street now littered with cops and flashing lights and this woman who's called danger down upon them all. She can also feel his eagerness to leave—he *needs* to flee, with his record—but she hasn't given him permission to do so.

And she won't. Not yet.

"She's outside now," he says, scrambling for the information she wants. Anything so she will let him go. "She's smoking and leaning against a fancy car."

"What kind of car?"

"Not sure. Some vintage number with a soft top. Nothing ever meant to crawl the streets of this neighborhood."

"Is she Law?"

"I don't think so," he answers. "She's too . . . girly to be a cop. She looks like some sort of, I don't know. Pinup girl."

"I don't care how attractive you find her," the woman snaps. "I want to know if she's dangerous."

More rustling. "She's Anglo, like me. Dark hair, loose curls. Slim. No, doesn't look a bit martial."

Neither do I, the woman thinks, gazing out her own window at the gray, empty street. "But she is motivated?"

"She broke a window and went inside by herself."

By herself. What good is it to have a watchdog with no bite? Maybe she should show Tomas what teeth really look like. "And you just let her?" she snaps.

"She was after something." No bite. Just a whine.

The woman sighs, and closes her eyes. There is nothing to be done with a man like this. Nothing but use him for his brawn, and eventually turn his greed against him. She remains silent for a long while, pondering just how to do that, knowing he'll wait for as long as she wants.

"Follow her," she finally says, opening her eyes.

"But the cops—"

She stops him there. "I want to know what she knows."

This time he knows better than to argue. "Done."

"Tomas." The silence following his name is loaded. She knows he's spoken to some of the other men, *her* countrymen. She also knows—they'd told her—that in their language she is sometimes called "mother" and "bride." But to Tomas, she is the least motherly or maidenly woman he's ever meet, and that's how she keeps him tied to her, close, on a leash. "We're too near to our goal to allow some random stranger to trip us up."

"I know what to do." And that's *why* she keeps him at all.

"Make sure she doesn't see you," she says in parting, and waits for the answer that should have come. *Of course. I'm not stupid. Nobody ever sees me.*

Instead he says nothing. She curses silently, knowing then he's already been seen, but she doesn't call him on it. Instead she hangs up, letting him believe he's won a little something with the deceit. She will allow him to follow this newfound trouble, and get the answers she needs first. It will allow her to remain hidden. Smoke and shadows, after all, are where she thrives.

She will take care of Tomas—who knows too much, yet does too little—after that. And the strung-out kid in the abandoned house that this useless man was supposed to be watching?

He'll be considered lucky in comparison to Tomas's coming fate.

CHAPTER FIVE

The Sierra Vista Rehab Center was located on a busy intersection only one block from an affluent residential enclave that included a country club and guarded gates . . . not quite what Grif had expected. Other than the nurses' station and the white-tiled halls, the interior wasn't what he expected, either, and skewed toward homey rather than institutional, or at least like an exclusive private school. As Grif and Kit followed a nurse to the head administrator's office, he wondered how many of his preconceived notions were taken from the cinema, black-and-white flickers where wild-eyed patients were wheeled from room to room by stoic attendants, their straitjackets crisp, gazes empty, mouths slack.

He saw no such examples now, though they hadn't been allowed into the patients' ward, and were instead being led to the administrator's offices, presumably for last-minute instructions on how to interact with the patients in general, or at least with Mary Margaret. It wasn't until they were seated across from Ms. Lucinda Howard, with a wide, glossy desk looming between them, and her certificates and diplomas splayed across the wall behind her, that he realized something was wrong.

"How did you say you knew Ms. DiMartino again?"

Kit and Grif looked at each other. They hadn't, though Ms. Howard had their visitor's request form squared in front of her. They'd submitted it five weeks before, but had obviously left out the part about Grif's having known Mary Margaret fifty years earlier.

"We're old friends of the family," Grif said instead. "Mary Margaret's nephew, Ray DiMartino, told us where to find her."

Ms. Howard dismissed the familial bond with a sniff. "You understand this is highly unusual. It's rare that people outside of immediate family are allowed to interact with the patients. At least while they're under direct care."

"Mary Margaret doesn't live here full-time then?" Kit posed it as a question, but she, too, already knew the answer. She was just reminding Ms. Howard that they could, and would, eventually talk to the woman. Within these walls, however, the outcome of that meeting could be observed and controlled.

"No," Ms. Howard answered, with a tight smile. "Mary Margaret is a high-functioning patient. She had great results with our psychosocial rehabilitation program and had been living independently for over twenty months before this latest . . . incident. Your paperwork indicates you're already aware of this, which raises the question: why?"

"Why what?" asked Grif.

"Why disturb her with questions about her past? You're aware of her history. Yet you're not doctors, so you can't deal with the feelings and possible fallout that raising these issues outside of therapy might cause. Is there any particularly good reason that you might disturb the mental health of an individual who is already teetering on the brink of yet another breakdown?"

"We certainly don't want to cause Ms. DiMartino any distress," Kit said, leaning forward. "But we're looking for someone who disappeared a long time ago, and she might be able to help us locate their whereabouts."

Ms. Howard's lips tightened like a string, and she glanced back down at the paperwork, but the top sheet gave explicit familial permission for their visit. Mary Margaret had been consulted, and accepted the appointment when Kit called the facility five days earlier, so no matter what Ms. Howard's reservations were, there was little she could do about it now.

"Very well," she said, standing so that Kit could see straight up her narrow nose. "I'll see that she's ready. You'll be visiting in the atrium, our common area. There will be nurses there to assist you, and her, if needed."

And she strode from the room, spine ramrod-straight, without a backward glance.

"Was that a warning?" Grif muttered, when she'd gone.

"Do we look that threatening?" Kit replied, glancing down. Grif didn't bother looking at himself—he'd been stuck in the same clothing for more than fifty years—but since they were waiting anyway, he took the opportunity to give his partner a good once-over. They'd stopped at home after leaving the abandoned tract house, and she was now wearing a navy Japanese kimono dress that wrapped tightly across her chest and flared into an A-line skirt trimmed in red. Her bag and hoop earrings, both bamboo, matched the wedges on her feet, and the crimson flower behind her ear contrasted boldly with her onyx hair, currently tucked into a black snood pinned behind her bumper bangs.

She's like living, breathing origami, Grif thought, studying her from toe to head. She took a new delicate shape every day.

"Well?" Kit said, when his gaze finally reached her eyes.

One corner of Grif's mouth lifted. "I'm not scared."

Kit snorted, but sobered quickly as Ms. Howard reentered the room. She'd been gone less than two minutes, and though Kit and Grif automatically stood, she returned to her position behind the desk, and took a seat.

"I'm sorry," she said, folding her hands, not looking apologetic at all, "but Ms. DiMartino seems to have had a change of heart. She no longer wishes to see you. In fact, her preference is to have no visitors at all for the remainder of her stay."

Meaning, Grif thought, don't have her nephew call and try to convince her otherwise. The speed of Ms. Howard's return indicated she certainly hadn't tried.

"Did she say why?" Kit asked, hands clasped.

"She doesn't need a reason," Ms. Howard said, lifting her chin. "Here at Sierra Vista, we teach our patients 'no' is a complete sentence."

"Of course," Kit said quickly, though her voice was tighter now. She tried clearing it. "It's just that we're . . . disappointed. We were hoping she could help."

"Ms. DiMartino's first priority is to help herself. Frankly," said Ms. Howard, looking pointedly at Grif, "I was surprised she agreed to see you in the first place."

Maybe he *should* have given himself a good once-over, Grif thought, frowning. "Why's that?"

"She's not that fond of men, Mr. Shaw. She doesn't trust them, will never abide being alone in their company, and certainly doesn't consider them friends."

"Strange," Grif muttered. "She wasn't like that when I knew her."

"Excuse me?" Ms. Howard said, eyes narrowing sharply.

"Nothing," Kit said quickly, and Grif shifted uncomfortably. Looking all of thirty-three years old, same as when he'd died, he certainly couldn't explain to Ms. Howard that he'd known the now sixty-two-year-old woman when she was only twelve. "We're just surprised her nephew didn't say as much."

Ms. Howard shrugged. That wasn't her problem. "I'm afraid there's nothing I can do."

"Well, thank you for your time," Kit said warmly, though Grif just stood and left.

"Why do you bother being polite to such people," he said when Kit finally caught up to him halfway down the sterile hallway. He gave the double door leading outside a violent push. "You can't sweeten up vinegar."

"Because it's not about the war, darling. It's about the win."

Grif stopped dead and looked at her.

Kit stared back. "That means being surly doesn't help our cause."

"And being polite does?" he said, resuming his stride, though his anger had deflated and his shoulders slumped.

"Of course. Ms. Howard said Mary Margaret doesn't like men. That's you, not me. So being polite keeps the dialogue open. She'll be out from under Ms. Howard's eye and thumb in just a few days. I'll try again then."

"I don't know, Kit," Grif said, reaching the passenger's side of the car. "Maybe we should let her be. I have no idea what happened to her in the last fifty years, but some people got a reason not to remember the past. Plus, seeing me, like this . . ."

He gestured down the length of his body, indicating all of it—the suit, the shoes, the face that hadn't aged a day in half a century.

Kit paused, the car door half-open. "Honey, she's locked up in a mental-health facility, and drugged up to her eyeballs. And that's when she's *not* trying to drown her memories in a bottle. You really think she's forgotten anything? Take it from someone who's been there. Mary Margaret's past is chasing her down."

Kit began to climb in, but Grif held his hand up over the roof of the car. "Back up. What do you mean you've been there?" He pointed back at the sterile building. "You mean . . . *there*?"

Squinting up into the sun, she sighed. "Not Sierra Vista, but yes. One like it."

"But you're . . ." Grif couldn't help it. He made a face like he'd just swallowed a bitter pill. "Cheery."

Kit barked out a dry, humorless laugh. "Yes, and I had to make a conscious decision, and do a lot of work, to get that way. Starting when I was seventeen."

"After your father was killed."

Kit just nodded as she climbed in the car. Grif was slower, but only because he was putting it all together.

"That's when the rockabilly thing started, too, right?" he said, once he'd pulled his door shut, angling his body toward hers.

"Yes," she murmured, and Grif knew the memories were bad, because she didn't chide him for calling her lifestyle a "thing."

"Locked up, drugged up . . . shut up." Though the car was silent, her hands were propped stiffly on the glossy wood of the steering wheel as if it was holding her in place. She finally looked over at him. "That's not how I wanted to live, you know? So being *cheery,* as you call it, being rockabilly, and being a damned good reporter is my way of keeping the dialogue open."

"With whom?" he asked.

She blinked at him, then said, "With the world."

Grif simply reached out and placed his palm against her cheek.

The transformation was instant. Her hands fell to her lap, an enormous smile bloomed on her face, and a blush sent color rushing to her cheeks. He'd never met anyone who laid her emotions bare more easily than Kit. It made him want to cover her up, mostly, though lately it had started making *him* feel naked. So, for them both, he drew her close, held her tight, and rested his lips atop hers. He kept her there until they both were steady again.

"Don't worry," Kit said, glancing back to the building where Mary Margaret was hiding. "If there's one thing I'm good at, it's getting people to talk."

As if on cue, her phone rang. Checking it, Kit smiled, then flashed him the number. Detective Dennis Carlisle's photo flashed with it. "See?" she said cheerily, before answering it.

Grif just shook his head. Looks like they were headed to the dead house. Maybe, he mused, her communication powers extend to the deceased.

Then again, that was Grif's beat.

The coroner's office was housed in a building that was better-looking than most of its last-minute guests, though not by much. The brick face had clearly been laid decades earlier, though it'd been painted over so many times it looked like it was shedding its skin in the Vegas sunlight. The doors were steel, and the security guard inside had eyes of the same material. They didn't warm even when Kit gifted him with her brightest smile.

However, he did let them pass. "Second door on the left," he said, without emotion, and Kit mentally thanked Dennis for coming through yet again as they made their way down the peeling linoleum hall.

"Look," she told Grif, who was back to being annoyed with her after leaving the Sierra Vista facility. "What does it hurt to ask a couple of questions?"

"Depends on who you're questioning," he muttered.

Kit knew he was just worried for her safety, but his tone made her want to hiss. "I seriously doubt the coroner will whack me for wanting to know what happened to some street kid in an abandoned home. But I'm so glad you've got my back. Just in case."

Grif grunted, still annoyed, but held open the door to a small anterior room with the most uninspired desk she'd ever seen. A buzzer sounded behind the door opposite them, in what was likely the autopsy room. It opened a moment later, and in backed a man with fierce red hair, both too long and too short to be of any purported style. They'd obviously caught him in the middle of his work, because he was wearing scrubs, gloves, and a paper mask that cut deep indents into his flushed cheeks. His blue eyes stood out brightly against his skin, making him look wild.

"Sorry. My assistant went for coffee." The words were wry, and Kit sympathized. Budget cuts all around. The paper was experiencing them, too.

"You the coroner?" Grif asked.

"Medical examiner." The man stripped off a glove, held out a hand. "Dr. Charles Ott."

Grif shoved his hands in his pockets. Kit merely brightened her smile.

Ott laughed. "They're fresh. I'm just back from lunch."

Kit couldn't imagine downing a burger and then coming back to this job, but maybe that was what kept Ott so skinny. If the budget at the paper got cut too much, she might consider a career change. The autopsy room could be her key to being as svelte as Dita Von Teese.

"I'm Kit Craig," she said, finally taking the hand, "and this is Griffin Shaw. I believe Detective Carlisle told you we were coming?"

"He did, but you should know that I prefer to work alone. Don't like newshounds or detectives looking over my shoulder, you know?" He said it with a wink, but the words were clear enough. *Don't question my work.*

"Of course," Kit said.

The mask widened as the coroner smiled. It didn't make him look any less crazed. "But then I got a load of the deceased and thought a little tit-for-tat might be in order." He didn't wait for them to agree. "I'd love to know where the hell this kid learned to make *krokodil*." He pronounced it like "crocodile."

Kit looked at Grif.

Ott motioned to the door behind him. "Come with me."

"Should someone look that laid-back about death?" Kit whispered, edging close to Grif as they followed the coroner into the autopsy room.

"Not on this side of the Everlast," Grif muttered, and drew her even closer.

"Excuse the mess," Ott said, leading the way to a sheet-covered body in the room's center. "Nobody around here cleans up after themselves."

Har, har, thought Kit, swallowing hard as she neared the body. She averted her eyes, as if staring at the dead would be rude, her gaze scanning the long counter opposite them, and the sink rising in its middle. It was as cold and unwelcoming as Kit would've thought, if she'd ever really given thought to the workings of a morgue. Though the drains beneath the autopsy table were scrubbed clean, and the scale next to the body gleamed under the bright lights, Kit shuddered. Feeling her tremble, Grif gave her hand a little squeeze.

The doctor checked his hanging clipboard. "Jeap Yang . . . what kind of name is that anyway?" He didn't wait for an answer. "Age nineteen, sixty-eight inches tall, and he's a featherweight. You know anything else about him?"

Kit looked at Grif, who shook his head, so she said, "He wanted to be a chef."

"Well, the only thing he's been cooking lately is poison. There are traces of heroin in his system, probably the gateway drug for this one, and a quick-and-dirty hair sample shows residual cannabis, but any cash he had lately, and I guarantee there wasn't a lot of it, went into this drug. He'd have died even without the last few doses." Niceties over, Ott yanked back the sheet, and pushed at Jeap's white, mutilated arm with his fingertips. "Blood poisoning had already set in. Gangrene in several areas—the arm is only the most obvious. His groin, probably his first and most oft-used injection site, is the worst." He rolled the sheet back even more. Kit cringed. "The drug certainly lives up to its name. It's a fucking beast."

"What the hell is it, Doc?" Grif stared at the infection site, his voice tight, and his face so pale that his freckles stood out like constellations against his skin. Kit gave his hand a squeeze this time, and he glanced at her gratefully.

"Don't feel bad," Ott said, seeing it. "Even I haven't seen a green scaly groin before."

Kit blew out a hard breath. "I had an infected hangnail once, and that alone had me screaming for antibiotics." She couldn't imagine having an open wound on her body. Or in it.

"It's called desomorphine," Ott said, pushing the rotted flesh aside with his thumb. "The street name is *krokodil,* or 'crocodile' to us English speakers. It's a Russian street drug."

Kit drew back. "Russian?"

"I know," he said, shaking his head. His hair bloomed like a troll doll's. "I never thought I'd see it in my life, certainly not stateside. It's incredibly powerful and brutally addictive."

Kit's own vices didn't extend past caffeine and smokes, but she had friends who'd tried to shake off addictions before, some more successfully than others. "More powerful than heroin?"

The doctor scoffed. "A heroin substitute, but it makes powder look like a sugar high."

"No kidding." Grif's mutter made him sound more like himself.

Ott shoved his fingers someplace they shouldn't be, and the fetid smell of rot bloomed in the room. "It's not just the symptoms, though. Necrotic skin is bad, but the withdrawal is what ambushes the user. One hit and you're hooked, but try to quit and that's when it really takes hold." He glanced up. "Ever experiment with drugs?"

"No," Grif said.

Kit shook her head. "I don't like the feeling of being out of control."

"Big surprise," Grif muttered. She elbowed him.

"Well, I did," Ott said, bending to peer at places not meant for the human gaze. He was so intent on his search that he missed Kit's surprised frown. "Started popping pills right after med school, then gradually moved on to X, coke, heroin, meth. That's why they don't let me work on the living anymore, and it's how I got into this business. Personally, I know what it's like to be addicted. Professionally, I know what the chemicals are doing to the addict."

"You're very lucky to have that sort of perspective," Kit said softly.

"You're lucky you're still alive," Grif said, and Kit caught him studying the air around Ott's body. He'd once told her that he could see the imprint near-death left on those who'd narrowly escaped it, and he read those etheric outlines as easily as a palm reader scanned a hand.

Ott's must have been bad for Grif to mention it, and the man confirmed it with a dark, drawn nod. "My last hit was eleven years ago, and it put me down hard. The withdrawals lasted about ten days, or so they told me. I lost count."

"I bet even an hour is like a lifetime when you're in that kind of pain," Kit sympathized.

He moved his shoulders, as if the memory made him uncomfortable. "And all you have to do is shoot up to make it all go away."

"So how is *krokodil* different from that?" Grif asked, as Ott covered Jeap's chest cavity.

"Other than a desperate need to keep using it even after your flesh starts decaying?" Dr. Ott blew out a breath. "Imagine that painful week of detox being extended a whole month."

"After how long of using?" Kit asked, eyes gone wide.

"One hit," he said grimly. "And that month of agony is non negotiable. You can't tough it out. A colleague of mine went to Russia, did a paper on it. He said they had to tranq the patients just to keep them from passing out."

Kit let out a low breath, gaze flicking back to the scaly sites on Jeap's upper body. "Now the name makes sense."

"The Russian doctors call desomorphine addicts 'the walking dead.'" Ott shook his head, staring at the remains of what had once been a whole, if not perfect, boy. "The drug literally eats you alive."

"C'mon, Doc," Grif said, tone round with disbelief. "Surely word spreads on the street about a drug like that. If people know their flesh is going to fall from their bones, and their mind will break if they try to quit it, why would they still do it?"

Now the doctor looked amused. "Because they're poor, Mr. Shaw. Making illegal drugs more expensive doesn't result in fewer junkies, just more desperate ones. Come here." He motioned Grif closer to the corpse, and when they were all as tightly gathered as they were going to get, the doctor bent low and sniffed. "Smell that? It's acrid. Like ash if it could still burn."

Grif looked at Kit, and she knew he wasn't going to be sniffing anything. Kit wasn't exactly excited about the prospect, but she was curious despite herself. The more she learned about this drug, and what it'd done to Jeap, the more ammo she had to chase down its supplier. She sniffed, and immediately pulled back. "Irritating."

"Think how it felt to him," the coroner said.

Hands in his pockets, Grif finally leaned over as well. "What the hell is that?"

"Iodine," the doctor answered evenly. "And some lighter

fluid, maybe some industrial-strength cleaning oil, and—most important—some over-the-counter codeine."

Kit waved a hand like she could rewind the conversation. "Like in cough syrup?"

"Over the counter?" Grif tilted his head. "Sounds harmless."

"That's just the thing," Ott said, inhaling deeply, though he appeared more fascinated than repulsed. "It's only over the counter in Russia. You need a prescription here. And it's not harmless once you put those things together. Then you've created a poison the body can't resist."

He gestured again at Jeap's body, and Kit's gaze followed the movement. The white bone of Jeap's elbow lay exposed, perfectly formed and almost pretty through the tattered tissue.

"It's cheap." Kit closed her eyes to fight back the tears. And Jeap had been poor. And desperate. And in the end? Alone.

"Heroin has to be grown," Ott said, covering the body. "Someone has to plant poppies, convert them to opium, turn that into heroin. Then they gotta transport it. None of that's necessary with *krok*. It's a synthetic, so anyone with the recipe can whip it up. Ol' Emeril Lagasse over here probably did all this with a kitchen spoon, a lighter, and a syringe."

"You do know a lot about it," Grif commented.

"I wasn't just an addict, I was an addict with access to the medical library."

"And would you have ever done something like this?" Grif asked, jerking his head at Jeap's destroyed remains.

"I'm lucky I didn't have to make that choice," Ott replied, frowning. "*Krok*'s relentless. Thirty minutes to cook, but only a ninety-minute high. Using this shit is a full-time job."

One you couldn't quit, Kit thought, breathing out again.

"See that?" Ott said, pointing at a wound that had oozed openly on the corpse's neck.

"Least of his worries," Grif muttered, though Kit cringed at the open sore.

"The last in a long line," Ott confirmed. "His hands would have been shaking, either from the withdrawals or the pain. He missed the vein. That creates an immediate abscess."

Grif fell silent. The lunch Kit forgot to have rose in her throat. Dita's dress size, she thought dizzily, might not be out of reach after all.

"What really stumps me," Ott went on, "is where the hell did he get the recipe?"

"Good question," Grif said stiffly.

"Well, let me know when you get the answer." Dr. Ott was replacing the sheet over Jeap's face, but paused at Grif's pointed look. He gave a humorless laugh. "Don't worry, it's the professional in me that wants to know. Because personally?" The doctor's face darkened, the crazed look fell away, and his face went as dead as Jeap's. "I'd check myself into rehab the moment I even *thought* about doing that."

CHAPTER SIX

K it was on her phone before the morgue doors even slammed shut behind them, the Q&A between her and her aunt rapid-fire as she slid behind the wheel. Marin's raspy staccato was an evenly matched rival as they exchanged information, and despite the long night and day, Kit had to smile. It was good to be able to move quickly beyond the niceties and get right to the point.

It was, Kit thought, good to have family.

Kit was still wearing a faint smile twenty minutes later, when she stepped into Marin's office at the *Las Vegas Tribune*. However, the expression fell as she searched her aunt out over the mounds of papers and books threatening to topple from her desk. Kit heard the clacking of computer keys as she crossed the room and finally caught sight of Marin's dark, spiky hair, though her shoulders remained hunched, her head bent.

"What the hell happened in here?" Kit asked, gesturing at the mutating pile of dead trees.

"What the hell are you wearing?" Marin shot back, never looking up, and not missing a key. Someone, Kit thought with a wry smile, was on a deadline.

"I've been up since three A.M.," Kit said, wishing she'd said nothing when Grif, who'd trailed her in, gave her a knowing scowl. "But I still managed to spruce up."

"Of course you did." Still typing, Marin added, "I see you brought your lap dog."

"That's guard dog to you, Wilson." Grif perched himself on the only free edge of Marin's desk.

Her aunt looked up then, eyes narrowing into slits. "And how're you doin' on that count, champ?"

Grif jerked his head at Kit. "She's still walking this mud-flat."

Marin leaned back in her chair. "Yeah, walked right into a drug den this morning. Where were you then?"

"That's enough." Kit stepped forward, and Marin's hard gaze shifted. Marin and Grif might like sparring, but Kit's idea of sport stopped short of drawing blood. "Grif's only mistake was in trusting me too much."

Marin turned back to her work. "Ran into that problem a few times myself."

Grif said nothing, but Kit sighed. "And if it weren't for Grif we would have never known about this Russian street drug."

"*Krokodil,*" Marin said, mouth twisting like the word itself was poison. She punched a key, then shifted her laptop around so they could see the images she'd gathered there. "Crap makes chemo cocktails look like Kool-Aid."

Not to mention chemo was meant to help its host, Kit thought, looking her aunt over. Three years past her last treatment and Marin was thriving.

"Yeah, we already got the Technicolor version of that," Grif said, jerking his head at the gangrenous images offered up from the bowels of the Internet. "Question is, how'd it get here?"

"Know how to read Cyrillic script?" Marin asked, hitting a button on the computer so that the screen flashed to Russian text.

"No," they both replied.

"Well, if you did you could print this baby out here and cook up your own fresh batch of crocodile soup. I've been using the Latin alphabet to transliterate it and decipher at least some of the ingredients. Did you know they put paint thinner in this garbage?"

"Don't forget codeine," Kit added. "Lots of it. So who'd be able to secure enough of it to boil it down into a street drug?"

"A doctor," Grif guessed.

"Aren't we smart?" Marin then switched her screen to another, this one in English. "A Russian one, in fact. I've already begun searching Russian surnames in the valley. It's a long shot, and total cultural profiling, but it's a start."

"Ever hear of delegating?" Grif asked her.

"Ever hear of 'no'?" she said, reclaiming her computer.

Kit interrupted again, trying to get them both back on track. "Ever hear of the Russian mafia plying their drug trade on the Las Vegas market?"

"The Rusanovka *bratva*. They're small, and not too powerful . . . except when they are." And before either of them could ask, Marin said, "Meet Sergei Kolyadenko, originally from

Kiev. He's the *bratva*'s comrade and leader. He's also a felon with ties to drug trafficking, weapons smuggling, and money laundering."

"He's fond of action words, I see," Kit said, writing it all down in her beloved Moleskine.

"He's damned crafty, is what he is. He was out of the country most of last year, returned to his motherland to be treated for an undisclosed illness, but now he's back and word is that he's reasserting his strength."

"Think he brought *krokodil* back with him?"

"I think he's not above making radical statements. And *krokodil* would certainly do it." Marin swiveled, yanking the photo she'd just downloaded from the printer, and handed it to Grif. "Sergei and his crew fly under the radar, mostly because they have the great good fortune of looking like the majority of the populace, at least until they open their mouths. It's very hard to hide a Russian accent, not that most of them even try. English is barely a second language to the *bratva*.

"As for the alleged dealers and launderers, the individuals enter and leave Vegas as they please, departing when the heat gets turned up, though not before entrusting someone else with their role. They give the local law enforcement fits, because police never really know who they're looking for. You know those pasty white men. They all look the same."

Grif passed Kit the photo of the Rusanovka gang. Sergei was as handsomely nondescript as Marin had said. So was the handful of men staggered behind him. However, the woman next to Sergei was a different story. Kit's gaze slid over her milky face, down plentiful curves, and dropped to her name, printed just below. Yulyia Kolyadenko. Sergei's wife.

"So how is Jeap Yang involved?" Kit wondered aloud, hand-ing the photo back to Grif. The kid's dark skin tone had spoken of a different background. "He can't be Russian."

"So what exactly is he, Asian?" Marin asked sharply as Grif handed the picture back. She shook her head—it was meant for them—so he silently pocketed it.

"Working on it," Kit replied, already cringing, because she knew what was coming next.

"Dammit, Kit," Marin snapped. "Don't just come to me with questions. Come to me—"

"With answers," Kit finished for her, nodding. "Jeap's background check is up next. Including who he was spending his time with most recently. Dennis is going to see if his family will talk to me—"

"Us," Grif corrected.

"And we know he was hanging out with a new girl." Kit huffed, blowing her bangs from her forehead. "She was the one who introduced him to the stuff."

"What a sweetheart." Marin folded her hands. "She got a name?"

Swallowing hard, Kit dropped her gaze. "Not yet."

"Goddamn it, Kit."

"Hey, easy—" Grif started.

"No." Marin stood so quickly that her chair cracked against the wall. The tower of papers on her desk wavered as she slapped her hands on either side of her computer and leaned forward. "No, I will not go easy on one of my reporters who brings me a half-baked story with more holes than a sea sponge, and asks me to do the majority of the legwork."

"This is your niece," Grif tried, but he'd never seen Marin in one of her full-blown tirades. Kit had, which was why she said nothing at all.

"No," Marin snapped. "Right now she's one of my employees, and she knows better than to cross that threshold with more questions than answers." Marin turned her attention away from Grif, and Kit felt a familiar warmth flush over her cheeks. "Don't waste any more of my time. Do you want this story or not?"

"Yes."

"Then give it some weight, Ms. Craig. Facts, not speculation." Yanking at her chair, she took a seat. "That's the only thing that's going to help Jeap Yang. Not your pity, not your horror."

"Yes, ma'am." Chagrined, Kit turned away.

"Give me something that I can put in black-and-white," Marin yelled after her, leaving out that Kit had gotten ahead of herself. That she'd been so shocked by the horror of *krokodil* that she was forgetting to dot her *i*s and cross her *t*s. That emotion was clouding her judgment.

But Marin didn't have to say it. It was on the faces of everyone in the pressroom who'd overheard the command. And it was in Kit's heart, too, berating her with every beat.

Hey!"

Kit paused to run a hand over her head as Grif clomped down the stairwell behind her. She wanted to be composed when she reached the ground floor, so she'd opted for the stairs.

"Kit!" Grif yelled again, but Kit was counting stairs, and rummaging for cigarettes in her bag, pissed at herself for not doing better. *Being* better.

What was wrong with her? She knew not to let her enthusiasm get away from her like that. She might be a bit impulsive—and maybe Grif was right that she was a tad flighty, too—and passion was fine in one's personal life. "But not in your professional one," she chided aloud, and kept counting down.

Old accusations of nepotism and favoritism and other "-tisms" rattled off the old stairwell, and as much as Kit tried to ignore them, they also rattled in her brain. Yes, there were those who believed she worked at the paper solely because it'd been started by her great-grandfather, but none of those people really knew Marin Wilson. She hired, and kept, only the best.

"Hey," Grif huffed, finally catching up with Kit halfway down the second-to-last flight. "What was that all about?"

"That was me being an idiot," she muttered, wincing again as she remembered the disdain in Marin's stare. Kit worked hard to prove to her aunt that while she might be the mercurial Shirley Wilson's—Marin's sister—daughter, her father's stalwart blood roared in her veins, too. It burned that she could blow it so damned easily. "I didn't prepare before I went in there. I didn't give her anything to work with or bring anything new to the table. I failed."

"Failed?" She could feel Grif staring at her. "Honey, you've barely begun."

"Exactly."

Grif remained silent for a moment. "But there was more. That was . . . personal."

Kit reached the ground floor, and pushed steel, emerging into the open air. The heat ambushed her, and she blew out a breath against it. "She expects a lot from me."

"More than the other reporters?"

"Of course." Tucking her head, she lit her cigarette.

"Because she hopes you'll take the editorial reins someday?"

Inhaling deeply, Kit looked at him, thinking maybe if she

said the words aloud they wouldn't weigh on her so very much. "Because if I don't, then I'll be just like my mother."

Grif spoke softly. "And what's wrong with that?"

"Nothing. Unless you were her sister." Kit smiled wryly, then shrugged. "My mother was . . . golden. It was hard on Marin."

"You're standing up for her," Grif said, with a tilt of his head.

Kit took a drag, then sighed. "Being my mother's daughter wasn't easy, either."

Shirley Wilson-Craig—the beautiful black sheep of the Dean S. Wilson newspaper fortune—had married blue-collar, and at the time it was a scandal among the Vegas elite. Shirley had reveled in it, which made Kit smile . . . but it also meant Kit had a mother with a high-class pedigree and no sense of duty, and a father who valued duty but possessed an utter disregard for class.

Kit disregarded nothing. She was twelve when cancer claimed her mother's life, and sixteen when that bullet felled her father. After she'd grieved the second time—broke down, as she told Grif, and put herself back together yet again—she swore that whatever remained of her tenuous life would hold meaning. That's why she was so upset now. She hadn't just disappointed Marin. She'd disappointed herself.

"I thought you loved her," Grif said, not understanding.

"I did. Still do." She spoke quickly, because her heart came near to bursting every time she thought of her mother. "She was perfect. Beautiful, graceful, aristocratic, wicked smart." She smiled wistfully, but the smile faded as a thought ambushed her: If I were more like my mother, Grif would have already forgotten Evelyn Shaw.

"You're all of those things, too," Grif said, his timing uncanny.

Kit snorted, but waved away his raised eyebrow by saying, "Marin has some other words for me . . . but, look, she's under a lot of pressure. Most newspapers are worth less than the paper they're printed on, these days, and the fate of ours weighs on her. So, no, I'm not standing up for her, but I don't blame her, either. Besides, a dead woman can still cast a long shadow. If anyone knows that, it should be you."

She hadn't meant to say that last part. It slipped out, more of a murmur around her cigarette than a statement, but Grif's hearing was impeccable, and his hand was immediately on her arm. "What does that mean?"

"I just meant that your wife's death, even though it was over fifty years ago . . ." Kit ducked her head. "It still haunts you."

" 'Course it does. But it doesn't cast . . . what'd you say? A *shadow* over me."

"No," Kit said, and finally looked up. She swallowed hard. "Just everyone around you."

Grif's hand fell away. The look on his face was so injured and stunned that Kit wanted to reach for him. But she'd finally said what had been haunting *her* for so long, so not only couldn't she stop, she didn't want to.

"Look, what do you think it feels like?" Flicking her cigarette away, she crossed her arms. "To know the man I love spends most of his waking hours thinking of another woman?"

Hurt shifted to confusion as he drew back. "I'm not thinking about her all the time."

"No, but you're chasing her down." She laughed humorlessly. "And sometimes it feels like she's chasing you, too."

"What?"

Kit shook her head. For a smart P.I., he could be so stupid. "You say her name in your dreams all the time, Grif."

"That's what this is about? I'm not even *conscious*."

"Have you ever dreamed about me?"

"I don't need to. You're here."

Kit felt her expression turn to stone. Grif swallowed hard. "Wrong. Answer."

She turned away, and when his fingers wrapped around her arm this time, she gave it a violent shake. She shouldn't have let herself get drawn into this conversation, she thought, striding to her car. But all it'd taken was one slip in thought, one reminder of how hard it was to be compared to someone who was perfect—someone who would always be perfect now that time had also made her saintly—and Kit was suddenly doubting everything she was.

But what's to doubt? She wasn't perfect, but she was vibrant and smart and, yes, cheery.

She was also *alive*.

So, with the safety of her car between them, she finally looked up. Grif was on the other side, his reply waiting, too. "I don't compare you to Evie, Kit."

"Maybe not consciously," she conceded, "but the shadow of her memory is in your eyes every time you look at me. You should at least know that."

Grif just continued to stare at her so blankly that she knew he'd never even given it any thought. Shaking her head, Kit wished the whole conversation away. Then her phone rang.

Wish granted, she thought, answering without viewing the number as she climbed behind the wheel of her car. Still silent, Grif slid in next to her. "Kit Craig."

"Detective Carlisle." Dennis's voice teased at her formality, though it sobered again with his next question. "How would you like to visit with a junkie who spent all of last weekend with one Jeap Yang?"

Right now? Kit thought, blowing out a hard breath. "I'd like nothing more," she said, and busied herself by pulling out her Moleskine. A little conversation about drugs and rotting flesh might be just what she needed to banish her worries over a dead woman.

CHAPTER SEVEN

Thirty minutes later, a very *tense* thirty minutes later, Grif trailed Kit into a bar just a shade shy of full dark. Probably best, Grif thought, eyeing the sag of the industrial ceiling, and the bumps in the uneven concrete floor. It would be charitable to call the place a dive. A permanent dark stain led directly to the bar, where vinyl swivel stools sat in uneven clumps, the seat-backs damaged and slumping, not unlike the men occupying them.

It was nearing four in the afternoon, so the after-work crowd had yet to arrive, but there was still a handful of customers lined along the scarred bar top. One listlessly plunked quarters into a flattop video poker machine while two others watched a ball game above the bar with the same lackluster enthusiasm. A fourth man simply stared into space, face blank above his half-empty beer glass.

Choice digs, Grif thought, then returned his gaze to Kit's ramrod back. Her uncharacteristic cheerlessness matched the mood of the room, but it also confounded him. He still wasn't quite sure what'd happened in Marin's office, or what led to their strange conversation in the parking lot afterward.

Did he dream about her?

That wasn't the Kit Craig he was used to. His girl was relentlessly optimistic, dogged, and thick-skinned. Her overflowing confidence, despite any odds, was one of the things he loved about her. And she lived in emotional sunlight. A shadow cast over her? By Evie?

Hardly.

But he didn't need to understand it to see she was truly upset, and the conversation wasn't over, though he'd have to wait to ask her more. Detective Carlisle was already waiting.

They crossed the room to the far corner, where Carlisle hovered over a man who wobbled in his seat. There was nothing wrong with the chair, but the man was disheveled, unwashed, and sour-smelling, and currently picking at a wound on his forearm with unswerving fascination. With thin, brittle hair and a pocked face, the man was lean but not fit, long-limbed but lacking strength.

The most telling thing about him, though, was the solid ring of plasma outlining his body, a bright strip that only Grif could see. Not long, Grif thought, refocusing on the man. Not if he kept up this way.

The man's expression didn't alter when he spotted Kit and Grif standing there, his gaze sliding away after a mere moment, his hands renewing their restless fidgeting.

"This is Trey Brunk," Dennis said in a normal tone, though Brunk appeared not to hear. "He's a heroin user, as he'll readily tell you, and he has his rages, which is how we had the great fortune to meet. But he's not so bad."

Clearly accustomed to Brunk's lack of focus, Dennis leaned close, startling the man by putting a hand on his bony shoulder. "Hey, Trey. These are the people I was telling you about. The ones who are trying to help me find out what happened to Jeap."

Thin lips pursed tight, Brunk shook his head. "Hell, I know what happened to him. He went floatin' on a pile of shit. Once you stop caring about the crop, man, you step on the dime."

"He means Jeap's drugs were bad," Dennis translated. "And that's what killed him."

Grif huffed as the plasma outlining Brunk's frail body pulsed. This man's "good" drugs weren't exactly being kind.

"So where were you when Jeap took his final trip?" he asked Brunk.

Brunk held up his hands like he was fending off charges. "Hey, man, I was asleep for most of last week."

"Including yesterday?" Kit asked.

His head bobbed once. "Asleep," he said definitively.

"You sleep a lot, Mr. Brunk?" asked Grif.

Brunk's rolling gaze circled back up and almost stuck on Grif's. His eyes were watery, though. Like the life inside him could pour right out of his sockets. "That's how I break the cycle," Brunk said. "I got this theory. Down the dozers and I can sleep through the super flu. Then I don't got to face the evening. Get it?"

Grif and Kit both looked to Dennis for translation.

"He means if he takes enough sleeping pills he won't have to feel the heroin withdrawals."

Which could last a week, Grif thought, remembering Dr. Ott's words. From the looks of things, Brunk spent every other week sleeping.

"Why did they call him Jeap?" Kit asked.

"Called himself that. Short for J.P., but I don't know what that was short for." Brunk snorted as he looked up at them. "I called him Chevy sometimes. Or Ford. And I'd add it to the other half of that Chinese sign, just to fuck with him, you know?"

"You mean 'yin'?" Kit said, following along admirably. Grif was already half-lost. "Like Chevy Yin?"

"Yeah, he hated that." Brunk laughed nostalgically, picking at his arm before moving his fingers, worrying his face. His hands were moving faster now that he was more alert. "He said he was the light side of the yin-yang circle thingy. You know, 'cause he was so light-skinned and all."

Kit and Grif looked at each other. Death pallor aside, Jeap was dark-skinned. At least compared to them. Brunk read their confusion. "I know! But he said he was white where he came from, so . . ."

Grif looked up at Dennis, but the officer just shrugged as well. "Jeap Yang was his legal name. I'll dig for more."

Kit nodded, then returned her attention to Brunk. "What about a girl? Someone new who he was hanging out with recently?"

"Oh, sure." He blinked rapidly, then jolted when he remembered. "Brandy. Or Britney." He blinked again. "Bianca?"

"Think, Trey," Kit said, then softened her voice and her face with a smile. "It's important."

But Brunk shook his head. "I really don't know, man. She liked those wigs, you know? Different colors. Pinks and blues and yellows. She was very bright actually." He squinted like even the thought hurt his eyes.

"And she was the one who introduced him to the crocodile?" Kit asked.

"All I know is he wasn't using it, and then suddenly he was." Brunk shrugged, growing bored—or, more likely, tired—with the conversation. He slumped farther in his seat. "But if anyone knows what happened to Jeap, it'd be Brandy."

"Or Bianca," Grif muttered.

"Britney, I think," Brunk said, bobbing his head until it fell to his chest. Kit looked at Grif and sighed. Waste of time.

But, surprisingly, Brunk rallied, head snapping back up. "Good guy, that Jeap. Laid-back for a tweeker. I think he really believed in all that mystical Oriental bullshit. Thought it would help him get clean, so one day he could work in a restaurant. And then he could own a restaurant. Those other burnouts would laugh, but they were assholes. I never laughed."

"That was nice of you," Kit said, as if that made him less of a burnout.

Brunk nodded. "Well, he was the best cook."

The fact that he'd lost his most reliable heroin cook dawned on Brunk then, and his nostalgic smile melted. He picked at his arm for a moment, then looked up at Dennis. "I'm thirsty, man. Got anything for me to drink around here?"

Dennis shook his head, impatient now that he knew Brunk couldn't help. "I look like a waitress to you?"

"You said you'd make it worth my while, bro." Brunk's eyebrows lowered, and so did his voice. "C'mon. It'll help me sleep."

"Shit." Rolling his eyes, Dennis pushed from the wall.

Brunk's head sagged as Dennis walked away, as if the retreating detective were pulling all his energy away with him. His chin dropped onto his bony chest, and a soft snoring started up almost immediately.

Grif jerked his head at the slumbering junkie. "Didn't give us much."

"And we still don't know how the Russians tie in." Wincing, Kit flopped into the chair across from Brunk. "Marin's going to have my head."

"That's too bad, sweetheart," Grif said, pulling out a smoke. "I like it where it is."

"You're just trying to make me feel better."

"No, actually it balances you out."

She rolled her eyes, but didn't smile.

"Fine." Grif shrugged, and blew out a stream of smoke. "Maybe she'll stuff it and mount it over her office door. You could chin-wag at her all day long from that position."

"Yeah." Kit finally smiled back. "She'd hate that."

Grif's reply was cut short by Brunk's head unexpectedly swiveling around on his shoulders. It popped up on his neck like a jack-in-the-box before snapping straight. The tinny tune was still bouncing through Grif's mind when he caught sight of Brunk's eyes, which were suddenly star-pricked and darkly alive with interest.

Kit gasped.

"Hello again." Brunk's whole face shifted as someone else's smile raised his cheekbones high. Though still gaunt, his face looked wide and almost healthy. His body straightened in his chair, and his fidgety hands folded together. "I thought we might make a formal introduction."

* * *

What the hell are you doing here?" Grif whispered, dropping close to Kit, palms on the table. Shocked into silence, still staring into those overbright eyes, she didn't move at all.

"Just visiting. Same as you . . . Griffin Shaw."

The fallen angel's voice remained light, but its words had the weight of knowledge, and each syllable emerged from Brunk's thin lips in a way that made the human look like a ventriloquist's dummy, which wasn't too far off. It was merely animated flesh instead of wood.

"Oh, yes," it said, at Grif's lowered brow. "I know all about you now. I've been asking around, you see."

"Wait," Kit said, recovering, though she clutched Grif's biceps in her hands. Grif didn't blame her. An icy breeze enveloped them every time Brunk opened his mouth. "He can possess the living?"

"It can possess those who have no possession of themselves," Grif said shortly. "And it's not a he."

The fallen angel scrambled Brunk's features into a scowl, but they smoothed out once the onyx stars in his eyes shifted. "There you are. Katherine Craig. Reporter, native Las Vegan. The girl who lives in the moment, but dreams of the past. The girl who loves the truth."

"How do you know me?" Kit whispered, color draining from her face.

"I torment dead people," it whispered theatrically, then laughed so that Brunk's Adam's apple bobbed madly.

Swallowing hard, Kit lifted her chin. "Then someone should have told you that it's Kit, not Katherine. Only my parents called me that."

"Don't engage, Kit," Grif warned. Everything was ammo in the warped wings of the Fallen. Besides, Jeap Yang's words were pinging around in Grif's mind like hard marbles. *It's going to circle back for her . . .*

"Yes. You changed it once they were both dead," it said now, eyes twinkling darkly. "The name they gave you hurt your ears in the wake of their deaths, so you reinvented yourself."

"And what's your name?" Kit asked, without missing a beat, though Grif knew her well enough to see she was rattled. Worry always caused a dent above the bridge of her nose.

"Nice of *someone* to finally ask," it answered, flipping Brunk's lanky hair. "I am reigning statesman of the Third, formerly of the Cherubim tribe, keepers of knowledge, guardians of the Celestial Records, and the once-Pure, now charged with maintaining the chronicles of the Fallen." Brunk's strange smile returned. "But you can call me Scratch."

"As in Old Scratch," Grif said, finally gaining its attention.

"Very good," Scratch muttered, though it didn't look happy or impressed by the interruption. Leaning back in the chair, it folded Brunk's arms. "You know your Germanic myths."

"I've been doing my research, too." Grif kept his eyes on the animated body, but addressed Kit in a low voice. "Old Scratch is a popular nickname for the devil, also interchangeable with '*devils.*'"

"Yes, we are One and also many," it said, and showed rows of teeth.

Grif ignored it. "*Scrat* or *waldscrat* means 'wood spirit' in Old Germanic. It ties in with the forest."

"It ties in," Scratch corrected, "with the Garden."

"*The* Garden?" Kit asked.

"Maybe once," Grif said shortly. "But now both are well out of God's presence."

"Yes. Shame, that." Feigning a large yawn, Scratch stretched and turned toward the bar. "Where is that drink? Hey, nurse!"

"I thought your kind feared liquids," Grif said, when it turned back around.

Surprise flashed in the cunning gaze, before it went suspiciously blank. "'Fear' is such a strong word. It's more of an aversion, really. Mostly to water."

"Especially holy water," Grif told Kit.

"Ah, but fortunately there's not a lot of that floating about in these fine establishments." Scratch plunked its elbows atop the table again. "However, firewater is right up my alley."

"You have no right to feed that poor man's addictions," Kit said angrily.

"I have no right?" Scratch frowned, mimicking her outrage, before slumping again. "I have every right. He handed it to me when he shot the very first load of trash into his body. Trey Brunk hasn't been clean, or *pure,* in nine years. He doesn't need any help feeding his addictions. He'll never stop."

"You don't know that."

"Of course I do. I'm *in* him, silly girl. He *let* me in," he added, before she could protest. "And now I know what he knows."

"That's awful."

"No, it's quite fun actually. The tweekers are the best sport. Paranoid little bastards." It winked at Kit. "Gives new meaning to being chased by their demons, don't it?"

"Seems like a pretty full existence, Scratch," Grif interrupted. "Torturing moral criminals in the Eternal Forest, and possessing the sick and addicted here on the Surface."

Scratch studied Brunk's fingernails. "We stay amused."

"Yet you still find time to track down the Lost."

"You're talking about Jeap Yang, yes? About five-eight. Terrible hair-stylist. In love with the vein in his left forearm?"

Grif just stared.

Flaring its eyes, Scratch stared back. "What? He was standing on the corner of life and death with his thumb sticking out. I just offered him a lift."

"That's a crock." Straightening, Grif shoved his hands into his pockets. "You've been targeting the Lost and confused."

Scratch smirked. "Gonna go tell Daddy?"

"I don't understand," Kit interrupted, shaking her head. "Why would you hurt an innocent soul? One that's not even destined for the Eternal Forest?"

"Why would I—?" Baffled, Scratch tilted its head at Grif, and pointed as if to say, *Get a load of her*. But without waiting for a response, it turned back to Kit. "Because I can. Because I like it. Because I'm *bored* with blighted souls, unfit for Paradise, and each with a narcissistic psychosis that makes them think their predilections are the most original and devious and evil."

It rolled Brunk's eyes, first the left, then the right. "And I'm tired of torturing the terrible souls who deserve every heinous thing they have coming to them. I want something new and fresh and novel. I want those who are tottering right on the edge of moral depravity, and who will tip my way given just one little poke. I *want* the Lost. Better yet, I want something pure that I can *make* Lost."

It stared at Grif in bald challenge, but Grif just shook his head. "Too late, Scratch. I'm a Centurion, both angelic and human. You'll never touch me."

"Who said anything about you?" And it turned to Kit, gaze like glue, sticking where it shouldn't. "But I'd love a chance to climb inside you, Kitty-Cat."

"Sit back, old boy," Grif said, his voice a low growl.

At the same time, Kit whispered, "Don't call me that."

Scratch ignored them both, leaning forward. Brunk's top lip elongated into a thin sneer. "I'll call you what I like, and I'll take what I want. You think I'm merely bound to those pitiful humans who invite chaos into their lives through addiction? Think again! I *feed,* as you put it, on the emotions that prompt those addictions. Drugs and alcohol are nice little hors d'oeuvres, but rage and envy and doubt are the entrées I savor most. *That's* when the Chosen—any of you!—are truly possessed. And that's when I'm at my fucking best."

A whimper, near to a keen, escaped Kit's throat as she edged back again, and she looked up, waiting for Grif to contradict Scratch's words. Grif just shook his head. He knew a lot, but he didn't know this.

"The damned belong to me," Scratch continued, seeing it had them both rattled. "That's not in question. And the Lost are just the damned-in-training, though they don't know it. But you, *Kitty-Cat?* You, with your bright soul and open heart?" Phrase and lips twisted around each other like invading roots. "You are just some choice bit of beauty that I have not yet broken."

Grif's hands were around Brunk's neck before anyone took a breath. He squeezed, and heard branches snapping in the man's trachea.

"Uh, uh, uh," Scratch chided, even as its eyes rolled back in Brunk's head. "Hate the sin, not the sinner."

Growling, Grif released Brunk's throat. It was right. Hurting Brunk wouldn't let him touch the spirit inside. "You will never touch her, hear me?"

"That's right," Scratch said, clearing its throat. "Because I don't want to touch her. I want to possess her."

"What's going on here?" Dennis was back, but, unsurprisingly, none of them had seen him arrive.

"Ah," Scratch said, glancing down as it pulled a pair of shades from Brunk's shirt pocket, shielding the stardust in its eyes from Dennis. It didn't want the human to interfere, but it wasn't quite done yet, either. "Finally. My drink."

It held out Brunk's hand, but Grif snatched the shot glass up as soon as Dennis set it down. Scratch's attention immediately swerved to Grif as it lowered Brunk's chin. "Give it."

"No."

It tilted Brunk's head. "What? A trade?"

Grif inclined his head. "The drink for the others."

"You mean, the Lost. Like Jeap?"

Grif nodded once. Scratch had inhabited Jeap's body, so it not only knew the boy's thoughts and feelings, it possessed his knowledge as well. That's how it'd located Brunk, who ran in the same crowd. If Scratch was hunting Lost, he'd know whom else Jeap was hanging with.

"Two more," Scratch said, confirming his thoughts.

"What the hell is he talking about?" Dennis asked.

Scratch ignored him. "I want the drink first."

Grif jerked his head. "I don't think you need another drink, after all."

"Withholding a man's addictions from him isn't an effective deterrent," it snapped, slamming palms on the table before composing Brunk's features into false stoicism. "Take it from a seasoned sinner, that's no way to give up a vice."

"Then how?" Dennis asked, still thinking he was talking to Brunk. He missed the cold calculation in the responding smile. Grif did not.

"Well, first you have to pick a specific sin. You must commit yourself to it fully. Then"—it paused for a beat—"you gotta throw yourself into it."

And Brunk's body was suddenly hurtling toward Kit, reaching for her shoulders. She squealed, but she'd been taken by surprise and was slow. Meanwhile, Grif, holding the drink, backed away, not wanting to spill a drop, so it was Dennis who stepped between Kit and Brunk, grabbing the man's filthy shirt and tossing him back in his seat.

Scratch let Brunk's hands drop, and gazed up at Dennis in fascination. "Oh, this is interesting."

"What the hell is wrong with you, Brunk?" Dennis shook him so that the man's head wobbled on his body.

"Keep that thing away from me." Kit, still standing, folded her arms protectively around her body.

Grif slammed the shot glass down in front of Scratch. "Here. Just drink it and leave."

Dennis shifted away, shaking his head at Brunk's strange behavior. Scratch adjusted Brunk's T-shirt like it was straightening tuxedo lapels, then made a show of lifting the shot glass. It toasted Kit with the golden liquid.

"I'll leave," Scratch said, enunciating each syllable sharply, "when I'm *damned* well ready."

And it threw back the firewater, licked its lips . . . and began to scream.

"What the hell—" Dennis grimaced and the air around them grew cold, and Kit backed up even more, but Grif just stood there, palming the glass vial he'd been concealing, now empty of its contents.

"Good-bye, you soul-stealing bastard." Grif's voice was so low that only another angel might hear it. Scratch howled in reply, straining against Brunk's flesh, causing the man's neck to pop—*snap, snap*—as it twisted Grif's way.

"I know you now!" Wind and leaves whipped through every

syllable. "You won this round, but I won't forget! I *never* forget!"

And the fallen angel left its host body as quickly as it'd arrived. Brunk slumped forward, face slamming against the tabletop with a sick, fleshy thud.

"Jesus," Dennis said, rubbing a hand over his face. His expression was stunned. "He looked . . ."

"Possessed," Kit finished, swallowing hard. Grif glanced down and saw that her hands were shaking. He took one in his own and gave it a small squeeze. He'd done what he had to. Scratch wasn't going to get to Kit.

Brunk's gaze rolled back in place. The whites of his eyes were pristine, the irises dark as molten chocolate.

"Trey?" Kit asked gingerly, leaning forward.

Brunk took one good look at her face, glanced down at empty shot glass in front of him, and vomited all over the table.

Rearing back, Kit barely saved her bamboo handbag. Filth spewed from Brunk's body, noxious and acidic and seemingly endless. Only Grif knew why. The liquid he'd prepared after he'd caught Scratch trying to wrangle away Jeap's tortured soul comprised something Pure. It expelled all impurities from mortal flesh, including fallen angels . . . and the addictive matter Brunk had been poisoning his body with for years.

It took a while.

Kit was at Grif's side, giant question marks in her gaze, but he shook his head. He'd bring her up to speed later.

"Jesus, Brunk," Dennis said, when there was a break. "What the hell are you on?"

"He's okay," Grif muttered. "He's just . . . detoxing."

And now that he'd had a taste of real Purity, Brunk might even be able to beat his addiction. What was unholy could never exist alongside what was Pure.

Waiting until Brunk was between spasms, Grif reached out and put a hand on the man's shoulder. Dazed, dizzy with all the fresh oxygen zinging through his every mortal cell, he took a moment to focus, but when he did, his eyes were clearer than they'd likely been in years.

"Two more tweekers, Trey," Grif said, holding the gaze. "Just like Jeap. Where are they?"

Tears of understanding welled in Brunk's eyes. "Oh, God."

"Where, Trey?" Grif demanded, because Scratch had the knowledge, and he'd gotten it from this man.

But Brunk was having an extremely delayed rush of survivor's guilt. Without the addiction as a barrier between him and his emotions, he was facing for the first time what drugs had done to him, and his friends. "I hid the last of my stash. I wouldn't share. They didn't have any more money, so when Jeap told them about the croc, the crocodile," he clarified, with a shudder, "and how cheap it was, they jumped on it."

"*Who*, Trey?"

"Tim and Jeannie." He covered his face with his filthy hands. They were no longer roving, no longer tweeking, but they shook with guilt. "You gotta help 'em. They can't stop, just like Jeap couldn't stop. They stole his stash and left him in that flop, but they took the codeine. He'd already showed them how to make it. It's my fault. I wouldn't share."

"No, it's their choice," Grif said, over Brunk's blustering sobs. "But you can help them by telling us where they are."

The distraught man lifted his head, and squinted at Grif. "They stay with Timmy's mother mostly. She kicks them out, but they know her bingo times, and they sneak back in when she's gone."

"Where?"

"Shangri-La Apartments, in Meadows Village."

Grif shook his head. It meant nothing to him.

But Dennis jerked his head toward the door. "Got it."

Yet it was Kit who led the rush from the bar. And as the sounds of retching resumed behind them, Dennis and Grif had to run to keep pace. Meanwhile, the men at the bar—each attending to his own vice—never even looked up.

CHAPTER EIGHT

Meadows Village wasn't far, yet rush hour was just beginning, and traffic was bad at every turn. Grif took the time to fill Kit in on what'd happened at the bar. Or at least what he knew of it. He'd been as surprised as she was to learn that Scratch could inhabit the living through their negative emotions as well as their addictions. He'd have to talk to Sarge about it, but it made sense in theory.

"The fraction of the Host that turned against God was one-third of all angels. That's why the fallen are called the Third. They were immediately banished from God's presence, and cast into a place it would never be felt again."

"The Garden of Eden," Kit said.

Grif nodded. "Now the Eternal Forest. They're reluctant inhabitants, but they're a part of it, too. Both are withered and decayed, completely lifeless."

"Except when they possess the living."

Except, Grif now realized, when the living somehow gave up possession of themselves.

"And so the people who die and end up in the Forest? They're the same?"

"They're the only source of energy, entertainment, and power that the Third possess." Grif pursed his lips tight. "But don't feel too bad for them. Nothing good or pure can exist when blotted entirely from God's presence."

He waited, but Kit remained silent as a violent shudder worked its way down her spine. Her beautiful lips were pressed tightly together, too. She was trying to keep from crying.

"It's the Forest, Kit," Grif said softly. "Not a walk in the park. You felt how cold his breath was. Magnify it fivefold. Shelter and food? Nonexistent. Same with water, though the Third despise it anyway. Water is a symbol of life—of baptism and rebirth—and nothing that truly lives can exist in the Forest."

"It sounds . . ." Her voice trailed off as she tried to let the Forest bloom in her own imagination. Few humans, though, had a place in their minds for this kind of madness. "Hopeless."

"Hope is a gift from God," Grif said softly. "The Third rose up in mutiny against God, and humans do it on a case-by-case basis. The perversion of free will, God's greatest gift, lands you there. The Forest is those perversions made manifest."

"And what about me, Grif?" She glanced over, and there were tears in her eyes. "It said it wanted me, but I can't imagine living in a place without hope or love."

"Of course you can't." Grif wanted to comfort her, but there was little he could do while she was driving. "You're made of those two things, with a healthy dash of grit thrown in just to spice things up."

She didn't look comforted. "It can touch me. It wants to possess me."

"It . . . imprinted on you somehow." Grif shook his head.

"Like what? Some evil baby chick?" Her nerves were getting the best of her, and she jerked the wheel. Grif reached out, and held it in place.

"You were the first person it has seen in, well, God knows how long. The first who wasn't evil or dirty or doomed. Or Lost. It said you were bright, and light—"

Kit shuddered, and Grif felt helpless. He opened his mouth, but Kit was already pushing past the moment. "How did you destroy it?"

"I don't know how to destroy an angel." But he was damned well going to try to find out. "It's only banished."

"So how did you banish it? What was in that bottle?"

"Love," he finally answered. He glanced over when she only stared. "It's more toxic to them even than water. In fact, if it were to wash over Scratch like the baptism they so hate, I bet then you could destroy it."

Kit tilted her head. "How did you bottle love?"

Grif shrugged. "After we found Scratch possessing Jeap, and I knew it was targeting the Lost, I also knew it'd be back. So I harvested some tears."

Goggling, Kit missed the car braking in front of her, and had to come to a hard stop behind it. While they waited for a green light, she turned to him. "Because tears are made of water?"

"Because tears are made of water *filled with emotion*. Infused with heartfelt memory. Love is only between mankind and God, Kit. It's poisonous to beings that were created, not born. They've never felt it."

"Even the Pure still in heaven?" A horn honked behind Kit, but she waited for Grif's answering nod before driving. "So the human element in the tears that banished Scratch . . ."

"And the Pure element that cured Brunk."

Kit was silent for a long minute. "They were yours?"

Grif tried to keep his shrug nonchalant. "Where else was I going to get something so precious on such short notice?"

"But it said it knows you now, Grif." Her tone said he'd better not try to evade.

"It's not a possession thing, okay? Not like Brunk. It only gained knowledge of the emotional memory responsible for those tears." Grif braced himself for the inevitable, and uncomfortable, questions by looking away. *What do you love so much that it makes you cry? Or whom?*

Yet they never came. Glancing back, Grif wondered why, then remembered Kit's earlier hurt. *What do you think it feels like to know the man I love spends most of his waking hours thinking of another woman?* "So that's why you let Dennis intercept when Scratch tried to reach me." Though muted, there was still a note of accusation in her voice.

"Dennis didn't intercept," Grif said, immediately defensive. "I let him run a pick."

Kit blew out an annoyed breath. "You know I don't understand your stupid baseball analogies."

Grif just shook his head. "Look, *I'm* the one who got rid of Scratch." At least for now, he thought. "Besides, it just wanted to scare you. You're the best person I know. No way are you ever destined for the Forest."

"Well, I'm scared, okay? It knew things about me. It called me 'the girl who loves the truth.'"

"One of your enemies told it," Grif guessed. "Someone who ended up in the Forest instead of the Everlast. Someone it could torture for information once it . . . saw you."

Because while it'd been surprised that Kit could see it the first time, it was ready for her the second. And aggressive, Grif thought, swallowing hard.

You are just some choice bit of beauty that I have not yet broken.

Kit, busy blowing her Betty bangs from her forehead, didn't notice the shudder that rocked Grif in his seat. "I'd like to think I don't have enemies terrible enough to warrant an eternity of torture in the Forest."

"Chambers?" Grif reminded her, causing a wince. Bringing down that local kingpin, a man who'd tried to kill them both, was the first case they'd worked together. Chambers had died terribly . . . though not as terribly as he'd lived. *That's* what landed a soul in the Eternal Forest.

"I wouldn't even wish Scratch on him," Kit said solemnly.

Grif didn't say it as they drove on, but neither would he.

Where the hell are we?" Grif asked, taking a deep breath. They needed to change the subject, and regroup. Someone in the valley was feeding young kids a drug that had skin falling from their bones. As a distraction from soul-stealing angels, it was a good one.

"There is no hell, remember?" Kit muttered, knowing what he was doing, but allowing it all the same. "Though if there were, you wouldn't be too far off. Meadows Village is one of the oldest neighborhoods in Vegas. It used to be the first place newcomers wanted to live, but now it's the last. It's located in Naked City."

"Oh, sure," Grif said, the old memory revisiting slowly. "I've been to Naked City."

Silence filled the car. It was the briefest of pauses, but it'd been happening more and more lately. Grif would mention something he'd seen or done, because the memory was somehow closer now that he was back on the Surface. Sometimes he could even smell the old scents, as light as the pressed powder Evie used to use on her skin. Other times he could hear the East Coast accents trailing behind trouble boys walking the casino floor, even though he knew they were long gone.

And sometimes the places Grif recognized on this second go-round were less real than those dogged memories; the casinos and restaurants and mom-and-pop hash houses seemed like shells to him, more fragile somehow now that the original owners were gone. But it was the natural order of things, and tucking the past away was how the living could go on.

Thing was, despite Kit's love for all things of his era, she could never really know what came before. Maybe the silence that kept rising between them meant she was beginning to understand that. But how to keep her from worrying over it?

Have you ever dreamed about me?

"When?" she asked now, shaking him from his thoughts.

"When what?" Grif cleared his throat, his mind. "You mean when was I here? Just over fifty years ago, I guess," he said, beginning slowly. "Evie and I had just met. I'd finished up the case that'd brought me to Vegas, and she had a girlfriend, Jane, who lived in Naked City. She worked the center bar at the Jolly Trolley."

"Oh, I've heard of that." Kit gave a small laugh, getting into the telling. She was a sucker for nostalgia and thinking of her city's heyday always made her dreamy. "It was supposed to have the best steak in town."

"Dollar ninety-nine," Grif confirmed. He and Evie had eaten there right after visiting Jane, though he didn't mention that now.

"So Jane was a showgirl?" Kit guessed, and Grif nodded, because that's how Naked City had gotten its name. The women, mostly single, lived there like a coterie of hens, due to the location's proximity to their jobs on the Strip. They also had a habit of sunbathing topless in groups on the buildings' roofs to avoid tan lines, which could cost them their jobs.

"Well, the place took a spectacular swan-dive from famous to infamous in the years since you were last there," Kit said, and Grif was glad to hear her voice was back to normal, though her driving was still lousy. He cringed as she zigzagged between two cars and a delivery truck ambling on the two-lane road. "Those women would be sunbathing on our finest crack houses today, and Naked City now references prostitution, not chorus lines."

Grif shook his head. "Evie would be so disappointed."

This time the silence rose between them like a wall.

"We're here," Kit said softly, as they turned into a lot that sagged and tilted. Grif caught her wrist as she shoved the gear into park.

"Baby—" he began.

Though her smile was more of a wince, she closed her other hand over his own. "I know."

And she let the tension, the past—the worry over Evie and Grif's misplaced dreams—roll from her shoulders just like that. She gave his hand a squeeze, took a deep breath, then got out of the car.

A single patrol car was already parked sideways at the Shangri-La apartment complex, along with Dennis, who'd somehow managed to arrive first. Kit headed his way, but Grif held back to observe events from the Duetto's bumper. A curious crowd was already beginning to gather on the sidewalk . . . though not so curious that they wouldn't take note of a vintage convertible sports car in a neighborhood littered with vehicles that looked like tuna cans on inner tubes.

Staring down a teen already eyeing the rims, Grif leaned against the hood. Kit was right. The neighborhood couldn't have gotten any more run-down if someone dropped a bomb on it. And the Shangri-La was damned well the same complex Jane had lived in all those years ago. Its white facade had been re-stuccoed in a nauseating pastel pink, and green doors popped along the top railing like dark bruises. Fifty years ago, a tidy row of rose bushes had burst with blooms along the ground level, proudly attended by all the pretty residents. But nothing thrived here now, Grif thought, eyeing the chipped tile of the in-ground pool in the front courtyard. Algae had stained the rim to match the complex's doors.

"What they looking for this time?" A kid, small for his age, and barely into double digits, sidled up to Grif. He was dark-skinned, but not exactly African-American. He had a rat-a-tat accent, too, so likely had roots someplace south of the border. Someplace warm. But he shivered now, alert with nerves, as he waited for Grif's answer.

"Get home, kid." Grif crossed his arms as he watched the officers begin their door-to-doors. "It's not safe around here."

"No shit it's not safe around here, *pendejo*. It's my 'hood."

Grif did a double-take at the kid's language, then asked, "Know it well?"

Motioning with his arms, the kid tilted his head. "Man, what'd I just say?"

Yeah, the kid was street all right, and after the day he'd had, Grif couldn't help but wonder where this soul would be in another fifty years. Not in Naked City, that was for sure. This wasn't a place that sustained life.

"What's your name?"

"*Oye*," the boy shot back. "I'm the one asking the questions around here."

Unblinking, Grif lifted an eyebrow.

The boy, either unused to being seen, or too used to being watched, fidgeted, jerking on his jeans. Poor kid. Didn't even have a belt to his name. "It's Luis, man. Why you wanna know?"

"We're looking for a couple of junkies, Luis. A man and a woman."

Luis just motioned behind him, at the block of mismatched homes leaning and tilting in varying degrees of disrepair. Chain-linked fences surrounded some, while others sported crumbling front porches. Grif spotted a rusting tricycle among the weeds of a yard penning in a wide-shouldered dog, but all signs of real life, a real neighborhood, were gone.

Grif thought back to Brunk's tearful confession. "The man is named Tim. The woman's Jeannie."

The kid tucked his hands into his baggy front pockets, echoing Grif's body language. "They like you?"

"What do you mean?"

"White-bread." Then, with a sly look, he added, "And not too bright."

Grif jerked his head. "They do drugs. That sound bright to you?"

Now Luis's gaze darkened, and the face that'd just begun to open shuttered completely. "Drugs don't mean you're stupid."

"You're right," Grif said quickly, as Luis turned to walk away. "Wait."

Luis just waved him off.

"Here," Grif called out. "For your trouble."

The twenty was gone from his hand almost before the kid had turned around. Didn't have to offer it up twice, Grif thought, as Luis tucked the bill away, looking around.

"I think the people we're looking for are probably . . . light." Brunk was white, not that he'd have noted whom he was hanging with, as long as they had drugs. Yet Jeap had described himself as being different, too. "And they stay with Tim's mother, it's her place. She, uh, likes to play bingo."

That was all Grif had to offer, other than the twenty, yet to his surprise the kid's face lit. "Oh, *esa loca*? She plays keno, too, but she don't like anyone to know, cuz *that's* stupid."

Grif straightened from his slump. "You know her?"

"Everybody knows Crazy Lettie. But she don't live there." The kid pointed in the opposite direction of the Shangri-La, at a weed-choked doublewide with dingy sheets curtaining the small windows. "She stays there."

And Grif immediately knew Luis was telling the truth. A silvery shimmer of wafer-thin plasma glided into the trailer through cracks in the windows and under the doorframe, twining between the cinder blocks it was mounted on.

"Kit!"

One thing about his girl. Even when annoyed with him, she listened. She turned, saw where he was pointing, and whirled back around without even questioning it.

"Dennis!" she called. "It's not the apartments! It's over here! The house!"

Dennis, in turn, listened to Kit. The urgency in her voice had the detective running, and the uniformed officers following in a quick jog. Though able to enter the home in a safety sweep, they made a show of rapping loudly on the peeling wooden door first.

"So do I get some kind of reward or something?" Luis asked, drawing Grif's attention away from the officers clustered on the sagging stoop. Kit stayed back, lingering on the property's periphery.

Grif ignored the outstretched hand. The second twenty wasn't going to be as easy. "You see anyone coming or going from that place?"

"I see everything, *maricon*."

"Don't call me that."

"It means 'sir' in Spanish," the kid said, eyes sparkling.

"How do you say 'bullshit' in Spanish?"

"*Mierda*," the kid answered, relishing the word. "Now do I get a reward?"

"Yes. The prize of knowing you just saved two lives."

"Shit, man." The kid kicked at the ground with the worn toe of his sneaker right at the same time one of the officers kicked in the door, and said the exact same thing. The three of them disappeared inside, and a moment later the youngest came out retching.

"Or maybe not," Grif muttered, and studied the grounds around the trailer for signs of a Centurion, wondering who got the Take. Unsurprisingly, he saw nothing. If someone was dead inside, the Centurion had whisked them away before mortals arrived. "You said you see everything in this neighborhood, Luis. How many people are in that trailer?"

"Far as I know, just two. Loca Lettie can play the slots for two, sometimes three days at a time. Her tweeker son got here just after she left and hasn't been out since."

Kid really did have the lay of the land. "How long ago?"

"Yesterday."

"Time enough to die," Grif muttered, turning back in Kit's direction.

"Shit, *coño. You* already been here long enough to die." Luis's gaze darted to the left, over Grif's shoulder, then back just as quickly, as if he didn't want to be caught looking.

Grif shifted to find a man watching the action from the far side of a yard surrounded by a chain-link fence. No, Grif thought. Not a yard. Some sort of business butting up against the neighborhood. The man held a cigarette in one hand, and was idly stroking the muscular head of a pit bull with the other. Grif wondered exactly what kind of business he was in. Five other men lingered behind him, watching darkly, and calling to one another in soft voices across the small lot as they lounged in the fractured sunbeams of late afternoon.

"That him?" Grif asked, turning back to Luis.

The kid thrust out his bony chest, but Grif saw the knowledge, and fear, skitter across his gaze. "That who?"

"The one who runs this 'hood?" Grif guessed. Why else house a business on the backside of this societal abyss?

"You don't want to know who that is," Luis answered, eyes hard.

Grif smirked. "Does the guy I don't wanna know got a name?"

Luis just looked at him.

"I thought you said you knew everyone in Naked City, Luis. Don't tell me you don't know a hot dog like that."

"I know enough not to be talking about him with the Five-Oh."

"Fine. Then you can stay here and watch the car while I go ask him myself," Grif said, turning away.

"Screw that."

"Another bill in it for you."

"I don't need your money," Luis called out, almost sounding tough.

"*Mierda,*" Grif said, and crossed the street. He halted in the middle of it, though, a bright movement catching his attention from the corner of his eye. Kit, he saw, had just finished a quick exchange with Dennis, and was headed Grif's way. Actually, he thought, frowning as she zeroed in on him, she wasn't just headed toward Grif. She was striding.

No, Grif amended, right before she reached him. She was *barreling.*

Slamming her palms into his chest, she sent him flying backward two full feet. To Grif's surprise, and Luis's hooting delight, she rammed him again, and would have done so a third time if he didn't reach out and grab her wrists.

"Why did he do that?" Kit asked, jerking free. Her fists were clenched at her sides, and her eyes were filled with tears, but she didn't wipe them away as she continued to stare him down with that accusatory gaze.

"They're dead?"

"Why, Grif?" she asked again, confirming it.

"I don't think Brunk knew—"

"Not him," she said, with an impatient growl. "I mean *it*. Scratch. That fallen *angel*." She spat the word out, made it sound like a curse. "Why did it taunt us about these two if it was already too late?"

The truth wasn't much of an answer, but it was all Grif had. "Because that's its job. That's what it does."

"Its job?" Kit echoed disbelievingly, and Grif had to admit it sounded lame.

Grif tried again. "It wanted you to feel this—"

"No! It's more than that," she said, pointing back to the trailer. "It could have led us here sooner, and I'd have felt exactly the same. Why did it have to wait until they were dead? Is it really that cruel?"

Worse, Grif thought, but said, "You know who else didn't stop Tim's death? His mother. She's out pouring her paycheck into a one-armed bandit while he's rotting on her floor. You know who else didn't stop it, Kit?"

She looked at him, jaw clenching reflexively, but didn't answer.

"Tim didn't stop it. He did this to himself. Angels, even the fallen ones, aren't responsible for every damned action."

Kit looked away, then huffed, exhaling the last of her righteousness. "Well, Tim isn't here, so I can't kick his ass about it."

"But I am." Grif shoved his hands into his pockets.

She lifted her chin. "Sorry."

"Yes, I can tell." He put one hand on her ramrod-straight back, and steered her around until she was facing the other end of the street and could easily view the men clustered there. "There's someone else who didn't stop it, either . . . and I think we should go make his acquaintance."

CHAPTER NINE

That was all he needed to say. Kit instantly snapped into her reporter mode, glancing back once at Luis, then at the small commercial building, the men—the attack dog—in front of them. She had an ability to put two and two together faster than anyone Grif knew, and she also understood this era better than he did. Sure, men who loomed over neighborhoods like dark clouds had always been around, but she might be able to see something in the situation that he didn't. Besides, try to leave her behind, Grif thought, and tough little Luis would really have something to laugh about. They'd be safe enough with the heat poking around a few doors down.

He watched the six men straighten from their bored slouches as Kit and he approached. "Lost, *macho*?" said the man in front, sliding along the fence's perimeter as if pacing it.

"I'm not Lost, no," Grif answered, earning an elbow in the

ribs from Kit. He glanced over at the sign out front that'd previously been obscured by construction on the side of the building. LITTLE HAVANA. A restaurant.

The man—skinny as wire and tobacco-dark—squinted as
he leaned against the front gate, trying to ferret out disrespect
in Grif's words as they came to a stop before him. Then he
turned an equally calculating gaze on Kit. He held it there so
long, licking his lips, watching her with eyes like burned-out
bulbs, that she squirmed and folded her hands in front of her.
A smile lifted one corner of the man's mouth before he turned
back to Grif.

"Don't want no trouble with the po-po."

Grif didn't correct him. The assumption that he was a cop
might help. Grif glanced behind him as if to call Dennis over,
but he was, in fact, checking to see if the real detective was
watching. Dennis was occupied with the dead, though, so
Grif shoved his hands into his pockets, and turned back to the
living. "No trouble. Just some questions."

"What makes you think I got answers?"

"You look like a man with answers."

He looked like a man who'd dust them if he didn't like
the way they blinked. Tattoos coiled his body from neck to
wrist, with four dots forming a box cradled in the webbing of
his right hand. These were different from the tattoos worn by
Kit's friends. Those were ornamental, expressive, joyful, and
kitschy. These looked like blue veins that'd been pulled to the
surface from within the man.

Grif lifted his gaze. The man's nose had been broken, probably more than once, and never reset. His hair was short and
thickly gelled. He cared, Grif saw, deeply about appearance. At
least in his own way.

"Got nothing for you, *macho*." The man jerked his head. "'Sides, I got customers to worry about."

Grif let his gaze canvass the empty lot. The restaurant was undergoing an extensive renovation; Little Havana wouldn't see customers for months.

"Maybe I got answers for you, then," Grif said.

The man's eyes steeled over at that.

Kit fiddled with her phone, as if uninterested. The man looked her over, and smiled. "We can talk. My house is just there."

So they left Little Havana for the single-story home, followed by the other men. Kit was nearly vibrating with nerves, and Grif would have reached out to calm her, but he didn't want the men following them to know she needed it. She wouldn't want it, either.

The home was as down-at-the-heels as the rest of the neighborhood, and stuccoed like the rest of the city. A dog run stretched along its north side where, after a brief exchange of staccato Spanish, one of the men deposited the heavily leashed pit bull. Good. Animals sensed Grif's otherness in a way people didn't. More mutts had attacked him in the months he'd been back on the Surface than all of the thirty-three years of his "first" life.

There was no sidewalk, as the entire front of the lot had been paved over, as if concrete was the only thing keeping the thing upright. Errant weeds sprouted among the cracks like escaped convicts, yet the yard was swanky compared to the home's interior.

Ducking in behind the man, Grif emerged in a living area with a popcorned ceiling, dingy gray walls, and a corner altar. The furnishings were sparse; just a sagging sofa and a dark recliner huddled around an empty coffee table, but he sensed an air of care to the place. Grif and Kit ventured farther inside, and the door snicked shut behind them.

The other five men remained outside.

Grif glanced over to gauge Kit's comfort level. The hairs on the back of his neck had risen as soon as the door shut and the gloom closed around him, and he could see Kit struggling to find something nice to say, like, "It's a lovely home you have here."

The man saw it, too. The dark craters in his eyes sparked. "Seen enough?"

Not waiting for a reply, he jerked his head and turned toward the open kitchen. A refreshing odor wafted from within, meat stewing, thick and warm, as they made their way down a hallway studded by the gaze of silent saints.

"We're not looking to interfere with dinner . . . or your business," Grif said, trying to make up for Kit's silence. "We just have a few questions."

The man disappeared around the corner. "Like?"

"Like what's that smell?" Kit asked suddenly. She almost looked as shocked as he did that she'd found her voice. But her eyes were alive now and she was leaning forward, genuinely interested. Grif almost smiled. "It's fantastic."

"My *abuela*," the man said, gesturing to an old woman at the stove. "She's making *ropa vieja con arroz*. Our family's recipe. It has made Little Havana famous."

The two exchanged words in Spanish and the old woman looked up at Kit and smiled. There were holes where most of her teeth should have been, and enough wrinkles to fashion a map of the world across her face, but her gray hair was thick and neat, and there was the hint that she'd once been beautiful. "Let me guess, she's always been the best cook in the neighborhood?"

"I think so," the man said proudly; not any more friendly, but not any less.

Grif nodded thoughtfully, then said, "Maybe you should put the word out."

"We're a family business. We ain't planning a franchise," the man retorted, flopping back in a vinyl chair, again suspicious.

"Someone else is trying to drum up business on your turf, though," Kit said, crossing her arms. "And I don't think your *abuela* would approve of what they're cooking."

This time, when the man stared at Kit, it was with raw hatred, not surprise. Even Grif was taken aback at the hard look, while Kit swallowed audibly beside him. This time her discomfort failed to appease the man. Echoing her body language, he folded his arms over his wife-beater, and continued to use his gaze as a weapon. Kit took a step forward beneath that hot stare. "Mr. Baptista, do you know a young man by the name of J. P. Yang? He goes by Jeap?"

Grif startled, and immediately tensed. The old woman stopped smiling, the holes in her mouth disappearing as she, too, fell still.

"How you know my name?" Baptista said lowly.

Kit flashed her phone, which contained his image, and gave them both a distant, professional smile. "Public record, Marco. Your family has owned Little Havana for a long time."

Almost snarling, Baptista tilted his head at Grif. "You let your woman talk out of turn, *cabron*?"

The way he said it made Grif want to check the gun at his ankle, and back carefully away. But Grif had only four bullets in his .38 snub-nose, and that was strapped down tight. Baptista's friends were outside, and so was the dog, while Dennis and company were too far away.

"She's her own woman," he said instead, slowly tucking his hands in his pockets. "And she speaks when she wants to."

"I'm also a reporter. Kit Craig." And she stepped forward and held out a hand. Grif held back a groan. Baptista stared, then slapped her hand away, rising to his feet as she reeled back. Grif slid a hand around her waist, but otherwise didn't move.

"You come in here pretending to be with the police, asking me questions, and upsetting my grandmother?" He pounded his chest, the sound somehow reverberating, both hollow and loud. Grif cut his eyes sideways. The old woman remained by the stove, as alarmed by the outburst as Kit and Grif, but she didn't look upset. She looked resigned. Baptista jerked his chin at Grif. "You a reporter, too?"

"I look like a reporter?" Grif asked calmly.

The calculation had long disappeared from Baptista's gaze, and the anger faded now, too. Without blinking, he jerked his chin. It was acknowledgment. Respect. He saw enough of himself in Grif that he managed to settle again. "Come with me."

Baptista rose, and crossed the room, too close to Kit. He paused next to her, looking down. "You stay in the kitchen."

After a graduated moment, Kit merely nodded, and Grif blew out a relieved sigh. He'd make it up to her later.

So?"

"We," Grif started, letting Baptista know that Kit was still very much a part of this, even if she wasn't in the room, "need to know about a new drug in this neighborhood. It's made from things that shouldn't even be in a landfill. It's both cheap and highly addictive."

"You got nerve coming into my home and asking me about drugs, *cabron*."

"We think it's Russian," Grif added.

Baptista's gaze flickered, then he pursed his lips and sank into the sofa. He didn't offer Grif a seat. "Yeah, those *maricons* are dangerous. They're *huevones* compared to La Nuestra or Las Emes, of course, but dangerous enough."

"So you know them."

"Only one. Sergei Kolyadenko." He paused to see if the name meant anything to Grif, and Grif nodded. It was the same name Marin had given them. Baptista pointed to a tattoo, the number fourteen, which meant nothing to Grif. "We served together in Soledad. Now you give me something."

"All right. This him?" Grif asked, pulling out the photo Marin had given him.

Baptista glanced at the copy. "Maybe."

"Know what he was in for?" Grif asked, tucking the picture back in his jacket.

"Drugs. Weapons. Money laundering. He was too pussy for more than that."

"Did he deal while you knew him?"

"We was all dealing back then . . . as your woman probably saw from my record," Baptista added, voice hard. He threw an arm over the back of the sofa and sprawled. "But I ain't in that shit anymore. Didn't you hear?" His face grew a smile. "Crack is whack."

"We're not looking for crack, Mr. Baptista," Grif said, his own voice crisp. He might be in Baptista's home and on his turf, but he wasn't going to roll, either. "We're looking for *krokodil*."

Baptista lifted a shoulder. "Never heard of it."

"You will. It's affecting people in this neighborhood, and it's dangerous."

Some softer emotion skittered across Baptista's gaze, but it was gone too quickly to identify. "Is that what J.P. was on?"

"So you do know Jeap?" Grif said.

Baptista scoffed. "Don't say it like it means something. Everyone knew Jeap. My *abuela* and his family knew each other on *La Isla*." He jerked his head toward the kitchen where the old woman and Kit could be heard murmuring softly.

"And when was the last time you saw him?" Grif asked.

"Two, three weeks ago. With some hot chick and the tweekers you just found dead in Crazy Lettie's place."

Grif tilted his head. "How do you know they're dead?"

"Because the heat don't come to this neighborhood for the living." He cocked his head. "And neither does the press."

"And this hot chick?" Grif asked, wishing for Kit's always-present notebook. "What did she look like?"

Now Baptista smiled, face almost going handsome. "Stacked. Long legs. Great ass. Crazy damned hair, though. Blue, the first time I saw her. Pink the next."

And he shook his head as if to say, *Kids these days*.

"So she was here more than once?"

Baptista stopped shaking his head and sent Grif another piercing look. "I know you might find it hard to believe, but people do come here more than once."

"Catch a name?" Grif said, undeterred.

"Why would I need a woman's name?" Baptista said coolly.

Grif sighed, stared, and hoped Kit was having better luck in the kitchen.

*   *   *

The men," the old woman began, surprising Kit, because she hadn't been sure Baptista's *abuela* spoke English. "They talk like they play cards, no? Their hands held close to their chest. Tea? I made it myself."

Kit nodded once and took the seat that Marco Baptista had vacated. "Thank you, Ms. Baptista."

"Josepha," the woman corrected, eyes crinkling as she smiled. She placed a cup of steaming tea on the table, and Kit realized that she really had made the tea herself. Leaves and stray roots floated on the surface. The color was uneven, but it smelled of lemon and something muskier and unnamed.

"Don't worry," Josepha said, settling across from Kit, palms cupped around her own mug. "The men will argue some and when it's all settled they will tell us their plans. We can then agree, or change their minds for them."

Kit laughed, though she remained on guard. Hospitality usually made her melt into the moment, but the voices from the other room—the way Baptista had looked at her like an object instead of a subject—had her on edge. That, coupled with the foreign language and the corner altar and the exotic smells, made Kit feel as if she were in a foreign country without a map or guide or rudder to steer her back home.

"You're very pretty, Ms. Craig. You look like the girls did when I was young." Josepha smiled slightly, eyes far off as she remembered, nodding at Kit's red-trimmed kimono dress. "I used to wear things like that, back on the island."

And she'd probably been beautiful, Kit thought, because despite her humble home—and the wrinkles and the miss-ing teeth—there was something regal about Josepha Baptista. Something her grandson, and life, hadn't yet knocked out of her. Kit recognized it, and liked it.

"I wish I could have seen it all back then," Kit said. "The fifties is the era I love the most."

"An era you never lived?" Josepha asked, then laughed at Kit's responding nod. "I suppose that's why it holds sway over you. Illusion is often stronger than reality."

Kit didn't correct the woman. She had long stopped trying to defend her rockabilly lifestyle. She loved things because she loved them, and that was reason enough.

Instead, she glanced over at the carved statues spaced along the top of a multilevel platform. The altar had been behind her when she walked in, so this was the first opportunity to study it openly. If she'd known she'd be visiting the Baptista family, she'd have brushed up on her knowledge of Afro-Cuban religions.

"Ever see a Santerian shrine before?" Josepha asked, catching Kit's look.

Kit shook her head, studying the lit black candle, the bell and bowls surrounding it, the incense smoking into the statue's unblinking gaze. "I know that's your saint, though."

"Orisha, yes. That's Chango."

Chango additionally had bowls of seeds and beads and mirrors scattered at his feet. Kit wanted to ask Josepha about that, but the woman was lighting another candle between them, this one white. Kit would've assumed she was just setting the mood, but it was broad daylight in the middle of summer.

Eyeing the silky flame, Kit said, "The Christian religion ascribes meaning and ritual to almost everything, though this seems different somehow. It's more . . ."

"What?" The word was clipped, defensive. Like Kit's lifestyle, Josepha had likely been forced to defend her religion more than once. Santeria, after all, was synonymous with voodoo.

"It seems more vibrant. Dense. Almost pregnant with meaning." The shrine was different from any altar Kit had ever seen. It looked the same as a full belly felt, engorged with flavor, tipping into too much.

Josepha laughed. "Of course! The original priests in Santeria were all women, you know. We founded almost all branches of the religion, led all the major ceremonies, carried out all rituals."

"Really?"

"Yes. I, for example, was named after one of the most famous and most powerful Cuban priestesses. Of course, once there was power to be had, the men took over." Josepha shrugged, and gazed at the smooth flame between them as she sipped from her mug. "But we originally started out as a matriarchy. Oh . . . hear that?"

Kit turned to the doorway. "I don't hear anything."

"Exactly. They'll be done soon." Josepha smiled, yet as they turned back to the table, her smile fell. "Why did you do that?"

Kit stiffened at Josepha's alarmed tone. "What?"

"Why did you blow it out?"

Kit frowned at the white candle, now curling with black smoke. "I didn't."

Josepha's face drained of color, gaze flicking quickly between Kit and the candle, drawing meaning out of something Kit had never—and probably would never—understand. "Marco!"

Baptista appeared so quickly it was like he'd been waiting outside the doorway. Grif appeared, too, alarm scrambling his features. Josepha and Marco exchanged rapid-fire Spanish and suddenly Kit was being lifted by the arm and dragged to the front door.

"Mr. Baptista," Kit tried, feeling bruises already forming beneath his grip. "I didn't mean to offend . . . I don't know—"

"Hands off her, Baptista." Grif was suddenly between them, and Kit thought that if she could see his wings, each blade would be drawn sharp. Marco did release Kit, then, but only because they'd reached the end of the hallway. Behind him, Josepha was still ranting in Spanish.

"Sorry, *cabron*," Baptista said, holding the door wide. "But you can't stay for *ropa vieja*."

"That's okay," Grif countered. "We'll visit Little Havana once it reopens. Like you said, people do come back more than once."

Baptista just held open the door, hard gaze fixed on Grif. He didn't even acknowledge Kit as she passed. Yet she felt better as soon as she stepped outside. Back, she thought, where she knew the meaning of things. Back in her own country.

"Keep walking," Baptista called as they passed the litter of weeds and men in the concrete yard. "And good luck getting those Russians outta my city."

"Your city?" Grif half-turned.

Baptista's outline hardened in the harsh light, and Kit tugged on Grif's arm. "Like you said. My family has been in Las Vegas a long time."

Grif returned his hand to the small of Kit's back, and tipped his hat. "Good-bye, Mr. Baptista."

"Adios, *comemierdas*."

And as the smoky chuckle of a half-dozen dangerous men rose behind them, Grif gave Kit a grim smile. "Remind me to ask Luis what the hell that means."

* * *

What the hell did you say to Baptista's grandmother?" Grif asked, keeping his pace steady. They were still being watched, and by more than one guard dog in the scrappy lot.

"Nothing," Kit said, digging for her cigarettes. "Her stupid candle blew out and she went crazy. Sometimes illusion is stronger than reality."

"What does that even mean?" Grif said, squaring on her.

Kit shook her head, lighting up. "Just something Josepha said."

"So why'd she get so upset about the candle?"

"Gee, I don't know. Let me just check my handy-dandy pocket guide to religious cults."

"It's not funny, Kit. I get the feeling that if Baptista had waved to his buddies with his right hand instead of his left, we'd be locked in the side yard with that mutt."

Kit frowned, turning serious as well. "Baptista told you the Russians are dangerous, but so is he. I can feel it."

"Yeah? Your phone tell you that?" Because pulling Baptista's information up while still in his house had also been dangerous.

She held the damned device up again, where the same stony gaze he'd just faced was frozen again. "Yes. Marco Baptista. Served four years for armed robbery and possession of narcotics. I can't dig deeper until I get back to the office, but I bet there's more on his sheet than that."

"Do you really think he'd knowingly allow this junk into his own neighborhood?" Because Grif couldn't see it. If Baptista considered Vegas his city, how much more possessive would he be over his personal stomping grounds?

Grif glanced back at Baptista's posse. Dollars to doughnuts, each of them lived nearby. Would they all just stand around and watch their friends and families get strung out on something like *krokodil*?

"No," Kit finally said, following his glance and thoughts. "But I can't help but think 'his' city would be a lot better without him, too."

"Good." Turning back to her, Grif shoved his hands in his pockets. "Then I won't have to worry about you sneaking down here for more information. Besides, we've got our tie. He knows Sergei Kolyadenko."

"And?"

"Doesn't seem to like him."

Kit blew out a hard stream of smoke. "And the woman?"

Grif shook his head. "Same info. Lots of wigs. A new face in the crowd . . ."

And suddenly Kit had flicked her light away, and was crossing to the other side of the car. The pool at the Shangri-La Apartments sat still and clouded behind her, murky enough that even the sun's relentless rays couldn't penetrate more than an inch beneath the surface.

"Where are you going?"

Grif hoped Kit's answer would be one Baptista would like, because Luis was still loitering, listening intently, and Grif had a feeling it'd reach Baptista's ears before Kit was even out of sight.

"If heaven isn't going to help, I will," Kit called back, not caring who heard. She paused with one foot inside the vehicle, one out. "I'll flush the Russians out like quail in a thicket."

"How?"

She leaned forward, one arm resting on the soft top. "With words, Grif. I'm going to write it down, then write it up. These dealers might operate in the dark, but I have the power to bring it *all* to light."

Grif crossed to her quickly, dismayed to note a good half-dozen people staring at them, including Luis. "You sure that's wise, Kit?" Grif said, voice low as he reached her side.

Squaring on him, she lifted her chin. "I don't run away from my problems by sticking a needle in my veins, so I'm not vulnerable to these people. But these kids," she said, motioning to the trailer where Tim's and Jeannie's bodies had been found, then at Luis and the others gathered on the street, "they are. And no one, including your high-and-mighty feathered friends, is protecting them."

Grif winced, because she had a point. "Fine, but you are vulnerable."

"You mean Scratch." She swallowed hard at his nod. "I can control my emotions, Grif. I'm in possession of myself."

"I know that."

"Good. Then let me work on this in the only way I can. I . . . need that."

Grif shoved his hands in his pockets and nodded. Trying to discourage her would only stubborn her up anyway.

Kit bit her lip. "Look, I know there are boundaries you can't cross, that they come with the halo and wings, but don't forget what it is to be human. It's impossible for me to see all that we have and not try to help."

"I know." It wasn't in her nature not to help. "And I'm doing the best I can, too, doll."

She hesitated, then folded into him. Nothing had changed. The world was still hard, the danger still there, but as always, her shape and warmth and softness—her *goodness*—eased the aches of the day. Grif closed his eyes, as she whispered, "I know that, too. And I love you for it."

Then she slipped from his arms, patted his chest, and climbed into the car.

"Hey," he said, before she could shut the door. She gazed up at him, and he managed a smile. "I love you, too."

Even before answering the phone, the woman knows who it is. Tomas is watching the Craig woman and her companion, but *she* is watching Tomas.

"Speak" is all she says as she watches the sun set over Naked City.

"I'm watching them now. They're leaving the neighborhood." He pauses, but the woman only waits for more. "I also know every place the Craig woman visited since this morning."

"Are you following her now?" The intimation is that he'd better be.

"Yes. Craig's in the car, but it looks like she's leaving the man behind."

Yes, she sees that, too. "Stay on Craig. She's going to be trouble. And Tomas." There is a pause. "You did well to see where she was going. I find it very interesting that she tried to visit Little Havana."

Even from a distance, and as he starts his car and begins to follow the Craig woman, she can see Tomas straighten, and preen. She smiles to herself. It is good that he still desires to prove himself to her. She can still use that. Yet it also emboldens Tomas. "I can take care of her if you'd like."

It is a thought. That's what he does best, and it is why she's hired him in the first place. Wrapping one arm around her middle, she asks, "You say she left the big guy behind?"

"Yes. But I can take care of him, too," he says, and she smiles again, and relaxes. He wants so badly to show her what he is capable of.

"Maybe later," she says, and imagines Tomas deflating a bit. He is gone from view, doing her bidding. "I don't want to risk that kind of attention right now, although . . ."

Tomas waits.

"It wouldn't hurt to scare the girl a bit."

There is a blare in the background, likely caused by Tomas blowing through a red light to keep up with Craig, but there is also a smile in his voice. "I can find an angle."

"Good. Make some noise in her life. Nothing direct, though. Be creative. Make sure it can't be traced back to us. Maybe she'll rethink what she's doing. But Tomas?"

"Yes?"

She thinks of Katherine Craig circling, writing articles, questioning people who might eventually lead to her. "Whatever you do? I want her reeling."

"I'll give her a good scare," he says immediately.

"Do more than that, Tomas," she says in a low voice. "Put the fear of God into her."

CHAPTER TEN

Kit couldn't sleep. She'd burned up the bulk of her anger doing exactly what she told Grif she would do, going home and pounding the computer keys so hard that she broke a nail. Even amid her moral outrage, she managed to construct a story about a drug that stripped flesh from the bone, and a dealer—faceless, nameless, remorseless—who preyed upon the poor. She'd submitted it electronically, and then had a tense fifteen-minute phone call with Marin before her aunt agreed to approve the story and run it by morning. The only thing Kit left out—in print and in words—was the heartlessness of angels who stood by and watched as man—and woman—fell.

That, the confounding senselessness of it, was what had her tossing and turning alone in the bed she and Grif normally shared. Or maybe her sleeplessness was precisely because she was alone. Sorry she'd run him off, she had called Grif just after nine, but he said he was following "a lead" and would be a while.

A private lead, she added silently.

So, even though it was already late, Kit decided to go out, too, and knew as soon as she was showered, warm, and in motion that it was the right decision. The mere act of stepping into her closet cleared the worry from her brow. She inhaled deeply, immediately feeling more certain, more herself, when surrounded by all her things. She touched a strand of estate pearls, and felt a smile reach the corners of her mouth. She let her fingers roam: Bakelite bracelets, antique brooches, vintage furs, and peacock feathers.

The black-and-white skulls and cherry prints—yards and yards of cherry prints—kept it from looking too much like her grandmother's closet, as did the silk stockings and frilled panties, the colored eyelashes reserved for special occasions.

It wasn't that she was a clotheshorse, Kit thought, sliding on a pair of seamed fishnets. Though that was true, to a degree. But she had specifically chosen every item in this closet. Every single piece had its place. Her entrée into the rockabilly lifestyle had not only come at a time when her life had lacked style . . . it'd lacked *life*. After her father followed her mother into what she now knew was the Everlast, Kit had suddenly, brutally, found herself in a family of one. It took some time before she came around to the idea that she, alone, was enough to build a new family around her.

She'd had Marin, of course. Her prickly and pragmatic aunt had coaxed her from her depression with more tough love than compassion, yet it'd worked, and in her own way, she'd shown just as much love as Kit's mother would have. That was why their relationship was so very complicated. She was not the woman Kit had wanted, yet she was the one Kit had needed.

Still, Shirley Wilson lived on in her daughter, and after re-emerging into the world an orphan, Kit vowed to let nothing into her life that didn't make at least one of her senses explode. Every bit of furniture adorning her home was carefully considered—from the vintage record player to her meticulously curated collection of Depression glass. Same went for the clothes she donned, from the corsets to the Mary Janes.

Even the food she put *in* her body had to be wanted more than needed. Kit didn't want merely to be sustained. She didn't want only to exist. If a physical item didn't speak to her in a voice as enticing as a lover's whisper, then it had no place in her periphery.

So what if the majority of people considered the rockabilly lifestyle eccentric or weird? Those who didn't know her thought only that she wanted to live in the past. What they couldn't know was that the rockabilly lifestyle actually simplified things for her in a way that someone driven by the latest fashions and fads couldn't enjoy. Having set lifestyle parameters took the angst out of deciding what car to drive or how to dress. Wouldn't the masses be amazed to learn that, in living an extreme lifestyle, Kit was actually playing it safe?

Which brought her to Griffin Shaw.

Kit sighed, letting her hands fall still and her eyes close. How ironic that even though the man was from the era she most adored, the one that she honestly believed kept her safe, he was the first thing she'd allowed in her life that was decidedly unsafe. With his straight-razored pomp and wing-tip shoes, he certainly looked like her kind of extreme. Even strangers commented on what a great-looking couple they were when walking hand in hand. Kit wouldn't argue that, though those same strangers would call him crazy if they heard his claims of being an angelic messenger.

Yet this unsafe man had saved her, the crazy one had actually shown her his wings, and if anything about him was extreme, it was that he brought all of Kit's senses to life at once. In short—in fifties' terms—Kit was completely gone over him . . . and she hoped never to return.

That's why the thought of Grif crying without her there to console him made *her* want to cry. She'd wanted to ask if the tears he'd bottled to banish Scratch had been tears of joy or sorrow, but had been too afraid of the answer. And now she couldn't even think of it. She had to keep her emotions in check—the jealousy she barely acknowledged, the envy she tried to ignore.

The stupidity she felt over playing second fiddle to a dead woman.

Closing her eyes, Kit tried to clear her mind. Then she remembered the way Scratch had looked at her through both Jeap's and Brunk's starry black gazes. A chill broke out along her spine.

You are just some choice bit of beauty that I have not yet broken, it'd said, branches scratching in Brunk's throat. *I don't want to touch her.*

I want to possess her.

"Shut up," Kit said aloud, like it could still hear her now. Who knew? Maybe it could.

"Shut. Up." She said it again, just in case.

Because if she was going to live—and she and Marin had made damned sure of that a long time ago—then she was going to love whom she wanted without fear, and she was going to follow her heart. The loss of the most meaningful people in her life had struck her like a lightning bolt. So why the hell shouldn't the addition of a great love do the same? Passion was a positive emotion, right? And the willingness to be open to another person was a strength, not a weakness.

So, as Kit combed through the carefully edited world of her closet, her mind gradually settled. Outside was a world she couldn't understand, where desperate people injected their bodies with drugs that caused their flesh to rot from their bones. Outside, too, was the man she adored, working alone to avenge the death of a woman he'd loved fifty years earlier. If she'd fallen short in her understanding of that, it was only because that, too, was another world she could never really know.

Yet Kit was well versed in all things rockabilly, and *that's* what she needed tonight. Jiving and swinging to wash away the dregs of the day. The retro-inspired beauty and liveliness of her pinup friends to remind her that this world was also good. Sailor Jerry tattoos would remind her of simpler times, and a greaser with a comb in his back pocket and a naughty gleam in his eye would work wonders on her mood with one spin around the dance floor.

What Kit needed right now, she decided, was to sip an Old Fashioned and smoke a Lucky through a gold-tipped holder.

"And I might as well do it," she said, holding up a cocktail dress with a built-in bullet bra, "while watching someone shake. Their. *Tassels.*"

The dimness upon entering the Bunkhouse—all rockabilly, all the time—was similar to the dive where Kit and Grif had met with Trey Brunk, and yet the two places couldn't be more unalike. The Bunkhouse was a dance hall, spacious and clean, and brightly lit when there was a Lindy Hop, though tonight the stage was set for cabaret. There was a cash bar just inside the door, unnecessary with the cocktail waitresses sashaying about in leopard satin, but it was ribboned in gilt, and added to the feel of a twenties speakeasy.

Outside of early to midcentury, rockabillies weren't particular about their eras. They could mesh the roaring of the twenties with the war-inspired tiki torches of the forties, and top it all off with a cupcake dress from the sixties . . . and the girl inside was the cherry on top. The Bunkhouse did all this and more, so that it was cheery, a bit raucous, and tonight it was teeming with life.

Kit's heart swelled as she crossed the threshold, and handed her vintage mink cape to the coat-check girl, who exclaimed admiringly as she took it. The canister footlights were dimmed at the stage, and the red curtains drawn, but they were backlit so that the next performer's silhouette was purposely displayed, teasing hip swivels combined with a boa to keep the audience in their seats.

Scouring the room for her own seat, Kit blinked in surprise as she caught sight of Dennis from across the room. He stood to wave, but blended well with the other greasers in his bowling shirt and sideburns, and she smiled and waved back, because it was good to see him here. God knew he deserved a break after catching two *krokodil* cases in a row. My fault, Kit thought, with an inner wince.

Then again, Dennis had been dipping his toe back into the rockabilly scene a lot more since the case that had reunited them four months earlier. Before that, he'd believed that donning his uniform meant putting away his alternative tastes. Kit liked to think she'd brought a bit of fun and nostalgia back into his life. More than most, Kit thought, the men in blue needed a good, solid place to escape.

Just then, Kit spotted her own much-needed escape, a

bird-bright, long-limbed looker with a crimson hairnet and a wooden parasol . . . one used to casually jostle and jab those who wandered too near her table. Nobody cared, though. The woman was just playing. She was also one of Kit's closest friends, Fleur Fontaine.

"Hello, dolly," Fleur said as Kit arrived, ruby-red lips wide and smiling. "Thought for a while that you were going to miss the show."

"Not a chance," Kit said, plopping down between Fleur and her tablemate, another of Kit's nearest and dearest, Lil DeVille. In contrast to Fleur's retro kimono and finger waves, Lil was wearing a navy-blue sailor shorts suit, probably a thrift-store find, and red pumps that had her towering over six feet. She toasted Kit's arrival with her Schlitz, flashing red fingertips and a long-lashed wink. Kit settled in with a sigh, and signaled to the waitress for her own drink, wondering why she'd ever considered staying home.

"Where's Joe Friday?" Fleur asked, propping her arm on the table so the mermaid inked there flashed its emerald tail.

Grif had called to say he'd gone to a strip club to question Ray DiMartino, the owner, about Mary Margaret and his old case. But Kit didn't say that. She was just starting to feel good and didn't even want to think about it. Placing a cigarette in a vintage holder, she said, "Out gumshoeing the streets alone. He told me to stay home with my hens."

"Sexist pig," Fleur scoffed, giggling as she used the tip of her parasol to poke at a passerby in a zoot suit.

"Lovable sexist pig," Lil added, because they all knew, and approved, of the way he doted on Kit. She just hoped that letting him question DiMartino alone in the bowels of Masquerade would give him the answers he sought. She knew why he'd gone alone. Grif hated taking Kit into that environment, yet as the music swelled throughout the Bunkhouse, and the curtains rose to reveal a platinum blonde covered in little more than glitter and feather fans, she couldn't help wondering what he'd make of *this* one.

Doesn't matter, she decided, as her Old Fashioned arrived and the woman onstage began to flutter her plumes. Let Grif have his haunted past and pedestrian strip club for the evening. This was *hers*.

Besides, Kit thought, sipping as the fans fell away and the audience began to whistle and hoot. It wasn't where Grif was that bothered her, or what he was doing. It was what he was *thinking*. About another woman. About that *Evie*.

Something of her thoughts must have been revealed on her face, because Fleur turned to her as soon as the act was over. "Spill" was all she said.

Kit looked away. The stage kitten, dressed in fishnets and a bustier, sporting victory rolls, was sweeping glitter from the stage so the next performer wouldn't fall. Lil was flirting with the whole table of swing boys next to them. She could confide in Fleur without interruption. Yet Kit didn't feel like voicing her worries just yet. Voicing them, she thought superstitiously, might make them real.

"I'm just all junked up with this story I'm working on," she said instead, tapping her cigarette holder against a crystal ashtray. "It's the most disturbing, disgusting, vile thing I've ever seen."

Lil caught the end of the statement, and leaned close, propped her elbows on the table. So Kit told them both about young Jeap Yang, his addiction to a drug that stripped the flesh from his body, untethering health from the inside out, and about Tim and Jeannie as well. She ended with the new information Marin had shared about him after Kit had submitted her story. "His real name is Juan Pedro Perez. You guys got feelers out in the Hispanic community?"

"Where's he stay?" Lil asked, all of her playfulness gone.

"What does that have to do with anything?"

"Because we're not like you Anglos, *mamita,*" Lil replied, falling into the accent that made her trill. "We stick together."

"Whether we want to or not," Fleur agreed, equally serious. "We pile our immediate family atop each other, and pile extended family atop that. And extended includes pretty much anyone we've known since childhood—neighbors, children of neighbors . . . their dogs."

"I still remember my first pet fish, may he rest flushed in peace." And Lil lowered her head, closed her eyes, and made the sign of the cross.

Kit smiled at her dramatics, thinking the whole cultural dynamic sounded claustrophobic . . . and nice. "He's from Naked City. That's where the two tweekers died today."

"Shit, girl, he probably ain't Mexicano." Screwing up her beautifully painted mouth, Lil drew back to regard Kit with disdain. "You think us Latinas all look alike."

"No, I don't," Kit said defensively, but the two women gave her matching stares, arms folded across their chests, perfectly plucked eyebrows raised in identical doubt. "You two, for example, look better than anyone I've ever seen in my entire life."

"Good recovery," Lil said immediately, turning back to her drink, cultural slight forgotten as a woman in red took the stage, twirling long ombre sashes as if each were a cape and the audience were her captivated bull. They were certainly transfixed when her tassels began swinging in opposite directions, and Kit added her own applause to that of the crowd.

Evie Shaw had probably been just like that, Kit thought, watching the woman present herself to the crowd like a gift. But without the tassels.

As the set ended and the applause soared, Fleur turned back to Kit, renewing the conversation exactly where they'd left off. "Naked City is the old Cuban *barrio*," Fleur explained, cradling her parasol on her lap. "They pretty much took over the neighborhood in the early eighties, because the rent was cheap and they could all stay together."

"But that was a long thirty years ago," Kit pointed out as the MC gave a mid-show shout-out to the legendary burlesque star Tart Ta-Tan. An older woman in polka dots and pearls stood to give a Miss America wave. "Surely there are Mexicans there now."

"Yes, but the Cubanos had an added defense. A way to keep newcomers, at least the smart Latinos, out of the neighborhood," Fleur said, and Lil—who'd rejoined them—gave a concurring nod.

"What?"

Fleur pointed the handle of her parasol at Kit. "The Marielitos."

Kit tilted her head. "Mariel-what?"

"Remember the 'freedom flotilla'? The Cuban boatlifts from Mariel to Miami? The way America welcomed the refugees only to have the crime rate skyrocket?"

"No." Kit put out her cigarette, then leaned on her elbows.

Lil sighed. "Think *Scarface*. Think drug runners using white powder to control their new world." Fiddling with her swizzle stick, she shook her head. "The Marielitos have a reputation even among the Cubans, and they make the PIRU look like children playing in a schoolyard," she said, naming one of Vegas's most violent gangs.

"So, then, I need to talk to a Cuban," Kit muttered, scouring her mind for sources.

"*Ay,*" Lil said, rolling her eyes. "Get a Cubana talking and you might never shut her up again."

Kit drew back as Fleur scoffed her agreement. "How come you can both be prejudiced, but I get chewed out if I even say the word *chola*?"

"Because we're Latinas," Lil said, as if that explained everything.

"*Sí,*" added Fleur. "But even I would be very careful about questioning a Cuban in Naked City about one of their own. From what I hear, it's still a different world."

"What do you mean?"

"She means they still kill chickens in their backyards." The voice, low and resonant, popped up directly behind Kit. She turned to find Dennis close, palming a cold Pabst, smelling faintly of spice, probably his pomade. Probably Suavecito.

Kit narrowed her eyes as he pulled up a wooden chair. "How long have you been standing there?"

"Just arrived," he said, straddling the chair, beer can dangling from his fingertips.

"Really?" Fleur said. "Then you'll react in total surprise to find Kitty-Cat here is playing investigative reporter again."

"Yeah, but you were the one who mentioned the Marielitos," he pointed out.

"So you *were* eavesdropping."

"Most of the Mariel descendants are good people," Dennis said, expression gone serious as he turned to Kit. "Besides, you're not going to get someone in that neighborhood to talk to you, Kit."

"He's right. Forget that you look like a Vargas girl," Fleur said. "To them you represent establishment, and a world where they don't even want to belong."

Sipping at his can, Dennis nodded. "When you're marked as an outsider, even in your homeland, and then you move somewhere else where you're both outsider and outlaw, you tend to live by your own rules. Obviously not all of the Marielitos were criminals, but they're still very insular. They trust no one."

Kit thought of Marco Baptista's grandmother, of her broken teeth and orishas and candles. "Okay, but the boatlifts were decades ago. Fortunes change. Families change."

Lil draped an arm over the back of her chair. "You really are so white."

Dennis sipped his beer and smiled. "Memories are as long as lineage."

Kit was certainly learning that. "Well, I wouldn't ask them anything they find threatening. And this new drug makes cocaine look like cane sugar, you saw it. Besides, the two junkies who died today weren't even Latinos, yet they resided in Naked City. So I think someone's bringing 'crocodile' into the poorest sections of the city and setting it loose on the kids there."

Lil whistled. "Then it'll be a crocodile against a sleeping dragon . . . and you'll be poking that dragon."

"It's a good analogy," Kit said, and a part of her thought it might even be a just reward. "Maybe a drug that creates an inferno inside the body can only be fought by a monster capable of breathing flame. Fire against fire."

Dennis ran a hand over his head. "As long as that fire isn't directed your way."

"Oh, look! It's Layla's turn!" Fleur grabbed her spinning rattler off the table and stood as Layla Love—their sometime frenemy and the city's self-appointed neo-burlesque queen—

began to gyrate to a raucous bump-and-grind. "Come on—let's go cheer her on!"

But Lil just kept looking at Kit. "Not me, *mija*. I'm going to stay and watch this show."

"What show?" Kit tilted her head, then blinked when Fleur unceremoniously dragged Lil away. O-kay.

She turned back to Dennis. "Friends," she told him with a shrug.

He leaned on the table so their elbows touched, warm, comforting, and close.

Kit leaned forward, too. "So what do you got for me?"

This close, there were sparks to Dennis's eyes, a brilliant yellow ring around his irises that flared like warm stars when he smiled. "Gotta get right to the point, don't you?"

"People are dying," she said, raising her voice to be heard over the catcalls and rattlers.

"And knowing what I've 'got' isn't going to stop it."

Kit lifted her chin. "It could. If I think fast. Act faster."

"You're right." He inclined his head. "It already did."

Kit blinked. "What do you mean?"

"The tweekers you led us to today?" he asked, as if she could forget.

"Tim and Jeannie," she said, because she never would.

"Tim Kovacs and Jeannie Holmes," he confirmed, then shook his head appreciatively. "It was good work, Kit. Damned good work."

She couldn't see how. "Because?"

Now a full smile bloomed, causing the stars in his eyes to dim in comparison and the spotlights and music to fade. All Kit heard were his next words . . . and they truly were beautiful. "Because one of them survived."

CHAPTER ELEVEN

One of the tweekers destined for death—one of the fates Grif had sworn they couldn't change—had survived? Kit shot so straight in her chair she was almost standing. "Which one? Who?"

"The female. Jeannie Holmes." Dennis held up a hand as Kit opened her mouth to ask more. "But don't get too excited. The doctors aren't sure she'll make it. She already coded once and she's being kept in a coma because of the extent of her wounds."

"When can I—" Kit started, then caught herself. "I mean, when can you talk to her?"

"Did you hear the coma part?" Dennis shook his head and his eyes lost all their satisfaction. "This *krokodil* is no joke. It will take weeks to wean her from it, and that's only if she survives that long."

Kit recalled Dr. Ott's words. A month to recover fully. By then there'd likely be more dead.

Dennis read her mind. "Even then we don't know how much good it'll do. She might have fried her brain, too. I don't know how this drug works."

"Does she have family?"

He nodded. "A mother. She's at the hospital now."

Kit bit her lip and waited.

"Kit." Dennis sighed, exasperated.

"You wouldn't even know about this case, or *krokodil,* if it weren't for me," Kit pointed out. "And Jeannie wouldn't be alive."

"And?" he said. He was going to make her ask it.

Fine. She lifted her chin. "And maybe her mother will be so thankful that she'll be willing to talk to the woman who got her daughter help in time."

Dennis sighed again, then looked away. "I'll ask," he said, after another moment. "But stay away from Naked City."

Kit decided not to tell him about her run-in with Baptista, and would've lunged to hug him if his eyes weren't currently glued to Layla's blinding, glittering tassels.

"Want a closer look, dear?" she teased, bringing Dennis's gaze back around.

"Nah," he scoffed softly, glancing down as he lifted his drink. "I have the best view in the house."

And he looked back up, directly at Kit.

Kit stared back, stunned as applause rose up all around her. What the hell was going on?

"I mean it," Dennis said, glancing away, missing her frown. "You look amazing tonight. Our girls are all babes, of course, but you have a way of filling up a room. It's like a giant bouquet of roses in a banquet hall. Everything else looks artificial next to something so real and alive."

"Dennis," she said, then paused, unsure how to continue.

"I know," he said, holding up a hand to stop her. "You're in a relationship, and your man would kick my ass just for the way I'm looking at you now."

"Yes," Kit said, though Grif had too much confidence and self-possession to get worked up over another man's aspirations. He wouldn't pummel Dennis because of that look. He'd pummel him on principle.

"So let me just say this," Dennis said, and Kit held up a hand.

"You really shouldn't."

He knew that, of course, and just smiled. "Ever since the Chambers case, when you popped back onto my mental radar, bringing this world"—he motioned around—"back with you, I feel more alive than I have in years. You reminded me of how much this meant to me. Sometimes I wonder why I ever gave it up."

Yes, she could see that. He looked fully alive in his cotton and denim, errant glitter winking off one cheek. He lived as she did, too, with nostalgic admiration for the past, but feet firmly planted in the here and now. It was something Kit could appreciate tonight, while all alone but for her girlfriends and cherry-infused Maker's Mark zipping into her veins. Besides, when it came down to it, a charged moment between longtime friends meant little.

Kit, very simply, was in love with Grif.

Hesitating, she finally placed a hand on Dennis's arm. "Thank you for telling me, but . . ."

"I know," he said, rising so that her hand fell away. "I just wanted you to know, too."

She smiled. "I'm glad you didn't give it up. All this, I mean."

"Me, too. Though it does make me wonder."

"Wonder what?" she asked, head tilted up.

Lifting her hand, he dropped a kiss atop her fingertips, his own giving a light squeeze before he let it drop. "What else I gave up too easily."

And Kit had nothing at all to say to that.

Without another word, Dennis rejoined the gearheads at his table, leaving her gaping in his wake. Fleur materialized almost instantly.

"So, that's interesting," her friend said, and Kit knew that despite Layla's mesmerizing act, Fleur had seen everything.

"No, it's not," Kit replied quickly.

"But it could be."

"Sure." Kit, mobile again, lunged for her drink. "If it'd happened, I don't know, six months ago."

"Because of the man who's torturing you with his absence tonight?" Fleur asked, raising an eyebrow.

"Just because he's not here right now doesn't mean he's gone." The most important people and things in life rarely needed to be present to sustain their hold. "Grif is the first thing I think of in the morning and my last lingering thought at night. He's burrowed so deeply inside of me that he could take up permanent residence there. I couldn't get him out even if I wanted to."

"Okay," Fleur said, waving away the deep declaration of love. "But you shouldn't look like you want to call for an exorcism when you say that."

Kit drew back. Did she?

"Wanna talk about what's really bothering you?" Fleur said, now that the two of them were alone. Lil had disappeared backstage to congratulate Layla.

Kit held her friend's knowing gaze. "Not really."

"Which is why you must," Fleur said practically. "You gotta exorcise your worries, cast them out like demons."

The word made Kit think of Scratch, and she shuddered. But Fleur was right, and she also realized that this was really why she'd come here tonight. To commune and connect. If circle skirts and cherry tattoos were her oxygen, her friends were her lungs.

"Grif isn't just wandering randomly," she told Fleur, leaning forward on her elbows, wanting to get the story out before the next act began. She had time. The stage kitten was still flirting with the crowd. "He's researching the murder of another woman. It's a very old case, half a century, actually, but it's something very . . . personal to him. I know I should want answers for him, for them both, but he's . . . I don't know. Obsessed."

"How obsessed?" Fleur asked when Kit looked away.

Kit thought about it for a moment, then lifted her gaze. "We can be sitting, having a perfectly nice dinner," she said, not adding that it was one she'd spent hours planning, shopping for, and prepping, "and he'll suddenly get this faraway look. The food disappears—the textures, the taste. The candlelight no longer touches his eyes. The hand holding his fork falls still."

Fleur listened intently, but said nothing.

"Or we'll be watching a movie and I'll feel a kind of shift, and even though he hasn't moved at all I'll just look over and he'll be gone, same way. That seeing, but not seeing. And I know he's with her."

Fleur wrinkled her nose. "With this old woman? This old case?"

Kit nodded, and caught pity crossing Fleur's gaze before it was erased.

"Okay," Fleur said, still trying to understand. "So what do you know about the woman in question?"

Evelyn Shaw had been beautiful. She'd been a perfect siren. She'd been married to the man Kit loved.

And he dreamed of her still.

"I know she's been dead for years," Kit said, "but he thinks of her every single day of his life. What more do I *need* to know?"

Fleur slapped the tabletop with her palm, causing Kit to jolt and the couple next to them to stare. "Every. Damned. Thing."

"What?" Kit asked, drawing back.

Not breaking her stare, Fleur grabbed Kit's hands. "Learn all you can about that woman. Research her the same way you do your stories. Pretend you're going to put a byline beneath anything you find. Look into this . . . what was her name?"

"Evelyn," Kit answered, though that wasn't what Grif called her. *Evie.*

"So research this Evelyn and learn about her—what she did, where she worked, who her family and friends were. Learn her secrets." Fleur's eyes narrowed as she jerked her chin. "I bet if you look close enough, you'll find she wasn't so damned perfect. Even if she did have the advantage of being alive in Elvis's golden years."

Kit's sigh lifted the bangs from her forehead. "Yeah, but I can't go to Grif and say, 'Look what I found out! This woman you were obsessed with gossiped with the neighbors, carried a canteen of gin around in her handbag, and flirted shamelessly with the milkman!' That'll only reflect badly on me."

"So don't go to him." Fleur shrugged. "That's not the point anyway."

It wasn't?

Fleur patted her hand, and smiled. "*You* need to know she wasn't perfect. I see the way he looks at you, Kit. You two were destined for each other. But if you need more security in your relationship, then you gotta create it yourself. Dig for it. I mean, that's what you do, right?"

That *was* what she did, Kit realized, straightening. Why, she investigated stories like this all the time in order to give her subjects the truth and, whenever possible, solace. Why wouldn't she do the same for herself?

Glancing up at the next performer, a woman with glitter on her eyelids and in her left glove, Kit nodded. *She* was the one who was warm and alive and real and here on the Surface. *She* was the one who held Grif when he awoke gasping from nightmares. And she would continue to do so, because she *was* his soul mate . . . and not by default.

Fleur was right. Why not dig a little deeper on the beloved, doomed Evelyn Shaw? Kit sipped at her drink, and watched tassels begin to swing. Find out a little something that would allow both Grif and her to shake off Evie's ghost once and for all. Then Grif could remain present during both his waking *and* sleeping hours. Then he'd dream of Kit and no one else. And maybe then, she thought, Griffin Shaw would be as alive in her arms as she was in his. And the saintly, perfect, haunting Evelyn Shaw could stay tucked in the past.

Right where she belonged.

CHAPTER TWELVE

If Ray DiMartino were a zoo animal, he'd be a meerkat—slender, with a tapered face and dark, shining eyes. And the Masquerade Gentlemen's Club, Grif decided, as he sat with Ray in the owner's booth, would be his natural habitat. Music and lights pulsed, no matter the time of day, and female dancers—made up, dolled up, trussed up—flirted boldly, sliding and gliding to show off every curve of flesh, no imagination necessary.

Yet despite the club's sweaty, red-faced, sexual pulse, it still felt lifeless to Grif. It was as if everyone knew they were just acting, desperation pulling each of them back into a twisted childhood where pretend was the only thing that was real.

Grif supposed that's why Kit didn't mind when he came here alone. She called the place dull, uninspired, and sexually jejune. Whatever that meant. She'd been here once, wearing a dress that'd completely covered yet accentuated her femininity and managing to simultaneously blend in and stand out. Grif recalled her looking like an exotic bird amid a forest of green foliage.

Ray remembered, too.

"How's that pretty lady of yours doin', Shaw?" the man said, sprawling in the red leather booth like he was wearing it. He didn't wait for Grif to answer. "Shoulda brought her in. She was going to talk to me about incorporating some new moves into some of the girls' routines."

Ray was never going to see any of Kit's moves. Not if Grif had anything to say about it. "She's at a burlesque show with her girlfriends," Grif answered truthfully. She'd left the message on his cell phone an hour earlier.

"All tease and no tit, huh?" Ray shook his head, as blind to subtlety and nuance as to the way Grif's fist curled on the table, and sighed. "Ah, well. To each his own."

"Crying over lost customers, Ray?"

Cupping his palms around a cigarette, Ray scoffed. "We're in a recession, didn't you hear? Times are never so good as when they're bad."

And wasn't that a sad societal statement, Grif thought, looking around.

"Got some new girls," Ray said. "In case you want to play while the Kit-Kat is away." He wriggled his brows knowingly.

"You know why I'm here, Ray."

Pursing his mouth like the cigarette had gone sour, Ray looked away. A woman writhed on the center platform, but he watched her like one of those newfangled reality shows this generation was so crazy about—like it was happening to someone else far away. "Still digging up old bones?"

"You said you were going to help." Grif had given the man four months to get back to him, four months to go through his mobster father's belongings and scrape up a name or two that might help Grif discover who'd killed him more than fifty years earlier. But Ray had none of his father's enterprise. Whereas the old man had virtually run this town from the underground, Ray sat out in the open, showing his white belly.

"Came up empty." Ray shrugged his shoulders, no big deal. He'd rather risk nothing and gain the same. "Anything Pops mighta had was either lost or thrown out as trash." He paused, making a face. "Unless that bitch, Barbara, took it with her when she fled to California. God knows she took everything else."

Yes, Barbara DiMartino. Old Sal DiMartino's second wife. Grif had never known her—she'd come along after he'd been dusted—but for some reason she knew him. And for some reason, Ray had reported, she hated Evie and him both.

Barbara said that both Shaws got exactly what was coming to them.

"No word from her, then?" Grif asked, reminding Ray of their previous conversation. "You still don't know where she might be?"

Ray flicked his fingers, scattering ash on the floor. It disappeared unnoticed. "She remarried damned quick after moving to Cali, and probably again after that. She wasn't one to mourn too long over a cold grave, if you know what I mean. Not when there was still plenty of the living to cash in on. Don't matter. Like I toldja before, we didn't get along. I don't ever expect to hear from her again."

Turning away, Grif rubbed his chin with the back of his hand, fighting not to punch something. This Barbara was the best potential lead he'd had. She'd hated him at the time of his death, and Grif wanted to know why. "Maybe you can help me with something else, then. I've been remembering some things about that day."

Ray swiveled his head, staring Grif square in the face. "What do you mean, 'remembering'?"

Grif cursed inwardly at the slip. He was doing that more and more these days. The longer he remained on this mudflat, the more the past and present got mixed up in his mind. Borrowing Ray's nonchalance, he shrugged the look away. "You know, just bits and pieces I heard over the years. Thought maybe you could confirm or deny."

"Confirm what?" Because they both knew that's what Grif really wanted.

"That there were two guys, not one, who attacked Griffin and Evelyn Shaw in their bungalow that night at the Marquis."

Ray shrugged. "Man, I didn't hear that *they* were attacked at all."

No, he'd heard that Grif had killed Evie, left her to die, and disappeared. "Trust me," Grif muttered. "They were attacked. And I believe at least two men died that night. Shaw and one of his attackers."

The third had left him and Evie to bleed out on a cold marble floor.

"Man, I was just a kid," Ray said, shaking his head, but Grif already knew that. He remembered Ray as a seven-year-old brat running dice in the back of his father's liquor store. Now fifty-seven, Ray was so mistrustful of his memory, and eyesight, that he believed Grif only greatly resembled the man he once knew.

"You're not being very helpful here, Ray," Grif said. And why was that? They'd parted last time with an agreement between them, if not an alliance. Had he come across something in his father's files to change that? Or, like a bored zoo animal, had he simply lost interest?

"Look, I've told you what I know, all right? I run a strip club. I ain't in the Life. Those days died with my pops." Disappointment flashed across Ray's gaze, erased with the next strobe of light and forgotten in the following pulsing beat.

"You're right," Grif said, blowing out a breath. Ray's father had been the most influential, feared mobster in this town when feared, influential mobsters were damned near celebrities. And Ray? Well . . . Ray was Ray. "It was a long time ago. I'm sorry."

Looking away, Ray jerked one shoulder, but Grif could see he was still steamed.

"How 'bout these folks, then?" Changing the subject, he reached into his pocket. "Know them?"

"Shit, man." Ray glanced down, then quickly away. "Why you asking me about the Kolyadenkos?"

"A case I'm working on. A new one," he clarified, and jerked his head at the couple in the photo. Ray's dad was gone, but there was always someone to take a mobster's place. "We think they're getting kids hooked on this new drug, but we don't know why or how."

Ray picked up the photo, then whistled quietly under his breath. "Not surprised. They call her the Viper, you know? On account that she's so deadly."

Grif blinked a few times, feeling suddenly like he was playing catch-up. "She?"

"Yeah, man . . . wait." He chuckled, then allowed the sound to bloom into a full, rounded laugh. "You think this guy, Sergei, is running the action? Oh, man . . . you're as out of the loop as the heat."

"You mean . . . Yulyia?" Grif frowned, looked at the photo again, anew, trying to wrap his mind around this new information. "She took over when her husband got sick?"

Ray reached for his beer. "That was just an excuse to amp up the action. She's always run that crew, though up until recently only those close to the Kolyadenkos knew it. She's gotten bolder lately, though. Like I said, striking fast, hard. Remember that killing atop the tower last year?"

"Yes," Grif lied.

"They say that was the Viper. Pinned the guy up there and let him spin—or ordered it. Sergei is just a front. He looks every bit the Russian general, but make no mistake. Mrs. K calls the shots."

Grif sat silent for a bit, drinking his beer, reordering his thoughts.

"I thought you were out of the loop, Ray," he finally said. "How do you know all this?"

"'Cause the only way to *stay* out of the loop is to know where not to step." He pointed at Grif. "Something you obviously haven't learned."

"Yeah, yeah."

"Besides, a babe like that comes on the scene, everyone notes it."

Grif looked around the room at all the girls nobody really noted. Sidelong, he glanced back at Ray. "Marco Baptista note it?"

Ray's face shuttered the same way it had when Grif had asked about his own dark past. "*No habla Español,* man."

"C'mon. You can't *stay* out of the loop, and not know this guy, Ray."

"Yeah, I know him." Ray jerked his chin. "I know enough not to talk about him."

Grif just waited.

Pulling a face, Ray cursed. It took another minute after that, but he finally looked at Grif. "There is a story."

Grif settled back. "I like stories."

And Ray had a doozy. It went back eight years, though that didn't dilute the telling. There was a gorgeous woman involved, and worlds were upended because of her. Not a new story, no, but in this telling it was Marco Baptista's world that got the shake, right when he was running a drug operation to rival the kingpins of old.

There wasn't a woman Baptista couldn't bag, Ray said, either by enticement or by force, though one look at the long-limbed blonde who'd stridden in to buy a cache of hash, and he wanted her to come to him by her own neediness and will. On her knees, he said. Begging and desperate, as he deserved.

"That's how Yulyia Kolyadenko got into the neighborhood." Ray leaned forward, relishing the telling despite himself. "She sat across from Baptista in his own restaurant, eating Cuban pork and drinking rum he'd smuggled from the homeland, and got him to talk."

Yulyia learned who the players were in Vegas, which cops to press on vice, and what attorneys and judges turned a blind eye in exchange for a pocketful of green.

"Baptista thought he was bragging to secure a righteous lay," Ray said, nodding. "He thought someone who was newly arrived to this country would find his tales exciting and very New World and shit. That she'd look up to him for guidance, and feel a little knee-scraping gratitude."

But what Kolyadenko found was a blueprint to the city more detailed than the tattoos webbing Marco's body. Without giving up a single kiss from her glossed lips, she overtook giant swaths of the city's drug trade with new, stronger product, and *huevos* most men didn't possess.

And Marco, Grif thought, shaking his head, blustering and full of macho Latino id, never even saw her coming.

"He fell for it hook, line, and sinker," Ray confirmed, stubbing out his own cigarette. "He never respected women before, but man, he despises them now."

Not all of them, Grif thought, memory winging back to the humble house held up by an altar and faith, scented with spice. "He lives with his grandmother, you know."

"Yeah, and have you seen her teeth?" Ray asked, miming gums. Miming fists. Then he shrugged. "Ack, well. Women make men do crazy things."

He gestured around the room where men traded bills for sins of the flesh. Yeah, Grif thought wryly. They were all being strong-armed.

"Thanks, Ray." Pocketing the photo, Grif rose to leave. It was a good story, but it was clearly all he was going to get tonight.

"Hold on, man." Ray held out a hand, just short of touching Grif. "About your grandpops . . . there might be a guy."

Grif waited.

Ray shrugged. "Old Al Zicaro is still around."

Grif squinted, recalling the name. "The newshound?"

He remembered Zicaro vaguely from his first lifetime, accusatory headlines that'd blared like horns while Grif had been working to find Sal DiMartino's niece. Grif had even caught a few choice arrows flung in his direction, though Zicaro had never been able to do more than intimate that Grif was made. Because he wasn't. He was just there to collect a paycheck for finding little Mary Margaret.

But the memory of those last weeks bum-rushed him now. Zicaro had been young and eager, always waving that pad and pen, jaw flapping a mile a minute. Grif suddenly recalled wanting to punch that motor mouth on more than one occasion.

"He's gotta be in his seventies now, but the bastard always had a mind like a steel trap." Ray's lip curled, remembering Zicaro with the same fondness Grif did, and he added, "Of course, you're betting on him playing with a full deck in the first place. That bum ran stories about spaceships filling the desert sky right next to beefed-up mobsters whacking everything in sight. He saw a conspiracy in everything, but verified nothing. Ask me, it made him crazy."

Grif would take crazy over nothing. "Know where I can find him?"

To Grif's surprise, Ray did. "Sunset Retirement Community, last I heard," he answered immediately. "The *Trib* did a piece on him a while back, honoring his years of—get this—service to the community. The piece said he was still chasing down stories, but he's using the retirement home's copier to print them, and he hand-delivers them to the other residents' doors every morning. Like I said, nutso."

Grif agreed, but just shoved his hands into his pockets. "Thanks, Ray."

Ray shrugged. "I wish I could help you more. I really do. Your grandpops was a good man, always took time for me, and not everyone did that. Not everyone really . . . saw me." Ray frowned a little at that, then shook it off. "Anyway, if what you say is true, and someone whacked Old Man Shaw and his pretty little wife . . . well, I hope you find 'em."

Grif thanked him again, then exited the club into a night still heated by the runaway sun. The doorman motioned a

THE LOST   163

cab forward from the queue, but Grif waved them both away. Hoofing it helped him think, and the night held a nice enough breeze that he could do so comfortably for miles. Besides, despite the neon's nightly onslaught, desert pockets and darkness still bloomed here and there in the industrial district. So Grif put his hands in his pockets, tucked his head low, and headed into it. There was something else he wanted to try as well. And it was best if he did so alone.

Grif waited until he was sure the darkness had covered his tracks, and was far enough from Masquerade to know he hadn't been followed. He reemerged from the desert scrub onto a lost side street, where streetlamps pocked the deserted sky like unwilling sentries, half of those busted. Pausing beneath the faux awning of a closed pawnshop, he glanced around once more, celestial vision pulsing, looking for heat, making sure he was alone.

Once satisfied, he lifted the fedora from his head, studied it, and flipped on the switch hidden in the lining of the brim. A light flashed. Nestling the hat back atop his head, he decided Kit's gift was kitschy, insulting, and damned annoying.

Question was, did it work?

Taking a step forward caused the brim to emit a short, shrill beep. A series of increasingly urgent trills allowed Grif to ascertain that that pawn shop's front faced south. He swiveled that way, and was trying to figure out how to adjust the volume, when a voice popped up behind him.

"Bro, why is your hat beeping?"

Jolting, Grif jerked the hat from his head as he turned. It began beeping madly in response and he fumbled for the off switch. Glancing back up, he mumbled, "What the hell are you doing here?"

Across from him was a kid with scrawny semitransparent shoulders and jagged wings glistening with dew from the Everlast, feathery tips trailing off into smoky wisps. They were ruffled, but still magnificent. Good thing, too, Grif thought, eyeing the Centurion. It kept the focus off the kid's parachute pants and Members Only jacket. Not for the first time did Grif give thanks that he hadn't been offed in the eighties.

"I'm slumming, G-man." The kid, Jesse, gave him a sidelong grin. "Why else would I be on the mudflat?"

Grif cut his eyes to the wavering form of a woman, wingless, next to him.

"Oh, this is Mei." Jesse jerked his head at his Take. "She's newly dead."

"I can see that."

She was also compact, Asian, and wearing sensible black heels and a crisp pantsuit. Must have been working late when she'd been bumped. Grif didn't know how she'd died—death wounds never showed in the ether—but she was lucky no matter the method. Dressed like that she could spend eternity with a little dignity.

"Good to meet you, Mr. Shaw," said Mei.

"You know my name," Grif said evenly, before turning a dead-eyed stare back on Jesse. "Why does she know my name?"

But Mei was the one who stepped forward and answered. "We've been speaking of you, Mr. Shaw."

He glanced at her, but busied himself lighting a cigarette. "You're pretty calm for someone who's just been slugged."

As she and Jesse were still pounding mud, she'd been killed within the hour, and probably half that, since her etheric form hadn't yet begun the Fade. If Jesse didn't see her back before it faded altogether, she'd disappear entirely, and ghosts were almost impossible to find, even for a Centurion.

But Jesse didn't seem worried. "Mei's a psychologist. Or she was, until one of her clients decided she was a whack quack."

"It was that asshole, Collins. I just know it." Her professional demeanor dropped for a moment and she shook her head. "He's a narcissistic manic with a coke problem and mommy issues. I should have buried him in his eval."

"So how's it going, homes?" Jesse turned to Grif, deliberately using the eighties slang Grif hated. The first time Jesse had said it, Grif thought he'd meant "Holmes," as in Sherlock.

"Naw, it means you're my homie," Jesse had said, punching his biceps, and bouncing backward before Grif could return the punch. "My brothah. My friend."

But Grif wasn't any of those things, so as he lit a stick, he told the other Centurion the same thing he'd told Luis earlier in the day. "Don't call me that."

Kids these days, Grif thought, shifting the now-silent hat on his head. No respect for their elders.

"Whatever, dawg. I'm just the messenger." Jesse fluttered his wings, enjoying the play on words.

Grif flicked ash. "You're molting, messenger."

Jesse made a face. "Sarge wants you back in the Everlast, bro."

"Sarge is fine with me here. He gave me a Take. In fact," Grif said, crossing his arms, "I'm helping find the Lost."

Mei's long hair swayed as she took a step forward. "Sympathizing isn't the same thing as helping, Mr. Shaw."

Freezing, Grif shifted his eyes to her. "Charming bedside manner, Doc. Can't imagine why a client would wanna dust you."

"Ouch, Grif. Mei's just trying to help."

Flicking his stick aside, Grif shoved his hands into his pockets. "Didn't ask for it."

"I told her about you because Sarge says that the longer you stay on the mud, the more you're going to remember, and—"

"You been talking about me with Sarge, too?" Grif interrupted sharply. "Gee, *homie,* you've been talking about me a lot lately."

Jesse just shrugged. He knew Grif couldn't touch him in his etheric state. Not while Grif wore flesh. "It's not just me, bro. It's everyone. Your return to flesh and the Surface is the most interesting thing to happen since the Fall. Manny is even laying odds that you get offed twice. Courtney thinks you're just biding your time till you die of natural causes. Or are they unnatural, if you're technically already dead?"

Grif didn't want to know what the over/under was on the former, and he ignored the latter. Tilting his head, he asked, "You really want to help me, Jesse? Tell me what you know about the Third. In particular, about banishing them from the Surface."

"You can't banish the Third," Jesse scoffed. "Technically, they aren't really here."

"They are. I saw one. It told me they could possess souls that weren't in possession of themselves. It said they can even possess those who give themselves over to negative emotions."

"Sure, but that's not *real* possession. They're like Mei and me here. We're talking to you now—"

"We're influencing your mood," Mei added, voice detached and clipped.

"Yeah, and *mood* is how they getcha," Grif said.

"True. They can possess bodies for short periods, but they can't displace the resident souls."

Grif thought about that. So even if Scratch did get into Kit, it wouldn't be forever. But it didn't take forever to make someone go mad.

"What about water?" he asked.

"They can't stand it."

"I know that, Jesse," Grif said through clenched teeth. "Can I use it to get rid of a fallen angel if one of them is possessing a human body?"

"I suppose. Being dunked would be a sort of reverse baptism for a fallen angel. It'd kill them rather than save them. But like I said, they won't go near the stuff. Why you asking, bro?" Jesse asked, eyes narrowing.

"No reason," Grif said quickly. He didn't need Jesse reporting the query to Sarge. If Frank even thought Kit was in danger, he'd force Grif to leave her side for sure. Turning to pace, he caught Mei giving him a cool sidelong stare. "What?"

Mei only lifted her pointed chin. "Please, Mr. Shaw. Don't waste the short time we have together with unnecessary defensive emotion. I'm here to help."

Grif looked back at Jesse. "You brought me a shrink?"

This time—etheric state or not—the young Centurion did step back. "C'mon, homes. I want to help you solve your life's, and death's, greatest mystery." Jesse splayed his fingers wide and whispered dramatically, "*Who killed Griffin Shaw?*"

Grif felt a vein begin to pulse in his head, and turned back to Mei. "I don't need your help."

"And Katherine?"

"The name is Kit," he said quickly, because what he really wanted to say was *Go pound sand,* but he didn't talk that way to ladies.

"Maybe you should reconsider whether you're good for Kit," Mei said evenly.

Maybe he should reconsider the way he talked to ladies. "You know you can't charge me by the hour for this, right?"

"Kit is going to age, Mr. Shaw. Did you ever think about that?"

"No," he lied.

Mei smiled tightly. "Well, maybe you should. She's twenty-nine now, but *her* mortal clock is ticking. Soon she'll be thirty-three, same as you when you died. Soon after that she'll be *fifty*-four. A cougar." The smile widened. "You'll be her boy toy."

Grif thought of the changes he'd seen between now and his first go-round on the Surface. Men married older women now. Shoot, men married men now. "It won't matter."

"Of course it will. You, Griffin Shaw, are a stopwatch while Katherine Craig is an hourglass. You should quit her now. Let her live the life she was meant to live, with someone from her time and era. Sure, it'll pain her in the short term, but she'll eventually heal, find some mortal man to wed and have babies with, and they'll grow old together. Just as God intended."

Grif stared at Mei for so long the silence almost snapped. Then he turned to Jesse. Seeing the look in his eyes, the other Centurion held up his hands. "Don't shoot the messenger, bro."

That's exactly what Grif did. His ankle piece was in his hand so quickly it surprised even him, and he blasted a hole through Jesse's semitransparent body before anyone else spoke. Mei was newly dead enough that she actually screeched, and cowered behind Jesse's frayed wings. Jesse just stared at his belly, then whirled to regard the new hole in the brick wall behind him. "You shot me!" he yelled, also incensed.

"And I'll do it again, you meddlesome little pansy!" Grif waved the snub-nose in their direction. "Get out of here, both of ya!"

But Jesse didn't know when to stop.

"Know what your problem is?" he yelled, hands on hips, parachute pants flaring wide.

Grif shot him again.

Jesse didn't flinch this time, pointing at Grif instead. "You're straddling worlds, bro!"

"I ain't your bro." Grif aimed.

"Oh, save your bullets," Jesse scoffed, fully recovered now. "You don't belong to the Everlast *or* on the mudflat anymore. You don't belong anywhere."

"Get out of here, Jesse," Grif said in a low voice. "Cuz you and I aren't always gonna be on opposite sides of the great divide."

"Yeah, yeah." Jesse waved him off, turning away. "See if I ever help you again."

He turned his back on Grif and pulled open the pawnshop door, motioning for Mei to follow him into the yawning maw of the Universe. Recovered from her mortal scare, she paused to regard Grif with a hard, cold eye.

"Jesse told me that the longer you wear flesh, the more you remember. Be wary of that, Mr. Shaw. Memories are stronger than we think. You'll want to find out who killed you, do it quickly, and leave."

"Why should I?" he huffed.

"For the woman you love, of course," she said, and Grif wasn't sure if she meant Evie or Kit. Mei knew it and smiled. "Katherine Craig is totally alive in the moment, Mr. Shaw. But you are completely lost in the past." And with a swish of her dark hair, she followed Jesse through the doorway, into the cosmos, and Grif was again alone.

CHAPTER THIRTEEN

Kit couldn't remember the last time she'd slept so poorly. She'd drifted off around three-thirty, when it became clear that Grif, for whatever reason, wasn't coming home. She'd woken to the sounds of her paperwork on the Marielitos tumbling to the floor, around five. Unable to fall back asleep, she decamped to the living room, where she settled in to work through the sunrise. Having dozed, she was startled to awareness by the thump of the paper on her doorstep just before six, and had been awake ever since.

At least it was Sunday, she thought, sipping her first cup of coffee. She was curled up on her modular velvet sofa, wearing a white cotton nightgown identical to the one Audrey Hepburn wore in *Roman Holiday,* with a steaming mug at her side and chenille throw over her knees. The paper lay in front of her, and her computer hummed on her lap. She kept her eyes glued to it even when she heard the door open . . . even as the alarm she knew was set remained silent. She looked up only when Grif remained at her periphery, lingering uncertainly in the foyer.

"You finally made it home." She winced inwardly, hoping she didn't sound like a nag. Or worse, needy.

But Grif only inclined his head. "I had some things I needed to work out."

And he couldn't be in two places at once, Kit thought, looking away.

"I'm sorry, Kit." When she still said nothing, he lifted his fedora, ran a hand over his head, and sighed. "My head is . . . screwy."

"I . . ." She wanted to say "I understand," or "It's okay," or "It doesn't matter," as she always had before, but none of that was true. He'd left her alone to wonder and worry while he was out chasing memories of another woman, and they both knew it.

"I know," Kit finally said.

Edging over, he sat on the sofa beside her, elbows on his knees as he toyed with his stingy brim. "The hat works."

Despite the lingering low-grade tension, a smile slipped onto Kit's lips. "It beeped?"

"And how."

Now a true grin bloomed. So she *had* been with him, then. In a way. "You wore it."

"I wore it," he confirmed, edging closer so that their hips touched. He tilted his head, eyes meeting hers. "And found my way back."

He leaned over and kissed her then, and the tension she carried all through the long night slid from her shoulders. It wasn't a kiss you gave to someone in second place. It wasn't flavored with distraction or misplaced emotion. His mouth claimed hers like he was taking ownership, and making up for the empty night. His lips firmed like she was his hunger, then softened like she was also his need. It was the way Kit longed, always, to be kissed. By the time he pulled away, her hair was mussed, her vision blurred, and her loneliness almost forgotten.

Almost.

"How are you, doll?" he said, with that low scratch of a voice.

Kit's heart skipped in double beat. She loved it when he called her that. And she wasn't going to squander this moment—*hers*—by dwelling on worry. Sure, the night had been long. But Kit was ever looking forward. It was morning now, and Grif was back, with fingertips entwined in her hair as he nestled in tight to her side. *This* was real. Not the brittle, buried past. Not another woman's ghost.

"The story ran," she said, thinking business might steady them both. She pointed to the coffee table, where the morning edition of the *Las Vegas Tribune* lay flat. "Marin agreed to put a rush on it after I swore on my life to dig up more on the Kolyadenkos."

"Probably that of your firstborn, too," Grif muttered, reaching for the paper. He began skimming the article, but quickly looked up. "It's her byline."

"Really?"

He held the paper out so she could see Marin's name printed there.

"Hmm. Must have been the autocorrect on her computer. She proofed it before sending it to print." Kit waved the inaccuracy away. "Anyway, I don't care who gets credit for breaking the story. As long as all our resources are marshaled to solve the damned thing."

Grif continued reading, then stilled. "You mentioned the Russian mob by name? Jeez, Kit." He looked up at her. "That's a good way to get killed."

Kit huffed, and lifted her mug. "Maybe in the fifties. These days it's a good way to let them know we're onto them, and get them to stop distributing this crap. Besides, *I* didn't mention them by name. It's a direct quote from 'a source close to the investigation.' They said it, not me."

Grif just frowned, then nodded at her printouts. "And what's that?"

"Just some additional leads my girls gave me on the Naked City population. Did you know that historically it's been largely comprised of Cubans? More notably, it's been home to a boatload of Marielitos. Literally."

Kit filled him in quickly on the history of the Mariel boatlifts, and the influx of immigrants fleeing Cuba, stigmatized by Fidel Castro's inclusion of the island's criminals and mental-asylum population. All had occurred after Grif's death in 1960.

Then she leaned over and pulled out a sheet of paper buried under the others. "Our friend Marco Baptista is second-generation Cuban-American, and direct descendant of one of those Marielitos. He also has a rather impressive prison record, though it pales in comparison to his father's rap sheet. But, more important, I discovered there's been a recent turf war in Naked City between two rival gangs, allegedly in pursuit of control of the local meth market. Care to take a guess as to which individuals control those two gangs?"

"Kolyadenko and Baptista." Grif looked impressed. "You've been busy."

I've been jittery. I've been worried. I've missed the hell out of you.

Making sure her hand was steady, Kit lifted her coffee mug and said, "And I'm not done. Baptista mentioned a woman, a looker who dresses in wigs and tight clothing. If my hunch is right, and the Russians are targeting addicts in Baptista's neighborhood, I think they're using this woman to do it."

She pulled up an image that'd been minimized on her computer, revealing a stunning blonde with a cascade of curls framing glossy red lips, cold blue eyes rimmed in smoky hues, and a creamy heart-shaped face that dipped at cheek and chin in slanting angles. Diamonds the size of thumbnails winked at her ears, while lace curled delicately along her long, slim throat.

"Yulyia Kolyadenko." Grif recognized Sergei's wife from the photo Marin had printed out. He looked at Kit.

Kit set down her mug, then angled toward him. "Tell me if this plays with you, or if I need more coffee, but what if the Russians are trying to pick off their Cuban rivals by targeting their kids and families? Fleur and Lil were telling me just last night how closely knit the Hispanic community is. Generations often live with generations."

"As we saw with Baptista and his grandmother." Frowning, Grif glanced again at Yulyia's image. "And you think this is how they're doing it? Sending in . . . teasers? Then letting the addiction spread?"

Kit pulled her knees up tight and nodded. "Like a virus. Once begun, it's practically unstoppable."

"Maybe." Grif began to nod. "Because they can't get clean due to the withdrawals, yet they can't live long if they don't get clean."

"Nothing clean about this drug," Kit agreed, glad to see he wasn't dismissing it outright. Feeling steadier, she cleared her throat. "And what about you? How'd you spend your night?"

"Not shooting lighter fluid and drain cleaner into my veins."

"That's a relief," she replied, keeping it light.

"Not flirting with a bunch of greasers at a burlesque club, either."

Kit stilled at that before she caught the twinkle in his eye. "That would be a different cause for worry," she replied, voice steady as she shoved the memory of Dennis's unexpected flirtation out of her mind. "But you saw Ray DiMartino again?"

Grif nodded, his frown returned. "He had nothing. Said his father's old files were clean, probably picked through both before and after the FBI moved in. Claimed there wasn't even anything on Mary Margaret's case, or the work I did on it."

"And Sal DiMartino's second wife, Barbara?" Kit asked, because that's what Grif was really after.

He shook his head. "Ray doesn't know where she is. Doesn't want to find out, either."

"I'm sorry, Grif," Kit said, and sighed. She'd like nothing better than for him to get a handle on his past, just as she had with her parents. After all, that's what the living did.

Grif shrugged. "It's okay. He gave me another lead. Al Zicaro."

Squinting, Kit searched her memory. "I know that name."

"You should. He once worked at your paper."

Kit snapped her fingers. "Old loony Uncle Al!"

Grif lifted an eyebrow.

"Pet name around the paper," Kit explained quickly. "He was always seeing, or inventing, some conspiracy theory about the local mob. My aunt said he was as nutty as they came."

"Doesn't make me hopeful about getting any good juice outta him," Grif muttered.

"Where is he?"

"The Sunset Retirement Community," Grif confirmed.

"Hmm." Kit settled against the sofa. "Sadly, I've never met my loony uncle."

Grif tilted his head. "You'd go with me?"

"Of course. I love a good conspiracy theory. They always contain at least one or two kernels of truth. According to my dad, Zicaro had a pack-rat memory. Ask him the right question, and we might actually get the answers we need."

And then Grif could bury them along with the memory of his death, his first life, and—yeah—his first wife.

"Thanks, Kitty-Cat." And Grif said it so softly that Kit knew he was aware of what he'd cost her last night. It was still there, between them, but maybe if she left it unvoiced, it, too, could get tucked away.

"But talking to DiMartino couldn't have taken up your whole night," she said instead.

He reached for Kit's mug and sipped. "Mary Margaret is out early."

Kit held out a hand and he passed the coffee back. "Then we should visit her, too."

Grif's expression went wide at that, like he was opening to her, and there was wonder in his eyes. The look should have comforted her . . . and would have, moments earlier. Instead, for some reason, it made her want to pick up her coffee mug and smash it against the wall.

So, when her phone buzzed, she took the opportunity to gain a little distance, and reached for it, causing Grif's outstretched hand to fall away.

Kit put down the mug, then smiled, reading the text. "It's Dennis."

"And?" Grif said, sidling up beside her.

Kit put a hand on his chest, preventing him from drawing in closer, though his gaze remained fixed on her lips. "One of the kids from Naked City survived, Grif."

His eyes opened wide.

"Jeannie Holmes," she said. "And her mother has given us permission to go see her."

"Right now?"

Kit shook her head. "Not until ten."

"Good." He relaxed again. "Because I can think of a better use of our time just now."

And wasn't now all they really had? The past was gone, Kit thought, as Grif's arms came about her. The future unknowable. And possibility lay between them like a pair of dice waiting to be tossed. Kit didn't know if Zicaro or Mary Margaret, or even the elusive Barbara DiMartino, had the answers that would forever put Grif's mind, and Evelyn Shaw's ghost, to rest.

But *right now* Grif was leaning Kit back, looking at her like she was a natural wonder, and making her want to open as well. It was a good emotion, and it was what she'd really been waiting for throughout the night.

"It's nice to have you home, baby," she whispered into his mouth.

Grif slipped one strong knee between her thighs. "I'm not quite home yet."

So Kit arched up to him, and showed him the way.

CHAPTER FOURTEEN

By the time late morning rolled around, the summer heat had been switched to full-blast, scorching the air and setting Vegas's blacktop streets to broil. Grif had his sleeves rolled, but wanted to strip down to his undershirt as soon as the sun's rays hit his body. It took a while for Kit's classic convertible Duetto to cool, and he couldn't help but think of the sun's violent plasmic state—all that fire and cosmic fuel burning the atmosphere.

So deep, Grif thought, that there was nothing it couldn't split, sunder, or touch.

And speaking of deep, Grif thought, stealing a glance at Kit. There'd been something deeper niggling at her when he'd arrived home that morning. More than just worry or irritation over his absence. He'd sensed it as soon as he entered the living room, the same way he sensed a soul recently loosened from its body. It might have been the dregs of their conversation about Evie the day before, and Kit's harebrained idea that Grif somehow compared the two women in his mind. It was a talk he'd been determined to revisit, though he wasn't so sure now.

Do you ever dream about me?

No, he didn't really want to bring that up again. And there was no comparing Kit and Evie anyway. They could have been alive at the same time, same era, and still wouldn't exist in the same universe. Evie was moody and melancholic and prone to fits of passion, good and bad. Grif had often held his breath when she entered a room, waiting to see which it would be, sighing in relief when she turned the beautiful moon face his way, a calming force over the wild sea.

Kit, on the other hand, was like a newly opened soda pop. All effervescence and sparkle and fizz. It was a strange feeling when a woman's smile made you want to hold her inside of you just to feel more of her cooling effect. So her mood yesterday had cold-cocked him. He didn't know what to do with her when she was flat.

Thankfully, whatever was bothering her had melted away during the course of their lovemaking. What started out as sweet and tentative on the living-room sofa transitioned into a wild vertical roll down the hall. They'd ended up back in their bedroom, where they eventually slept, as if trying to make up for the missed night.

God, but this woman made him forget himself. It was such a complete lapse in purpose and reason that it almost worried him. Should he react to another person like she was an addiction? Or allow himself to burn with a need so fiery all he wanted to do was add more fuel?

Half the time, Grif thought, he didn't even know he was

craving her—her touch, voice, nearness. Then the need climbed into him like a bandit, and it was only after he was already bruising her lips with his and devouring her flesh like an animal that he realized how hungry he'd been for her at all. By the time they were done, both sated and sweaty, loose-limbed and exhausted—he could barely remember his own name.

He even forgot why he was here.

Grif shoved that thought—all of them—away. The important thing was that Kit was back to her normal self, volleying theories on the Cuban-Russian connection like she was playing tennis with herself. By the time she'd come to a halt in the hospital lot, she was armed with plans to confront the Kolyadenkos, Mary Margaret, and Al Zicaro in one fell swoop.

Five minutes later, though, after following the ER nurse's directions to the hospital's cafeteria, they were faced with a sight that made them both fall still and silent. Jeannie Holmes's mother was already waiting.

The woman's hollow gaze skimmed Kit first, wistfulness blooming, before dying on the next blink. Seeing the look, Kit shoved her bag into Grif's hands, and rushed to take the woman's hands in her own. "Thank you for agreeing to see us, Ms. Holmes. I know this is a terrible time for you."

Ms. Holmes's face damned near turned to dust. Her head fell, and she dropped back into her seat, and slumped. Yet her fingers remained locked with Kit's, who moved to sit next to her. Grif remained standing across the Formica tabletop.

"Call me Jann," she said, finally looking up. "Detective Carlisle told me you'd be coming. And that you saved my daughter. Thank you. No one else ever tried."

"I wish we could have done more," Kit said softly.

Grif sat, too. "We'd like to do more still."

Jann jolted at his voice, and her expression hollowed out again as she drew her hands away. Grif'd seen this look in women before, cowed and withdrawn and mistrustful. He both understood it and didn't, but knew Kit would have to take the lead on this one.

"I want to show you something," Jann said, pulling a battered brown handbag from the adjacent plastic chair. She rummaged until she pulled out an old photograph, and handed it to Kit. "Jeannie wasn't always like this. Three years ago she was beautiful, bright. So smart I would have sworn on my life she could never get involved with any drug. Certainly not this."

"I don't think smarts have anything to do with it," Kit said, gently thumbing the worn photo. "These kinds of drugs can take over your mind in one fell swoop. They shut down the pathways that lead to healthy decision-making and burn new cravings into your mind."

"They eat you alive." Jann winced like she'd bitten into something bitter, and she dropped her face into her hands. "She used to sing, you know. She had a voice like an angel. The kind that could have taken her somewhere."

Kit rubbed her palm along the woman's arm, Jann Holmes's pain etched across her own brow. It made Grif want to pull her close and protect her from herself.

"We're working hard to get *krokodil* off the streets and to take down the people who put it there."

Sniffing, Jann's eyes narrowed as she glanced up at Grif. "You're the couple who busted up that prostitution ring a while back, aren't you? They said at the time that the man who was running that ring, that Chambers character, was untouchable in this town. But you touched him."

Grif just nodded.

Jann glanced back at her lap, and the photo that she cradled there. "More rich men doing what they want, making money off the poor . . . or the cravings of the poor." Mouth pursed tight, she looked at Kit. "I can't tell you much. Jeannie and I haven't been close in years, not since she started using. I'm ashamed to say that I kicked my own daughter out of my house. I knew she'd already shot every dollar and dime she had into her veins, and when the money I worked so hard for began to disappear from my wallet, well, I'd had enough. I've just . . . I've had enough of people taking things from me."

"So had you ever met her friends? Tim Kovacs? Or Jeap Yang?"

"Tim was the one she was found with, right?" Jann asked, but immediately shook her head. "No, she obviously picked him up somewhere on the way to rock bottom. But, of course, I'd met Jeap. They dated for years. I think he's the one who got her into that life. Started with the light stuff, but that was like putting a match to a fuse for my Jeannie. She's like me. I get hooked on something, and it don't ever stop. That's why I don't ever start."

Jann lowered her head again.

"Ms. Holmes . . . Jann. This isn't your fault." Kit leaned close. "Nothing could have fated this addiction. It was her choice. But she *was* given a hand in getting there."

"Only someone without a child could say I'm blameless." The permanent frown deepened between Jann Holmes's eyes. "It's a mother's job to protect her child. I brought her into a dangerous world. And then I failed her."

Jann rose, and hefted her bag over her shoulder. It looked like it weighed a thousand pounds. "I— I think I'm going to go home for a bit. I've been here since they brought her in. I've already told her nurses that you can go in, but I don't know what you expect to accomplish by seeing her. They say she might never wake up." She huffed humorlessly. "Just don't get your hopes up. That girl will break your heart every time."

And she walked away without another word, steps as monotone as her voice, until she disappeared from sight.

"Ouch," Kit said softly, finally breaking the silence.

"What *do* you expect to accomplish here, Kit?" Grif asked, because it was the one thing that hadn't made sense to him on the short, hot drive over. She'd been chatting too rapidly for him to get a word in edgewise, but in the wake of Jann's dejection, he couldn't help but wonder the same thing. "Chances are Jeannie's not going to miraculously wake from a coma just to help forward our investigation."

Kit's chatty demeanor made a sudden detour. She looked away, all at once overly interested in the vending machines. Grif narrowed his eyes.

"I could use a granola bar about now," she said. "You want a granola bar?"

"Ki-i-it." The word elongated into a growl. She turned back to him with wide, gamine eyes—à la Hepburn, à la Evie, à la every woman who'd ever tried to pull the wool when getting what they wanted. Grif crossed his arms. "What. Are. You. Doing?"

She licked her lips slowly, as if testing the words for flavor before answering. "I'm baiting . . . it."

Grif shoved back from the table. The pop and effervescence and fizz of her personality suddenly made his head want to explode. "Hell no."

"There is no hell," she quipped. "Remember?"

Grif shook his head. "For the life of me, I cannot figure why you're always bound and determined to throw yourself in the line of fire."

She clearly had no argument, as she waved the concern away. "Scratch reached out to us through Trey Brunk, and I bet we could have squeezed vital information from it if we'd been prepared for it."

"How do you propose we prepare to face off against one of the Third?"

"Not we, silly," Kit said, rolling her eyes like he was the nut job. "Scratch would never talk to you."

Now Grif stood.

Kit stood, too, and suddenly they were toe to toe. In that moment, with determination in her eye and her jaw clenched tight, he decided she looked *exactly* like Evie.

"No." Grif meant to walk away, clear out of the hospital without looking back—heat be damned, along with Kit's harebrained ideas—but he whirled back before he'd taken three steps. Pointing, he said, "Scratch wants to possess you. It wants your soul!"

"So let me use that," she implored, palms up.

"Over my dead body."

"I don't think anyone with a dead body has ever said that before," Kit said, crossing her arms.

Now he did turn to leave.

But Kit appeared unexpectedly in front of him, leaning forward, all of that energetic willfulness curled into her fists, like he was the one in the wrong. "Grif, when I told you Jeannie was still alive, you got a look on your face that contradicted that fact."

Grif said nothing.

"Is she destined to die?" she asked, and then clarified, "Is she your next Take?"

He unclenched his jaw only long enough to answer. "Yes."

"Soon?"

"Yes."

Shaking her head, Kit glared. "So we don't have much time, and we have even fewer leads. It's worth a shot."

Laying a palm on each side of her face, Grif whispered fiercely, "It's not worth all the fortune in the world."

Placing her palms over his, Kit squeezed. "Let me do this, Grif. I don't have wings. I can't fight using fists or brute strength. All I have is my mind, and the knowledge that this Scratch creature is . . . interested in me. And . . . ouch. You're hurting me."

Realizing his palms had fallen to her shoulders, he released her immediately, but he didn't back away. "Scratch is stalking you."

"I'm counting on it."

Grif slammed his fist on the table next to him, causing the rest of the room to go silent and still. He didn't care. "Don't say that like it's a good thing! It's obsessed! Didn't you see the way it looked at you?"

Kit only lifted her chin higher. "Yes. I know exactly what that sort of obsession looks like."

He stuttered into silence and cocked his head. Was there some sort of double meaning in her words?

"I can do this, Grif," she said before he could give it more thought.

Grif jerked his head. "It's too dangerous. It will try to use your emotional weaknesses against you."

"So I won't show it any." She shrugged.

"It has a bead on you, Kit, and I don't know what to do about it! Not yet, anyway."

Kit jabbed a finger in the center of his chest. "Then let me use that obsession! Let me get what we need from Jeannie through it by doing what I do best."

Grif cursed and paced away, blowing out a hard breath as he yanked the hat from his head. Running a hand over the top of it, he stood for a moment, feeling her eyes hard on his back. When he was sure he was calm, he turned. "If we muck it up, Jeannie could be Lost."

Kit stood there, her pretty face and cupcake dress completely at odds with the steel in her spine. "Then we don't muck it up."

And what about you, he wondered, but couldn't say. He didn't want her to know how worried he was for her, partly because he didn't want to admit it to himself. But Scratch was the scariest creature he'd ever encountered . . . and he had absolutely no idea what to do about it.

Grif didn't answer for a long while. Visitors and orderlies and nurses mulled around them, but nobody paid much attention to the man and woman in an obvious standoff. They were probably used to the drama. And Grif was used to Kit. He knew that look on her face. If he demanded she leave here now, she'd just return once his back was turned. Better to stay close so he could keep watch.

So he sighed and asked the inevitable. "What's your plan?"

And he was unsurprised to find that it included him.

The curtain did little to separate Jeannie Holmes's bed from the rest of the ER, and the human drama playing out behind and around Kit seeped into the dreary enclave in the form of intermittent moans, rhythmic beeps, and constant drips. A machine also beeped in the corner of Jeannie's cubicle, Kit saw, but that was the only life behind that curtain. She wanted to ask Grif if plasma ringed the girl's pale, limp body, but for now, as planned, Kit stood utterly alone.

Edging closer to the bed, she studied Jeannie. She looked a fraction better than Jeap had when Kit found him, though the fresh-faced girl in Jann Holmes's photo was long gone. This face was pocked with scabs that stood out angrily against sallow gray skin. Chapped lips were sunken slightly, indicating where teeth should have been, and her hair was lank and brittle.

The wounds left from the crocodile injections had been cleaned and were bound tight, so maybe Kit only imagined that a cloying sweetness lingered beneath the room's antiseptic scent. At least the girl's brow was smooth, indicating a total lack of consciousness. Regardless of what'd gone on before, Jeannie would feel no pain at her time of death.

"Jeannie and Jeap," Kit murmured, feeling her resigned study shift to overt sadness. "I bet you were a cute couple at first." The girl who sang like an angel. The boy who liked to cook.

"I wish I could speak with you," Kit said softly, leaning nearer. "Because I'd really love to know . . . what was your longtime boyfriend doing with some new woman?"

It was a rhetorical question. Kit knew exactly what Jeap had been doing. Same thing Jeannie had been doing with Tim Kovacs. Getting their tweek on.

But how had Jeap then passed his crocodile addiction on to her? Kit's gaze skittered briefly to the girl's bandaged limbs, then she looked away and leaned against the side of the bed. "I bet he couldn't quit you, huh? You were the love of his life. Even if the drugs were telling him differently."

It was a statement that could be seen as silly, a regret only a girl could sigh over . . . at least that's what Kit was counting on. Still, Jeannie didn't move, eyes immobile behind her paper-thin lids, and the only sound within the sad, little chamber was the *beep-beep* of the monitor. Either Scratch was doing a crappy job of stalking Kit or she had to put some more *emotion* into it.

"Remember," Grif had told her. "The Third feed off negative emotion, and if you reveal even the slightest hint of it, Scratch won't hesitate to use it against you. Don't let it. If it tries to goad you into rage, you combat it with patience. It says hate? There's no stronger emotion than love."

"I know that," Kit said softly.

"I know you do, doll," Grif replied, the intensity washing from his face as he placed a palm to her cheek. She knew he was genuinely scared for her. That alone was all the reminder she needed.

She'd then given a humorless smile. "I just have one question."

Grif cocked his head.

"Why are the Third the only ones who get to wield the sharp emotions?" Hate, vengeance, rage, greed—all cutting, all dangerous.

"I don't know, Kitty-Cat," Grif said. "But I'm sure I'd lift a blade in my love for you."

He was just trying to shore her up, yet Kit still smiled. "Griffin Shaw, you say the most unintentionally romantic things."

Fortified by the memory, Kit stared at the glowing green line of the monitor and continued to address Jeannie as if she were conscious. "You know, I was once lost as well. I don't know if you can see it from where you are, but that dark time marked me similarly to the way the *krokodil* has marked you.

Not physically, but psychically. Can you see the ring of a former sorrow around me? A Pure angel once told me he could."

Nothing.

"Anyway, I understand the need to hide somewhere safe. But where you are now?" Kit shook her head. "That's not safe. That's not anywhere. You're going to have to leave there soon, because your body is going to give out, but you want it to be by your choice. You don't want to be Lost."

The silence deepened, and the machine's *beep* punctuated it in shrill stabs. For all Kit's awareness of angels and the Everlast, she received no more answers than anyone else who'd ever stood by a sickbed, waiting for a miracle. Kit wondered if Grif was right, and she was just wasting time. Jeannie wasn't going to wake. The doctors said so, as did Grif . . . and he had the advantage of celestial eyesight.

Kit squinted, trying to blur her mortal vision so that she, too, might see the plasmic outline fating Jeannie to death, but there was nothing fantastical about Kit. She was merely mortal, and saw only what she was meant to.

Yet she *could* communicate this way. Scratch had addressed her directly using Trey Brunk's drug-altered state. And the . . . *thing* wanted her, right? So Kit took hold of the girl's lax fingertips, leaned closer to that destroyed young face, and whispered, "I don't care what you've done, Jeannie Holmes. I don't think you're weak at all. You're human, and you've made mistakes, but beneath this fragile flesh? I think you're incredibly strong. And I think you should leave this mudflat on your own *damned* terms."

It was the curse that did it. Or maybe the strength of her conviction, or the anger behind it. Grif said not to allow in any negative thought, but Kit couldn't help it. And this was *righteous* negative thought. It was bullshit, she decided, that kids like Jeannie had to live in a world where such a gruesome death was possible. It was additionally offensive that heaven's celestial heralds didn't lift a feather to help.

Jeannie's fingertips twitched, then tightened over Kit's to the point of pain. Kit lifted her head in time to see the girl's face stretch wide, but it was with a grin she'd likely never worn before. The entire room seemed to pulse, and a rolling sound, the ripple of leaves on an accelerating breeze, undulated along the privacy curtains before settling again. Then Jeannie's bruised lids whipped open like window shades, and twin stars shone where pupils should have been.

The anger and frustration that'd flared after Jeap's death rushed over Kit again, but she damped it down and played dumb. "J— Jeannie? Is that you?"

The head moved up and down woodenly. Kit barely resisted an eye roll. Kit would have to be on *krokodil* herself not to see that this wasn't Jeannie, but she played along, heart pounding so hard she could almost taste the beat in her throat.

"I knew you were strong," she said, managing a shaky smile. "I'm so glad you decided to speak with me."

It nodded.

"I don't think we have much time, though," Kit continued, trying to ignore the cold air now being exhaled in her direction. The hand clutching hers grew icier degree by degree. "Someone will be coming for you soon. A Centurion. They're a kind of angel, one that used to be human."

The fallen angel blinked. "Not like you, then. You're . . . like me."

Kit caught the sound of leaves rustling deep in Jeannie's throat, and fought back a shudder. She wasn't *like* this thing at all.

"I'm human," Kit confirmed, fighting her nerves by lifting her chin. "And I'm a reporter. I'm trying to find out who did this to you."

Jeannie laughed at that . . . or, at least, Scratch did. "I did this to me."

"You had help," Kit said gently.

"You mean J.P., right?" Scratch said, accessing Jeap's real name through Jeannie's memories. As with Trey Brunk, it now possessed the thoughts of the body it ruled.

Swallowing hard, Kit said, "I mean the woman who gave him the recipe for crocodile. Britney. Or was it Brandy? No, Bianca?"

This was the information she needed, and she held her breath to see if Scratch—so eager to reach her—would release it.

"You mean Bella," Jeannie/Scratch said, and Kit's heart leaped in her chest. "She popped up out of nowhere. Glommed on to Jeap like he was God's greatest gift. Said he was just the man she was looking for." It scoffed. "Her and those stupid wigs and that clunky, annoying accent."

"They hooked up pretty quick?" Kit asked.

"You know how men are," it said, rolling Jeannie's eyes so the black stars in them pulsed. "Professing to be lone wolves, but unable to be alone with themselves. Right?"

Scratch was fishing for a reaction. Kit changed the subject. "And what happened when he lost his job and the money ran out?"

Kit didn't know for sure that Jeap even had a job, but even the most dedicated tweeker wouldn't pump lighter fluid into his veins if he had another choice.

"She had that recipe," it said, fishing that answer from Jeannie's memories, too. *Bingo.*

Kit resisted a full-blown smile. "And didn't you mind? I mean, about them getting together?"

"You would have minded, wouldn't you?" it answered. "If it'd been your man longing for another?"

"Yes," Kit answered honestly, because she couldn't see the harm in admitting that, but added, "Though my man tends to go for a more traditional gal."

"Oh, but Bella was whatever you wanted her to be. She wore those stupid wigs and bright clothes, but they were more like costumes than anything. She knew the guys loved it." Scratch crossed Jeannie's arms, ignoring the tubes and tape and bandages holding Jeannie together. "I just thought she looked like a clown."

"Maybe that was the point," Kit said, crossing her own arms, trying not to shiver. The curtained cubicle had to be ten degrees cooler now. "Bella didn't want any of you to be able to identify her. But was there anything noteworthy about her? A scar? A personal tic? Some physical item she favored?"

Jeannie/Scratch shook her head. "Her clothing was always different, but always the same. Low-cut. Tight-fitting. Cheap bling. That was never J.P.'s type before, you know. He liked the way I dressed. Solid, like I was going somewhere."

A wry smile flashed this time . . . and it fluttered wistfully at the edges. Edging back, Kit stared. Could that have been Jeannie? Could she hear Kit? Did Scratch's power or magic or whatever enable *her* to talk to Kit as well?

"I want to show you a picture," Kit said quickly, and yanked the photo of Yulyia Kolyadenko from her bag. "Is this Bella?"

Jeannie's head tilted, and while the star-stamped pupils remained, they were dull and softly edged. Almost, Kit thought, human. Finally—she, it—*someone* said, "No. That's not her."

Kit's hopes plummeted. "Are you sure? Imagine her with a wig."

"Not her." The woman who might be Jeannie shrugged. "Even with the right earrings."

Kit paused. "What earrings?"

"The basketball hoops that hung down to her damned shoulders." The twin stars in Jeannie's eyes pulsed, brightening at the curse word. "I commented on them every time I saw her. The wigs varied in length, but the earrings never did."

Kit bit her lip, thinking. She couldn't see the meticulously groomed Russian wearing hoops that large, but then she couldn't picture her flopping with Jeap, either. So, a lackey? A female underling in her organization to do her dirty work?

"I don't like it here anymore," Jeannie said suddenly, and gave a great shudder. "It's too cold."

It was. Kit reached down. "I can pull up your covers—"

"Can you take off my flesh? Because that's the real problem. It's weighing me down like an icy anchor." Kit froze, unsure who was talking now, and the voice shifted, frail with memory. "When I was using croc, it felt like I would never be cool again. I was either shooting up or burning up."

"I'm so sorry," Kit said, and meant it. Shooting *krok* might have begun as a personal choice, but once the drug took hold, choice became a luxury viewed from afar.

"Because you, too, know what it is to burn, don't you?" A lilt tinged the flat tone, and Kit's ears suddenly wanted to pop, like during an altitude shift on a plane. "You once wished for death and longed for oblivion."

Don't engage it.

As Jeannie's gaze blazed, pricked with the twin stars, Kit decided to follow Grif's advice. She had what she wanted. A name, and clues to Bella's identity, if not a full description.

"You're looking a little parched, Jeannie," she said, reaching toward the bedside tray. "Would you like a little water?"

Jeannie's features immediately twisted, as if they were made of pale putty pressed atop a skull-shaped rock. Scratch wasn't trying to hide anymore.

Kit backed away. "Let her go."

"No." And with its otherworldly gaze fixed on her, Scratch began manipulating Jeannie's expressions, pressing them into anger and horror and sadness, often at the same time. The raw hatred glowing in the irises completed the aspect of possession. It seemed there was nothing at all human left inside the fleshly shell. "I'm going to drag her into the Eternal Forest. I'm going to see to it that she's never warm again."

Kit shook her head. "She hasn't earned a place in the Forest. You have no right to her."

Scratch scoffed, and a glacial wind cut past Kit to whip at the curtains behind her. "Don't deign to tell me my rights! I was fashioned by all that is Pure! I was created of the finest material in God's great universe! Back when the Forest was still known as the Garden, before I was cast—"

"*Was,*" Kit interrupted, her own indignation growing. "Was, was, was. And are no more! And even if you hadn't fallen, what's Pure never trumps what is Chosen." Kit knew that much. God loved mankind . . . not the feathered beasts created to protect them.

She also knew that she should shut up, and that Grif was probably cursing her from his hiding place. But she was hot now. Jeannie's life had been wasted and her death hard. Her passage into paradise shouldn't be the same.

She just hoped Grif was making a move now that Scratch's attention was on her.

"Temper, temper, little *deva*." Because, of course, it sensed the downgrade in her emotions. "If you think this is a neat little example of possession, you should see what I have planned for *you*."

"No." Kit shook her head. "I'm Chosen, one of God's own. And so is Jeannie."

Scratch drew a smile across Jeannie's face, sickly sweet. "And yet here you both are."

Kit managed a smug smile of her own. "Yes. And thanks for your help."

The brow on Jeannie's face drew overly low, and all was still. The seconds stretched, then snapped. Star-struck eyes flew wide, the light within them flaring like torches, then Jeannie's body stiffened, and the stars in her eyes snuffed like matches.

Kit inched forward. "Jeannie?"

Scratch lunged, and bandaged arms ripped at Kit's shirt. The stars in Jeannie's gaze were blotted out, but the eyes had flipped to the backside of her skull, and the attaching muscles stretched before Kit like taffy. Kit fought to escape, fought for a scream, but the body jerked back just as suddenly, as if yanked by the center of the spine.

Kit twisted from the frigid grip as the body convulsed, and the room swelled with the sound of something living being uprooted. Jeannie's whole body fell onto the bed like a discarded ragdoll, and lay exactly as before, as if it'd never been possessed by a sadistic fallen angel. The wind-washed howl of dead leaves and snapping branches slid from the cubicle, and on Kit's next blink, all was still.

The heart monitor beat steadily, same as before. The chill left the curtained chamber. The noise on its other side rose again, in relieving and unbelievable normalcy.

Shaking, Kit bent to peer beneath the bed where Grif had been hiding.

Gone.

"If a fallen angel can possess her body, so can you," she had told him, back after Jann Holmes left the hospital crying.

Grif jerked his head. "It's technically not allowed."

"But you've done it before," Kit pointed out, and he couldn't argue that, because he'd done it in the case that'd brought them together. He'd done it to her best friend, Nicole Rockwell.

"You lined up your pulse points with hers," she reminded him, and he frowned, obviously wishing he hadn't told her. "You fueled them with your angelic energy. Do the same with Jeannie, bind yourself to her, and Scratch won't be able to touch her soul. Or, at least, it'll have to get through you first."

"And doesn't that sound peachy," he muttered, but he hid beneath the bed anyway, because they both knew Jeannie Holmes didn't deserve to spend her afterlife fleeing Scratch in the Eternal Forest.

And then he'd done it. While Kit had Scratch's attention, Grif had slipped *inside.*

Rising again, this time truly alone in the room, Kit could only wonder what happened after that. Wonder . . . and settle in to wait.

CHAPTER FIFTEEN

Two angels battling over the same body. Grif grounded himself in the reality of Jeannie Holmes's blood and bone, and thought, This is bound to get ugly.

Lying on the cold hospital floor beneath Jeannie's bed, the first thing Grif did to prepare for entry into Jeannie's body was force his own blood to thicken, gel, and cease circulation. His angelic nature allowed his flesh to easily go malleable and light. Like atoms, his cells could disperse and travel through the cold and unyielding wilds of the Universe, as long as he kept a clear picture in his mind of where he was going. That's how he delivered souls into the Everlast, and that's how he entered Jeannie Holmes's body.

But Jeannie was having none of it. He'd been careful to line up his energies with hers, felt their chakras click into place, but fumbled blindly for her precariously tethered soul. She was hiding. Thus the darkness.

Don't let go yet, he thought, just as her pulse points flashed, and a jolt of lava-hot electricity shot through his etheric form. Her energy lit like a landing strip, but her body temperature immediately dropped twenty degrees. Scratch had arrived.

Grif looked around at the reality illuminated by the fallen angel's presence, unsurprised to find an exact replica of the cubicle where Jeannie's mortal body rested. The curtains, the bed, the sounds of the ER were all the same, and Grif approached the bed, surprised at the thoroughness, though he shouldn't have been. Even on the Surface, even fully conscious, people always created their own individual realities.

So while Jeannie might've been wearing a hospital gown back on the Surface, in this reality she wore a cotton shirt, jeans, and lace-up boots, all black. Her skin was unmarred by open sores, her eyes alert and clear, and she was a slightly older version of the Jeannie who'd stared back at him from Jann's well-worn photo. It was how she really saw herself.

Yet even here, her plasmic outline was a violent ring of red flame. It seared the space around her like a solar flare, and sent heat radiating throughout her body. Jann Holmes, Grif thought, was going to have her heart broken one last time.

Worse yet, this Jeannie lay bound to the bed by thick, winding coils of enormous tree roots and dead branches. Grif didn't know enough about possession to know if this was how she felt, or if Scratch had placed her there once it'd entered her body, but she was trapped, and clearly unable to free herself.

Grif rounded the bed, flexing his shoulders so that his wings flared. "He's after me," Jeannie whispered, as he leaned over her.

He paused, the onyx blades of his wingtips glinting in the light. They could appear softer, like dew-tipped smoke, if he willed it. Sometimes he did, depending on the skittishness of the Take, but there was a reason God gave angels wings like weaponry. Sometimes the rise and fall of a waterfall of spears was the tool needed to navigate through the silky Universe. Like now.

"It," he corrected softly, then began sawing at the deadened roots, ears pricked to Kit's and Scratch's voices rumbling, and setting the surrounding curtains to sway as he worked.

But after a minute, Jeannie whispered. "It's after you, too."

Grif looked at her and she nodded. So this was Scratch's handiwork, and probably the reason Jeannie had not yet died. It'd tethered her soul to her decaying flesh. It was using her as bait. Grif worked faster. "Just hang on. I'm going to get you out of here."

So they fell silent, listening to Jeannie's vocal box rumble in her throat, and Kit's replies, tinny and farther away. Jeannie listened intently, the conversation beginning to relax her into interjecting her own intermittent answers about Jeap and Bella, and the *krokodil* that had wrapped itself so violently around her life.

Meanwhile, Grif labored, cutting through the deadened bark until his shoulders screamed, and branches and bramble lay in jagged mounds around his feet. Another minute at most, he thought. And then he could scoop up Jeannie's soul and have her in the Everlast before Scratch even knew he'd been here. The thought had him smiling up at her. She half-smiled back.

"I like your wings," she said.

"Yeah? Play your cards right and you could have a pair just like 'em."

Yet the words were barely uttered when her smile suddenly froze, and the blood in her veins roared to life. Adrenaline rushed around them, so loudly and rapidly that Grif hunched low, feeling like a stone at the bottom of a hot river.

The taste of metal flooded the back of Grif's throat, so fast and full that he almost choked. Fear, he thought, recognizing its slide beneath his tongue. The heartbeat fueling Jeannie's body sped up. The ceiling throbbed in a rapid, unsteady beat. The curtain hemming the cubicle began a misty fade to black, which was her vision narrowing. Suddenly they were someplace that was nowhere, back in a body that no longer worked.

Grif looked at Jeannie's face, but her gaze had hollowed out. "He knows you're here."

Grif didn't correct her this time. New vines shot from nowhere to reclaim her body, and the vision Jeannie had so carefully constructed around her gave way to the darkness of the Eternal Forest. A movement caught Grif's eye as shadow separated from shadow, and a creature emerged from the gnarled stumps and protruding brush.

Grif had never seen anything like it on the Surface or the Everlast. Pure angels could look either human or monstrous, depending on their purpose, but they were never obscene or grotesque, and that was what this was. Made of kindling and thorns, it had the gait of a giant praying mantis, but with arching bramble flaring from its back where wings once grew.

It was exactly what one might think a creature outside of God's presence looked like: a hollowed-out husk housing withered sentience, a spirit without soul, and a splintering, endless hatred.

"So you really are both angelic and human," Scratch said, studying Grif's own sturdy frame and billowing wings, though it cringed from the weak glow of Jeannie's remaining strength. "How did you manage it? Someone impregnate a mortal? God get bored with the existing species? Or maybe you're the bastard product of some bi-worldly war?"

Grif didn't answer because if Scratch knew his name, it knew his story. Besides, Grif'd seen hatred before, shredded resentment behind mortal and immortal gazes, but the way Scratch looked at him now was entirely new. That look was spring-loaded with spikes and teeth, and countless deadly triggers. Of course, there was double reason for this skinny, hunched creature to hate him.

Feeling large and healthy and powerful, Grif stepped forward. "Get out of this body."

"It is rather crowded in here." Scratch feigned wiping a hand over its brow. "Toasty, too."

It turned to Jeannie. "You hot, Jeannie? Cuz you look like you're burning up."

Jeannie just began to cry.

"Of course you are," it said patronizingly. "You're just one big human bonfire these days, aren't you?"

"Leave, Scratch," Grif commanded.

It simply tapped one lean finger against its chin, ignoring Grif. "Say, it's nice and cool in my neck of the woods. Why don't you take my hand, little lady? I can show you the way."

And as it extended that hand toward Jeannie, the vines around her creaked and loosened.

Grif lunged, but roots immediately shot from the floor, impeding his progress and, a second later, his view. He dodged, expecting Scratch to counter again, but the creature just watched Grif from the corner of its shimmering, starry eye.

A smile snapped over its face as Grif pulled up short.

"She's not goin' with you." Grif sidestepped the root, and another shot up. This one began a slow, screeching crawl toward his ankles.

Scratch's splintered smile widened. "But can't you feel the heat emanating from her every molecule? I'd be doing her a favor." Hunching, Scratch propped its bony arms on its hips, and scowled at Jeannie. "Look what you did, you stupid girl! You destroyed the only body and life God gave you!"

Jeannie began crying in earnest.

"Stop it," Grif ordered.

"You don't deserve to be in His divine presence," Scratch continued, with a reptilian leer. "You don't deserve to be any-where good!"

"Don't listen to it, Jeannie, and don't judge her, you rancid bit of celestial trash. You've never lived. You were never born so never had the chance to fail or thrive. You don't know the hardship of a real choice."

"Doesn't make me wrong," Scratch snapped.

"No, it makes you Fallen." Grif kept his attention on Scratch, but tried to soothe Jeannie. The fallen angel was too close to her. If its lies swayed her and she accepted its hand of her own free will, then Grif could do little to stop it. And Jeannie would be Lost forever.

"You can't see it in this light, but there are two open sores on that thing's back. Its wings were plucked when it betrayed God. They still bleed like a river, and they'll never stop."

"Wings are for the weak," Scratch interjected, circling now.

"You tell the archangels that?" Grif countered, circling as well.

"Those glorified pigeons have no sense of humor," it scoffed. "The fallen ones get a kick out of it, though."

"I want to go home," Jeannie said, blubbering now. Branches snapped in the darkness around them, her mind cracking, and Scratch smiled. "Please, I just want to go—"

"You have no home, you thankless wretch!" Scratch screamed. "You are unwanted and unloved! I am the only one who cares what happens to you now!"

Again, it held out its hand to Jeannie. This time she looked at it.

"No," Grif told Jeannie, and another vine shot up next to him with a resounding snap. He ignored it. "Scratch is a world-class liar bent on your destruction. But its power is confined to the Eternal Forest. Wingless, it can never ascend again. It certainly can't overcome anyone bathed in God's light."

"But Jeannie's not *in* God's light, is she? She's dirty and vile. A disgrace to the God who made her."

"Oh God, oh God, oh God . . ." Jeannie sobbed, but there was no hydration left in her body, and no tears to be had. She was also becoming more inflamed along with her emotions. Her slipping soul would soon be entirely untethered. Scratch, Grif realized, was just biding its time until it could seize her.

It was also forming a meticulous patch of briars around Grif. Though spaced to give the illusion of randomness, the jagged mounds could easily intertwine to form an impenetrable hedge. Grif's own personal forest in the wilds of Jeannie's mind.

"Don't listen," Grif told Jeannie, because she was the key. "There's a place for you in the Everlast. Loved ones wait for you there. You'll forget your mistakes, you'll forgive yourself. There is more after this, and it's all there just waiting for you."

"What would you know about it, *Centurion?*" Scratch spat Grif's title like chewing tobacco. "You're just as Lost as she is."

The blades in Grif's wings scraped as he shrugged. "So leave her be and take your chances with me."

"Rest easy, old boy. I've already carved out a place of honor for you in the Forest. But for now"—it glanced at Jeannie— "I'm going to add to my collection."

And with a fracturing curve of its spindly spine, it leaped, bridging itself over the girl's shaking body. Its limbs squeaked as they elongated to form a hovering cage atop her, and leaves bloomed on twisted boughs, dying instantly and falling to the ground.

Grif whirled on bent knees so that the blades on his wings brought down the deadened boughs and briars as easily as if slicing through cheese. He prepared to leap over the short hedge, dead yet already sprouting again, but Scratch turned its head, bared its teeth, and let loose a gusting, glacial howl. The raw wind cut at Grif, and though he could hear Jeannie's anguished cry, brittle leaves whipped into his face, obscuring his vision.

I need water, Grif thought, wishing he could shed—and somehow cast—at least one defensive tear. I need more blades and time and help.

I, Grif realized, with a panicked start, need *God*.

Teeth chattering, suddenly freezing, he whirled again so that the leaves fell away, and the hedge was again cut low. Scratch, he saw, had already removed all of Jeannie's ties, but it hadn't yet touched her. She lay there, vulnerable and frozen, but she was still God's child. She had to choose it for herself.

"No, Jeannie!" Grif screamed. Icy air howled back at him, and a branch rose from nowhere to wallop his back. Thrown forward, he barely dodged the shoot that threatened to impale his chest, instead bracing himself against it with one hand.

Vines immediately wrapped around his wrist and caught him there.

He screamed into the raw wind. "Don't accept his hand! Trust me, Jeannie—you'll only be exchanging one personal hell for another, and there's no escape in that one. You are not meant for the Forest."

Gnarled roots slid over the top of Grif's feet, trapping him in place. That's when he remembered his piece. It was strapped to his ankle here, just as when he died, and before the roots could recover and trap his right hand, too, he yanked the snub-nose from his ankle holster and shot Scratch right through the chest. The fallen angel was blown from Jeannie's bedside, rib cage splintering into chips. Grif shot again, skull this time, but a second spear ripped through Grif's side. They both cried out at the same time, and the shadowed forest shook around them.

That's when the globe appeared over Jeannie's bed, a translucent sun spun from the filament of crystals and precious gems. For some reason looking at it made Grif want to cry and laugh at the same time. It made his heart swell like it was engorged with light. Even Scratch fell still, marveling at its beauty. But Jeannie, frozen beneath the floating orb, reacted the most strangely. She stared up at it before giving a slight nod, then closed her eyes, and opened her mouth. Scratch gasped and reached out from where it'd fallen, but it was too late. The sun lowered and slipped into Jeannie's mouth like a glistening wafer.

Scratch's body exploded with light, screams shooting in every direction as blinding rays burst through its splintered core. The heat inside Jeannie's body rose again, but in the instant before it became unbearable, it began to rain. Scratch howled and writhed with the first drop, but there was no escaping the gentle deluge. It curled into itself, and the rain's effect on the rest of the forest was the same. Vines and trees and shadows and bramble dissolved like vapor, and the illusion of the forest began to disappear.

The charred, sodden thicket that'd been the fallen angel tumbled like a weed, but it managed one last neck-wrenching pulse of its eyes before rolling into oblivion. "You tell her . . . tell her I know her now, too!"

And then it was gone.

Silence rushed in with a wave of emptiness that would've crushed Grif's eardrums if his breathing hadn't been so ragged.

Unencumbered, Jeannie sat up in her bed. "How did you do that?"

Grif just looked at her.

"How did you make that light appear over my bed?"

Instead of answering, Grif closed his eyes and slumped. Then, slowly, he licked his lips, tasting the rain as it continued to fall over his face, its sweetness and relief filling him with peace and the warm glow of acceptance and love. He sat there until the deluge lessened, just letting it wash over him, and only when it stopped did he find his feet. He rose, staggering slightly.

"You're crying," Jeannie noted, when he reached her side.

"It's nothing," he told her, holding out his hand. He needed to deliver her to the Everlast quickly, just in case Scratch recovered and returned. But inside he *was* crying, much like Jeannie had been earlier. *Oh God, oh God, oh God.*

Inside, he was thinking only of Kit.

Kit paced Jeannie Holmes's ER cubicle, wiping her cheeks, though they were now dry, and stealing glances at the girl's still, silent form. What the hell was going on? Grif had been gone only ten minutes, but they were the longest ten of Kit's life. Each passing second weighed on the previous one, so that before long the heaviness in the cubicle threatened to halt her breath.

But why should I worry? Kit silently reasoned. Grif was an angel and a protector and he had wings that could slice open the strongest foe.

Yet she *was* worried, because Grif was also alive—maybe only half so, and maybe by default—but alive enough to matter. Alive enough that she would feel his absence if he was suddenly gone.

And that's why, when Jeannie's body began writhing in a way that mortal bodies simply didn't, and the machines failed to register it, Kit coaxed the possessed girl's mouth open, and poured her tears inside. Though "pouring" wasn't exactly accurate. One tear had done the trick. The writhing stopped immediately, and Jeannie had been still for so long that Kit felt on the verge of tears again.

So when Grif appeared, rising from beneath the bed on the other side of Jeannie, Kit gave a startled yelp before skirting the rails and rushing him. "Oh, thank God!"

She pulled him to her so that his "Oomph" was muffled against her shoulder, then pulled back just as quickly to study him. "You're okay? Is Jeannie okay? Did you . . . you know. Take her?"

Face ashen, Grif shook his head, and staggered to the plastic visitor's chair behind him. Slumping, he sighed. "She's still here. I have to draw her spirit directly from her body in order to Take her."

"Oh, right." And Kit would have to leave the room for that,

but that was fine. What mattered was that Jeannie's soul was safe, Grif was here, and Scratch was gone.

So why was Grif's face ashen, and his expression pulled so tight that it looked like it would crack if he moved?

"Honey," he began, and his voice did crack. Like a bad motor, he couldn't seem to start it up again without turning it over a few times. Finally, he looked up. "What the hell did you do?"

But he knew. She saw that, and just swallowed hard. "So it worked?"

He only managed a mute nod.

"So Jeannie's not Lost anymore?" She pressed when he still didn't answer. "Right?"

"It doesn't matter, Kit—"

"Of course it does! Scratch thinks it can drag the Lost souls into a fate that's not their own but—"

"Scratch isn't after the Lost anymore, Kit! It's after *you*!"

She drew back. "It can't touch me. I'm Chosen. And I'm not vulnerable. I'm . . . good."

Face crumpling, Grif shook his head. "You gave it your tears, Kit! It has your memories. It knows your emotions—"

"That's right!" she said, because she didn't need to be attacked by him, too. "I fed my tears to Jeannie, cried them right into her mouth, because her body was convulsing and her head was jerking side to side, and I didn't know what the hell was going on! I wanted to help! Did I? Did I help?"

It took a while, but Grif finally whispered, "Yes."

But he looked like he blamed himself for it. Kneeling before him, Kit wondered what exactly had gone on between him and Scratch. She took his hands, icy cold, in hers. "Then it was worth it."

"Not to me."

Kit had never seen Grif this way. Though fully clothed, he looked naked somehow, like something had been taken from him. She swallowed hard. "You're scaring me."

He opened his mouth but the words didn't come. That just scared her more.

"I have to go," he finally said. "I'm her Centurion. I have to . . ."

But he couldn't seem to voice what he had to do. It was as if he no longer knew.

"I understand," she said, and straightened as if to stretch, though she really half-pulled him to his feet. "You need to secure her soul safely in the Everlast. I'll leave and you'll have your privacy."

She led him to the bed, telling herself she was saying good-bye to Jeannie, and not showing Grif what he needed to do next. Yet when she turned to leave, he stopped her with a hand on her arm. It was still cold, like he'd just come in from a winter storm, but at least it was now steady.

"It was right, you know."

Kit didn't understand. "What?"

"Scratch," Grif answered, and he frowned and winced at the same time. "It was right when it said that you were a light. Your soul . . ."

"What?" Kit repeated, with more alarm this time. What was wrong with her soul?

Still shaking his head, Grif closed his eyes. "It was the most beautiful thing I've ever seen. And then your tears began to fall, and I've never felt so loved and at peace and . . . pure."

Stunned, Kit said nothing.

He opened his eyes again, and it was a steadier gaze that

found hers. Good. He was coming back around. And yet his face was blank, the expression blasted from it. Grif, she realized, was terrified. "I couldn't stop it. It would have had Jeannie. And it didn't even want her, not really. But . . ."

"But it's fixed on me," Kit finished for him.

"It craves you like a caged lion, one that's been malnourished for centuries." He shook his head. "What were you thinking of when you . . . you know."

"When I started to cry?" Kit asked, and Grif nodded. "You."

Grif sighed, also nodding after a moment, before he jerked his head at Jeannie. "I have to take her. Now."

"Okay." She turned again.

"Kit." He spoke her name sharply as she reached the curtain that led back into the bustle of the ER. She turned back around to find him more solemn than she'd ever seen. "Keep your emotions under control. I think that's how it plans to circle back around."

Kit swallowed hard. "When will you be back?"

"I don't know. I need to deliver Jeannie to incubation. I need to talk to Sarge about Scratch and the Lost. I have . . . some other questions while I'm there."

"But time runs differently in the Everlast, right? I mean, you can arrive anywhere you want back on the Surface?" She meant anywhere in the future. He just couldn't go back to the past. Join the club, Kit thought, blowing a hard breath as he nodded. "Okay, so meet me right outside the hospital . . ."

"That's less than five minutes. It's tight."

Kit just stared.

"All right." He finally nodded. "Of course."

Kit sighed in relief. All she had to do was walk through these curtains and the ER, into the main hospital, then stand right outside the doors where they'd entered. It was safe here, and there were other people around. Then Grif would be there, probably holding his hand out to her before she'd even crossed the threshold. Together they'd figure out what to do about the fallen angel that'd swallowed both of their tears. That'd inexplicably fixed on her.

That craved her like a malnourished lion.

Kit counted her footsteps as she left the ER, just to keep her mind busy. No negative emotions, only steady action, forward motion. A shout and then running feet sounded behind her as she hit the double doors leading to the lobby. Jeannie's name followed, clattering like a chaotic pinball off the walls of the ER, and she paused for a moment to look back.

She felt sorry for the nurses, because she knew their work would be in vain, and for Jann Holmes, who was getting some well-deserved sleep somewhere in this city but would soon be woken by a peace-shattering call.

And she was surprised to find that she also felt sorry for herself.

Outside, she lit a cigarette as she waited, trying to keep that thought from blossoming into something more. The only way to do that was not to think about it at all. So, shielding her eyes against the sun's rays, she emptied her mind and searched for Grif.

Kit glanced at her watch; seven minutes had already passed. Where was he?

Then a bounding, boisterous tune burst from her handbag. Kit jumped before she realized it was the ringtone she'd assigned to Marin. The song matched her aunt's nonstop energy. Digging for her phone, Kit shunted her smoke aside and glanced at her watch. Past eleven on a Sunday. The paper would be silent, the presses cooling between printings. Even her workaholic aunt took the morning off.

Squinting against the unrelieved assault of the sun, Kit scanned the lot as she answered. Still no Grif, and he should already be there. She needed him now, God knew she did, and he was never . . .

"I'm at the paper," Marin said, without preamble. "In the employee lot. Oh, Kit. Kit—"

"Marin?" Kit froze. She'd never heard her aunt's voice so panicked before. Not even in the worst throes of her cancer treatments. And never at work. "Are you okay?"

But there was a clatter, and Marin's voice, more distant, curled into a scream. "Oh, God . . . please, no! Please don't!"

The connection went dead mid-cry, and Kit was suddenly running. She glanced around the lot one last time as she yanked open her car door, but Grif simply wasn't there, and she couldn't wait. Someone had Marin.

CHAPTER SIXTEEN

houghts of Jeannie and *krokodil,* of Scratch and dangerous emotions—and even Grif, wherever the hell he was—
were gone as Kit peeled haphazardly through Vegas's urban
core. But a buzzing filled Kit's head—Marin's tattered cry
on perpetual repeat—while her heart pounded hard enough
to breach her chest. She dialed 9-1-1. She gave the operator
Marin's location. Then she rocketed toward the newspaper's
offices, determined to get there first.

The hospital and paper were each pinned in the middle of
the city, but so was the police station, so Kit was surprised
to arrive at the *Trib*'s grounds first. No guard, Kit realized,
as she whipped through the open gate. It would have given
her pause—why did it feel, suddenly, like danger lurked
everywhere?—but she'd already spotted the small figure
propped like a doll outside the employee exit.

"Marin!" Kit was out of the car, screaming as she ran toward her aunt, only vaguely conscious of sirens rising into the air somewhere behind her. There was blood. There was her aunt, glassy-eyed and slack-mouthed, head rolling Kit's way.

There was a needle taped to the inside of Marin's arm.

In it, a viscous yellow substance was primed, and pointing dangerously at the delicate blue vein of her forearm, held in place by a dirty makeshift tourniquet. Masking tape, yards of it, secured Marin's other arm so that it was pressed tight and useless at her side.

Kit's knees burned as she dropped down next to her aunt, gently edging a finger beneath the needle, and carefully angling it away. "I can't remove it. It's too tight."

Sirens wailed closer behind her, but not close enough. Kit searched Marin's free arm for marks, but the blood seemed to have all come from her face. A split lip. A bloody nose.

"J-just hold it clear until they get here."

"Okay. I— it's okay," Kit lied, lifting her head to find Marin's shocked gaze trying to locate her own. Her aunt— who single-handedly ran the city's newspaper, and had fought off cancer like an Olympic gold medalist—managed a wobbly smile. Kit nodded and lowered her eyes again, studying the poisonous contents. *Krokodil.*

She fought back tears along with the shakes. She—and, more to the point, her aunt—couldn't afford for her nerves to rise. Still, it was a lot to ask of someone whose sole living relative had just been attacked. Marin, who never missed any damn thing, realized it.

"Talk to me," she said, voice weak, though the command was suddenly there.

"About what?" Breathe, thought Kit, breathe and stay focused. "Where's Grif?"

Damned good question. Kit jerked her head.

"Okay, the case you're working on, then."

You mean the one that did this to you? Kit wondered, but didn't say. The one that put you in danger?

"Did you find out any more about the dealers?" Marin pressed.

Amazed, Kit just stared. The woman had just been attacked outside her own workplace, probably by those very same dealers, and while her blood was still wet on the pavement around her . . . she wanted to talk shop?

Kit shook her head. Yet there was a waiting in the silence. Marin needed a problem to solve, and focusing on that might keep Kit's emotions under control as well, so she swallowed against the dryness in her throat and tried to gather her thoughts.

"Okay. Okay, well, I visited the user who survived. Jeannie Holmes. She was comatose, though. She couldn't tell me anything."

"It was worth a shot," Marin said, wincing against some unseen pain. "I can't tell you how many times I've come up with nothing only to circle a story from the other side and hit pay dirt."

Marin's breathing was beginning to steady, and the sirens finally seemed to be getting closer, allowing Kit to catch her breath as well. Perspective dawned with the passing minutes: this had been a warning, not an attack meant to hurt.

Somewhat reassured, Kit blew out a hard breath. "Well, maybe it just looks like nothing. I mean, as I was sitting there

with this unconscious girl, I couldn't help but think of negative space. Sometimes what's not there is just as important as
what is."

"Elaborate, please."

Kit almost—almost—smiled at that. It was one of Marin's
favorite directives. So she nodded. "Well, it's like when I deco-
rate my home. I first consider the layout of the room, its shape
and form and function. Then I place the large pieces, sofas
and tables and beds. After that, I layer in the medium pieces,
the side tables and lighting. The small touches come after that,
vignettes and tablescapes and all the knickknacks I own and
love."

Marin's eyes began glazing over . . . and it wasn't from
shock. "The point?"

"Editing," Kit said, just as shortly. "I go through the rooms
and subtract twenty percent of what's there. Clean it all up.
Simplify. Make it look pretty."

Marin wrinkled her nose at that, but in Kit's world, pretty
was always the point. "It's the subtraction of detraction, Marin.
That's what makes a space impactful. It only *looks* like nothing
is there. Follow?"

"Feel free to push that syringe," Marin retorted.

Kit winced, then noted the closed-lip smile on her aunt's
face. In a chaotic situation, she'd once again taken control.
"I'm just saying that it's the same with people. You look past
the obvious, and into the negative space they've left behind,"
Kit said, like it was clear. "We still don't know who this Bella
woman is, but she's not Yulyia Kolyadenko."

And then three squad cars suddenly squealed into the wide
lot, and steel-toed boots sounded behind Kit before hands were
gently pulling at her arms. Voices rang in her ears, shouts rain-

bowing over her head and shattering the air's stillness in relieving arcs, but before moving away, Kit made sure the needle was
freed from Marin's soft, delicate skin. Then the paramedics
arrived, too, and they all backed off, and Marin was no longer
alone.

"It was just a warning," Kit heard someone say, a palm
easing around her shoulder. Kit realized she'd sunk to the
ground next to the exit. Her head had fallen into her palms
and she was shivering despite the blazing heat.

"Grif?" She sat up, shaking off the image of blood and that
needle and the horrified expression on Marin's face when she'd
arrived.

"It's me, Kit," the voice said, and her name settled her spinning mind.

"Dennis."

"It was just a warning," he repeated, palms warm on the
sides of her head. His jaw clenched as he studied her face.

"Yes," Kit said mechanically. It was a terrible one.

"Where *is* Grif?" he asked, voice strained.

Kit looked around at all the officers, at the paramedics, at
Marin, then back at Dennis. She finally shook her head. "I
don't know."

All she knew was he hadn't been where he said he'd be.

CHAPTER SEVENTEEN

Grif strode down the hospital corridor for the second time that day, though this time there was an urgency to his step that had been lacking before, one that had the few people he did pass at this late hour stepping quickly to the side. The pocket phone Kit had given him, the damned thing he never bothered to check, had been blinking for he didn't know how long. And though the message had sat there for hours, the elapsed time did nothing to erase the urgency in Kit's voice.

Marin's been attacked. Come as soon as you can.

By the time he found his girl slumped on a cold plastic chair at the end of a long, bright hallway, her urgency had obviously burned away . . . yet something else had burned away with it. She turned her head, saw Grif coming, and instead of standing to greet him, simply sighed and put her head back in her hands.

"It was a warning," she said, before he could sit or even ask. "The Russians, in retaliation for the article that ran this morning. At least, that's what they told Marin. She said before that they moved fast when wronged. I should have listened."

He knelt before her, hands on her knees. "What did they do, Kit?"

"They left a note. It said, 'This is for shooting off your mouth. Next try shooting this.'" Her gaze was watery when she opened her eyes. "They had her hooked up to a load of *krokodil,* Grif."

The memory of decaying flesh on a living body revisited him, and Grif wavered in his crouch. "Did they . . . ?"

Kit shook her head hard, cutting him off. "The drug didn't touch her."

"It was in the syringe, though?" he asked, and she managed a nod as footsteps fell behind him. Grif turned, then stood when he saw Dennis coming down the hall, a cup of steaming joe in each hand. When the hell did he get here?

Accepting the coffee, Kit answered the unvoiced question. "Dennis brought me in. He was there when I found her."

Grif's jaw tightened so much it hurt. "Good. Thank you."

"Of course," Dennis said, then jerked his head at the door across from them. "I'm going in. See if she can tell us anything more."

"Thank you. For everything." Kit put a hand on his arm.

Very slowly, Grif followed the touch with his gaze, angling up to settle on the man's face. Silent, seething, he kept it there until Dennis nodded and left. Then he shifted and sat, only to find Kit giving him an equally aggressive look.

"Where were you?" she asked softly.

Grif drew back. There was something thin and metallic—and somehow wedge-shaped—in her voice. It rose up between them and put a bump in his chest that had his own words speeding up. "I delivered Jeannie to incubation. She's safe and clean and out of pain."

"And then?" Kit asked, not looking at him.

Grif licked his lips. "I still had time . . . or so I thought. So I asked Sarge about the Third, about Scratch in particular—" He saw Kit's jaw tighten and hurried on. "*You* gave it your tears, even after I told you not to—"

"This isn't about me. Where were you?"

He hesitated. "Sarge, well, he mentioned Evie—"

Kit sighed.

"And it was the first time he ever brought it up himself, so—"

"So you thought you'd stick around."

"It wasn't long. Two minutes, more or less."

"A lot can happen in two minutes."

"Kit, I didn't know."

"I know you didn't know." She shook her head. "But you left me alone."

"I was doing my job," he defended himself. "I was watching after the dead!"

"Maybe you should care a little more about the living," she said, then held up a hand as he drew away. She shook her head, and he could see she wanted to take it back. "I'm sorry. I didn't mean that."

"You're sore—"

"I'm not mad, Grif. I'm hurt and I'm scared. Marin was attacked because it was *her* name in that byline and not mine."

Of course. The article that'd run that morning, naming the Russians, reporting the drug.

"And, Grif, I was alone. I needed you."

The damned hallway seemed to shift at that. Jesus, he thought, rubbing a hand over his face. What was wrong with him? "I'm sorry."

"Don't be sorry." Exhaustion infused her sigh. "Just be *here*."

Grif opened his mouth, but she pressed a finger to his lips.

"And I will be there for you, too. We're a team, remember?" Grabbing his hand, she enfolded it in her own. "You don't have to sneak off to the Everlast for answers to Evie's death. Neither one of us has to be alone."

Words rushed out of him like a flood. "Yeah, but things are different lately, Kit. I mention her name and you flinch. I don't want to hurt you if you learn things about me that I can't change. I'm trying to protect you. Don't you see?"

"Don't try to shield me from your feelings, Grif." She shook her head. "Because that's what really makes me feel alone."

Grif drew back, dumbfounded. Was that what he'd been doing?

"Kit?"

They both looked up.

Dennis was peering from Marin's room. Grif wondered how long he'd been standing there, and how much he'd heard. "She's asking for you."

Kit gave a jerky nod, and rose. Grif re-sighted on Dennis as she disappeared.

You, Griffin Shaw, are a stopwatch while Katherine Craig is an hourglass.

Grif shook the reminder—the *bullshit* reminder—away, and stood. "Was it really the Russians?"

Tucking his thumbs into his pockets, Dennis shrugged. "Looks that way. They retaliate quick when wronged."

"That's what Kit said." Ray had said it, too, though Grif hadn't taken him seriously. Especially the rap about Yulyia Kolyadenko . . . the "Viper." But it suddenly seemed Grif hadn't taken anything seriously enough. He jerked his head toward the door. "She get a look at them?"

Dennis shook his head. "Snuck up behind her when she was leaving the building. Same with the guy in the guard box. Bump on the head. Coulda been worse."

Yes, Grif thought. It could have been Kit.

I needed you.

They stood in the sterile silence for a bit, the aromas of cleaning supplies and bitter coffee pervasive in the air around them. Grif realized the same scents had been present in the ER earlier in the day, with Jeannie, but he hadn't noted them as much then.

What else, he wondered, looking at Dennis, had been right in front of him that he hadn't noted?

"Did you know her dad?" he asked suddenly.

Surprise lit Dennis's face, but he shook his head. "Before my time. Knew of him, though. Asked some of the other guys on the force about him."

Bet you did, Grif thought, clenching a fist.

"He married blue blood, but the man was blue-collar all the way. Straight-up patrolman. Never wanted off the streets. Helped the rookies, had the respect of his squad, his lieutenant. Cared about the job like it was a part of his family, too, and cared about his family more than anything."

They were silent for a long moment.

"You know she was institutionalized for a time, after his death."

Grif frowned. "What do you know about it?"

"Same as you, probably." Dennis shook his head. "She doesn't like to talk about it, and you'd never think it, right? Not with her 'nothing's gonna get me down' attitude. She's got some steel in her, though, and even that didn't affect her for long. Reinvented herself, her family, and her dreams. Shit, her makeup might as well be armor. For all the crinoline and hair flowers and glamour, she's one strong woman."

Grif looked at him, and in the uninspired acrid hallway, they took size of each other—how fast was he? How strong? How motivated?

Grif thought angel wings and experience trumped whatever this buck with a badge and a growing crush on his girl might have, though he still had to fight the impulse to punch first and think later. But he didn't, and for all those same reasons. Dennis might wrong Grif, but he'd never harm Kit.

"I like you, Shaw, which is why I'm going to give you some free advice."

"Let's hope it's worth more than that."

"There's plenty of pain to be had in this lifetime. Doing this job has taught me that much." Dennis gave his head a small shake. "You don't have to go looking for any more."

"You don't know what I'm looking for." Or who, he didn't add. Although Kit did, and maybe that was the problem.

Shrugging, Dennis began backing down the hallway. "Just do the right thing by her."

"Or you will, I suppose?" Grif asked, voice raised.

"Hey." Still walking, Dennis put up his hands. "Someone should be there for her when it counts, right?"

Grif's hands clenched in his pockets, and he wished he'd gone for the punch. He'd forgotten how many ways there were to clobber a man. And though Dennis was just that—a man, and not an angel like Grif—he was one from Kit's time. One whose life was also hourglass-shaped, and not an endlessly ticking clock like Grif's.

Quit her now. It'll pain her in the short term, but she'll eventually heal, find some mortal man to wed and have babies with, and they'll grow old together, just as God intended.

"Push off," he muttered, watching Dennis disappear around the corner, not sure if he was talking to Dennis, or Mei, or both.

As for Grif, he felt like he'd just been shaken awake. Scratch had hijacked Trey Brunk's body in order to get to Kit. Jesse had visited with Mei in order to plant doubt in Grif's mind. And here on the Surface, Dennis was suddenly on point.

It's all part of a greater plan, Grif realized, as he began to pace. And he'd bet the house that Sarge was behind it. Who else knew the things that rattled around inside Grif's head and chest? Or the guilt that haunted him like a ghost?

You might find you have more in common with Jeap Yang than you think, he'd told Grif. *Some guys spend their entire lives searching for a place to settle . . .*

But that wasn't true. Grif'd found Kit in this lifetime. Saved her, even. And, in turn, she grounded him. Made him feel found, not lost.

Grif thought about that a moment longer, then nodded once to himself, before he reached for Marin's door. Sarge and Mei and even Dennis might be convinced Grif should let Kit go, but that wasn't going to happen. Instead, he'd put away the things that haunted him, at least for a while, just as Kit had done all those years ago after her father's murder. He'd be fully present in *this* life, at Kit's side, and there for her in the same way she was there for him.

Ironically, to do that, he needed to go. Now.

"I'm coming with you," Kit said, when he pulled her back into the hall.

Grif shook his head, and slipped a hand around the back of her neck. "Remember how you said you needed me? Well, I heard you, I did. But Marin needs you like that right now. And I think I've got another way to help you both."

"How?"

By focusing on solving Jeap's, Jeannie's, and Tim's deaths. Proving there was a place for Grif, and no one else, at Kit's side. By solving this attack on Marin. By caring, as Kit said, about the living, and starting now.

Starting, he corrected as he bussed her cheek in farewell, with the Russians.

As always, when tragedy struck her life, and she didn't know what else to do, Kit got to work. Even though she left the hospital later that afternoon, it was just for a quick stop home to shower and change before returning to Marin's private room. Dennis had pulled some strings, and a cot had been set up for her in the corner. Marin would have protested, saying she didn't want or need Kit to be put out, but Dennis had pulled more than one string, and the drugs forcing her aunt to rest took care of that as well.

Kit shut the door, set down her belongings, and stood by her dozing aunt, who was lost in a sleep additionally fueled by fatigue and stress. It seemed a lifetime ago that Kit had found Marin slumped outside the newspaper's building, but time was like that, a trickster when it came to fielding regrets. Shaking off the memory of that poisoned needle scraping against her aunt's soft arm, she bent and kissed the sleeping woman's forehead.

Then she got to work.

Using Marin's food tray, Kit set up her laptop so that she was facing her aunt, both so she could remain bedside and so the light would be less likely to disturb her aunt. At first, the silence of the room pressed at her ears like leaded earmuffs. Kit always had music going at home—Wanda Jackson or Imelda May, or, if she really needed a wake-me-up, the HorrorPops— but she soon settled into the quietude of the room and sunk into her own mind.

Sipping from her travel mug, she brought her computer humming to life. The hard drive in Marin's office was what she really needed, but this little baby had cloud connection to that, and was updated constantly by both Marin and Kit. Its last date of entry was that morning.

So Marin had been updating her files at the same time Grif had been battling a fallen angel, and Kit had been feeding that same creature the information in her tears.

A shudder played at her spine, and Kit swallowed hard. Grif had freely admitted he had no idea what to do about Scratch, but whatever the answer was, surely they could find it together. And though it'd been hard to talk openly with Grif about Evie, she was glad she had. She felt closer to him now that they'd addressed the invisible elephant in the room, and facing it was another thing she was determined they'd do together. Then, maybe, Grif would be free to forget the past.

Refocusing, Kit typed in the password that only Marin and she knew, gaining access to the family archives, and a lengthy menu popped onto the screen. The family archives were not high-tech, just an orderly collection of disorderly anecdotes, thoughts, and half-baked reports on happenings in the Las Vegas Valley, but that was part of their appeal. The information in these files couldn't be googled or keyword-searched or cached on the Web. Much of it wasn't even substantiated, which was why it'd ended up on Marin's hard drive instead of hard print.

Yet Kit's family had long known that coupling salacious, outlandish, or even just eyebrow-raising bits of gossip with known information—then adding in a reporter's well-honed instinct—could unearth something even better than cold, hard facts. It provided possibility. Nuance.

Negative space.

And that's what Kit needed to unearth more regarding Sergei Kolyadenko and his merry mob of Russians. The attack on Marin wouldn't stop that. In fact, after her aunt was settled in her hospital room, and the strangers taking blood and tests and statements had all gone away, Marin made Kit promise to pursue this story through to the end. "Don't let them get away with this!" Marin snapped, glaring at the IV in her arm. "I'd go after them myself if these quacks would just cut me loose."

"Auntie," Kit said quietly. "They had a syringe filled with addictive poison taped to your forearm."

Marin just stared, gaze stubborn and hard, hands knotting within Kit's own. They were fragile against Kit's, almost brittle, and not at all the way they appeared when flying across computer keys, or pointing and waving about in the air as she gave orders. Marin's personality was so forceful that she appeared physically stronger than she was, and Kit suddenly realized that despite the cancer, it was her aunt, and not Grif, whom she most often considered immortal.

Which made the attack all the more shocking. Marin simply couldn't, *shouldn't,* be touched.

"Dangerous shit," Marin had agreed, nodding with vigor.

Her hair was flattened on one side, giving her a tilted look, but the resolve remained. "That's why we must get it off our streets."

Kit, refusing to be guilted into anything, shook her head.

"I'd die if anything had happened to you," she said, heaving the plate of guilt back Marin's way.

"You thought you would die once before," Marin pointed out. "And you didn't."

Kit shook her head and pulled her hands away. "Let someone else do it. It's not worth it to me. You're all I have left."

"It's always worth it, Katherine. And I'm not all you have left." Marin reached out, surprising Kit with her speed, and again with that strength. "You still have *you*. You always have you."

And how could Kit argue with that?

Besides, Kit also had three dead addicts, all teens, an aunt who'd been threatened because of Kit's investigation into those deaths, and a mystery woman who disguised herself as an over-aged Katy Perry while spreading disease and death all over the city. *Kit's* city. Finding this woman, she knew, was key.

So she pulled up the file photo on Yulyia Kolyadenko, and studied it. Fifty years from now, people would probably look back on this snapshot in the same way Kit viewed those from the midcentury years. They'd think this woman glamorous, classic, and chic. Who knew, she might even be those things . . . though she might be the opposite of them, too. Either way, Yulyia was stunning.

Yet there was a hardness there as well, Kit thought, studying the jawline, the lips, the eyes. Skepticism shellacked the clear blue gaze, a look that said she'd seen and survived more than her share of trouble. There was an almost brittle curve to her sharp mouth, like life was one big laugh and the joke, comrade, was on you. She was not kind, either, Kit decided. There was a lifelessness to her artifice that Kit had always considered a shortcoming in a woman. She was so perfectly groomed she might as well be a prop or a doll.

Question was, was she a weapon in some man's arsenal meant to control Vegas's drug-fueled underworld? Would she wear cheap leather? Multicolored wigs? Hang out with junkies in the city's dankest holes?

Kit's gaze settled on those thumbnail-size diamonds. "No way."

And she didn't think the man the files described as proud and imperious, Sergei, would ask or allow it of his wife, either.

Another woman, then. Kit scrolled through the digital files, eyeing the slim Slavic faces of those with known ties to the Kolyadenkos' *bratva*. It would have to be someone close, trusted, and with an investment in seeing the Russians pick off Marielito progeny—or as close as they could get—one by one. Kit paused on a photo of a woman named Anna Vaganova, mentally imposing a brightly colored wig on her delicate features. Yet Kit also couldn't discount the power of coercion, and that turned the woman she was seeking back into the proverbial needle in the haystack.

Leaning back, Kit blew the bangs from her forehead, because that was the most likely answer. The *krokodil* itself was like a neon arrow flashing in the Russians' direction, so why not send a native English-speaker to do your dirty work?

Yet Jeannie Holmes said the woman who fed them the *krokodil* recipe had a clunky accent. "I have new drug to try. You weel love eet to death," Kit attempted and winced.

Talk about clunky. As easy as an Eastern European accent was to identify, it was almost impossibly hard to mimic.

Kit scrolled back to Yulyia Kolyadenko's photo again.

Maybe Jeannie had it backward? What if this mysterious woman wasn't trying to hide her Russian accent? What if she was trying to put it *on*?

Like the earrings, it wasn't something Grif or Marin—or someone willing to inject lighter fluid into their veins—would pay heed to, but Kit did. A woman who was particular about the things she put in and on her body could spot a fellow acolyte, regardless of time period, age, and ethnicity.

"I voodn't be caught ded een cheep hoop earring," Kit tried again, channeling Yulyia . . . badly. Yet Kit smiled anyway, then switched to her own voice. "So what about a woman from your rival Cuban gang, then? Could that be the source of our mysterious Bella?"

Frustrated, Kit switched screens to locate her own private files, but caught her breath when an archived photo jumped out at her. The pain she'd managed to shunt aside all night ambushed her as Grif's face—the sprouting stubble and hard lines and probing stare that Kit loved so much—gazed back at her in black-and-white . . . though, of course, he wasn't really looking at her at all.

At the time this photo was taken, Kit didn't even exist.

But the woman his arm was draped loosely around had not only existed, she'd been his entire life. The same hand cupping that slim waist sported a thin gold wedding band, and there was an answering diamond on her finger, a chip of a thing that, though not large, winked in the photographer's flash like a taunt. Kit wondered why Grif's wedding band never reappeared on his body at four A.M., same as everything else he'd died in. Obvious answer? He hadn't been wearing it when he died, though he swore he had. So had someone removed it just before that? Had he simply forgotten to don it earlier?

Kit took her gaze off the diamond, and moved it up to the woman's open, direct stare.

The monochrome tones did nothing to diminish Evelyn Shaw's peaches-and-cream complexion, and cheekbones as high as the Rockies sat beneath eyes that shone with amusement and mystery. Her clothing was business casual for the day—a tidy, if sexier, Jackie Kennedy—though Kit knew Evelyn Shaw hadn't had a job—at least not at the time this photo was taken, just before her and Grif's deaths. This was obviously a special occasion, and Kit's gaze briefly dropped to the accompanying tagline.

Yes, it was the week Grif had brought little Mary Margaret DiMartino back home to her family. Her kingpin uncle, Sal, was in the foreground with arms splayed wide, and he was the real focus of the photo, while Grif vainly attempted to skirt the press's view. Kit's eyes shifted again to Evie.

She wasn't shying away from anything. She was in a lean-legged stride halfway between both men, head tilted toward the blazing-hot photographer's bulb. Unlike Grif, his wife clearly relished having her photo taken, and she wore the same knowing, closed-mouth smile in every photo. Kit frowned, wondering exactly what Evie knew. That Grif loved her? That he always would?

That Kit had to rival her for his love?

"You're obsessing," Kit muttered, reminding herself to be careful. She had to keep her feelings, especially regarding this woman, under control. If there was any danger of slipping into negativity, this old love epitomizing everything Kit had ever wanted—the era, the lean looks, the man—would be the trigger.

Kit could easily see herself losing control then, burning up inside, just like Jeannie, and without ever touching an invasive drug.

Learn her secrets.

Fleur's voice visited Kit in memory.

I bet if you look close enough, you'll find she wasn't so damned perfect.

What the hell, Kit thought, copying and pasting the photo of Grif and Evelyn into a new file. Ignoring this dead, now near-mythic woman hadn't worked. Grif couldn't move on while fixated on the past, so Kit began compiling an action list, beginning with calling on Mary Margaret again to see if she might be up for a private visit with Kit. She'd find out for herself just what hold Evelyn Shaw had over Grif. What magic she possessed from beyond the grave that even Kit—flesh and blood and *here*—couldn't seem to break through.

"And then what?" Kit muttered, fingers falling still over the keys.

"Then you ruin his every loving memory of her . . . just for fun."

Kit's hands fell still, and she looked up to find a fallen angel sitting up in her aunt's hospital bed, wearing Marin's flesh along with its own knowing smile, and watching her with a darkly glittering gaze.

CHAPTER EIGHTEEN

Yulyia Kolyadenko had a serious shopping habit. This hadn't been referenced in Grif's gathered data. Ditto the almost disturbing affection for something that looked like a cross between a gerbil and a rat, yet barked like a dog. She carried the shivering, useless thing for three long hours, never allowing its painted pink toes and sweater-clad underbelly to touch the ground. Grif knew this because he'd trailed her and two bodyguards as they wound their way through a cavernous place that reminded him of one of the lower levels of hell. The indoor monstrosity was serpentine, brightly lit, loud, and hosted a population of screeching young girls. It was called a mall.

Dodging cart vendors who inexplicably kept trying to put lotion on his hands, and others who wanted him to buy T-shirts stamped with the names of places he'd never been, he watched Mrs. Kolyadenko enter stores with a brisk, confident gait, yank clothing and belts and jewelry and shoes from the racks, purchase most without trying them on—thank God— then hand the packages over to the men flanking her, essentially turning them into beefy bellmen. Grif started to believe his hunch was wrong—how could a woman so obsessed with red-soled shoes run an entire network of foreign mobsters?— and he'd just decided to abandon her and her pampered fur ball when she slipped through a pair of discreetly placed side doors, and into a waiting stretch limo. Pausing halfway into the car, she turned slightly, then marched back through the porte cochere and directly up to Grif.

"You are following me." Her voice was husky and low, her eyes cerulean and sharp.

Grif glanced down at the fur ball, spotting eyeballs and a pink tongue. It was definitely a dog. "Yes."

"I don't like it when strange men follow me."

"I'm not that strange," Grif replied.

Yulyia remained still and cold, like a Siberian ice sculpture.

"Besides," he added, flicking his gaze at each of the flanking bodyguards, letting them know he saw them. "I'm a detective."

She sneered. "First a cop. Now detective. I am starting to get paranoid, I think."

"A cop?"

"Yes. This morning. He requested a meeting with my husband." She lifted her chin. "He got me instead."

Disquiet settled in Grif's stomach like a stone, weighing him down at the center. "Detective Carlisle?"

"You know him?"

Grif inclined his head.

"Of course you do." Yulyia flipped her hair, and her voice turned thin, honed. "All of you *followers* know each other."

"I'd like to talk to you, Mrs. Kolyadenko. If you have a few minutes."

Yulyia just turned and walked away. "If you're trying to use me to get to my husband, Mr. . . . ?"

"Shaw," Grif said, keeping stride. "Griffin Shaw."

Yulyia paused as before, one heel perched inside the waiting limo, right arm thrown over the open door. "Mr. Shaw. My husband has not been well and he is getting tired of being harassed." She drummed her long red nails on the window. "I'm getting tired of it."

Tired? Grif mused. Because female or not, given the look in her cold blue eyes, he'd have said "furious."

"You're the boss," he replied lightly, tucking his hands into his pockets, but Yulyia's head whipped up, gem-like eyes narrowing. She held up a hand before her bodyguard could close her door, and Grif let a closed-mouthed smile grow on his face.

"Get in," she told him, and the bodyguards headed his way.

Grif had never been in a limousine before, and took a moment to study the interior—the creamy leather, the thick carpeting, the bar, and the glossy woodwork—but ignored the bodyguard currently trying to drill holes through Grif's head with his eyes alone. Instead, Grif shifted to face the Viper and the real danger.

"Now," she said, as the limo pulled smoothly from the curb. "What could you possibly want from me?"

"I'd like to know why your *bratva* attacked a woman in a parking lot, and left her bloody and terrorized with a drug-filled syringe attached to her arm."

Yulyia laughed and folded her hands over her knee. "Why would I do that? Who is this woman?"

"Why would *you* do that?" Grif asked.

"We," she corrected so quickly the word emerged like buck-shot.

"We?" Grif echoed, widening his smile.

Yulyia, though, was no longer amused. "I mean Sergei, of course."

"Of course."

Hands cradling her small dog, Yulyia began petting it in quick strokes. "You should not look at me in such a way, Mr. Shaw. Bare so many teeth, and someone might think you came here to bite."

Placing his elbows on his knees, Grif leaned so close to Yulyia that she would need only to extend her index finger to touch him. Yet, her knuckles were white, bones showing as her hands fell still, and after a moment her little dog squealed. With a jerk, she relaxed her hold, and looked away.

Grif did not. "Why was the editor of the *Las Vegas Tribune* left lying in a parking lot with *krokodil* kissing her veins?"

Surprise widened Yulyia's deep-set gaze, but she instantly blinked it away. Marin's attack hadn't hit the wires yet, so of course she wouldn't know about it . . . unless she was a very good actress. By the time Grif had completed that thought, Yulyia was stroking her rat-dog again, fully recovered. "Mr. Shaw," she said, slanting her legs to one side and nestling into the plush leather. "Do I really look like a woman who deals drugs?"

"I don't care about the drugs, Kolyadenko," he snapped back, using her surname, same as he would a man. "I care about the woman."

For a moment Yulyia looked like the Viper that Ray had likened her to—body taut, head tilted, blood all but vibrating beneath her skin. Yet she didn't strike. Even the oversize rat in her lap remained still. Grif wondered what he'd said that'd stunted her aggressiveness.

"The Rusanovka *bratva*," he went on when she still said nothing, "which your husband is known to head, is infamous for its drug trafficking, weapons smuggling, and money laundering."

"Yes, I've heard that, too." A deep frown appeared on Yulyia's forehead. It did nothing to detract from her beauty. "But, again, I ask you. Do I look like a woman who deals drugs?"

She looked sleek and sexy to his mortal eyes, and his celestial ones didn't detect even a tinge of fatalistic plasma, and if she'd ever done drugs, even long ago, it would be there. Staring at the crystalline etheric outline, Grif had to wonder if she'd ever had a cold. She was a blank canvas . . . minus the canvas. There was simply nothing there. Grif finally answered, "No."

"That's right," she said, tossing that thick, golden mane, and settling her dog next to her. Even with all the fur obscuring its features, the little animal looked relieved. "And has anyone been able to prove that the Kolyadenkos are anything but good American citizens?"

"Not that I know of." Grif shrugged.

"Exactly. People are jealous. People are stupid. And people make up things that they can't prove. *Krokodil*," she scoffed, infusing the sole word with Slavic disdain. "I'd have to be stupid to bring that trash into this country."

Grif didn't point out that she'd never asked what *krokodil* was in the first place. "And who would like to make you look stupid?"

Eyes narrowed, she leaned so close her breath shocked him into a shiver. "What is your angle, Mr. Shaw?"

"No angle," he answered shortly. "Just wondering about

your enemies. It's only a theory, but maybe other outfits have designs on your drug territory."

"I told you. I don't do—"

"Maybe," Grif went on, "Marco Baptista."

The hitch was slight, but Grif caught it, and Yulyia knew it. She lifted her chin and ran the tip of her tongue across her bottom lip. The move was both thoughtful and provocative. Grif thought he heard the bodyguard next to him swallow hard.

"That Cuban," she finally spat. "That nothing of a man who likes to hit women."

The description married with Grif's gut instinct about the man. "He beats women?"

"How do you think his own grandmother lost all her teeth?" Yulyia scoffed, though Grif couldn't tell if the disdain was for Baptista or his grandmother.

Grif trained his gaze on her placid face and not the long, bare legs in front of him. "He doesn't seem to be a big fan of the fairer sex, does he?"

"Unlike you?" she retorted, scorn slithering through her words.

No, Grif decided, he wasn't wrong about her. Although, locked in the back of a speeding vehicle with that look, along with an armed man next to him, Grif wasn't feeling very self-congratulatory about it. "Unlike me."

"Pull over," Yulyia called to the driver, then addressed the man across from Grif. "Get out."

His gaze flicked to Grif, but he left the car as soon as it came to a halt, without comment or question. Yulyia pressed a button, raising the privacy shield between her and the driver, saying only one word before he disappeared. "Drive."

Grif thought better about waving to the meathead outside the car. The tinted glass would keep him from seeing it anyway, and the man already had his head down as he trudged along the gravel next to the asphalt, the rocky terrain a better choice than the still blazing street.

"What is your interest in Marco Baptista?" Yulyia asked, dropping her head against her soft leather headrest and observing him through a half-lidded gaze.

Grif held out his hands, palms up. "Two of the kids using *krokodil* died in his neighborhood."

"Then maybe you should be questioning him."

"I have."

"Good. Because he's known for dealing trash. In fact, he has a lot in common with the drug's namesake. He lurks in the murkiest of places. He feeds on other living beings. He lives like an animal."

Grif said, "And how would a woman like you know that?"

"And what kind of woman do you think I am, Mr. Shaw?" She uncrossed her legs at the ankle, lifting the right, draping it over her other knee.

"I think you're calculated. And driven," he answered immediately. "I think you once stood for so many hours in a breadline that you swore you'd never go hungry again," he said, paraphrasing a line from the most famous movie of his childhood. "I think you'd do anything to keep from doing so again."

Yulyia stared at him so long that the road ribboning beneath their tires took on a musical quality as they slid back onto the freeway, as if it could go on forever, and so could a breadline, and so could a stare.

"What did you mean earlier?" he was surprised to find himself asking. "When you called me a follower?"

"Just what I said. If you had any initiative at all, you wouldn't be taking the orders, Mr. Shaw. You would be giving them. Then again, followers have their place in the world, too. We can't all give orders."

"Like you?" he asked.

"I like to be heard, if that's what you mean. But that's not what makes me different," she added, preventing him from having to ask. "I have a gift for seeing a situation both as it is and as it could be. Most people merely long for the world to be as they wish it."

"You're not a dreamer?"

"Dreamers are easily deceived."

"So you're a realist?"

"I am . . . settled."

Some guys spend their entire lives searching for a place to settle . . .

Grif frowned, Sarge's words hitting him as hard as the paper had the morning the Pure angel appeared in a paperboy's flesh. Was this what he'd meant? That Grif had more in common with someone who was Lost, like Jeap, than the coolly self-possessed woman who sat across from him now? He didn't mind the contrast with Yulyia, of course, but he didn't think that made him a follower.

Yulyia had been intensely quiet during Grif's musings, but she tilted her head to the right now, interrupting his thoughts. "I like your hat. May I see it?"

Grif shrugged, then handed over the hat Kit had given him. Yulyia spotted the button to activate the navigation feature immediately, and Grif quickly explained what it was. He didn't want her dropping her pretty pooch and reaching for the lady's pistol she no doubt had stored back here. The bodyguard might be gone, but the danger was not. "It's just a tool to find my way around the city. Like an electronic compass."

Turning the hat in her hand, she still looked suspicious. "Why do you need electronic compass in hat?"

"I get lost easy." Grif shrugged, his genuine embarrassment causing Yulyia to laugh, possibly her first genuine emotion during the day. Smiling, she placed the hat atop her head.

"Why do you do it?" Grif asked her as she adjusted the fedora into a fashionable tilt.

"Do what?"

"Hide behind a man." Which would disappoint Kit. It put Yulyia firmly out of the running for Bella. "We both know your husband isn't the one running the *bratva*. So why pretend it's him?"

Yulyia propped an arm against the door, tucking the long red fingernails beneath her chin as she stared out the window. "I am Russian, Mr. Shaw. In my country, women are traditionally subservient to men. Like most men who came of age in Soviet society, my Sergei still lives in past. Such men are obsessed with honoring their fathers and family name, and doing something that will make those old, dead men proud. Yet I am woman."

"I noticed," Grif said.

"And as woman I am charged with looking forward. I must create my own future."

"Only women do that?"

"Women know, as most men can't, that we must choose fate before it is chosen for us." Outside, the city passed by with frightful speed. Yulyia licked her bottom lip again, this time more slowly. "You are considering my words. That is also novel for a man."

"Can you cut the insults, please?"

"Only if you do the same," she said. "No more stupid questions. You and that cop. You know Baptista is dealing this shit. You know he introduced drug that originated in Russia to frame me." She narrowed her eyes. "And you also know that telling me all this means I have incentive to stop these horrible deaths."

"See," Grif said, not denying it. "I can be forward-looking, too."

Yulyia smiled at that, and if Grif wasn't mistaken, this smile, too, was genuine. There was a long stretch of silence where they merely studied each other. This, he decided, had to be how she derived her nickname. Not because of a swift offensive strike, but due to the intensity of that unwavering stare. No man would ever fear her physical strength, but all could fear that forward-looking resolve.

"I really do like this hat," she finally said, as the driver took an off-ramp. Uncrossing her legs, she slumped low in her seat. "I think I would like to wear this hat."

"You are wearing it," Grif pointed out, as they came to a stop at a red light.

Sliding lower, she propped one heel on each side of Grif's body. "I think I would like to wear it and nothing else, with you on your knees before me."

"I think I'd like my hat back now," Grif said.

Yulyia just smiled. "I will tell driver to take freeway again. You will put those big hands inside my thighs. You will split me with your tongue. Then you will thank me for allowing it."

You are a follower.

Grif fought to keep his eyes on hers. "I'll just take the hat."

"But you said all those lovely things about me." She lifted

her arms over her head, opening to him so that she was nearly reclined, and pressed the button on the hat's brim. It began beeping in insistent, even beats. "Don't you find me attractive?"

"You're very beautiful."

"Then what is problem?" There was a hint of anger in her tone, just a flash of that viper's flare. "You can't really be that attached to this hat."

Gently, Grif put a palm on each of her ankles, the skin smooth and warm beneath his calloused hands. She shivered, and though he didn't think she was feigning it, he still lifted one leg gently and crossed her legs for her. Yulyia immediately pushed into a sitting position. The dog squealed next to her. She ignored it.

Grif said, "Your beauty is not the problem. The problem is that touching you would be exactly like touching Marco Baptista. You both lurk in murky places. You both feed on other living beings. You both live like animals."

"Look around, Shaw. Do I abide in filth like that man?"

No. If possessions were the barometer, she couldn't be more different from Baptista.

He pointed at her chest, at where her heart was supposed to be. "I meant in there. You might be settled, sweetheart, you might be a survivor and a realist, and a leader of men who long for the good old commie days, but your heart is one of the ugliest things I've ever seen."

And the emptiness he sensed surrounding her suddenly made sense. There was a phosphorous gap around her etheric body not because she was clean, but because she was lifeless. Plasma didn't gather around someone who was already dead, and that's what Yulyia was inside.

Yulyia didn't strike at him, not like a viper or even a woman just scorned. But she did immediately stop the car. Grif had expected that, but he still sighed as he was dumped back in the early evening heat. It was a residential neighborhood, and in this city they all looked the same. He'd been hoping to get kicked out closer to the center of town.

"Good-bye, Mr. Shaw," Yulyia said coolly. He held out a hand, but Yulyia just gave him a closed-mouthed smile from beneath the brim of his beeping fedora. It was one of the most chilling looks he'd ever seen. "Don't forget to keep looking forward."

Then the window lifted, and she was gone.

CHAPTER NINETEEN

H ello again."
      It was here. Scratch had found her again, and was in her aunt's body. *The drugs,* Kit realized, and her breath caught like a trapped dove in her chest. It made no move to reach her, but Kit felt herself begin to shake. There was no angel under the bed this time. No ally biding his time to sneak up on Scratch from behind. This time Kit was truly alone.

And Scratch knew it. Its eyes gleamed, crusting her aunt's normally direct gaze with the same sickly-sooted stare that Kit had seen in Jeannie. It was blasphemous to see someone she loved defiled in such a way, so Kit's reaction was almost involuntary as she picked up the hospital's plastic pitcher of water and threw it on her aunt's face. Marin—or Scratch inside— sputtered. Her aunt's head dropped, and the shocked expression was blotted away, along with the water, by the thin sheet.

After a moment, Scratch came up smiling widely. "Nice try, dear, but you'd have to *drown* me in your tears to get rid of me now."

For the first time in almost as long as she could remember, Kit didn't know what to say or do. This was Grif's domain, not hers. She wanted to run, but she couldn't leave Marin with this . . . thing in her body.

"You know, from this perspective, you look just like your mother."

The jab, meant to push at old wounds, was exactly what Kit needed to collect herself. "You don't know my mother."

"Ah, but I do, even if it is only through Marin's dusty memories. And might I take this opportunity to add . . . it's fascinating to be privy to the secrets people will keep. Even from those they love."

The Third feed off negative emotion, and if you reveal even the slightest hint of it, Scratch won't hesitate to use it against you.

Remembering, Kit said, "I'm not interested in knowing anything Marin doesn't want to share with me herself."

"Suit yourself," Scratch said, its smile oily. "Her cancer's still in remission, by the way. She beat it back, and now she's tougher than ever. She's always had a hard time of it, though. It wasn't easy for her with Shirley as a sister, you know."

"Get out of her mind," Kit said evenly.

But it was too late. Scratch had access to Marin's innermost thoughts, and because Kit had given it her tears, it knew her dark worries as well.

"You couldn't possibly remember this," it continued, breaking up its syllables like footsteps over fall leaves, "but Marin and your mother fought like junkyard dogs. For sisters, they couldn't have been more different. Isn't that strange when such disparate people come from the same family? Your mother, the aristocrat. Marin, the Everywoman. They stood toe to toe when they butted heads. Marin always wondered if that was what all sisters did, or if it was only them."

"Stop it."

"You remind her of her mercurial sister with your flightiness, your careless nature."

"Marin loves me."

"Marin loved Shirley, too . . . she just didn't like her very much."

Kit ignored that. "My aunt is not Lost, and you can't have her."

"I don't want her," it said, looking directly at Kit. "And I don't need a vice in order to possess you. You gave me your tears of your own free will. It's like giving me a key to your house and letting me riffle around. I can tell you all about you now. Would you like that?"

No.

"Sometimes it's good to get an outsider's perspective on these sorts of things," it went on, winking. "Though I can hardly be called an outsider now, can I?"

Using Marin's fingers, bending them back so far they should've cracked, it began to tick off things it now knew about Kit. "You love your work, and you're good at it. You strive to live by the motto drilled into you by your patrolman father   "

"Don't talk about my father," Kit said through gritted teeth. She was trying to stay calm, but Scratch wasn't making it easy.

It feigned affront, and benevolence. "Of course not. Besides, your time would be better spent talking to Marin about him."

Kit frowned, unsure of what was behind the insinuation. But Scratch had already moved on, intent—as Grif said—on confusing and keeping her off balance. "We're talking about you, anyway, and what was it your doomed ol' dad used to say? 'Don't just find the easy answer, find the truth.' "

"You're not going to make me doubt myself or those around me. I've created a good life because I've built it on the foundation of those strong family ties. I have it all—friends, beauty, love."

"No, you merely have the hope of love." It held out its arms. "Now that Evelyn Shaw. She had love."

"You know nothing of it."

"Love is patient. Love is kind. Blah, blah, blah." It smiled. "And how do *you* love, Kit?"

"Passionately," she shot back, displaying some of it now. If it knew her well, it should know she wasn't going to just roll. "Wholeheartedly. Without restraint."

"I know how that feels." It met her disbelieving gaze with wide-eyed innocence. "I do. That's how I hate."

"Love is more powerful than hate," Kit immediately countered.

"Keep telling yourself that, sweetie."

"And you keep telling yourself that you're relevant just because you exist. But you were created, not Chosen. You're just a wrench in God's cosmic tool belt that can be picked up or discarded, used for good or ill. You exist, but you've never truly lived, so you can't speak to true passion. If you could, you'd know life *is* love."

"See that idealism? That's what I *love* to hate about you. You wear all your soft spots on the outside, exposed and just waiting to be pushed. Your blind hope is like a giant bruise."

"Don't say it like that's a weakness."

"Oh, I know it's a strength, and it's just the sort I *love* to break. It's fascinating how you refuse to harden yourself to life's disappointments. No matter who dies. No matter who lies."

"You're not going to turn me against the people I love."

"But Griffin Shaw and Marin Wilson have lied to you," it finally hissed, leaning forward, giving up any pretense of subtlety. "You! The girl who *loves* the truth. But I can give you their knowledge. Allow me to slip into your mind of your own free will for just a moment and I'll whisper their every thought into your inner ear. Use free will to choose something for yourself for once."

Kit raised an eyebrow. "Aren't you supposed to offer me an apple when you say all that?"

"You *want* to know how your father died!" it asserted, angering now.

"I know how he died," Kit said coolly.

"You know what they told you," it said, and the arctic chill in its voice was only part of the reason Kit went cold. "You're like your beloved Mr. Shaw in that way, haunted by an old mystery and by all the answers you'll never have. But"—it motioned down Marin's body—"I have answers."

"I don't want anything from you," Kit said, and rose to gather her things. She didn't want to think about her father or his death or what else Marin might know of it until she was well away from this room. And she had to get out now.

Scratch didn't lunge at her, or move to stop her at all, and it didn't speak again until Kit placed a hand on the doorknob. "You want to know who he'd choose."

Kit froze.

"If he could, that is," it continued, knowing it had her attention. "In the depths of night, when he's lost in his dreams and away from you, you wonder what would happen if you and

Evelyn Shaw were both alive, and all things were equal. Who, then, would be the recipient of Griffin Shaw's unconditional love?"

"It doesn't matter," she said, without turning. "That can never happen."

"But if you don't learn the answer to that question, your dreams will lie dormant and mute. You'll suffocate on your futile wish for true love, and like me, you'll want to destroy the object of your affection."

Now Kit whirled. "I would never hate like you! I don't care if you call it weakness, I'm going to stay soft and open and hopeful. *I'm* a child of God, you winged beast. *I* belong on this Surface, not you! And I have the right to love and be loved!"

"But you won't. Not ever," it said, and though the words were almost whispered, Kit felt as if she'd been punched in the gut. "I have your tears and I'm going to come after all the good things in your life, and dismantle them one by one. I'm going to claw my way into your heart. And then, I will destroy everything you love."

"*I'm* not at your disposal," Kit whispered. "I'm not Lost."

"Lost," it said, shrugging, "is just the opposite of Chosen. And who has ever really chosen you, Katherine? Griffin Shaw? He's so busy remembering a dead woman that he can't even see you. If I were you, well, that . . ." It shook Marin's head. "That . . . that . . ."

Its eyes pinwheeled in their sockets until they stopped dead on Kit's own.

"That would just piss. Me. Off."

Kit fled then, but not fast enough. Scratch's voice, ferried by hate and as chill as the center of the Forest, chased her down the hall. "Don't get sick, dear. And for heaven's sake, don't get knocked out. Be careful of even sleeping too deeply. Because I'm here, and I can wait lifetimes to get what I want."

Kit whimpered, and though she was rounding the corner of the long hall, she was sure Scratch heard her. She, after all, still heard it.

"Tick tock, Katherine. Tick tock . . ."

CHAPTER TWENTY

W hen Grif arrived home, Kit was on the patio, asleep on a lounger meant for daylight and drinks. The air still held a hint of warmth from the day, and sweat sat on her brow, but she looked comfortable enough on the patio, the blue-green glow from the kidney pool reflecting faintly on her face. Her vintage sundress would have been fashionable in Grif's first lifetime, and given the surroundings—if Grif allowed it—he could even pretend he was back in the fifties, home late from work, ready to kick up his feet and listen to ol' Jimmy Durante on the box, or noodle a bit over the $64,000 question.

But Grif kept his mind on the present, studying Kit a bit longer, hoping that the longer she slept the further she'd drift from her concern about Evie. Then maybe they could start over again.

"Why are you staring at me?" Kit suddenly asked, without opening her eyes.

Grif jolted. He'd entered the home without setting off the alarm, and she'd had the patio door ajar, so he hadn't made a sound. "Why are you sleeping outside?" he asked instead of answering.

Her eyelids lifted slowly, and she looked around like she was viewing a dream rather than waking from one. "It's beautiful, isn't it? Even in June the desert night can just whisk away the summer heat so that it all seems so far away. The temperature is exactly the same as the human body. I love that."

Grif tilted his head as she sighed. The light from the kitchen only revealed half her face, and her eyes—those clear windows to her emotions—had again fallen shut. There was a tumbler at her side, but it was still two fingers full, so he wondered if it was her first. She generally only drank for pleasure, but who knew after today? Maybe, like her eyes, she was using it to close her emotions off to him. Grif's heart bumped at the thought.

Kit had opened her eyes as the silence dragged on, and tracked his gaze to the drink. "I was hoping it would help me sleep. I'm overtired, but restless. Fatigue keeps dragging me under. Then it pulls me right back out again. But I can't bring myself to drink it."

"You're thinking too much." Not that he blamed her.

She nodded. "Yes. About Scratch, about Marin. You," she added, without heat. "And, still, about those desperate kids who add fuel to their veins just so they can feel anything good at all."

Grif edged closer, and she focused on him. "I saw Scratch."

Grif dropped to the foot of her lounger, and she scooted over, then put her head in his lap and hugged him tight.

"When?" he asked. "How?"

He held her as she told him about her bedside vigil, and how Scratch had used the drug-induced sleep to both possess Marin and reach out to terrorize Kit. Her voice remained steady, but he could imagine how scared she'd been. And Jeap Yang had been right. The fallen angel would've circled back for her even before she tricked it into divulging information about Bella and her case. Nothing Kit did, or didn't do, would've stopped that.

"Jesus, Kit." Grif ran a hand over her head, because what he was really thinking was, I should have been there.

Kit nodded. "You were right to warn me about my darker feelings. Scratch said that's how it would come for me now that it has my tears. It's . . . waiting." She said it matter-of-factly, but the tremor was there, between the words.

"I'm sorry, Kit. I'll talk to Sarge. See if there's anything we can do."

Drawing up her knees, Kit lifted her hands and held them beneath her chin as if in prayer. "There's more. I think it knows something about my father's death. In fact, I think Marin does, and she isn't telling me."

Grif jerked his head. "I told you. Its intent is to create chaos wherever it goes. It wants to confuse you."

"Doesn't mean it's not true, though." Kit pushed herself into a sitting position. "Someone took my father's life, Grif. Someone took him from me. And nobody has ever discovered who the killer really is. Don't you think that's a strange lack of concern for a cop killing? Especially an officer who was the brother-in-law to the nosiest, most dogged newspaper editor in the valley?"

He took her hands. "Don't let Scratch's words place a wedge between you and your aunt, Kit. You know that's what it's trying to do."

"If Marin knows something about my father's death that she's not sharing with me, then *she's* the one placing a wedge between us." Kit shook her head before he could speak. "You never knew my dad, Grif, but I wish you could have."

"Me, too," he finally said, and gave her hands a squeeze.

"Tell me about the Russians, did you find them?" She picked up the drink and took a sip.

"I had a little chat with that Russian mobster's wife."

Kit tilted her head. "And?"

He shrugged. "She liked the hat you gave me."

Raising a slim eyebrow, she waited for more.

"She spotted the navigation switch. I think she thought it was a weapon or recorder or something."

Pointing the glass at his head, she said, "So she took it?"

Because she sounded amused, Grif said, "After propositioning me in the back of her limo. With her little rat-dog watching."

Kit made a face. "Those pocket puppies are the worst."

"Right."

"That's all?"

"About it."

They stayed quiet for a moment and he said, "But it all got me thinking. The *krokodil* . . . what's the hardest ingredient to get a hold of?"

Kit squinted as she thought. "Lighter fluid is easy, so is iodine and paint thinner. But codeine. That's not so easy."

"Yeah, so I think we need to follow the codeine."

"Find the codeine, find the dealers," Kit said, nodding. "That's smart, Grif. You must be a P.I. after all."

"Thanks."

"So I'll see what I can stir up tomorrow on that. But first, got something for you." Kit jerked her head at the side table.

Glancing down, Grif spotted what he'd initially taken for a coaster. It was a slip of paper, he saw now, and he stared at the line scribbled across its center. "An address?"

"Mary Margaret DiMartino's address."

Grif nearly lunged for the paper. "How'd you get this?"

Smiling at his reaction, Kit pointed at herself. "Reporter, remember?"

Though every instinct was telling Grif to run for the door and this address right now, he managed to stay seated. But he felt like his whole body was vibrating, as if there were bees inside of him. As if he were an active hive.

Shrugging, Kit waved with the glass. "I needed something constructive to do after leaving the hospital. I didn't feel like being . . ." She was going to say "alone," Grif saw the word forming, but she changed it up and saved them both embarrassment. "Home. So I went by the club to talk to Ray DiMartino."

"Kit!"

"Oh, don't scold me out of some old-fashioned, misguided, and impossibly sweet notion of a woman's place."

Grif's mouth snapped shut.

"Besides, it turns out he really doesn't know where Mary Margaret lives, but he did know her last place of residence."

"And he told you, but not me?"

Kit batted her lashes. "Perhaps I'm more persuasive."

"How persuasive?"

"That's between Ray and me and the center-stage pole," she said, giving a little shimmy in her lounger.

Grif's eyes narrowed into slits.

"Oh, please." She waved a hand, dismissing it. "Anyway, it turns out that Mary Margaret's former landlord keeps all the

forwarding addresses of her onetime residences, less out of al-
truism, I think, than nosiness."

"So you got the address from the landlord, and went to
Mary Margaret's new place?"

"Yes. Well, her old-new place." Kit shrugged. "She's moved
again. Luckily, the lonely bachelor next door was extremely
friendly. I told him I was her niece. He said he'd been waiting
for her to send someone by as he was collecting her mail, and
could I please take it off his hands."

"And of course you were happy to oblige."

"It's not my fault if people like to give me things. Look, I'm
going to help you find the answers to yours and Evie's deaths.
Trust me. I understand how a lost love can haunt you."

"Which I suppose means you're going to confront Marin
about your father when she's better?" he said, still suspicious.

"Yes."

But how could he argue? He understood her need to know,
too. "You know, Sarge said I might have something in common
with the Lost—"

"No way. You're not Lost, Grif—"

"But maybe I am. Maybe after living and dying, but never
really moving on, maybe there's a part of me that won't ever be
found again." He frowned, not liking that, then shook himself
free from the thought. "But here's the thing. I always know
where my feet are on this mudflat when you're by my side. I
know which way is up when you're anchored above me, and
I can locate myself when I touch you below. You ground me
on this old mudflat, Kit. And I'm at peace when you're near."

Kit stared, and after a moment she let out a long exhale.
"Jeez, Grif. The things you say."

But Grif wasn't done. He slipped his hand around the back

of her head, fingers twining in her hair. He steadied her there. "Please. Don't give up on me. Not yet."

Because Grif didn't care what Sarge said. He *had* found a place to settle. And he was looking right at her.

In response, Kit rose. "Come with me."

"Where?" he asked, as she began backing up, his hand firmly clenched in hers.

She smiled. "To the bedroom, Mr. Shaw."

His own smile began to grow. "And why would that be, Ms. Craig?"

"Because I need comforting." Her seriousness was feigned, as was her drawn brow. "I need you to go on and on about how everything's going to be all right and . . . ," she said, unable to keep the smile away any longer, "if I recall correctly, the only time you really talk is in the bedroom."

He snorted. "And if I recall right, it's the only time you don't."

"Well," she said, tugging him into the house. "No reason why we can't both get what we want. We're partners, after all."

But as his suspenders fell away, and his shirt followed, he reached for Kit thinking he didn't want to talk at all. He wanted to disappear in *this* moment, drawing it out so that it was expansive and still, and let the past and future lie where they would.

Maybe it was their time apart, more than any since they'd first come together. Or maybe it was the sense of danger hedging them in on every side. Whatever it was, Kit's need to disappear alone with Grif was fierce. She wanted to go someplace only the two of them could go, not take him or be led, but make their way together. Like a pilgrimage, she thought. A hand-in-hand journey to commemorate the miracle that they were together at all.

The thought gave Kit pause, and she drew back to look at Grif. "I wish I could see it all the way you do."

"See what?" His gaze slipped over her face without finding purchase. He was looming over her in bed, but having trouble keeping his eyes focused.

"You know. God, heaven—"

"No one sees God." Shifting, he pulled, and Kit rolled onto his chest so that they were eye-to-eye. Using his wide, warm palms, he stroked her hair from her face. "And you'd be in trouble if you could see it like me."

"You mean dead, right?"

"I mean murdered," he said, and sighed into her hair. "Besides, I'm glad you can't. I don't want you broken."

"Oh, Grif." Kit slid a hand through his hair, thumb playing lightly atop his cheek. "You're not broken. You simply care, which is healthy. If anything, you care too much."

Grif huffed.

"You do. That's why you hung on to memories of Evie and of your life together through five whole decades. It's why you're still searching for her killer. And it's why you saved my life, a total stranger from another time and place, when you could have just let me die."

"Coulda, but here you are," he said, running his hand along her arm, eyes suddenly dark with different memories.

"Yes, and so are you, and that's no mistake." No matter what had gone on with him and another woman in the past, no matter what memories were stirred by finding Mary Margaret and questioning Ray DiMartino about the past, she truly believed Grif and she were meant to be together, here. Now.

Lifting one naked shoulder, she put on a wide-eyed expression. "Fact is, I'm so blown away by the miracle of us, together, that I don't even mind how tortured and stubborn and conflicted you are."

"Stop," he said drily. "You're exciting me."

She slipped a hand behind his neck. "Because you're also powerful and complicated and honest and good. That's not broken. That's human. That's . . . hot."

His gaze clouded again. "It is?"

A corner of Kit's mouth lifted as heat moved in her belly. Sliding atop him, she brought their faces closer. "Super-hot. My man has wings. And a nice, big . . ." She dropped a kiss to his lips, and whispered, "Halo."

Grif flipped her suddenly, his physical power flaring with his own need, and stoking Kit's. The heat in her belly rose into her chest, and her nipples tightened as Grif's irises grew wide. "You got it all wrong, cupcake. You make me sound like a saint, and I ain't no saint."

Slowly, Kit slid her tongue along her teeth. "Prove it."

His gaze fixed on her wide bottom lip. "I did. Lost my place in the Everlast for you. Got booted back down to this forsaken mudflat, still on the celestial time clock but with the limitations of the flesh."

Kit dismissed those epic sacrifices with a nonchalant shrug. "So prove it again."

So he drove himself into her in one smooth, warm thrust. Kit cried out with surprise even as she opened to him—she always opened to him and even so it was still never enough. Somewhere above her, Grif chuckled and muttered a belated reminder not to take anyone's name in vain, but then her legs were fastened around his waist, and he was the one who forgot to watch his language.

Kit could almost see the moment it happened, the dropping away of fifty years' worth of regret and worry. His shoulders dropped, his palms grew firmer. His mouth pressed harder and his eyes narrowed—on her, like he didn't want to miss a thing—but remained open. Kit smiled against his lips and lifted her knees, opening more. They rolled and breathed into each other's mouths and sweated and strained because they were here and alone, and they were *alive*.

Glorious, Kit thought, watching as he rose above her again, palms braced on each side of her head.

Yet glory meant something different to someone who was both angelic and human. He had the flesh and mind of a mortal man, but he was still a celestial creature and when he was exultant, when he gave thanks and paid reverence and took pleasure in something, it *showed*.

Kit remained fused to him, but momentarily put her own pleasure aside, knowing it would happen, waiting for it, watching. She slid her hands to his back, wanting to know the very moment he let go. She splayed her fingertips over the slight protrusions she felt there, and a shudder quaked through his body. Then, without warning, he arched.

"Let me see," she begged. "I want to see."

And so he lowered his head and kissed her so that the stark sizzle of ozone and iron flooded her mouth, and the entire cosmos flashed behind her eyelids. He shuddered again, causing an even deeper thrust, and though Kit cried out, he kept his mouth molded atop hers. The four seasons blew through her, starting with the crisp kiss of spring, and by the time autumn swept through her blood, she saw them: billowing black feathers raining over his back in two muscled arcs.

It was only in her mind's corner, a brief mental flash, but the soaring wings dripped with the dew of the Everlast, black as ebony and sharp as spears, the feathers overtaking Kit's vision before she was forced to breathe. Yet in that brief moment, Kit saw Grif as he really was, his mortal and angelic natures entwined like knotted roots, both at the forefront, both subsumed, and both, together, awesome.

Then her lungs filled, and the wings disappeared, but Kit didn't care. She held to the image in her mind, embellished it even, because this man, whole and healthy—not broken— belonged solely to her.

Grif's movements altered, growing liquid and smooth, like he was both melting her and shaping her anew. She felt golden inside, warm and divine, and she silently gave thanks for everything that'd allowed them to find each other, both good and bad. Because of Grif, and the raw miracle of him in her life, *Kit* was closer to God.

He set a new pace, both faster and more intense. That stray lock of hair she loved fell over his forehead, just above his closed eyes, and he stretched above her as he disappeared into the ritual of his thrust. Kit gripped him low, held tight, and timed it so that her release came at the same time as his. They had their lovers' rhythm. They would forever know what it was to be one.

"That must be what paradise is like, right?" she whispered minutes later, breath still ragged.

Grif, who'd dropped atop her in a heady tumble of dead weight, lifted himself to his elbows and cupped her head in one hand. Tucked in close, his chin stubble scratching at her cheek, he shook his head. "I don't know anything this good, Kit. Not in any world."

And then, still together, they slept.

CHAPTER TWENTY-ONE

Nobody could control their dreams. That was Grif's defense, what he told himself when he fell asleep inside Kit, but woke again a half a century earlier, walking hand in hand with his wife. Though the evening was studded with stardust, a material visible only to a Centurion's naked eye, Grif *knew* this night. Gripping Evie's hand tightly, he recognized the bite of winter's sharp edge, how it'd been too late for birdsong, and too cold for crickets, though something else had been stirring in the shadows.

Why hadn't he seen it the first time, he wondered, squinting at the towering silhouettes of the Marquis's imported foliage. The layers of greenery, gone black this late, made it even cooler, and Evie shivered beside him. It looked like a desert oasis, and was meant to. The guests in the resort's bungalows wanted to feel secluded and special and alone.

But in the remembering, Grif knew he and Evie weren't alone. They bumped hips as before, laughing and stumbling along the faux-stone path, giddy with the cocktails they'd consumed while gambling away the desert night. It was 1960, and they were in Las Vegas with a purseful of gaming chips and a room at the city's hottest resort, the Marquis.

What on earth was there to worry about?

Yet even as Grif smiled at Evie's drunken giggle, he cringed inside. These were his memories, after all, come alive in a dream, and ever since his return to the Surface, the nightmares detailing the way his first life ended had increased in clarity and severity. In this one, Evelyn Shaw—fifty years dead, yet dear to him still—was about to be attacked. She would scream. He would never see it coming.

Which meant Grif was about to be murdered, too.

He was wearing his favorite gray flannel suit, along with his Stacey Adams wingtips, and, of course, his fedora. They'd been celebrating that night, though for the life and death of him, he couldn't now remember why.

Evie wore heels and a dark cherry wiggle dress that caused her naked neck and milky face to glow as if lit from within. Her eyebrows were arrowed perfection, and white-blond hair lay obediently coifed around a gently pointed chin. Eyes of deep-set chocolate glowed as moonlight caught her knowing glance at him.

"I have plans for you, Griffin, my dear," she said, walking backward, holding both his hands in hers, her smile filled with promise. The fingertips of her right hand toyed with the wedding band on his left. Noting it jarred his consciousness. He hadn't felt the weight of that ring in so damned long. But then he lifted his gaze to Evie's, she smiled, and he slipped again into the past. "Just you wait."

But there'd be no more plans for either of them, just as there was no time to wait. He spotted the bungalow door, and, knowing exactly what lay beyond it, his heart began a mad scramble in his chest. Grif glanced up at the stars in the sky, the gateway to the Everlast, and prayed for a different outcome this time.

The night stared back, coldly indifferent.

Swallowing hard, Grif wondered if he'd have to relive being Taken, too. That first trip had been like journeying through an icy, open nerve, the Universe dense with dark matter and cosmic soot that pressed against the burning stars. Knowing that passage was once again only minutes away made Grif's chest ache with loneliness. And that made him think of Kit.

"What?" Evie snapped, halting before the bungalow's closed door, and turning on him as if he'd spoken aloud.

"Nothing," Grif said, in the dream and the past, though it'd all somehow shifted. This was wrong, he thought, swallowing hard. He hadn't said this the first time. He hadn't been thinking of any woman but Evie.

She hadn't looked at him like he had committed a crime.

"I just miss you. I miss spending time with you."

That soothed her enough that her response was once again melodious, a sweet dulcet tone that reminded him of spring. "We've both been busy lately. All your attention has been on that DiMartino case. But not tonight . . ."

Evie's was the voice of a breeze, Grif thought. A coy lull and tug that slipped smoothly into his groin, reminding him of whiskey and ice and the flare of a match. Not chirpy birds in the springtime, or flirtatious and incessant chattering. No, that was Kit . . .

"Who the fuck is Kit?" Evie demanded suddenly, and there was nothing coy or breezy about her voice now. Placing one hand on her hip, the other on the doorknob, she stood like a sentry between him and fate.

What was happening here? Grif wondered, blinking fast. Yet, on the heels of the thought, he already knew. This was no dream. In the same way Sarge had visited him as a paperboy, this was mythic . . . it was *vision*.

Don't fight it, he told himself. But how could he not, even knowing better? He didn't want to die again. He certainly wouldn't stand aside and let Evie be felled right next to him. No, this time he would fight.

But what the hell was he fighting against, he wondered, twisting to look behind him. Because this wasn't the way it'd happened the first time. Something was off, he thought, though he spotted nothing. Something was wrong.

"Answer me, Griffin," Evie said. She was the only one to call him by his full name, and though he'd told her before that it bothered him, he didn't say so now. Her voice was sharp, with a note of prim pique in it, which always meant trouble. It caused his gaze to slide away from the lone footprint he'd spotted embedded in the mud next to the door.

"I don't know," he finally lied, and tried to place an arm around her shoulders like he always had. But Evie jerked away.

"Cold," she said, shuddering at his touch. "Why is everything suddenly so cold?"

"I don't know," he said again.

Evie turned her pinpricked gaze on him. "Don't know much, do you?"

"Baby," he tried, but she shifted out of reach. He recognized the tilt of her chin as plainly as he recognized her dress. Evie would not be soothed.

"So are you enjoying your second life?"

She knew about that? Grif swallowed hard. "Come on, Evie—"

She lifted that sweet, stubborn chin. "Yeah, you're enjoying it. I can see you, you know."

Grif thought about that for a moment. Vision was a form of communication with the Everlast and those in it . . . but it wasn't a way to reach the dead. This, Grif thought, wasn't real. "No, you can't."

She stared, crimson lips thinning even further. "That's true," she finally said. "But I know what you're doing. You . . . and that other woman."

"It's been fifty years," Grif said, holding out his palms. "And you're dead."

"You're dead," she snapped.

Gesturing wildly, Grif finally snapped back. "Yeah, and I'm trying to find out why! I went back for us!"

"You went back for you!" she said, eyes narrowed to pins as she took in his face, forehead to stubbled chin. Then her hard gaze centered on his. "You think you're going to feel less guilty once you learn who did this? You think it's going to stop all the regret you feel for letting me bleed out on a cold marble floor? Letting me die while you did nothing?"

"I was ambushed!"

"You were my husband!" she said, voice cracking, tiny hands curled into fists. The diamond he hadn't been able to afford, but had given her anyway, winked against her white knuckles. "You were supposed to protect me!"

Yes. Love and protect, for better or for worse. 'Til death parted them . . . and it had.

Seeing Grif's argument deflate, Evie straightened. She was like a lock-jawed terrier when she got like this, and wouldn't let up until she'd shaken the life out of her target, even if it meant wearying herself and all those around her. Grif wondered how he could have ever forgotten that.

But Evie had a right to be angry. He hadn't protected her in the way he'd promised. So he just squared up and let fifty years of pent-up fury hit him dead-on.

"You're alive while I'm still dead," she said, melodious voice taking on an underlying scratch, like she was a record instead of the real thing. "Do you know what it feels like knowing that you're sleeping with another woman, heating her bed with your stolen flesh, warming her on the inside while I lie bone-cold in my grave?"

She grabbed at him then, not the loving embrace he'd come to yearn for but a grip on his throat that pulsed like a second death. Grif gasped as the chill from her fingers entered his chest, numbing his lungs and hobbling his breathing. Yet the rage remained in Evie's eyes, and her ruby lips curled in an ugly snarl. "Do you want to see how cold I really am, Grif? Because I can show you."

"No . . ." His mouth formed the word, but her touch had worked its frigid magic and no sound emerged. He clawed at his neck with his free hand, tried swallowing, but the effort only made him gag. Glancing back at the stars above, he prayed the vision away.

But it didn't work, and when Grif looked back at Evie, he cried out in the long-forgotten night. His wife's white-blond curls had lost all their softness and now lay flat and lank against the white gleam of her skull. There was no flesh on her face, no lashes or lids, no red lips to hide her wide skeletal grimace. He stared at the basic framework of the woman he loved, but it was an abstract shell of black shadows and white bone, and the previously clingy sheath now bagged around her body.

The brain still worked behind those hollow orbs, though. It both held his gaze and kept her fingertips tensile and tight. The look said that he hadn't been able to protect her, so she was going to protect herself . . . even from him.

Leaning in with a slow, considered glide, Evie looked for a moment like she would drop a fleshless kiss upon his lips. "You did this to me," she said, her breathless whisper bloated with the rotting blame of fifty long years.

"I know," Grif managed this time.

"Well, finally. Something you know." Evie's skull tilted like it might fall from her neck, yet her grip tightened. "Come on, *lover*. Let's go die so you can get on with your new life."

And she pushed him hard, shoving him through the bungalow door, back into the trajectory of the past where a man waited with a knife destined for Grif's gut. Back where another held a vase meant to shatter his skull. And back to where a Centurion would soon arrive to wheel him through the cold, unyielding Universe to his lonely post in the Everlast.

And knowing all of this, as he hadn't the first time, Grif cried out for Kit.

CHAPTER TWENTY-TWO

Kit had fallen asleep in her favorite spot, the warm, welcoming niche where Grif's shoulder met his side, nestling in so tightly against him the spattering of hair on his chest moved against her cheek like whispers. Then he tensed beside her. Not again, she thought, immediately awake. But he cried out his dead wife's name, and it entered their bedchamber like a thief.

"No, Evie!"

This time Kit hesitated in reaching for him.

Lost is just the opposite of Chosen. And who has ever really chosen you, Katherine?

Scratch had known exactly where to strike, she thought. She couldn't let the fallen angel's words alter her actions. "Grif, baby. Wake up!"

And so it went, as before. Grif was consumed with guilt,

over the past and what he was putting Kit through, too. She tried to reassure him, and thought she'd done a good job, but when he settled again, his back was to her, and he was curled up, as if afraid he might injure her more.

Kit didn't sleep. Instead, she watched Grif, and tried to bring back the image of his brow cleared of worry—because of her. She reimagined his breath, deep and strong. She comforted herself that even rousing from his nightmares, it was Kit he'd search out upon waking. *She* gave him release and contentment. Not like those furry-winged angels . . . those so-called Pures.

And not some dead woman whose ghost just wouldn't let go.

That's not fair, Kit chided herself, brushing back the hair from his forehead. It wasn't Evelyn Shaw's fault that she'd been murdered back in 1960. Kit could feel no less horror at that than she did at Jeap Yang's death, or Jeannie's and Tim's, or that of anyone who was taken before their time.

Yet Grif had escorted many souls to the Everlast, and had never chased down their murderers . . . not the way he was doggedly chasing Evie's. That was the difference, and though it shouldn't matter, she couldn't help but wonder what he'd choose if given the chance. This lifetime with her?

Or forever with his first wife, Evelyn Shaw?

"How the hell do I compete with a woman who is fifty years dead?" she whispered, before unconsciousness finally claimed her again.

In daylight, she shored herself up again by perfecting her pin curls and coloring her lips so red they screamed. Grif appeared fine. Neither of them mentioned his nocturnal visitor. They made small talk over breakfast, then left the house— partners in every way.

For now, the investigation involving dead junkies, the Russian mafia, and Cuban street thugs was Dennis's domain. Kit had called him upon waking, and told him about Grif's meeting with Yulyia Kolyadenko, though she left out the part where the woman had propositioned Grif. Truth was, Kit was trying so hard *not* to envision the gorgeous, powerful woman keying in on her man that she almost forgot to tell Dennis about the woman who did need mention. The one hooking the tweekers on the *krokodil* in the first place.

"She goes by the name of Bella," she told Dennis, as she pulled her car into the scarred lot of Vegas's oldest park.

"How do you know that?" Dennis asked. Kit waved away Grif's impatient growl as she tucked the phone beneath her ear and shoulder, and locked her car.

"Jeannie Holmes's mother," Kit lied, finally lifting the phone with one hand and taking Grif's hand with the other. It was in the high nineties, hot and dry, but not as brutal as it would be by summer's end, so Kit counted it as cool. "It's close to the name Trey Brunk was trying to recall."

"Her memory is undoubtedly better than his, too," Dennis said, and sighed. "I'll follow up with her later today."

Kit said nothing. The last thing she needed was for Dennis to catch her out in a lie, so she made a mental note to contact Jann first. She needed to offer her condolences over Jeannie's death anyway. She only wished there was a way to assure her that her daughter was in a better place.

"Hey," she asked Dennis, "have you checked the pharmacies and hospitals to see if any bulk amount of codeine went MIA?"

"First thing," Dennis said, and Kit deflated a bit. "I'm thinking it'd be too much for a pharmacy heist. Plus, all hospital drugs are logged, computerized, and locked tight. I'm not saying it's impossible, but it'd be hard to make off with an entire cache of codeine without raising some notice."

"What if you were a doctor?"

"Tough, even if you were the hospital director," Dennis returned. "My hunch is the drugs were procured over time, in smaller increments."

"Well, I have an idea," Kit said, "but I don't have the resources to follow it."

"Something you can't do?" Dennis huffed over the line. "Please, tell me."

"Check with the gang unit. Just see if any of the old Mariel families have someone working in the hospitals or pharmacies. Particularly Marco Baptista's gang."

Alarm popped in his voice. "Have you been researching Baptista?"

Kit winced. She still hadn't mentioned to him the run-in in Little Havana. "I'd start with records and administration," she said, trying to deflect. "Maybe H.R."

"Stay away from him, Kit." The alarm was gone, this was pure warning from Dennis the cop, not her friend. Halting beneath an overgrown pine, Kit tracked a couple of ducks that'd strayed from the pond, but she didn't really see them. She was remembering Baptista's cold stare, and shivered despite the heat of the day.

"Shoulda told me that earlier, Dennis."

A hissed curse came over the line, followed by a deep sigh. "I shoulda known better when you were popping off about the Marielitos at the burlesque show."

"Just be careful," she told him.

"Follow your own advice," he shot back, and the line went dead.

Kit sighed as she put the phone away. "He's mad."

"He should be," Grif said as they crossed a vast expanse of turf frying under the full Vegas sun. "You're a damned nosy reporter, and he's taken a liking to you."

Kit looked away. Like a hound, could he sniff out the other man's interest now that he considered her his marked property? She hoped not. Evie's ghost shadowing their relationship was already problematic enough.

"You don't think the Russians are distributing the *krokodil*," Grif said, having overheard the conversation.

"I think it's someone who wants to make it look like the Russians," she said, as they crossed the sprawling park. But she couldn't prove it. She certainly couldn't go to the police and paper—or even say to Grif—that her biggest hunch that the Cubans were setting the Russians up was based on a pair of earrings. "And Bella is a much more common name in the Hispanic community."

They made their way from shady tree to shady tree until the large pond came into view. "I don't know, Kit. The old-school Marielitos are toughs, no doubt, but I was thinking on this, too, and I just can't see them releasing this drug into their own community. Do you really think they'd allow their own kids to rot and die just to see the Kolyadenkos go down?"

Kit shook her head. "They weren't their own kids. Jeannie Holmes and Tim Kovacs were as white-bread as they come. Even Jeap was considered an outsider. And, yes, I think they'd see the lives of a few junkie kids as a small price to pay to own the bulk of the drug activity in this city."

Grif mulled it over as they headed toward the man-made pond. The park had been built before water restrictions were placed on the valley, and the recreation department was possessively hanging on to every blade of grass—no matter how brown and matted it might be. Grif—already sweating and less sanguine about the heat—angled her toward the shade of a tree that had been growing there for at least as long as he'd been dead.

"Look," Kit said, pointing at a woman walking on the other side of the pond. The woman's back was to them as she made her way toward a shaded concrete bench, but Kit was still sure. They'd followed the woman from the home that was Mary Margaret's last known address.

"That don't look like Mary Margaret," Grif grumbled, pushing from the tree to join her side.

"She was twelve when you last saw her," Kit reminded him.

"This isn't ever going to work," Grif said, trailing her. "It's nutso."

"I'm walking next to an angelic human," Kit returned wryly. "My definition of crazy is more expansive than it once was."

"I'm not talking about you," Grif said. "I'm talking about little Mary Margaret."

"And Mary Margaret isn't little anymore," Kit pointed out, walking faster as they rounded the pond. "She's a sixty-two-year-old, rather mentally disturbed woman."

Grif wrinkled his nose. "She'd have to be, to believe in . . . what was it?"

"Hypnosis. And it doesn't matter what you think of it," she went on before he could speak. "You don't know anything about it."

"And you do?"

"Of course not." Kit's sidelong glance was askew. "But Mary Margaret doesn't know that. Plus, she's on medication, which she mixes with alcohol, and she's also had psychotic breakdowns in the past."

"So we're messing with the mind of a severely compromised mental patient."

"No, we're just easing her into a new reality," Kit reasoned. "Besides, you want to see a real mental breakdown, show up on her doorstep looking exactly as you did when she last saw you fifty years ago. An attempt at hypnotism—even if I don't know the first thing about it—will be far easier for her to grasp than your fallen angel act."

And, finally, he had nothing to say to that.

Despite the heat, and the sweat already popping on her forehead, Kit linked her arm through Grif's as they rounded the pond's west end. "Look, she's already haunted, Grif. The drugs, the alcohol, the institutional stays prove that. Maybe being visited by a literal blast from her past will be just the thing she needs to help her move on."

They paused next to a palm tree with shedding fronds, and Kit squinted at the place she'd last seen the retreating woman. There was no one else out, given the strength of the midday sun, but yes, there she was. Sitting on the shaded bench, feeding the squabbling ducks from a bread bag.

"Stay here. Make sure she doesn't see you."

"I still don't like it," Grif called after her, but Kit was already on her way.

No, Kit thought as she trudged toward the woman, donning vintage shades against the onslaught of the sun. There was nothing at all to like about this situation, but it wasn't as though they had a lot of options. Mary Margaret was the only person who might remember the lives and deaths of Griffin and Evie Shaw.

The thought made Kit's heart pick up speed. It was the first time she had met someone from Grif's first life. What if all Mary Margaret recalled was how perfect he and Evie were together? How much he'd loved his wife? Grif didn't need the reminder, and Kit didn't want it, but she'd risk it if it meant he could finally move on.

Trying to look casual, Kit crossed directly in front of the woman, and drew her own loaf of bread from her raffia handbag. She felt the woman's gaze on her as she unwound the twist tie, and dipped inside. Some of the ducks branched off from the gaggle surrounding Mary Margaret's bench to see if what Kit was proffering was any better. It was merely different, but they were ducks. They didn't care.

A voice finally said, "Why are you dressed that way?"

Kit glanced over to find the woman frowning at her. She was wearing either short capris or long shorts, with a sleeveless blouse that showed pale, freckled arms. The gray in her undyed hair frizzed around her face, lying damp on her neck, and deep lines fanned at the corner of squinting dark eyes. Kit smiled, despite the censure in the woman's voice. It was definitely Mary Margaret. "What way?"

"Like that," Mary Margaret said, jerking her head at Kit's swooping skirt. "Like the women used to dress in the fifties. I haven't seen a dress like that since I was a little girl."

"The good ones are practically impossible to find. I made this one myself from an old Butterick pattern. I've always wanted one in cream," Kit said, as though they were best girlfriends, then shrugged. "But I'm rockabilly. That's what we do, how we live."

Mary Margaret wrinkled her nose. "What do you mean, 'rockabilly'? Like . . . Elvis Presley?"

Nodding, Kit tore up another slice of the bread she'd just

bought. "It's a subculture. It originally grew out of love for the music, but we also celebrate the fashion and the cars and the homes . . . the whole lifestyle, really, of the mid-twentieth century."

Now Mary Margaret was looking at Kit like she was crazy. "Why?"

Kit was equally puzzled why someone would wear a pair of shoes as ugly as Crocs in public, but she was also used to people questioning her fashion choices. "Because it's fun to live nostalgically."

Mary Margaret's frown deepened as she held out a piece of bread to the duck closest to her feet. "I don't think it's fun," she said, as the duck tore at the bread and backed away. "I think the past is full of pain."

Kit dipped into her bag again. "I guess I just like to dream about how it used to be back when the world didn't move so fast. Before there were computers and cell phones and fast food on every corner. The world was a simpler place then. Kinda like this place." She squinted up into the vast baby-blue sky. "Peaceful."

Mary Margaret scoffed. "You're dreaming, girl. It wasn't simpler. It was as hot and hard and mean as any time since."

Kit said nothing for a while, just let the chasm between her worldview and Mary Margaret's widen in the silence. She waited until the woman had balled up the empty plastic bag, slipped it back in her purse, and was readying to stand.

"You're probably right," Kit said, sighing. "But I'm also a hypnotist, so it helps to be a dreamer. It's easier to get people to let go and travel in their minds if I remain flexible in mine."

She nodded to herself as she tossed a sliver of bread as far as she could, watching the two largest ducks race for the prize.

"I've been told that it's easier for people to let go of their inhibitions and fears with me than any other hypnotherapist they've visited. I take them back in time and help them see what happened with new eyes. Some of my patients go back so deeply that I can almost see what they're talking about, exactly as they do—what used to be, what was supposed to be, and . . . well, now I'm bragging. Sorry."

"No," Mary Margaret said, sitting again. "Go on."

Kit flipped her hair back over her shoulder, and said, "Well, I just think that there's real value in reflecting on the past. Honor what came before, and you're better able to face what comes next. Or so I've seen in my work."

The skepticism returned. "And how much does it cost to get hypnotized?"

"It varies." Kit emptied the crumbs from her bread bag onto the bank, then gave Mary Margaret a full smile as she joined her on the bench. The woman stiffened, but slid over after another moment. "I only charge full price for those with insurance. Otherwise I meet people where they're at. So I'll do a session in a person's home, if they want, and let them pay what they can. In the end, we're each better off for the experience. Sometimes I even do it for free."

"Nobody does anything for free," Mary Margaret said, her voice so hollow that Kit felt a skein of guilt weave its way through her chest. But the real harm had already been done in Mary Margaret's life. Kit and Grif might be mining it, but they weren't adding to it.

Shrugging, Kit stood. "It's an honor to be able to help others."

Waving her farewell, she began walking back the way she'd come, counting down from ten. She'd only reached six before Mary Margaret called out. "Would you work with me?"

Kit turned, bit her lip, and walked back a few paces. "I'm sorry if I misled you, but I'm not like one of those psychics with a neon red palm-reading sign in their window. I don't regress people for fun. I only work with those who have serious trauma to work through."

She turned to leave.

"I have demons." The words tumbled out, pitched and hurried. Mary Margaret was standing now, too, and when Kit turned, she was close. "I have things that haunt me when I shut my eyes, and talk to me in my sleep. I know I need to let them go, because my therapist—not one like you, but a real one—she says that's the only way to truly be free of the past. That otherwise I'm only here part-time, but . . . I don't know."

"What don't you know?" Kit asked, drawing closer.

Mary Margaret tilted her head, and the strong sun reached down to dapple her cheek. "Why does so much of life have to be about letting go?"

It was a good question. Not just for Mary Margaret or Grif, or anyone haunted by events in their past, but for Kit as well. What was worth hanging on to? What was worth fighting for? What to release? When?

Kit thought of her father, of Grif and Evie, and then Mary Margaret as well.

"Will you work with me?" the woman asked again, heat and shade fracturing the pleading expression on her face.

Kit smiled. She might not yet know what'd happened to her father, and Grif's feelings for Evie were ultimately out of her control, but maybe she could help this woman see that the past—and letting it go—didn't have to hurt so damned much.

"I'd love to," she said.

CHAPTER TWENTY-THREE

Grif shook his head. The idea of hypnotherapy was so hokey he didn't see how anyone could believe in it, yet not only had Kit convinced Mary Margaret to let her accompany her home, the woman had insisted she come immediately. Kit's beloved Duetto was too small for Grif to be able to ride along and remain hidden, so he was left to hoof it in the relentless summer heat, the sun a hot griddle on his head and back. He left his hat on—his old, real one replacing the fedora Yulyia Kolyadenko had commandeered—but he'd removed his coat. Holding it over his shoulder with his right hand, he studied his cell phone's map guidance, following the streets as Kit texted them. He was beginning to like the damned thing.

Yet if the Pures were looking down at him now, they were surely laughing. He probably looked like a rat in a maze. He certainly felt like one as he turned the corner of yet another nondescript street. Still, that didn't lessen the smug satisfaction he felt after reaching the street named on Kit's final text, and catching sight of the Duetto parked in the cracking driveway of a cul-de-sac corner.

It was a working-class neighborhood, and it appeared everyone was doing exactly that, but Grif still stole sidelong glances at the nearby houses before ducking into the shade on the home's east side. He'd wait there for a few minutes and let the women get settled. He wasn't sure what was needed to hypnotize someone, but if he knew dames, they'd probably fritter away a good ten minutes making small talk before getting down to business.

Grif lit a smoke, and shook his head. Hypnotherapy. Phooey. Not that he'd gotten anywhere by more traditional means. Even if Kit failed in getting any new information from Mary Margaret, it wouldn't hurt the case. "Because there is no case," he muttered, blowing smoke back into the heated air.

A bigger concern was spending time with a woman with multiple addictions. Scratch had Kit's number now, and had already proven it wasn't shy about showing up. Kit assured Grif she was willing to take that chance, if only because he'd be with her this time.

Finished with his stick, Grif rubbed it out on the gravel, then slipped alongside the garage, careful to keep his shadow from crossing the front-room windows, though the shades there were drawn tight. He tested the front door and found it locked, so he waved his hand over the bolt, and entered anyway.

The stunted foyer was more afterthought than entry, but Grif paused there, listening for signs of life. He also listened for animals, though he'd already instructed Kit to text him if a dog lurked inside. Deeming it safe, Grif followed the low murmur emanating from deeper within the house, footsteps silent on the thin brown carpeting. He needed to time his reappearance in Mary Margaret's life, and not only to help Kit glean what information they could from the troubled woman's memory. It was rude, he thought, to drop in like some overgrown bird—feathered and friendly, but shocking enough to send a fragile mind back into the loony bin. At least she wouldn't actually be able to *see* his wings.

A dark stain rounded to the right, indicating a high-traffic area, so Grif headed that way. Emboldened by the low exchange of voices, he peered into a living area containing pretty much what he'd expected. An old television propped atop particleboard. Mismatched coffee and side tables. A sofa draped in a dingy gray throw, and a rip that bulged with white against the dark leather.

Drawn toward the voices—or voice; it was only Kit's now—he continued down a hallway that branched off in three uninspired directions. A half-bath lay directly ahead, while the room he'd passed from outside sat dark on the right. The one containing Kit's soothing, low voice was on the left. Again, peeking first, he headed that way.

"The brooch I've given you is what we call a focus," Kit was saying. "It's from the fifties, so if you feel yourself distracted by any thought or slipping back into the present, just run your fingers over it. Give it a squeeze. You can look at it if you need to, but return to your relaxed state as quickly as possible."

"Okay," Mary Margaret answered.

"I'm going to count backward from ten, and by the time I'm finished I want you to tell me what you were doing in 1959."

Grif entered the room. Kit was seated on a wooden chair that had once been a part of a kitchen set, and Mary Margaret was reclined on the bed, eyes shut, brooch clasped tightly in hands that rested between her breasts. He placed a hand on Kit's shoulder as he crossed to the center of the room, causing her to jump and glare at him, though her voice didn't hitch as she continued her countdown. Grif didn't dare risk making any noise by sitting in the chair by the window, or spook Mary Margaret by dropping to the side of the bed, so he just stood at the foot of it, and waited.

"Okay, Mary Margaret," Kit said, having finished her back count. "It is 1959 now, the month of . . ." She looked at Grif, who mouthed the answer to her. "August. How old are you, and what are you doing?"

"I'm twelve years old," Mary Margaret answered immediately. That was right, and Grif tilted his head, wondering if this hypnosis crap really worked. Immediately, he decided it did not. Mary Margaret wanted to be put in a trance, and Kit had openly admitted she was relying on that deep desire. Why not? Grif thought. The drugs and booze obviously hadn't worked.

But what the hell had happened to her, he wondered, trying to spot the twelve-year-old he'd known. Why hadn't anyone cared for her? How could things have gotten so bad that she was surrounded by cast-off things, and worse, looked right at home among them?

"I'm sitting in my room," she said, as if she could see it, and it was happening right now. "It's all white . . . sham and sheets and curtains. I have a Cissy doll, and she's in white, too. I'd begged my father for her, but he said I was too young and I'd break her. But Uncle Sal got her for me, and even Dad didn't cross Uncle Sal. I took good care of her. We always dressed the same, but then she got lost . . ."

Mary Margaret's voice trailed off, and though she didn't open her eyes, her face scrunched up as if in pain.

"When did she get lost?" Kit asked.

"When I was taken."

Grif felt Kit look at him, but he didn't move. Mary Margaret's word choice unnerved him, too. Lost. Taken. All because of something in her past. Maybe their *shared* past.

"Tell me about that day, Mary Margaret."

The hands tightened around the brooch, but Mary Margaret kept her eyes shut, and her breathing gradually steadied, still unaware that Grif was standing there.

"It's afternoon. Broad daylight. Safest neighborhood in the city. Safest house in the world."

Yes, she'd been at her uncle's house, Sal DiMartino, the day she was taken, which made the abduction especially nervy. The niece of the city's biggest kingpin, taken from his own front yard.

"My mother and aunt are at their weekly ladies' league meeting. They say they play cards afterward, but they pack flasks in their totes. Mother covers hers with her scarf and gloves." One corner of her mouth quirked up. "Dad never asks her why she needs a scarf in the summer."

"And where is your uncle?" Kit pressed.

"In his study. My brother, Tommy, and Dad are with him. They have the door shut. I know to stay away when it's shut but I want to show Cissy to my uncle. I want him to see I'm taking care of her. She's wearing her gloves and her pearls . . ."

"So you enter the study?"

"Yes."

"And what does your uncle do?"

"Nothing. Uncle Sal never got angry. He smiles, and Tommy ruffles my hair, tells me my doll is real pretty, but Dad shoves me toward the door, and I stumble. He yells at Gina for letting me in."

"Who's Gina?"

"My nanny."

Kit looked at Grif, who nodded. The police had questioned Gina repeatedly in the days following Mary Margaret's disappearance, but she hadn't seen anything. Shortly after that, Gina disappeared as well.

"She's angry with me, too," Mary Margaret continued. Her voice was light now, thin as a twelve-year-old's limbs. "She makes me go out back to play and tells me she'll bring lemonade. But she's sneaking my aunt's gin while she can, and she takes too long, and I want to play on the tire swing out front, so that's where I go. Me and Cissy. Both of us in white."

"So you're alone in the front yard, on the swing," Kit said, earning only a nod. "Then what?"

"The car comes out of nowhere. I see him running toward me, and I try to scream but he's too strong and fast. I'm in the backseat, and I still can't find my voice. Why can't I find my voice?"

Though seated feet away, Kit reached out, as if to soothe her. The calming action threaded her words. "It's okay, Mary Margaret. You're telling your story right now. You *do* have your voice."

"I don't want to be here anymore." And this time her voice was small.

Kit glanced at Grif, clearly wondering the same thing he was: where exactly did she mean? He circled his hand in the air, telling Kit to speed up.

"Okay, Mary Margaret. Let's fast-forward. Tell me about the day you were found. Tell me about the man who found you."

The tension left the woman's body almost immediately, and her arms loosened. "He is stronger and faster than them all. He's gentler, too—with me, I mean. On the day they find me, he gets to me first, even though the guns are going off and the police are screaming and the men are dying. He's picking me up, and whispering in my ear. 'You're safe. You're a good girl. That's a good girl.'" She was breathing hard now. "It's over fast, and he's tucking my head into his arm so I can't see. He's so gentle, you know? Why didn't Daddy find me? Why didn't he come and save me?"

It was exactly what she'd asked of Grif then. He shut his own eyes, and swallowed hard. He hadn't known how to answer the twelve-year-old, and he didn't know how to answer Mary Margaret now, but he was going to have to tell her something, because when he opened his eyes again, she was staring directly up at him, her own gaze wide. She surprised him not by screaming or panicking, but by saying the same thing she said when he appeared fifty years earlier.

"Take me out of here. I don't want to be here anymore."

She was so calm about it that for a moment Grif wondered if she couldn't also somehow see his wings. After all, his job was to take the Lost souls home . . . like he'd taken her home before. But she wasn't dead, and her vision was merely mortal, because then she said, "You look exactly the same."

"I know."

"I had a crush on you," she added unexpectedly.

Sure, she had. She was twelve. He'd saved her life. "I know that, too."

"But they killed you anyway."

The room fell as silent as the past.

"Who killed him, Mary Margaret?" Kit finally said.

But she didn't answer. Mary Margaret was no longer in the past, yet she wasn't fully here, either. She was in her own world, and she looked worried and unbalanced . . . yet somehow comfortable with both. "If I'd just listened to Gina, if I'd stayed in the back, then I wouldn't have been stolen, and you wouldn't have to find me, and then they couldn't have said that you did those awful things."

"And what was that?"

"Raped me." The words gushed from her as if launched from her throat.

It took a long minute before Grif could unstick his tongue. "I didn't . . . I would never."

"I know. But Tommy didn't believe me."

"Tommy?" Grif shook his suddenly clouded head. He thought he'd been ready for the truth, but how could any man—any decent man—be ready for this? "Your brother?"

Mary Margaret nodded. "He came to me the night I returned. He thought I was sleeping . . . and I was at first. But he was crying, and I'd never heard my brother cry before, so that woke me up. He put his hands in my hair, and whispered in my ear. He said he had it on good word that you'd been in on it with the Salerno family, and that you'd turned on them when things went south. He said, 'That bastard Shaw bragged about how he hurt my little sister, but now he's going to get his, family-style.'"

Grif had to work to unclench his teeth. "Who was his source, Mary Margaret?"

"Tommy disappeared," she said, shaking her head. "The

same night you and your wife were killed. And that was my fault, too. If only I'd stayed in the backyard . . ."

Mary Margaret's face crumpled, and she began to cry, but Grif didn't hear her. *Tommy disappeared the same night you and your wife were killed.*

"Grif?" Kit said, breaking character, seeing him when she wasn't supposed to. But her voice was as far off as Mary Margaret's, and Grif heard only static. He saw a blurred shadow knocking him against a wall. He felt the searing heat of a blade splitting his belly. He felt that knife in his hand and he reacted, slashing blindly.

"It was Tommy." Grif's whisper came out in a harsh rasp. Tommy DiMartino, all of twenty-two years old, nephew to Las Vegas's biggest mobster, full of swagger and wearing driving gloves and fury in his eyes . . . he was the one who'd attacked Grif and Evie in the suite at the Marquis.

And Grif had killed him.

Grif glanced back at Mary Margaret, because she didn't seem to know that. She'd said only that Tommy had disappeared. So whoever had cleaned up the mess had erased all evidence of Sal DiMartino's nephew having died along with Evie and him.

So who had attacked Grif from behind? Who busted the vase over his head, spilling his brains and life out on that white marble floor? Who felled Evie, too?

Was it Sal? Had the old mobster shaken Grif's hand and thanked him for safely returning his niece, all while planning and plotting Grif's and Evie's deaths?

"Did your dad ever ask you about it?" Grif asked Mary Margaret.

She shook her head, looking unsettlingly lucid and coherent, as if her past and present always collided in such a way. Who knew? Maybe they did. "Dad didn't even want to think about it."

"And had Tommy told your uncle what I . . ." Grif licked his lips, but he couldn't say it. Rape a child. He couldn't even *think* through a thing like that. "What he said I did?"

Mary Margaret nodded. "My uncle brought me another Cissy doll to replace the one I lost. He asked me about you. Not outright, but I knew what he was getting at. I told him you were gentle, and you saved me, and you'd never hurt me." Wonder clouded her gaze. "You really were the only one who didn't hurt me."

"Did he believe you?"

"He wanted to. He liked you, admired you." Her nodding stilled. "Now that I think about it, I think he was even a little jealous of you."

"Jealous? Why?"

"Because you had a normal life. It was something he could never have despite all his money and connections, or probably because of them. You also had honesty and integrity. Clean hands. And that beautiful wife who looked at you like you hung the moon."

Grif swallowed hard, and didn't dare look at Kit.

"But when you and your wife and Tommy died, Uncle Sal had no choice but believe those rumors. He was sad about it for years."

It burned. It tore a hole right in his gut that the reputation he'd worked so hard to build had been leveled with one targeted falsehood. Someone had set him up and framed him, but he didn't know who, or why.

"And then what?"

Mary Margaret gave a humorless laugh. "And then nothing. Life went on. Everyone forgot, or pretended they did. Dad
stopped speaking about Tommy, but he also stopped looking
at me. Then I was sent away to Catholic boarding school, and
the reporters went away, too. Life went on."

For some, Grif thought coolly. "And Sal?"

"I only heard him speak about it once. Thanksgiving, many
years later. Isn't that always the happiest family holiday?" She
gave the same barking, dry laugh, and shook her head. "He was
down, we could all see it, and he excused himself, and his wife,
the new one, not my aunt," she clarified, as if either of them
were new any longer, "she followed him, I followed them. Back
to the same study. Back where I'd taken that damned doll."

Grif jerked his head. He didn't have patience for her senti-
mentality now. "What did he say?"

"That he missed Tommy, and missed the way things used
to be. That for all the power he had, he couldn't change the
past. That he still couldn't believe Griffin Shaw would do such
a thing. Barbara told him to buck up. That it didn't matter
anymore, and that Shaw mattered even less."

"She didn't like him?" Kit asked, forgetting herself again.
Again, Mary Margaret didn't notice.

She shook her head slowly, and the intensity of the movement matched her gaze. "She hated you."

Grif drew back. Why the hell did this woman Barbara,
whom he'd never met—or didn't remember meeting—hate
him so much?

Mary Margaret shrugged. "You must have done something
awful to her. She won't tell me what, but it was bad enough
that her hate has lasted all these years."

For a moment, Grif thought she was getting her past and

present mixed up. He didn't even believe in hypnosis, and he was suddenly having a hard time distinguishing the two. Thankfully, Kit was fully present. "What do you mean, all these years?"

"Oh, she still gets plenty riled up over him." Mary Margaret let loose another of her dark, bitter laughs, then ran a hand over her face. "But at least someone isn't pretending they don't remember."

Kit and Grif looked at each other.

"You mean you're still in contact with your aunt Barbara?" Kit finally said.

"She's the only one who came to visit after my last big breakdown. We don't talk much, but she sends birthday and Christmas cards." Mary Margaret sat up in bed suddenly, squinting at the brooch in her hand like she'd forgotten it was there. "She said something strange the last time I talked to her, though. It rolled around in my mind, kinda itchy-like, you know?"

Grif didn't even trust himself to speak.

"We were talking about Vegas, all the changes and the economy and how nobody cares about their community or neighbors anymore, and the conversation shifted to how it used to be. I said that my childhood was idyllic, but then it changed, and it was all my fault. Funny thing was, she didn't disagree. All these years of people telling me that what happened wasn't my fault, and she just sat there, nodding."

"What a bitch," Kit said, surprising them all.

Mary Margaret looked at Kit for a long moment, gaze clearer than it'd been since they'd arrived. She finally laughed. "Yes. Yes, she is."

That seemed to surprise her, and she kept laughing until tears streamed from the corners of her eyes. "After I'd cried a bit, and she just sat there, letting me, she finally said that the past didn't matter anyway. That even though the Salerno gang had tried to use me to get to Uncle Sal, I wasn't a plaything, like a doll. I wasn't used. I was chosen."

"Chosen?"

"To bring Griffin Shaw down, she said." Mary Margaret stared directly at Grif. "And that I was special because of it."

Grif was clenching his jaw so hard his temples began to throb. Mary Margaret's gaze darted between Grif and Kit, and at last she said, "I'm not sure . . . but I think I've hurt you in some way, Mr. Shaw." Then confusion overtook her again. "I just don't know how."

Sighing, Grif stopped short of reaching out to her. He'd held her in his arms once, and told her she was safe, and look where that had got them both.

"You didn't hurt me, Mary Margaret," he said, and watched as her eyebrows tilted in surprise. Her eyes suddenly shimmered with tears. She seemed to deflate, fifty years of guilt sliding from her shoulders, and for the briefest moment he actually saw the scrawny, freckled kid she used to be—and the woman she *should* have been—all rolled up in one. Shaking his head, Grif offered up his own bittersweet smile. "They did."

CHAPTER TWENTY-FOUR

Y ou were sweet with her," Kit said, as they left the dark, womb-like confines of Mary Margaret's modest home, emerging once again into the sun's blistering heat. "Most people would just see a crazy woman."

"I see a Lost one," Grif murmured, knowing that his death long ago was partly to blame. Poor Mary Margaret, having that crime hoisted on her shoulders. And damn Barbara DiMartino for putting it there.

Kit followed his thoughts. "But we got a lead."

Clearing his throat, Grif tried to do the same with his expression. It wouldn't do to get emotional now. "Yep."

Barbara DiMartino—now Barbara McCoy. She'd married again at some point in the past fifty years. Grif knew this because Mary Margaret gave Kit the envelope from one of the woman's birthday greetings. It had McCoy's address, handwriting, and—though he hadn't opened it yet—a photo, too. Grif would finally know exactly who this woman was, and why she thought Evie and he deserved to die.

Sliding into the Duetto's passenger seat, Grif's heart beat against his chest, and rang in his ears. Kit's small car seemed to close in around him, not like a womb but a vise. His fingers trembled slightly against the envelope, which Kit surely saw as she keyed the ignition, though she said nothing. Pursing his lips, he glanced down and spied the edges of a photo—greenery, and water—either a lake or the ocean—and a white silk shirt on an arm propped against a hip. The arm of this Barbara, he thought, withdrawing it slowly. The arm of . . .

Kit's phone rang. Buddy Holly's "Oh, Boy." A tune Grif recognized from both past and present. Gritting his teeth, Grif dropped his hands, slapping the envelope against his thigh. "What does he want now?"

Kit raised her chin in response—he knew that blasted look—and answered the phone. "Hey, Dennis . . ."

Grif rolled his eyes. It was petty, he knew, but it felt intrusive to have another person in this car, in this moment. This was between Grif and Kit. Grif and Barbara. Grif . . . and Evie.

"Grif is here," Kit continued, flat gaze trained on Grif's face, like she was still reading his thoughts. He swallowed hard, and put the card aside for now. "He says hi."

Grif pulled a face. Very funny.

Yet Kit quickly grew serious. "Sure. Hold on."

She pressed a button on her phone Grif didn't even know existed, and static of background noise filled the tiny car. Grif hadn't known the phone could be set to speaker.

"You're on," Kit told Dennis.

"Do you guys want the good news or the bad news first?"

Excitement scored Dennis's tone, which of course decided things for Kit. Sighing, Grif tucked the card and photo into his jacket pocket. He'd have to wait until the future to look into his past.

"Good first. Always," she answered for them.

"I found Bella."

Jerking straight in her seat, Kit beaned her head on the Duetto's soft top. "No way. How? When? What did she say?"

"Let the man answer at least one of the questions," Grif muttered.

"After you gave me Bella's name, I cross-referenced it with the files we have on Marco Baptista and his crew. A Bella Maria Sanchez is the niece of one of Baptista's highest-ranking lieutenants, Manuel Sanchez. Mr. Sanchez has been employed for the last three years in the Sun Valley Care and Rehabilitation Center. He's a P.A."

"Physician's assistant," Kit whispered to Grif, then in a normal voice said, "And did you check to see if any large caches of codeine have gone missing under Mr. Sanchez's watch?"

"He's squeaky-clean," Dennis said, causing Kit to slump. "But a little more poking showed three more of Baptista's men similarly employed at rehab hospitals all over the valley."

"A very healthy bunch, these gangsters," Kit observed, easing from Mary Margaret's driveway.

Dennis hummed his agreement. "Yet they were clean as well."

"So what good is it to us?" Grif said, cutting to the chase.

Kit shot him a hard look as she left the cul-de-sac, but Dennis seemed pleased he'd asked. "Listen, my grandmother had a stroke a few years back and ended up in one of these places. She was so out of it she had no idea what year it was, never mind what drugs she was on. She certainly wouldn't know if they *weren't* giving them to her. One call to the narcs confirmed it . . . it happens all the time."

"So you think Baptista's crew has been pilfering from their patients? Stockpiling codeine for . . . what? Years?" Kit said, now thoughtful.

"A good three years, if my math holds up."

"That's about a year after the Kolyadenkos started coming on strong," Kit replied.

"Exactly."

"It would fit," Kit mused, biting her lower lip, slipping the Duetto through a yellow light.

"Sounds like you need to pay the Sanchezes a little visit," Grif told Dennis, intrigued despite himself.

"I'm here now."

"They actually spoke with you?" Kit said.

"That's the bad news," Dennis said. "I'm waiting for backup, along with the coroner to confirm, but the front door was slightly open so I knocked. When there was no answer I entered and found Bella, Manuel, and three others with point-blank shots to the head."

"Recent?" Grif asked.

"Very."

"And the rest of the joint?"

"Untouched."

Quick. Brutal. Passionless. A worry moved through Grif's belly. "So someone just came in, calmly shot them, and left?"

"Came in, *lined them up,* calmly shot them, and left."

Five homicides related to a case he was working on, and Sarge hadn't called him in for one of the Takes. Grif's worry intensified.

"Give me the address," Kit said, as they sped past the park where they'd encountered Mary Margaret.

"Well, that's why I called." Dennis's voice grew strange, and he grunted like he was picking something up. "I thought you might already know it."

Kit stomped the brakes, nearly bringing the car to a stop in the middle of the street before winging to the side. A horn blared as the car behind them sped past. Tilting her head, she said, "Why would you say that?"

"Because Grif's hat is here."

Kit and Grif turned to stare at each other. Then they both looked back at the phone in Kit's hand.

"His hat . . . ?" Kit began, but Grif cut her off.

"Get out of there," he said. His voice came out quieter than he'd intended, so he repeated himself. "Get out now."

"Sure. I haven't touched anything else, but the analysts will be here soon," Dennis responded, with more authority and less urgency than was needed. *Get out!* Grif wanted to scream. "You should probably come to—"

Come to?

Nothing.

Kit and Grif leaned forward. "Dennis?"

"What the hell is—?" Dennis mumbled.

Then a scuffle, the sound of the phone dropping, and the connection went dead.

"Oh God." Kit fumbled the phone as she redialed. "God. It's her, isn't it?"

Grif's voice came out hoarse. "She had my hat."

And now Yulyia Kolyadenko had Dennis.

* * *

It was all Kit's fault.

"Damn!" She hung up as Dennis's voice message sounded on the line, then punched redial. She wished he'd given her the address to Manuel Sanchez's home. Then she'd be driving there instead of sitting roadside, stymied and useless. Then she could do something.

"You need to call the cops," Grif said, as the phone continued ringing throughout the car. Kit was so focused that she actually jumped when he put his hand on her arm. "Call the cops," he said, when she looked up and met his eyes.

But the ringing stopped abruptly, replaced a moment later by the sound of a steady, insistent beep. Then the beeping faded and a voice came through the speakerphone, melodious but short, and utterly devoid of emotion. "Put Mr. Shaw on the line."

Holding the phone out to Grif, Kit closed her eyes and tried not to weep.

"I'm here." He held the phone crooked for Kit to hear.

"Good," Yulyia Kolyadenko said. "I thought it was you. I thought . . . you must want your hat back."

"Keep it," Grif said shortly. "I'll take the man."

"You will take what I am giving you, Mr. Shaw," Yulyia responded, accent severely clipped. "Just like everyone else. Do you understand?"

Kit watched Grif's jaw clenched as he swallowed. "Yes."

"So this reporter, this woman slandering my name in the papers, the one in bed with the Baptistas, she is the one you are with now?"

"She's not in bed—"

"I am asking for a simple yes or no only."

Kit nodded at Grif's troubled glance. "Yes."

"And did you tell her what I said?"

Grif shook his head, though the woman couldn't see it. "About?"

"Our burden as women. About how we must choose fate before it is chosen for us?"

Grif's eyes moved to Kit's. "I'll tell her now."

"But too late," Yulyia said. "Because now I am making choices for us all. For the dirty Cubans who are setting me up. For this stupid policeman who dares question me about my world, my business. And for you, who are working with him."

"We just want to stop the killing," Grif tried.

"If that were true? You would have never threatened me." Silence loomed on the line, and Kit and Grif waited. "No, the problem is, you think you know who I am. You sat across from me in my own car and called me calculated and driven and a realist. Realist. That is funny. But if you really knew me?"

A pause.

"Yes?" Grif said, because they all knew she wanted him to ask.

"You'd never come near me at all." The sound muffled as she snapped instructions in Russian that Kit couldn't understand. Despite that, an image of Dennis being dragged from a dingy, blood-splattered room flashed in her mind. She shut her eyes.

The sound cleared and Yulyia said, "You came to me with question. You wanted to know who hurt your newswoman friend. Then you said you respect women."

"I do."

"But Marco Baptista does not."

"We already know he's the one who attacked Marin Wilson," Grif assured her. "And we know he was setting you up."

"We also know that he introduced *krokodil* into this city to put the heat on your *bratva,*" Kit added, thinking it would help.

"Yet you do so little, you two people who know so much," Yulyia snapped back, unappeased. "That is main difference between us, I think. You know Baptista is dealing this disgusting drug, and you have nerve to question me. But I see it . . . and I make it stop."

"How?" Grif asked.

"That's what you need to figure out now, isn't it?" Yulyia said. "But know this: a viper's poison does not show on the outside. Not like Baptista's *krokodil.* Instead, it roils inside, hot like a fever, until it strikes you down. This is how I will attack Baptista. I will burn him from inside out."

That didn't sound different from Baptista's *krokodil* at all, but Kit wasn't going to say so to Yulyia. She couldn't put Dennis at risk.

"I hope you listened when I told you to keep looking forward," Yulyia continued, as if reading Kit's thoughts on Dennis. "Detective Carlisle is counting on you. Understand?"

It sounded final. It sounded like she was going to hang up.

"Wait—" Kit tried . . . because she had to try.

"No police," Yulyia barked over her, and the line went dead.

"Dammit." Kit looked at her phone, then slapped the steering wheel. "Dammit! She didn't give us anything!"

"Sure she did."

Kit glanced at Grif like he was crazy. "What?"

"She just told us she's going after Marco Baptista. The warning was to stay away and keep quiet. No paper. No police. Then Marco is gone and the whole issue of *krokodil* in the valley goes away, too."

Kit shook her head. "What about Dennis?"

Grif said nothing.

Kit searched his face, but his features were carefully blank. "Grif?"

He finally shook his head. "Let's hope she's just using him as bait."

Subtext: let's hope the Viper hadn't yet struck.

Forcing air through her nose, into her lungs, Kit sat and breathed and thought. Then she swung the car around in a sharp U-turn.

"Where are you going?" Grif's expression wasn't so blank now.

Kit didn't answer.

"Kit? What are you thinking?"

She felt so stupid for not having seen it or thought of it before. "Little Havana."

"What about it?"

She shook her head as she said, "It's under renovation, Grif. It has been for weeks."

"A perfect place to hide chemicals like paint thinner and propane."

"Not just hide them," Kit said. "It's their kitchen."

This is how I will attack Baptista. I will burn him from inside out.

"Stop the car," Grif ordered, his voice emanating from a deeper place in his throat than before.

Kit kept going.

"Stop the car, Kit," he repeated, clipping his words this time. "Because wherever you're going, whatever you're thinking, plasma is suddenly thickening around you."

Kit double-glanced at him. "Plasma? Like when you first met me? Like when . . . ?"

"When you were destined to die."

Kit eased up on the gas. Maybe Grif was right. Maybe they should leave Yulyia alone, and Marco to his fate, and hope she would let Dennis live. Just hope.

"That's better," Grif said, studying the air around her with squinted eyes. "Yes. That's just fine."

But Dennis was a friend, a good one. She could see him now: the way he carried his beer, Pabst dangling between two fingers, a lopsided grin on his face, pomade thick in his blunt-cut hair. Yulyia had him, this man who wore creepers and cuffed jeans, a comb in his back pocket, ciggies rolled in his T. He was a good man. The Viper had him.

And she *was* taking him to Little Havana. Grif's ability to sense the supernatural plasma told them that much. What it didn't tell them was how to stop it.

"You can call the cops," Grif finally said.

Kit shook her head. "She warned us to stay away. No police."

And no write-up in the paper after it was all said and done, Kit realized. Not unless they wanted to share Dennis's fate.

"But maybe we can save Dennis that way. And Marco and Yulyia will both get what's coming to them."

Kit thought about it. Yes, it might work. They might possibly rid the city of both the *bratva* and the Cuban gang in one fell swoop. Then Kit could write whatever she pleased. The truth would be out. Las Vegas would be safer than it was before.

But would Dennis live?

"No, Kit," Grif said immediately. The damned plasma must have returned even before she tightened her grip on the steering wheel. "I will sit on you before I let you anywhere near that restaurant."

"Then you'll have bite marks on your ass." The Duetto growled as she accelerated. "She didn't take Dennis just to kill him. She took him to make a point."

"The point is that she can touch anyone she wants at any time."

"But he's alive right now, and we need to help him."

"That's what you said about Jeap Yang, remember?"

"No!" Kit slammed her palm against the steering wheel. She refused to accept that this was the same, or that Dennis's death was already fated. "This is my friend!"

"It's not that simple," Grif argued. "Don't forget that Scratch is dialed in to your emotions. It'll also know if you're injured. So, yeah, it's Dennis, but it's also you. And it's me, too."

"Don't worry, Grif." The words were out of her mouth before she even knew they were on her tongue. "I don't expect you to go in. I know exactly where your priorities lie."

Kit held her breath. It felt like the oxygen had been expelled from the car anyway. She took a hard right. Almost there.

"What the hell's that mean?" Grif finally said.

"It means," Kit said, the grit in her voice matching his, "that if I do as you ask, do *nothing,* then I'll always wonder if I could have stopped it. And you will, too, because unlike Marco and Yulyia, and the violent paths they've chosen, this man is innocent!"

She let that hang between them as they waited for the light to turn green, and when it did, she followed Yulyia Kolyadenko's instructions: she kept looking forward. Moving through the intersection, picking up speed as Grif remained silent, she navigated the most direct route to Little Havana.

Choose our fates before they're chosen for us.

Well, Kit thought, maybe Yulyia had a point. And maybe, if they arrived at Little Havana first, they could do just that.

Something is going to happen. The woman knows it like she knows the beat of her own heart, because that is her gift, and so she begins to prepare. The only reason she takes time to answer Tomas's call is because she knows he has related information. Even the stupid Anglo can be used by the saints to carry her a vital message. That is the greatness of their strength.

"Don't tell me you've lost the reporter," she says in greeting, slipping her beaded necklace over her head.

"No, but I've had to pull back." Tomas's voice is unusually strained, causing the woman to look up from the table where she's gathered herbs, mini-sculptures, and bowls. "I'm using a tracer on her car instead of visual. That man who's with her, Griffin Shaw, he's sharp."

"And the problem?" Because this man only calls when there is a problem.

Tomas's swallow sounds loudly over the line. "They're on the move now . . . and I think they're headed back to Naked City."

And there it is. The knowledge inside her forms into a hard ball of certainty, rising in her chest like it has wings, and she is suddenly blessed with clarity. This is how it will happen: the two nosy investigators will arrive. There will need to be a prayer offered up to the orishas before that, then a ritual to ensure that her divine actions are concealed from the outside world. But then a deep cleansing can take place. The evil spirits that have beset her household of late will be banished, and the saints will finally be appeased.

"Want me to stop them?" Tomas asks, still under the illusion that this is a worldly concern. But Josepha Baptista has the gifted awareness of a high priestess. She can hear the saints calling to her, their voices slipping into her ear like the warm wind of her homeland. Sure, she wants to act quickly as well, but Josepha hasn't grown this old, this powerful, or this feared by giving in to impulse.

"No. Enough is enough. Let them come if they're intent on doing so. Today they will have the answers they seek. They won't like them, they certainly won't live to tell them, but they will know."

And then they will offer up their blood as a cleansing rite to her beloved Chango.

"I'll call the others," Tomas says in a voice so cowed that Josepha wonders if he'll come at all.

"Yes, do that" is all she says, because it doesn't matter. The orishas will deliver Tomas to her, too. "Meanwhile, I will end this once and for all."

CHAPTER TWENTY-FIVE

The front entrance of Little Havana was draped with a construction canopy and scaffolding. Usually meant for customers, it was blocked off for now, so Kit eased the Duetto around the corner for a look at the back, and the service entrance. The tall, dented steel door stood in stark contrast to the gleaming black stretch limo that was parked diagonally across the lot. It was out of place in this neighborhood, but even more noteworthy was the way it was being studiously ignored. All the curtains and windows and blinds were closed tight in the surrounding homes.

Grif shook his head and Kit kept driving, bringing the car to a stop two blocks from the restaurant. Silence engulfed them when she cut the engine, and she turned to Grif. "So what did you see?"

"Plasma spinning around the building like a cosmic web of silk."

Kit waited. Grif clenched his jaw, because he didn't want to say, but she already knew there was more. "And two Centurions on the roof."

She let her eyes close for just one moment, the knowledge that two deaths were imminent sinking in like quicksand. Grif thought it might give her pause, yet when she opened her eyes again, her hand immediately moved to the door. Grif settled a hand on her shoulder and pulled her back. "Did you hear me? There's plasma everywhere—"

"And Russians with guns," she added coolly. "And a Cuban drug lord likely inside. And Dennis trapped somewhere in between."

"You forgot something else," Grif told her.

"Did I?" she snapped back.

"The fallen angel who is stalking you." He shifted, squaring on her despite the confines of the car. "You can't be injured, Kit. Scratch will know. You can't get emotional. It will use it, and once it's in you . . . I don't know if I can get it out."

They stared at each other for a long time after that, or maybe it just felt that way. Loaded moments always did. Grif'd known enough of them in his two lifetimes, so he finally just swallowed hard, gripped the back of Kit's neck, and kissed her hard enough to have explosions going off behind his eyelids.

But not hard enough to displace the plasma toying with the strands of her raven hair.

When Grif pulled back, he tried to smile. "Stay away, baby. Stay safe. And remember"—he chucked her under her chin, hoping to lighten things up—"mind that temper."

Slipping from the car before either of them could change
their minds, Grif could only pray the reminder that Scratch
was angling to possess her would keep her safe. Meanwhile,
with Yulyia holding court out back, he was going to have to
enter Little Havana through the front entrance. With any luck,
the Russians hadn't gotten inside yet.

So, licking the taste of Kit from his lips, he used her flavor to
fortify himself as he ducked low and rushed across the scarred
pavement. Hidden by the scaffolding and tarp, he waved his
hand across the restaurant's front door, and the lock snicked
open. A moment after that, he was inside.

Kit's gaze remained on Grif's back until he disappeared
around the block. Then she got out of the car. Nothing had
changed about the neighborhood since their last visit. Glass
shards still winked up at her from weed-choked lots, and the
pool at the Shangri-La apartments was still murky, sparkling
with heat.

The only real difference, Kit decided, was the people. Or
lack thereof. Because while the rubberneckers had been out
in force the day they'd found Jeannie and Tim, the street was
strangely silent now. One might blame it on the heat, but not
with the activity going on behind Little Havana. There was a
limo nobody could miss, yet everyone was pretending not to
see it. If a turf war was about to begin, Kit didn't want to sit
here blind. She'd rather see it coming.

So she left the car where it was and headed in the direction of the back lot. Spotting a pair of Dumpsters belonging
to Little Havana, she decided she could watch from there, and
call the police—or Grif, already somewhere inside—if need
be. She made it just in time, too. The driver's door of the limo

finally opened, and Kit imagined the neighborhood holding its breath. A man in a black suit, liveried but bulky and carrying a pistol in one hand, stepped from the car, glanced around, then held open the car's rear door.

A moment later, Yulyia Kolyadenko emerged, lovely in a lavender pantsuit, gold winking at her neck and wrist, and holding a small dog. She certainly hadn't dressed for murder, Kit decided, and for some reason the thought struck her crazily, and made her want to giggle. That's when Yulyia shifted, and Kit's manic nervousness froze in her throat.

Yulyia did not wrinkle her beautiful nose at the boiling stench wafting from the Dumpsters, and her face remained placid as she scanned the nearest homes, even though a few curtains had shifted. Her pretty mouth twitched upward at that, and she tilted her head to the sky, and inhaled deeply.

Kit watched her, amazed. Yulyia had said on the phone that what differentiated her from Kit was that she acted when Kit did not, but that wasn't it at all. Kit acted—she was doing so now—but the woman before her did so without fear, without conscience, and without emotion. Kit, on the other hand, was like the dog in Yulyia's arms. A shivering thing, all emotion, all the time.

Because of that thought, Kit's gaze was glued to the dog as Yulyia placed the shivering creature back in the limousine right next to another of her possessions. This one was bound and gagged, with a bright red, swollen eye that shifted to follow the Russian, as attuned to the danger around him as the dog that disappeared into the car's long belly.

Kit let out a relieved sigh. Dennis was alive.

A second man emerged from the car, and Kit waited for more, but Yulyia snapped instructions to both him and the driver, pointing in opposite directions. The men split, one to the building, the other to the trunk. The driver carried a crudely hewn plank, which he wedged between the door handle of the restaurant and the pavement. A rudimentary tool, but effective. When he yanked the handle, it didn't move.

He nodded back at Yulyia.

Meanwhile, the second man reemerged with two large plastic fuel containers, one in each hand. While Yulyia strode forward and tested the jammed door herself, the two men split and began dousing the building.

I'll burn him from the inside out.

Kit searched frantically around her for her own rudimentary tool, one that could cut Dennis's bindings, and fast. A few long nails and large octagonal bolts lay at the edge of the Dumpster but—surprise, surprise—no knives or box cutters. Leaning to the far side, she spotted something shiny, though, wedged under the corner. A scrap of tin of some sort, maybe from the roof or a kitchen hood. Grasping it with both hands, she tugged it from the weight of the Dumpster, careful not to make it squeal as she pulled. The scrap tore and left her with little more than a comb-size, jagged piece of metal.

It would have to do.

Glancing between the unguarded car and the jammed door where Yulyia stood guard, Kit figured if she slipped around the Dumpster's edge, she'd be in Kolyadenko's blind spot. It was her chance to *act*, Kit thought, and when the men disappeared around opposite sides of the building, she did just that.

Bent low, Kit swallowed down her fear, and ran as fast as she could. She had opened the door and ducked into the still-cool limo within seconds. Kit shushed Dennis, who'd startled and turned, eyes growing saucer-wide when he saw her. Bound body weight, Kit soon realized, was like dead body weight, and Dennis outweighed her by almost a hundred pounds. He tried to help, inching backward caterpillar-style, but it was a struggle to lift him and still remain low. Showing Dennis the makeshift knife, Kit pressed it on the thick duct tape between his hands, yet the little fur ball rat-dog kept biting at her as she worked the metal.

"Stop it," Kit hissed, pushing the dog away. She could smell the gasoline now, its oily potential thick in the summer heat. Dennis must have smelled it, too, because he suddenly angled away, and shook his head. *Go,* he mouthed through the material pulling at his cheeks. The little dog head-butted her shoulder. Kit gritted her teeth and kept cutting.

Suddenly, the opposite door jerked wide, and arms stronger than hers yanked Dennis back. It was the driver, steely-gazed as he locked eyes with Kit. Barking guttural Russian, he bared teeth.

Kit hurried out the other door of the limousine, emerging with one hand cupped around the little dog's belly . . . and the other around its throat.

Yulyia stiffened in surprise when she spied Kit. Not such a big difference between us after all, Kit thought.

"Let him go," Kit said, heart thudding as she backed from the car.

The driver spat something unintelligible and began dragging Dennis backward.

But Yulyia yelled, "Stop!" and Kit thought, How odd to care more for a dog than a man.

"You want a trade, is that it?" Yulyia said, stepping away from the building.

Kit's pulse beat so hard it almost burst behind her lids, and the small animal's shaking had somehow transferred to her limbs. She wondered briefly if fear was an emotion that Scratch could use against her, and had to quickly push the thought away. "Yes. The man for the dog."

It was an insane trade, but then Yulyia had just killed an entire family. Kit wondered if the woman had been holding her dog while doing so, and that's why the animal trembled so. Yulyia's pretty blue eyes flickered, and for a moment it looked like she would agree. But when she only lifted her chin, instinct told Kit to turn around.

He was a dark blur in full sprint, but Kit recognized the second Russian just as he seized her, gasoline-soaked hands embracing her from behind. Yulyia screamed something about the dog as Kit fell, and he jerked her violently so she landed on her side, the dog safe. Then he whipped her back upright like a puppet, tucking the now-whining animal beneath his other arm.

"Good, Sergei." Yulyia reached for the plank beneath Little Havana's door handle and said to Kit, "Looks like there will be no trade after all."

"You don't have to do this," Kit tried, feet trailing for purchase as the Russian dragged her forward. Her eyes met Dennis's, and she saw the fear she felt laid bare in his gaze.

"Of course not," Yulyia said coolly, regarding them both. "I don't do anything I don't want to do. It is a good position for a woman, no?"

Kit shook her head. "Please—"

Yulyia scanned the empty parking lot as she stepped aside. "Throw the man in with Baptista. I want them to long for the flame even as it burns around their ears."

Kit had no idea what that meant, but she could intuit Sergei's response. *And this one?*

Yulyia waved her hand, gold bangles catching fire at her wrist in the sun. "Put her anywhere. She will escape . . . or she won't."

"No—!" Kit struggled, as the driver and Dennis disappeared inside, but even one-handed Sergei was too strong for her. Catapulted over the oily threshold, Kit landed in the dank hallway with such force she heard the crack of bone. Pain shot through her core and for a moment she could only curl into herself and relearn how to breathe. Then, moaning, she looked back at the open doorway.

"You disappoint me, Ms. Craig." Yulyia pulled out a lighter as Sergei rejoined her side.

"Please," Kit whimpered. "No . . ."

Yulyia withdrew a gold cigarette case from her pocket. "I have read your paper and thought you were smart in your own way, but as your man would surely tell you, smart isn't enough. This world requires a realist. By the way, where is Mr. Shaw?"

Kit didn't answer. Sergei, still holding the small dog tight, grunted and stepped toward Kit, but Yulyia halted him with a hand on his chest. "Maybe in your next life you will get to choose your own fate, Ms. Craig."

Flicking open the lighter, which flared in a slim scarlet glow, she smiled as she lit her cigarette. She must have expected Kit to flee into the belly of the building, but Kit remained frozen in place, her gaze newly fixed on the figure rising behind Yulyia and Sergei.

Specifically on the semiautomatic splitting their silhouettes in two.

Sergei sensed the danger first and drew his weapon even as he turned. A single gunshot cracked through the neighborhood. Yelping, the little dog slipped from Sergei's grasp, paws splashing fuel as it hit the ground and barely missed being crushed by the falling Russian. A red flower bloomed in Sergei's chest, opening quickly. The dog fled past Kit into the building, and Yulyia barely caught herself as she made to lunge.

Though she straightened, her pretty features were blasted wide as she watched the dog disappear. Without one glance at her fallen comrade, she slowly turned.

Now Kit began edging backward. Forget the petrol shining like black death in front of her. A dozen Cubans fanned the doorway in a lethal arc. Yulyia turned to face them alone.

"So we finally meet," she said as the woman in the middle stepped forward.

"And for that you can thank Ms. Craig," Josepha Baptista said, giving Kit a closed-mouthed smile. "After all, she's the one who led me here."

CHAPTER TWENTY-SIX

J osepha is a master at reading the power, or *ashe*, stoking any situation, and immediately sees what Yulyia Kolyadenko has in mind: a fire that will consume Little Havana, and—whether the Russian knows it or not—half the neighborhood with it.

Normally Josepha wouldn't object to a little flame. Fire is her greatest natural ally in her work as a priestess. She is adept at reading the light in candles, and using that power for spiritual cleansing and magical spells. She is a master at mixing incense and salts and herbs and oils to magnify the ability to control human behavior, but most of all, she enjoys the sizzle of freshly spilled blood fueling a leaping flame. It is a powerful way to transfer magic from the divine orishas to herself, and a purifying tool as well.

But Josepha knows she is not in control of this potential

fire—not yet—and she has to tread softly in this situation. Her dear Marco is somewhere inside Little Havana.

"Come to see our little kitchen, Kolyadenko?" Josepha says.

Yulyia takes a long drag, then leans against the doorframe, cigarette dangling low. "*Nyet.* I thought I'd do the cooking today."

Josepha has to give it to her. Outnumbered ten to one, and she still acts as though the saints favor her. If only all of Josepha's men had such balls. "But you're burning everything, you stupid bitch."

"I didn't say I was good cook." Yulyia shrugs, then purses her lips like she's just had an idea. "But we could ask Marco to teach me. He's just inside, you know."

Josepha's gaze drops to the ash lengthening on Yulyia's cigarette. Damn Marco for being so lazy, cooking the shit every Monday afternoon. It makes him predictable. But the *pendejo* can't get up in the middle of the night to work. Has to drink his *cerveza* and grab his crotch and watch those reality shows where nothing is real. How many times has she told him, habit is what defines a person. His reply? Stop reading all those self-help books.

But who will help you, Josepha thinks, if you don't help yourself?

She should just leave him to his predictable death. Should . . . but won't.

"And you are one tiny step away from the same fate, Kolyadenko. Drop that cigarette, and you burn, too."

"But then your secret is out," Yulyia says, taking another drag. "Everyone will know you've been cooking up *krokodil* on the same shiny stainless steel stove as your *frijoles*. Will your patrons like sipping propane along with their *postres*?"

"They will like the new kitchen it has paid for." Josepha smiles a grotesque smile.

"You are counting chickens before they hatch." Yulyia brings a lighter from behind her back, and flicks the flame. "One more step, and there goes the neighborhood."

The two women stare at each other, taking measure, their hatred and admiration mingling in equal degree. Question is, which of them is willing to set the world to burn?

Grif left the lights off in the restaurant's dining room, not that he could find them in the construction anyway. But even with his enhanced eyesight, his need for stealth had him sticking to the shadows. His gun was drawn, the same .38 that'd been strapped to his ankle when he died, but there were only four chambered bullets. Using them didn't concern him. Come four-ten in the morning, all four bullets would be back in place, just as they'd been when he died. What concerned him was staying alive until then.

Keeping to the walls, Grif came upon a hallway with two bathrooms, which he checked, but they yielded nothing. He moved quicker after that, back into the restaurant and to a side door. Locked. Cute, Grif thought, waving it open. Less amusing was what he found inside.

"So this is where death is cooked," Grif muttered, surveying the storage area. Oil solvent and lighter fluid were neatly stacked in combustible piles while gasoline and paint thinner littered the room, a chem lab gone bad. In the center was a folding table, stacked high with packages and jars and envelopes. Grif picked one up and stared at the white pills. A citywide supply of codeine. He canvassed the room again. A citywide supply of *krokodil*.

But no Dennis Carlisle, Grif thought, tossing the package down, and closing the door behind him as he left.

Instinct told him to find the kitchen, so he loped across the dining room's middle to the swinging door on the other side. It was metal, with a viewing glass, and Grif had to decide: push or pull. He pushed, and immediately cursed as a white blur tripped him up, then whisked past, whimpering and, if Grif wasn't mistaken, trailing urine behind it. He righted himself as he watched the thing disappear. *Was that a dog?*

The blow came from the side, so fast his snub-nose went flying. His hands shorted out in uncontrolled spasms—the same pins-and-needles shot through his legs—and his last thought as he fell was: I've died like this before.

"You think we wouldn't find out, Shaw?" A kick to the gut, already bloody and split wide. "You think you could screw this family—screw my little sister, you bastard—and that we wouldn't find out?"

Another kick, another deadly slash . . . but then the knife was suddenly in Grif's hand, and the blade sang again.

Then the crack of a pistol sounded, fifty years in the distance . . .

And suddenly Grif was back in the present, looking up at another man, who also held hatred in his eyes. This time there was no knife at hand, just indecipherable syllables raining down like shards around Grif's head. He well understood the fist that flew at him next, though. He knew the sound of bells ringing. That, at least, was the same in any language, and this man was nothing if not succinct. One shot, and then his footsteps, and Grif's vision, both receded.

* * *

Kit inched backward in a slow crab crawl. Palm, heel; palm, heel. She didn't want to draw attention—and the sights of all those guns—back to her. Twenty more feet and she could run into the place she'd fought to avoid minutes earlier. Find Grif and Dennis and the front entrance, she thought. And hope the Cubans hadn't blocked off that exit as well.

Palm, heel.

Only Sergei, body splayed just inside the threshold, had his gaze turned her way. Careful, he seemed to say—or the Russian equivalent. One quick move and Josepha might shoot. Yulyia might scatter ash. Because neither of them was the type to wait to burn.

Proof? Yulyia's next words: "We should team up, Josepha. Kill the P.I., Shaw, the woman." Kit froze. "The cop inside, too. When they're gone, we go back to our lives."

"And my Marco?" Josepha replied stonily.

Yulyia hesitated to admit the fate she'd had planned for Baptista. "He's in the freezer."

I want them to long for the flame even as it burns around their ears.

Kit increased her pace. Palm, heel. The freezer would be locked, Kit knew. Dennis's captor was seeing to that. But Grif could open it, if he knew Dennis was there. If she could get to him. Palm, heel . . .

But the slapshot vibration of running feet sounded suddenly, and Kit cringed, ducking aside just in time. Yulyia's driver made his grand entrance then, gun drawn, clearly reacting to the gunshot that'd killed Sergei. He was already growling as he turned the corner, and as he passed, Kit's palm-heel retreat shifted into a full-reversal sprint. She saw his gun arm lift to sight on the open entrance. It coincided with Yulyia half-turn—she, too, had heard his feet.

Everything blurred after that. Time tangled. Even fleeing, Kit could hear the bullets drubbing flesh, the clatter of steel and gold, the roar of instant flame and heat.

And the cries of two women caught in a web of their own making.

Grif and Dennis, Kit thought, running blindly. *Grif and Dennis.* It was all that kept her mind from sliding out of control as gunfire and flame overtook the world behind her.

CHAPTER TWENTY-SEVEN

Grif woke alone on the kitchen floor, vulnerable but fine, though a quick sniff told him something was burning. Groaning, he fumbled for his gun, then remembered the damned commie had knocked it out of his palm. His jacket was gone, too—so that's what the man had been doing when Grif stirred the first time. Turning out his pockets for more weapons.

Finding nothing in the jacket but an old greeting card—the window into Grif's past, offered by Mary Margaret—Grif saw that the man had tossed both aside. The card was splayed alongside the jacket, opposite the gun. He turned toward the latter, but a rapping noise behind him had him jolting in the reverse direction.

There was a face in the icebox . . . in the viewing window, that was. Grif pushed himself to his knees, then feet, because the face was also familiar. Dennis mouthed something, frowning as he pointed down, and Grif nodded. He put his hand to the door, and the lock clicked open, sounding a little like a trigger being cocked. Yet the door opened faster than it should, and the man who emerged wasn't Dennis. He was shaking, his dark skin gone ashen, but he was jacked up on fear and adrenaline, and he hit first—meaning Dennis first, then Grif—before he ran.

I am tired of being knocked over, Grif thought, and so was surprised when he was offered a helping hand. Dennis's palms were taped together, and damned cold, but they were strong and steadying—though his face was a mess. Still, Grif would have smiled at him if the ceiling wasn't suddenly curling with smoky edges.

"Which way did Marco go?" Grif asked, as he worked at the tight wraps of tape.

Dennis began shaking his head, but stilled as he stared over Grif's shoulder, and said something totally unexpected instead. "Kit."

The name was like a summoning. Kit was suddenly there, at his side—her moonbeam face directly in front of his own, her beautiful mouth moving, her voice right there but relegated to white noise as his own questions took over.

What was she doing here? How did this happen? How was he going to get her out again safely?

"Did you hear me?" she was saying, shaking Grif's shoulders. "There's a fire. We have to go, but I think the place is surrounded!"

It was. Grif knew, because tangled in the coils of poisonous smoke were streaks of silvery plasma, and lots of it. The mucilage of fate was creeping in. It would be sealed soon.

"Help him," Grif ordered, pointing to the tape-ends pulled from Dennis's feet as he worked the hands.

Sparks were slipping from the ceiling now, settling like fiery falling stars. A flare sizzled as one caught hold of something, and Grif's hands stilled as he saw what it was. Mary Margaret's card. *His* card.

His abandoned jacket could burn. If he lived, it'd return to him at four A.M. anyway. Ditto the gun. But that card was the only clue he had to that long-ago death. He hadn't even seen the photo of Barbara McCoy . . . the woman who was so sure he and Evie deserved to perish. He needed that card. It was a crazy thought, but if he died with it on him, he could take it with him to the Everlast, and more of that mystery would be solved.

"Grif!" Kit's voice spiked as he bent, and Grif's fingers had just curled around the edges when he saw that flash of white again. The dog. His knee-jerk reaction would have been to shoot it, if he'd had his gun. But the damned thing ran in circles, running for the sake of running, because running was the only thing it could do.

It was the only thing it could do . . .

It certainly couldn't open that big swinging door. Kit screamed again, and Grif turned and saw the shoes. Marco Baptista was back, his own pistol in hand.

And he wasn't cold or shivering anymore.

Kit had never been in a fistfight, much less a war, but she imagined that a warrior experienced the same heightened senses that she felt now, adrenaline sharpening every corner, searing colors at the edges, but slowing movement, as if the world were a fishbowl, and they were swimming somewhere at its core.

So Kit knew what happened next, and it occurred in exactly this order: Marco Baptista rocketed through the swinging door opposite them all, and then his face contorted in about three different directions when he spotted her. Forget the disdain he'd shown for her at their first meeting. This was pure hatred erupting across his features. This was *blame*.

Second sight: Yulyia's damned dog. Probably the only creature that was going to get out of this place alive.

Third: Grif—*her* Grif—Kit's angel and protector and goddamned partner, ignoring it all to reach for a greeting card on the floor. To reach, she thought, for the past while her whole world burned.

Those things happened at half-speed, like there was all the time in the world to alter the outcome. Then Baptista yelled at her, something in rapid-fire Spanish that required no translation, because his gun hand came up and suddenly everything sped up again. Sure, Grif finally turned back, but it was too late now. All he could do was look up at her, dumbstruck realization shifting to horror, as Kit, helping Dennis like Grif told her to, played sitting duck for a smoky hatred.

But the man next to her had shifted, too, moving before Kit even heard the report of the fired shot. Or maybe it was obscured by an almost imperceptible rushing of air-bound wings. All Kit knew was Dennis's body jerked in recoil before slumping in front of hers.

Crying out, Kit caught him, while over his shoulder, Baptista resighted.

Marco cursing, Dennis falling, the damned dog yelping, the ceiling burning, and finally—finally—Grif moved. Kit's scream was drowned out by a second blast that pulverized the air.

The crackle of the burning ceiling sounded like silence in the aftermath. Kit felt welts pop up on her body, like boils, and knew somewhere in her animal mind that they were burns, but Dennis was on his back . . . and Grif was, too. The smoke of his gun, held two-handed in the direction of Baptista's body, was lost in the smoldering room. Kit's ears buzzed, and her vision narrowed until all she saw was the blood pooling around Dennis's head. His ear had disappeared in a haze of red. Kit suddenly couldn't breathe. She felt like she was submerged in the ocean, if the ocean had gone smoky and silent.

The ceiling broiled above them like hot coals.

Crouched over Dennis's unmoving body, she yelled at Grif, "What kind of angel are you?"

Her voice registered lower in her throat than she'd ever heard it before. Her head shot up and she glared at the only other living person in the room.

Half-person, anyway, she thought with a snarl.

"Put down that goddamned card," she said, glaring at Grif, "and help!"

Grif's eyes shot wide. She scared him, she realized. She scared him and she suddenly liked that. He *should* be damned scared of her right now.

"Kit, please—"

Yes, she thought, beg.

"You have to calm down—"

She didn't have to do any damned thing she didn't want to do. She smiled to herself, suddenly in complete agreement with Yulyia Kolyadenko. It was a position every woman should be in.

Looking down, she realized she didn't want to hold Dennis's head in her lap anymore. So she let it drop.

"Kit!"

She ignored Grif's shocked cry. Dennis was going to die anyway. She could see the plasma swirling around him like flowing silk . . . how could she see that?

She didn't care how. She had the power now. For instance, she had the power to put her hands to his throat and squeeze. She did so, because she wanted to see the moment his soul left his body. As she pressed, she imagined Dennis's vision going as dark as hers, darker than the smoky sea where she now lived.

Darker, Kit thought, than even the shadows in the coldest depths of the Eternal Forest.

Grif saw the moment Scratch entered Kit's body. He heard the etheric snap like a bullwhip. She was scared of the fire, distressed about Dennis, and furious with Grif, and all of it combined to create the perfect emotional environment for Scratch's longed-for possession. The fallen angel had been lurking nearby, waiting for its opportunity to enter Kit, and now it was in.

As evidenced by her slim hands closing around Dennis's exposed neck.

The controlling consciousness was evil but the vessel was still Kit's, and Grif tried to keep that in mind as he squeezed between her and Dennis, his body creating a wedge between the two. Scratch's control imbued her with extra strength, so when she socked Grif in the jaw, faster and harder than he expected, his own fist curled automatically, and he loaded up to return the favor.

Scratch's eyes twinkled darkly, and it held Kit's body still for the punch. Growling his frustration, Grif redirected, and rolled her off Dennis, pinning her arms to her side.

Frowning, Scratch headbutted him. The blow sent tears springing to Grif's eyes, but not enough to shed. Besides, the fallen angel would bite him before allowing Grif's tears near its mouth again.

Grif bought himself time to think by blocking and parrying, but not throwing any blows of his own. Kit was scratching and spitting now, in the full throes of possession while the walls around them smoldered. The smoke was thick and black. If he didn't do something soon, they'd all die in this building.

Scratch would like nothing better.

Scrambling both physically and mentally, Grif dodged another hammering fist. Mindful of Dennis, he worked to keep Kit and Scratch away from the unconscious man, but was surprised when Kit used her leg strength to roll the other way.

Scratch propelled her body fast, heading directly toward a wall seething with sparks.

Grif had to lunge, throwing his body between Kit's and the burning wall. His wings were folded, one completely incapacitated beneath his own body weight, and hitting the wall felt like he was being branded, but he'd recover.

Kit would not.

Where the hell was the fire department, the emergency response, Grif thought, cringing from falling ash as he pinned her body with his own. He could really use a big hose right now.

That idea gave him another. Unexpectedly, he snapped Kit's head against the floor, not hard enough to give her a concussion but hard enough to make the stars in her eyes roll. In the fistful of moments that Scratch needed to recover, Grif dragged Kit's body over to Dennis's, and tucked them each under an arm. His wings snapped overhead, shielding them all from the singeing ash, though there was nothing he could do about the smoke but move fast.

He bounded back through the restaurant, darker than before, where the fresh construction wood and roomful of toxic propellants sat smoky and silent, like a ticking bomb. Kit's legs began wheeling, and a sharp pain shot through Grif's arm as her teeth found the flesh of his biceps, but he just squeezed her neck until her limbs fell still again. Sorry, sweetheart, he thought, dragging her along. But as long as Scratch was inside her, it was forced to live with her fleshly limitations. Grif had no choice but to use that.

Keeping his head low, Grif burst through the front doors and out into the open. Kit had told him the place was surrounded, but the building was ablaze now, and the Cubans had retreated. With one final marshaling of his strength, Grif tore past the onlookers as sirens wailed in the distance. A little late, Grif thought, falling to his knees on the cracked deck of Shangri-La's murky pool.

He left Dennis sprawled next to the turbid water as Kit swung and kicked and bit at him. Holding tight to her body, possessed by this creature, Grif wrested her arm and ducked the blows.

"You will die, Shaw!" Kit muttered, throaty and earthy.

"No. You will." Then he plunged Kit's body deep, and held her down.

Her limbs exploded in action. Grif knew Scratch was strong, but he hadn't been prepared for the violence of the reaction, and her face breeched the surface, black pinpricked eyes reeling madly as Scratch fought for purchase. Grif shoved her under again.

"Get out, you bastard," Grif growled, because as long as

those eyes remained starry, opaque points, Scratch was in possession of his girl.

Being dunked would be a sort of reverse baptism for a fallen angel, Jesse had said. *It'd kill them rather than save them.*

Grif hoped so. Because if this didn't work, he was killing the woman he loved.

CHAPTER TWENTY-EIGHT

K it knew what was happening. She knew despite being out of control of her body and her words and the thoughts that roiled over her own like crashing waves. Humans were dunked in baptism and could be reborn in life through water. Submersion should equal death for Scratch. Yet all she could think as she stared through the shallows at Grif was that four months ago this man couldn't bear to let her die. Now he couldn't let her live. Not, at least, with Scratch inside.

Scratch knew it, too. The fallen angel's thoughts became her own.

The Eternal Forest awaits you, Katherine. I will wrap you in the roots of the fallen Tree of Life. I'll tie knots around your soul. You'll reside among the black, brittle arteries of rotted boughs, which will hold you firm while I savage you again and again.

Kit tried to hold her breath, to be strong and control what

little she could—but Scratch was holding its breath, too. It thrashed to free itself from Grif's hold, while the pressure of its rotted thoughts stewed inside her skull like a second brain.

When you're dead, I'm going to make that Centurion watch as I carry you away. You'll be Lost to him forever.

Fighting the instinct to thrash against Grif as well, Kit forced her limbs to still. *No, the water is weakening you. And I'm still in control.*

And she focused on Grif's face, clearer now that the water was calming, studying her and willing her back. This was her body and life. That was her man. And she would prevail.

We'll see about that.

And Scratch played a slipstream of her memories back to her, her life flashing like previews at the cinema. She watched her mother die again. She saw her father laid to rest. She felt the fogginess of her brain while seeking treatment for mental heath. She remembered a man racing from the shadows to save her life; the first time she'd ever seen Grif.

Bring it, you bastard, she thought, holding her breath. Because all of that made me who I am . . . and I'm strong.

Scratch's growl scraped the inner walls of her skull, and she felt her eyes pulse with its anger. Above her, the water obscured Grif's frown as he noted the change. His jaw clenched and she felt his hands tighten on her shoulders, and Kit's vision dimmed again.

This time she saw memories that weren't her own.

She saw Jeap, jumpy but excited as he cooked his first batch of *krok.* The surge of drugs whipping through his veins shot her forward in time and she saw Trey Brunk laughing with Jeannie Holmes as Tim Kovacs shot up and immediately fell flat on his face. Then Jeannie joined him, blood vessels burning.

They were the memories of everyone Scratch had possessed, Kit realized. It'd been in them, so it knew their thoughts and secrets, too.

Did you say secrets?

And suddenly Marin snapped into view. She was secreting away a file from Kit's father's study. Kit recognized the room, and then she recognized herself as the scene flashed forward. She was sleeping in her father's nightshirt, as she had those six months after he'd died. Marin stroked her head and spoke aloud. "It's for your own good."

Scratch's cutting laugh sliced the memory in two.

Secrets, it repeated . . . and then Kit saw Grif.

Here's the memory he gave me in his tears. The exact emotion used to banish me from Brunk's body. Isn't it beautiful?

Scratch's question was rhetorical, but Kit had to agree. There was absolute beauty in seeing pure joy in the face of the man you loved, especially as he made love to you. Kit had seen this look before, brief flashes where he forgot himself and his duty entirely. Pushing to his palms, the Grif of memory arched his head and neck backward, completely open to his lover, giving everything he could. Kit almost smiled . . . and then he said, "Evie."

As she gasped, water filled Kit's lungs in an instant. She shook her head and tried to push and cough it out, but all she could think was: *Grif still makes love to Evie in his dreams.*

Inside of her, still holding its breath, Scratch smiled.

In this world, Grif began to cry.

Kit was losing. The weakening of her limbs, the numbness that'd sunk into her chest, and now the slowing of her mind. She stared up at Grif and tried to get the image of him straining toward another woman out of her head, but to do that

she'd have to simply release it. And to do that, she'd have to
let go.

"Fight, Kit!" She heard his words just above the water, the
scream ripping the insides of his throat.

But maybe letting go *was* another way of fighting. Maybe
knowing when to release something was what life was really
about.

Lifting one arm, Kit felt for the stubble of Grif's jaw, then
let her hand drop. Grif's tears fell with it, hitting the water
like liquid mercury. More fell, and there they congealed. Kit
knew it was the emotion in them that made them visible. Emotion he felt for *her*. So she watched the quicksilver tears spread
like oil over the water, thinning into a film over the surface.
The last thing she would ever see in this world would be Grif,
tinted in silver and shining. The last thing she would know
was that he cried for her, too.

She liked that. And hated it. And so Kit cried as well, and
her tears were cobalt-blue.

They rose to mingle with Grif's, tangling like magnetic
alloys, then fusing. They formed a new element in a color Kit
didn't have a name for, and she thought, That's a beautiful way
to go. Knowing your love has created something new.

Suddenly she realized Scratch had gone still inside of her.
That was important, she thought. It meant something, somehow. But it was too late to figure out what. So Kit just inhaled,
sucking in pool water and sorrow-tinted tears of silver and
blue. And when the color she couldn't name touched her lips?

Scratch screamed and took flight.

Grif didn't know what had happened, not at first. One
moment he was watching Kit die, Scratch's victorious gaze

burning like luminous coals, and the next she'd been launched from the pool as if from a catapult. Now she was on her knees, coughing and sputtering, hacking up the drink and the bile that came from being possessed by a member of the Third.

"I'm sorry, baby . . . be okay . . . I'm so sorry . . ." Grif was babbling, arms wrapped tightly around her, crying as her body convulsed and shuddered. Minutes dragged on, punctuated by sirens and yelling and the neighborhood coming back to life, but the attention was on the other side of the street. Nobody even turned their way.

Exhausted, Kit finally slumped and Grif pulled her onto his lap, stroking her hair from her face, and rocking her like a child. She stayed that way for a while, then finally tilted her head his way. "Our tears taste like a spring wind in flight. Our love is the flavor of a sunbeam biting cloud."

"Wait. You— you saw that?" He hadn't known she could.

"Scratch saw it," she replied, dropping her head back to his shoulder. "And I saw what it saw. Everything."

Grif didn't know what "everything" entailed, and didn't care just now. She was back, safe in his arms, and Scratch was finally—and truly—gone.

"The building . . ." she said.

He looked back. Little Havana was an inferno. "The *krokodil* is burning."

Then she stiffened in his arms, and Grif glanced down in time to catch the exact moment her eyes settled on Dennis. Reaching for him, she slid from Grif's embrace. "The whole damned world is burning."

CHAPTER TWENTY-NINE

Baptista's crew, who had indeed introduced *krokodil* to their own neighborhood, nearly blew Naked City away. The combustibles inside Little Havana burned through the night, but in the end, the place ended up looking pretty much the same. Meanwhile, Yulyia Kolyadenko died as she lived. Hard. Eyes open, and ever looking forward.

And Dennis was in a medically induced coma.

Unlike Jeannie Holmes, he had a room of his own: private, secure, and well-monitored. Kit brought her computer, setting up vigil just as she had with Marin. She thought having something to do would keep her mind off her friend's fight for life, but her search through the family archives for more information on her father's death suddenly seemed less important than it had only days earlier. The past was gone.

And the people she loved kept on dying.

"Please. Be okay," Kit whispered, staring at Dennis's impossibly still body. It was her incessant prayer. The words ran together in a river of supplication.

Grif had remained with her through the long, uncertain night as the doctors operated on Dennis, though she knew he believed her friend was already doomed. Yet for the first time since they'd met, Kit didn't care what Grif thought. After all, she'd read his thoughts involving a woman whose loss was his life's greatest sorrow—after Scratch had revealed Grif to her more thoroughly than he'd ever opened himself—and Kit didn't care if he remained with her or not.

Knowing all of this, Grif stayed. He remained still, and mostly silent throughout the night, perched near the window of the impersonal room like the Dark Knight overlooking Gotham. But angels weren't superheroes, Kit thought, keeping her back to him. For all the help they provided, those might as well be feather dusters on their backs.

Finally, near dawn, Grif stepped in front of her, obscuring her view and forcing her gaze up. "You've been staring at the same thing for hours."

"It's not a thing," she replied coolly. "He's a person."

His jaw clenched. "I meant the computer screen."

She knew that. But picking a fight gave her a place to put her anger and guilt and, yes, sadness. Because deep down she knew she could sit next to Dennis's sickbed and pray for a miracle, yet if God decided to pull the plug, then Dennis could be Grif's very next Take. Scratch might be gone, but no matter how many evils were banished from the world, it seemed there was always some new horror ready to break your heart.

"I'm going for coffee," Grif finally said, running a hand over his face. "Want to come?"

Kit's eyes burned from being trained on Dennis the whole of the night, but she shook her head. As long as he was here, so was she. She waited until Grif's hand was on the door before blurting out the only question she had left for him, the one woven like a black thread between the prayers looping in her mind. "Could you have done it to her?"

Silence was his answer. Maybe he didn't know what she was asking. Maybe, she thought, as she turned to face him, he didn't want to. Eyeing Grif coolly across Dennis's body, she clarified. "Could you have done that to Evie? Held her under water while she struggled for life? Watched her drown?"

He squinted, thinking about it, and finally nodded, giving her the truth—and her newest heartbreak. "Of course. Anything to save her."

Neither answer, yes or no, would have been right, but Kit still felt gut-punched. *Anything.* She turned back around, thinking, I'm tired of competing with the past. Grif wavered where he was, she felt him on the edge of saying more, but what more was there? He loved her, yes. But he still loved Evelyn Shaw, too. Kit knew *that* for a fact.

The door opened, and closed. Bowing her head, Kit almost sobbed. Yet the door swung right back open, and Kit straightened immediately. It was yet another doctor. She slumped.

"Well, that looks like a good way to pass the time." The doctor smiled, and pointed at Kit's forgotten computer. DR. MARKHAM was embroidered on his crisp white jacket, and there was a burning bunny pin on the left lapel. Whatever that meant. "Video games are a good escape. It's nice to disappear into another world for a bit."

Kit didn't bother telling him the Ms. Pac-Man ticking

across her computer screen was her screensaver. Somewhere in the night she'd lost her capacity for small talk.

"So how's our patient doing?"

Kit had been sitting in the room for almost eighteen hours, and hadn't seen this man once. Edging away from the bed, she stood to give him room. "You tell me."

Dr. Markham used a penlight to check Dennis's pupils. "It's hard to say with a GSW. It's an open brain injury, and there's been some hemorrhaging, but only time will tell."

But, Kit wanted to ask, would he be able to foxtrot and drink rum from tiki mugs and flirt like James Dean . . . or not?

"Is he your brother?"

"No. I was there when he was shot," she said, explaining why Dennis's family, and the department, had pulled strings for her. They wouldn't arrive until the next day, and they didn't want him alone.

"Boyfriend?" Dr. Markham pressed.

Kit shook her head. "Just a friend."

"That's good," Dr. Markham said, but before she could ask what was good about it, he bent over Dennis's chest, talking with his back to her. "You have to understand that Mr. Carlisle has experienced one of the most severe brain traumas possible. He may never think or speak normally again. Frankly, it'd be a miracle if he even wakes."

He was scribbling on his chart, so he missed Kit's wince, but flipped the chart shut a moment later and tucked it under his arm. "There's nothing more to do now but wait."

That was the extent of his medical care.

He smiled. "Guess I'll go grab a late dinner."

Kit looked at him. "It's six A.M."

"I'm just kidding."

Kit didn't smile.

"I am off my shift soon, though." He hung the clipboard on the peg at the end of the bed. "Maybe you'd like to take a little bedside break. Let me buy you a coffee?"

Kit's fleeting instinct was to wish for Grif, but no . . . she could handle this one herself. "Are you asking me out over my friend's sickbed?"

"He won't know the difference." Dr. Markham added a nonchalant shrug to his handsome smile. Behind him, Dennis's heart monitor continued its steady beat.

"Sure, he would," Kit said, in time to the beat.

The doctor tilted his head. "How?"

"Because every time you have a drink with an asshole, an angel loses his wings."

The smile, the invitation, and the doctor disappeared. "Ring the nurses' station if you need anything."

"Imperious bastard," Kit said, still glaring as the door clicked shut.

"Yes. That one has a serious God complex," said a voice next to her.

Kit whirled to find Dennis's eyes open wide, but there was no relief for Kit in the look. The blue depths swirled with liquid marble.

"No!" Kit said, leaping to her feet. The computer wobbled on the bedside stand, but she pushed it all away. "No," she said again.

"Oh, but I think I know a God complex when I see it." Dennis's face lifted, but it wasn't her friend's lopsided, heartfelt smile.

"Get out of there," Kit spat, grabbing Dennis by his shoulders, surprising them both. She gave him a shake. "Get out!"

"Relax, kid. Every life is improved by that which is Pure."

Not my life, Kit thought, and the expression across from her altered, as if whatever was inside Dennis heard the thought.

She tilted her head. "Who are you?"

"I'm Saint Francis of the Cherubim tribe, the first Pure to ever experience mortality as a part of God's divine will. But you can call me Frank."

The familiar name calmed Kit somewhat. "You mean . . . Sarge?"

"In the flesh."

Kit crossed her arms. "That's not funny."

"Admit it, Katherine. You've wanted to know more of the Everlast since you first learned of it. So here I am."

It was true. Ever since she'd seen Grif's wings flare from his shoulders in a rising wave of black smoke, and tasted forever in his kiss, she'd wanted to know more. She looked continuously for signs that angels walked among the living. She could admit now, under that roiling, marbled gaze, that she even searched for signs that she was favored. After all, she thought, staring back at the Pure, who didn't want to be one of the Chosen?

"I like you, Craig. You're what we in the Everlast like to call a Blender," Frank said, the swirl in his monochromatic gaze slowing to match his tone. "You might as well mix your faiths in a cocktail shaker. You bend dogmas to suit you instead of bending yourself to fit a dogma. You believe in God and angels, but you also believe in Satan and demons and ghosts and spirits and astrology and witchcraft and the evil eye and dousing. A Blender could say their Hail Marys on the weekend, then consult the Ouija board during the week, with equal faith in both."

"I've never played with an Ouija board."

"I know. Out of the same openness of faith." He paused. "Dennis is a Blender, too. That's why you can both so easily mix eras, combining your love for the past with the demands of modern-day life."

Kit brightened a bit at his use of the present tense. Surely he wouldn't use it if Dennis were destined to die?

"Griffin Shaw, on the other hand, was an Apostate." His mouth curled, the word a bitter pill on his tongue. "They believe only in what they can see and touch. The hard-core ones actively work to disprove the existence of God and angels and anything that is divine. The irony is that Apostates are actually closer to the angels than anyone. They're the ones who've already been touched by a miracle or a near-death experience. Yet it was so traumatic that not only do they not remember it, they harden their hearts to anything remotely mystical."

"Grif is a Centurion," she said, sticking up for him out of habit.

Frank huffed. "And he *still* doesn't believe in miracles. I ask you, who else has ever had a second chance in the earthly realm? Who do you know that is both angelic and Chosen? Griffin Shaw is one of the greatest miracles there is, yet he doesn't believe in himself."

"I believe in him."

"Why? He doesn't believe in you." He held up a hand at her indrawn breath. "No, don't get mad. You're the girl who seeks out the truth at any cost, are you not? You value it above all else?"

"I wouldn't say 'all else.'"

"And would you tune me out just because it's not what you want to hear?"

Kit took a deep breath and couldn't help but ask, "What do I not want to hear?"

"Griffin Shaw *will* discover who murdered him a half-century ago. It is destined. It is why we have indulged his return to his fleshly nature. But . . . it'll do nothing to bring the two of you closer together."

Tears immediately filled her eyes, even though the words weren't a surprise. It was only surprising to realize that it was something she already knew.

"He is not of this time, Katherine. He is only in it."

"He is Chosen," she pointed out. "Like me."

"Like you said, he is a Centurion. And you—"

"A mere mortal." She put her head down, and closed her eyes. "I know."

Frank was silent for so long that Kit thought he'd left. But when she glanced up, Dennis's gaze was still grainy and swirling and foreign. "Have you ever wondered what would happen if Shaw and you did live out your lives together?"

She'd dreamed of it.

Kit thought she saw sadness visit the churning eyes. "You would age, he would not. Eventually, it would worry you. As you know, living on while those around you die can be a special sort of hell."

Kit wrapped her arms around herself. "Why are you doing this to me?"

He surprised her by reaching out and touching her shoulder. Dennis's fingertips were ice-cube cold. "You have a gift, Katherine. An ability to see the bright side of every situation despite your insistence on, and knowledge of, the truth. You're cheerful by nature, and that is good. But the real reason you live so fully in the present, while still celebrating the past, is that you have the certainty, the knowledge, the *truth* that death looms ahead. So you do not sip of life, you gorge on it."

And Grif, because of his everlasting angelic nature, did not. His tomorrows lay before him on a road without end.

"This man," Frank said, gesturing down Dennis's body, "lives in the same way as you. He sucks out the marrow, seeks truth, bringing justice to light. He also cares for you, deeply."

"He's just my friend," she told him, as she had the doctor.

"But you want him to live."

"Of course." What did that have to do with anything?

"And, were things different, you could have feelings for him, too."

Kit wanted to argue, but as soon as the words were loosed in the room, she knew they were true. If circumstances were different—if she'd never met Grif—she may have developed real feelings for Dennis.

Biting her lower lip, Kit glanced at the door.

"Don't worry." Frank knew her concern. "I sent Shaw after a soul cowering in manhole beneath all this city's ridiculous flashing neon. He'll be gone for hours."

"You know that makes you sound like a jerk, right?"

"It's a job." He shrugged, and settled back into the pillows.

Kit glared, hating him for it. Frank glanced at her, churning eyes moving over her forehead as if reading a ticker tape. "Does it feel good to be Chosen?" he asked suddenly. "To be loved so deeply that He'd give everything for you?"

Angels, Kit realized, had wondered this for ages. It was the same question that drove the fallen angels to turn against God. Kit lifted her chin. "None of your business."

Frank barked out a laugh. "True enough. Let me ask you something else then? Since you are made in *His* image."

Arms crossed, Kit waited.

"Would you give up everything for someone you loved?"

"Yes," she answered immediately.

"Think about it," Frank sang.

"Is this rhetorical?" Kit asked.

"No, I can be very specific. What, for example, would you give up in order to prevent Dennis Carlisle's death at eleven A.M. this morning?"

Kit's gaze shot to the wall clock, and she read the time before her vision swam. Five hours, she thought, closing her eyes. *I hate you.*

"I know," Frank said lightly. "But people die. Life goes on."

"But not for Dennis," she said, standing. "Unless . . . ?"

"Walk away from Griffin Shaw," Frank said.

"No," Kit countered, folding her arms.

"Then Dennis dies, and you'll be left knowing you could have prevented it. Then your impossibly cheery disposition will begin to crack. Your moods will swing like a pendulum."

Frank continued to speak and watch her with utter impassivity. "You'll skip work, meals, eventually bathing. You will cease living life as you know it, and dwell only on your mistakes. In effect, you'll be addicted to memories that should already be buried in the past. You've seen the havoc that can wreak."

Kit shook her head. "No. That would never happen."

"That's exactly what will happen, and even having Griffin Shaw by your side won't be enough—"

"It will. It—"

"—because you'll wake up one day and realize you gave up a chance at a real life with Dennis for a love that is already dead. Then you, too, will be lost."

Lost is just the opposite of Chosen. And who has ever really chosen you, Katherine?

She looked at Dennis, then back at the wall clock marking his march to death. She thought of Grif, seeing and seeking Evie everywhere, even with Kit by his side. She recalled Mary Margaret's heart-rending words.

Why does so much of life have to be about letting go?

"Because that's the art of life," Frank said simply, reading her mind again. "And letting go is the only way you can take up something new."

And Grif had never done that. But . . .

"He might. I mean, he might still choose me, you know." Kit's voice was soft and shaky, and though she hated herself for doing so in front of Frank, she teared up, too. "In time, I could be enough."

"After fifty years?" Frank tilted his head. "Come on, Kit."

"I'm a good person." A single tear fell. The Pure tracked it with his surging gaze.

"I'm not arguing that. But I suppose to properly answer the question, you'd really need all the facts." Frank shrugged at her sharp look. "I have a secret that could change your answer."

A long moment passed. "Is it truth?"

He inclined his head. "But it's a hard one."

Kit placed her head in her hands. The angel was silent, though surely eavesdropping on every one of her tangled thoughts as she let her mind travel as far as it could down each fork in this decision. She felt the moment upon her like gravity itself.

Finally, Kit did what she always did when faced with a mystery. She lifted her head and leaned close. "Tell me."

He did . . . and her shoulders immediately slumped with

the knowledge. Her overactive, tired, and taxed mind slowed beneath its weight, and all of her options turned to dust.

She allowed a fleeting regret for not kissing Grif before he'd left the room.

Then she looked at the Pure, and swallowed hard.

"Let's make a deal."

CHAPTER THIRTY

Grif returned to the hospital just before eleven A.M., stripped to his shirtsleeves, jacket hanging over his left shoulder. He was hot, cranky, and because of Sarge's emergency Take, he still hadn't gotten that cup of joe. But he didn't dare stop now. Kit was no doubt wondering where he was, and probably sore at him all over again.

He'd just explain, he decided as he neared Dennis's room. Kit was a lot of things, but unreasonable wasn't one of them. Unkind wasn't, either. She'd be pleased to know another traumatized soul had been seen safely home. Still, things weren't easy between them right now, so his explanation, and apology, were on his lips even as he walked through the door.

"So I found the guy stumbling around in these underground tunnels. Said he was looking for 'the light.' I told him that wasn't the way it worked and the nut job ran from me, so

I had to send for another Centurion to corner him. She's the one who escorted him off the mudflat, which is why I couldn't return before now. I was stuck, here and now, and had to hoof it back in terrestrial time."

The rush of words felt like a train wreck, but when Grif finally paused for a breath, Kit still said nothing. She also, he noted with a quick skip of his heart, hadn't yet looked at him. "Kit?"

Leaning against the wall across the room, she continued gazing out the window, arms crossed and brow furrowed. Grif stared, trying to figure out what was off about her. She was totally still, but it felt like there was something rushing through her body, like a roaring river contained between the silent banks of her flesh. Something inside her was shifting, though she never moved. But what?

Then she looked at him, and that imagined sense of movement solidified in her gaze. The river freezing over, he thought, going cold himself. Whatever it was had settled.

"What do you see, Grif?" Her voice was wooden and distant, and seemed much farther away than the other side of the room.

He let his gaze roam, telling himself he was doing what she wanted, and not trying to escape the expression that matched that flat tone. Dennis still lay unconscious, the heart monitor bleating regularly at his back. The chart was at the foot of his bed—it looked like the doctor had been here, and signed it—but other than that, not much had changed. "You shut down your computer."

She wrapped her arms more tightly around herself. "I mean, what do you see when you look at me."

He saw his dream girl reimagined for the twenty-first century, that's what he saw. He saw the silk scarf holding back her hair, and her ladies' guayabera and her capri jeans and her canvas tennis shoes. Even dressed down, she was era-appropriate. "I see my girl."

Kit closed her eyes, and a small smile lifted the corners of her mouth. "Yeah," she murmured, the smile lingering a few moments longer. Then she opened her eyes. "But sometimes what you don't see is more important."

"What are you talking about?"

"Negative space," she whispered, giving him a sad smile. "The holes left by that which is no longer there."

Grif didn't say anything. The look in her eyes . . . he didn't know it. It was as foreign as Europe. As far off as France. It was like a place he'd never wanted to go, and for some reason it was here, in this room, in the very way his girl now held her elbows, arms across her chest, like she was holding herself together.

"You still love her," she finally said.

Grif swallowed hard, but kept his unblinking gaze on her strange one, willing her back from that far-off place. "Evie is dead, Kit. All I want is to—"

"It's okay," she went on, as if he hadn't spoken. "I mean, it's good that you still love her. A new love can't replace an old love. I always knew that. That's not what new love is for."

His heart began thumping in his chest. "Babe. You're just tired. Let's go home and—"

"I *am* tired." She nodded, but not to him, to herself. "I'm tired of trying to make you forget. I try with my words and my laughter and my hard work on your behalf. I try with my body." She laughed sadly at that. "I try so hard to be enough that you don't wake up every morning and wish you were someplace else."

Grif shook his head, almost violently. "You *are* enough."

"I know." She lifted her chin in that stubborn way he loved, and said, "I'm Kit Craig. Girl reporter. Rockabilly babe. One of the few humans who can talk to the Pure. And I love like a goddess. I'm passionate and devoted and open, with soft spots that can be pushed like bruises . . . and every single one of them was reserved for you." Her voice hitched, but she recovered it immediately. "*That's* how I love. And that's how I want to be loved. But I can't compete with her anymore."

He didn't even try to interrupt now. She had made up her mind about something in the short hours he was gone, but he couldn't be sure what it was quite yet.

"I can't compete," she said again, "and I can't get the knowledge from your tears out of my mind. I always told myself that I understood why you still cared for her, but I don't anymore. Now that I *felt* your greatest sorrow—loving and losing Evelyn Shaw—I can't find it in my heart to deny it. In your mind she'll always be perfect and beautiful and beloved."

Perfect? Grif thought, as Kit shook her head. Evie had been beautiful, yes. But not perfect. And Kit was already beloved. He opened his mouth to say so, but she didn't give him a chance.

"I asked you once if you ever dreamed of me. Well, now I don't have to wonder. I know your dreams like I know my own." She shrugged. "In a way, it's good. I can see that it's not my fault that you can't be fully present. There's nothing wrong with me . . . another woman simply beat me to the punch."

What the hell had happened while he was gone? Grif looked around the room like she'd told him to do earlier, as if that could provide the answer. And this time he saw it. The plasma ringing Dennis was gone. Grif's gaze shot to the heart monitor. His vitals were good. Normal, even. His color was fine. He was still unconscious, but etherically? He looked almost healthy.

Grif's exhalation shot from him in harsh rattle. "Who the hell have you been talking to?"

She looked down, causing a loose curl to drop over her forehead. An hour ago, Grif would have thought nothing of reaching out and slipping it back behind her ear. But not now.

"You have two loves, Griffin Shaw," she said, still not looking at him. "You have two lives. And one has to go."

Now Grif wanted to reach out to shake her, but the foreign look she gave him when she looked up again made him feel emptier than he had since landing back on the mudflat.

"You're lost, Grif," she said. "Lost to the past. Lost to me."

"I'm not Lost," he said, through clenched teeth. He had to force his jaw to relax just so he could get his next words out without biting them off. "And I love you!"

"I know," she said simply. "But I know something else now, too."

Kit glanced at Dennis, her neck working as she swallowed hard. It looked like she was on the verge of something, like leaping from a jagged cliff but even less fun. Studying her, he only caught the last part of her whisper.

"What did you say?" He tilted his head.

Kit swallowed hard. "I said every life is improved by that which is Pure."

Holding stock-still, Grif let his eyes alone canvass the room, squinting suspiciously at every shadow, then honed back in on Kit. "It was Frank, wasn't it?"

Her gaze fell.

"He came through in Dennis, right?" When she didn't answer, he yelled. "Did he?"

"We made a deal."

Grif actually backed up. The room spun, and he had to plant a hand on the wall to still it. The Pure had been planning it all along, he realized. He'd brought Grif that damned case, leading to Jeap and the other Lost souls. He'd probably known what Scratch was doing . . . and what it would take to stop the fallen angel. It was why he'd been so silent since assigning Grif the case. The Pure's only job was to see to it that the Centurions in his care moved on. And that still included Grif.

He looked at Kit. "Whatever you're about to say? Don't."

"Grif—"

He shook his head, mind spinning, finally catching up. "Frank is using your goodness, your thoughts and emotions, against you. Don't you see? He's been trying to drive us apart all along. That's why he sent me to Jeap. He knew you would go, start investigating it, that you'd involve Dennis."

Kit shook her head. "But—"

"What? You don't think he's capable of it? An *angel*?"

Kit finally blinked, and for a moment she was there, his girl, open to him. But only for a moment. She shook her head. "It's too late."

"No." Grif was suddenly next to her, his hands on her arms. "Whatever you did, we can fix it. Whatever deal you made, we can take it back. We can do anything as long as we stick together. We're a team." He shook her when she didn't answer. "Right?"

"Yes, but . . ."

"But what?" He squinted into her unreadable face, not understanding.

"But that's not what I want."

His hands dropped away, and suddenly he was floating, loosened and untethered, like when he free-fell through the Universe. But no. His feet were already on the Surface. "What?"

"I— I don't want to be chosen by default." And this time she didn't just glance at Dennis, she put a hand on his shoulder. She faced *him,* her back to Grif.

"Kit—?"

"She's here." Kit turned to face Grif, and he saw that a single tear had slid over her cheek. "And that means you're still a married man."

Glancing down at his ringless finger, the air exploding from his chest, Grif looked at the ceiling, under the bed, toward the private bathroom where someone with a Centurion's wings might be hidden. Meanwhile, his mind raced. Evie had come through incubation . . . when? And she was a Centurion now? Why hadn't Sarge told him? Why had he told Kit? And was Dennis to be Evie's Take? Her first?

Where the hell was she?

"No, Grif." He looked back to find Kit shaking her head, sheet-white as she watched his frantic search. She huffed, and managed a humorless laugh. "At least I know I made the right choice."

Grif threw up his arms. "I don't know what you're saying, Kit! Why are you looking at me like that? What do you mean she's here?"

"I mean your wife. Evie," she said, spacing her words carefully. "She's still *alive,* Grif. Evie's still alive."

The words sliced his brain in two, shorting out all thought, sending shivers into his limbs until his knees gave way. He braced himself against the wall, and looked around for more substantial support, but Kit remained far away.

Evie's still alive?

"Can I get some water over here, please?"

Both Kit and Grif jumped. Dennis was suddenly staring up at Kit, head tilted to one side with a smile. Aside from the bruised flesh peeking beneath his bandages, he looked no worse than if he'd just woken from a restful nap. Kit bent with a cry, and buried herself in a hug. It looked like she needed it more than he did.

"So that's the deal," Grif mumbled, throat tight as he straightened. He caught his breath, though his mind still whirled. Dennis's life in exchange for the knowledge that Evie still lived. And Kit, knowing what Grif would do—what he'd *have* to do—had accepted it.

Splaying his feet wide, mostly for balance, he shoved his hands into his pockets, and stood at the foot of Dennis's bed. He waited until Kit had straightened, and had no choice but to turn back to him. He shook his head. "Guess he knew exactly how to get to you, huh?"

She didn't ask who. Frank was as much a presence in this room as any of the living. But she shook her head. "He knew how to get to you, too."

Evie's still alive.

And Sarge had known it all along.

"You should go," Kit said tearfully. "I imagine you'll want to get right to work." And she turned back to Dennis, making it easier on them both for Grif to leave.

Next to her, Dennis frowned. He knew he was listening to a loaded conversation. Grif's gaze traveled between the two of them, both one-hundred-percent, twenty-first-century mortals. Both hourglasses, their time on this mudflat limited in years.

So Grif crossed the room and picked up his jacket. Maybe that shrink, Mei, was right. Let Kit have the life she was meant to have with someone from her time. Grif had just knocked into it like a meteor, a destructive force, sending it off track for a while.

Still, he paused with his hand on the door. "You should at least know one thing before I leave."

Because it wasn't like he hadn't been here at all. The time he'd spent with Kit, even if it did end like this, should count for something. The love they felt for each other didn't lose its meaning just because it couldn't stand up to a universal force.

"The knowledge in those tears that Scratch shared with you? Those old regrets you now hold against me? Yeah, they haunted me. They drove me back to the Surface to try to right old wrongs, and sure, they were the reason I got out of bed and paced almost every night, too.

"But every regret, every thing I ever cared for or about, and every wish I held in my heart about my first life, they all drowned with you, Kit." He shook his head. "I let them all sink to the bottom of that pool when I thought I was losing you. I cried new tears. And they were all for you."

Her brow furrowed. Of course she remembered. Filled with love, they'd mingled with hers to banish that soul-sucking bastard once and for all. But Grif needed her to know that he remembered, too.

"And as I cried," he continued, hoping like hell he wouldn't do so again now, "I prayed and swore to God that I'd leave those old torments behind. I'd let that old life go as long as I could have this new one. I swore nothing would ever matter again as long as you lived." He stared. "But I guess neither Scratch nor Sarge shared *that* with you, did they?"

Kit swayed, but it was Dennis who was next to her now, and he was the one who put a hand on her arm. Again, maybe that was the way it should be. Dennis was a good man. He and Kit were a good fit.

"I just thought you should know," Grif said, tapping his fedora back on his head and giving her a final nod. "You're the girl who loves the truth, and the truth is . . . I've loved you more than anything in my entire life."

And because his throat really did close up after that, and because Dennis was watching him without blinking, and Kit could barely see through her tears—and because she'd made a deal with Sarge that sealed her in place—Grif left. He strode down the hall blindly, concentrating on keeping his footsteps steady and moving forward. That way, maybe his mind and heart could follow.

"Grif!"

He stopped dead, too fast, and swallowed hard. When he turned, she was hanging back, half-inside Dennis's room, half-out. He suddenly understood how she'd felt all these months. Half-here, half-there.

Evie's still alive.

It was the thought that kept both of them rooted in place.

"Let me know." Kit cleared her throat. "When you figure it out, I mean."

Grif's head didn't seem to be working. She looked so different all of a sudden; someone he didn't know. Someone he couldn't touch. "Figure what out?"

"You know," Kit gave him a watery smile, looking briefly touchable. "Who killed Griffin Shaw."

He stared at her for a long moment, then gave her a grateful nod. That's exactly what he needed to do . . . or at least it was a reason to keep moving forward. The past, even the near past, was gone.

Now, Grif thought, as he turned and began walking again, all he had to do was figure out exactly where he'd left it.